The g... 
revolutio... ...rightful thane of the dwarves
ten years ago and cemented the rule of the mad idealist
Jungor Stonespringer.

The gates of Pax Tharkas are open, left that way
after the survivors of the revolution settled there.
It's not as though there's danger. The trap that saved
the dwarves during the War has been reset, and the
building itself is strong. And the gates of Thorbardin
have been sealed from the inside. The dwarves of
Thorbardin will not leave their home, free of the
contamination of humanity, sunlight, other dwarves,
to attack Pax Tharkas.

But now there is a new war. A new battle in the
Dwarfgate Wars that started after the Cataclysm and
never really stopped. This battle is between the hill
dwarves of Hillhome and the refugees of Pax Tharkas,
with a little help from the wizards in Kayolin, and the
secret of Pax Tharkas waits to be found.

For good or evil, the secret waits to be used.

# DWARF HOME

*The Secret of Pax Tharkas*

*The Heir of Kayolin*
September 2008

*The Fate of Thorbardin*
August 2009

# DOUGLAS NILES

Dwarf Home • Volume One

## The Secret of Pax Tharkas

**Dwarf Home, Volume One**
## THE SECRET OF PAX THARKAS
©2007 Wizards of the Coast, Inc.

Published by Wizards of the Coast, Inc. DRAGONLANCE, WIZARDS OF THE COAST, and their respective logos are trademarks of Wizards of the Coast, Inc., in the U.S.A. and other countries.

Printed in the U.S.A.

Cover art by Matt Stawicki
First Printing: December 2007

9 8 7 6 5 4 3 2 1

ISBN: 978-0-7869-4789-8
620-21632740-001-EN

U.S., CANADA,                                          EUROPEAN HEADQUARTERS
ASIA, PACIFIC, & LATIN AMERICA                         Hasbro UK Ltd
Wizards of the Coast, Inc.                             Caswell Way
P.O. Box 707                                           Newport, Gwent NP9 0YH
Renton, WA 98057-0707                                  GREAT BRITAIN
+1-800-324-6496                                        Save this address for your records.

Visit our web site at www.wizards.com

*To Juliette, Ben, Melissa, Buzzy, Sam, Jake, Emily, Kayli, Angela, John, and all the kids of Camp Nilesawhile*

*Thanks!*

# PROLOGUE

**Being a Proclamation of the Word of Reorx
Through the Vessel of His Most Faithful One:
The King of Thorbardin
High Thane Jungor Stonespringer**

My faithful dwarf children:

Our age is full of ill omens and dire portents. Know you all that it is only the resolute faithfulness of your leaders, and your own hearts, which holds mighty Thorbardin fast to its path of righteousness. Know you all that it is our cherished blessing to keep our gates sealed against the pernicious influences, the wicked and vile practices of the world that so relentlessly decays beyond the solid walls of our mountain home.

And know you all that there are those, even here among us, sharing the sacred protection of our keep, who would seek to undo all of the protections that our proud and all-seeing god has labored so hard to render into place.

I, your humble king, take this occasion to recount these threats, both the perils and successes of the recent past, and to warn against the looming menace that threatens all of our people should we fail to heed our stern and caring deity.

The vengeance of our righteous god is already manifest in the destruction of Qualinesti, our former neighbor to the north. The land of the elves has become subject to blight,

I

their once-great city rendered a poisonous morass—just punishment, to be sure, for that haughty and intractable race. The elves themselves are scattered and even now struggle to survive in a world where all are their enemies. Spare the elves no sympathy, my fellow dwarves, for their suffering is deserved. If Reorx has his way, we have seen the last of the elf race, which has ever been a scourge upon the surface of Krynn.

Nor need we dwarves concern ourselves any longer with the petty affairs of men, not deep in the sanctity of Thorbardin. But understand, my people, that humankind is ever a lingering threat, and the only real security, the only hope we have of avoiding inevitable contamination, is to avoid humans and treat them like the plague. Here, too, we are blessed by Reorx, for our steadfast walls and sealed gates offer us adequate protection, and no human could hope to penetrate our undermountain realm.

We are safe here from the ancient ogres, ever a danger to our race, and from the minotaurs that, Reorx in his wisdom has revealed to me, swarm the eastern lands of our continent like a pestilence of insects. Neither ogre nor minotaur can reach us in our undermountain sanctuary, and for this we owe our god, the everlasting Forge and Fire, most sublime thanks. Yes, even the wicked wyrms of dragonkind are barred from our realm, for the mountain summits, the granite walls, the great shell of Cloudseeker Peak, all will stand fast as bastions against these and other enemies.

It may be recalled by some that our Failed King, Tarn Bellowgranite, upon his exile some ten years ago, tried to terrify the dwarves of the clans with his claim of a fire dragon, somehow lingering since the Chaos War, still dwelling in the halls of the mountain city. Tarn Bellowgranite has been shown to be at best a misbegotten fool—though the proof came too late for the thousands of brave dwarves he sent to their doom in his mad quest to aid the elves of Qualinesti. The wrath of the gods smote Qualinesti, and it is to our eternal grief that the dwarf army, as well, was caught in the wholesale destruction.

That loss, that tragedy which still echoes in the silence of so many dwarven homes, is the legacy of the Failed King. His words were and are false, and his many threats—of dragon menace and internecine strife—have been seen as lies. For there is none among us, not a single dwarf of Krynn, who has seen any evidence of this fire dragon, and in those years since Tarn Bellowgranite has been banished, is there any doubt that it was a cruel hoax the Failed King tried to perpetrate on us?

No, my people, none of these dangers loom now. Yet there are new dangers that Reorx, in his benign kindness, has deigned to send me in a vision, that I might take the necessary steps to safeguard our nation. I regret to report, my beloved dwarves, that the threats which alarm Reorx have their roots not in elves and humans, nor even in rumored dragons, but lie within the hearts of dwarves themselves.

But take heart, my people, children of Reorx, for in this close threat we may indeed renew our hope of redemption. For a threat that is born of dwarfkind can be faced and defeated by dwarfkind. The struggle will require faith and courage, and everlong have we displayed those traits in abundance. It will require a discerning eye for treachery—and a determined and ruthless strategy to combat that treachery, to root out enemies within and obliterate them by whatever means necessary.

In this enterprise, we have been blessed by Reorx, for he has seen that Thorbardin is now ruled by a king and a council of thanes, who all possess the requisite wisdom and resolve to achieve ultimate victory. This is a virtual certainty.

The taint of the Failed King, it is known to all,

has been cleansed from our nation. He whose name is forever accursed dwells in exile now, a pathetic recluse in the hollow shell of a place that was once the great Pax Tharkas. That barrier, erected to mark the border between Thorbardin and Qualinesti, has concluded its purpose with the destruction of the elven realm. Let it languish now as a dwelling for exiles and enemies. Though a thousand dwarves, even a small army, might shelter there, they have no means to reach Thorbardin. From the Failed King, we in Thorbardin are secure.

Many of our people will recall the Mad Prophet, Severus Stonehand: he, too, betrayed his own and because of him the Daewar clan has fallen from high favor in Thorbardin. Even as the smoke of the Chaos War still lingered in our mountain halls, the Mad Prophet gathered the dwarves of his clan—those who were foolish enough to credit and follow him—and bore them away with him to the east in his doomed quest to restore the lost might of ancient Thoradin. That undermountain realm, so it is said, is older than Thorbardin, and at its height was nearly as auspicious as our own nation.

But that height was many, many centuries ago. Even before the Cataclysm, Thoradin had waned as a power, corrupted by the Kingpriest and the multiple impurities of commerce and traffic with the disparate realms of humankind. It is only right that Reorx, when he hurled the mountain down upon the surface of Krynn, saw fit to obliterate Thoradin. Now Reorx has revealed to me the true scope of the Mad Prophet's insanity, for the many Daewar who left Thorbardin with their leader were borne to a sea of fire, with three great mountains spuming smoke into a black sky and liquid rock pouring through the very fabric of the world. They found madness in the shell of Zhakar, and there, Reorx has shown me, they all perished. Their faithlessness in Reorx, their foolishness in adhering to false prophecy, was their undoing, and let it stand as a common lesson to all the rest of us, my people.

Nay, do not weep at their loss, my blessed fellows. Those few Daewar remaining among us owe gratitude to Reorx for their deliverance; it was their decision to stay here, within the safety of Thorbardin's walls, that has preserved their lives to this day.

Nor is there threat to our well-being to be found in the remote fastness of Kayolin, in the north. That nation of dwarves has long been lost to us, the once-true cousins. Reorx has revealed to me that the lord of Kayolin has taken to call himself "king"—as if dwarfkind could ever have two kings! Kayolin has opened its gates to men and hill dwarves, and the inevitable bastardization cannot but weaken the pure fiber of mountain dwarf sinew, the pure stream of mountain dwarf blood. Kayolin has become a land of merchants and shopkeepers, mocking its people's former greatness. Kayolin may be lost to us, but that is not a matter of concern; it grows weaker by the year and soon will fade as it flows forth and merges with the inconsequential world.

The ridges and slopes around our mountain fastness, wherein dwell a veritable plague of Neidar hill dwarves, are not the source of the dangers revealed to me by Reorx. True, hill dwarves have ever been a vexing annoyance, as they are well known to be arrogant, greedy, and stubborn as rocks. Our war with their kind cannot be said to ever be fully settled, not while any single Neidar, not one of the ill-bred, survive. But that will happen in time and is no cause for concern at present.

Hill dwarf perfidy is endless and never more transparent than in the case of the Failed King, who took a hill dwarf as his wife. Who is to say whether King Bellowgranite would have embarked upon his path of folly if it weren't for the seditious whisperings of his wife-from-beyond-the-mountain? However, the Neidar are barely worthy of our notice and, indeed, with our gates closed and sealed, they are a disease that has been quarantined. They cannot challenge us, they cannot steal our goods, they cannot add impurity to our bloodlines. They merely lurk without.

Where, then, lies the immediate threat to our future, to our purity, to our status as the favored sons of Reorx? You may ask this question, my people, and it deserves an answer. But it is not an answer that gladdens my heart, for the truth is painful.

For I repeat, the threat to Thorbardin, my dwarves, comes from within the hearts of its own people!

Know that I have labored with every iota of my being over the years of my reign to recognize and eliminate this threat. I have probed the full circle of our clans, the lofty Hylar, the proud Daergar, the clever Theiwar, the impetuous Klar, and those few who have remained of the lost and lonely Daewar. I have sought with my one good eye to investigate the weak and identify the cowardly—though sometimes it seems as though my eyeless socket, with its orb of smooth gold, sees with more clarity than true vision.

Over the years of my reign, I have presented the peoples of Thorbardin with important edicts, some seventy-eight of them to date. Every one of these new strictures has been designed to uphold the righteousness of this place, root out enemies, and hold my people fast to the true forward path of dwarf history. Though I, together with you, my people, have made good progress, our efforts have been only modestly successful.

That is not enough. Reorx has shown me more must be done.

I have been given visions of the terrible corruptions wrought among us by the females of our kind and come to know that, for too long, we as dwarves have tolerated the foibles of our weaker sex, allowed females to dictate, to weaken, to sully our greatness in ways that will, if unchecked, inevitably lead to our downfall.

I have been alerted to the growing dangers presented

by the outlaws who inhabit our realms, from the vile magics of the Theiwar wizard called Willim the Black to the depredations of the Klar criminal Mog Bogcutter, formerly a captain loyal to the Failed King. The former seeks to undermine our will while the latter and his ilk raid our food warrens and corrupt our youth with promises of treasure and adventure behind city walls.

I have seen too much faith placed in the heroes of the past and not enough loyalty given to the dreams of the future. By dwelling on the legacy of our people, we deprive ourselves of the wisdom and guidance of our current age, and this sin cannot be borne.

Perhaps most deplorable of all, I have beheld vile gully dwarves roaming carefree throughout our cities, bringing with them sickness, filth, and depravity. Ever immoral and ignorant, these worthless beings represent a slur on all the proud dwarf race.

Thus I have created new edicts, sworn as law with this posting, to counter these evils.

### Stonespringer Edict Number Seventy-nine: Regarding the Census of our Peoples

Commencing immediately, all family patriarchs are to compile a listing of all the male scions in that family. Such totals must be presented to the clan leaders by the end of the year, and the clan leaders must present their totals to their thanes within a fortnight following year's end.

The census shall count only males, as they represent the true core of Thorbardin's population.

### Stonespringer Edict Number Eighty: Regarding the Rights of Female Citizens

It has been recognized that the wily female, with her sexual allure, her soft words, her penchant for temporization and forgiveness instead of strength and resolve, has long been a weakening influence on the foundation of the nation. For too long, we have tolerated female ownership of businesses, female laborers working at our forges and mines, females as soldiers, even females as thanes of our clans. Females have inherited estates, and females have employed males as servants and laborers.

From this day forward, those roles are forbidden to the women of Thorbardin. No female may own property in Thorbardin. Property titled to female owners must be immediately transferred to a male relative. If no male relatives are available, the property shall be claimed by the female's clan thane for appropriate disbursement. Those females working in manufacturing, engineering, or at any military pursuit are hereby removed from their duties and consigned to their homes, where their husbands or fathers shall be expected to assign them proper roles. No male shall accept instruction or assignment of work or any other task from a female.

It will be noted that the former thane of the Theiwar, Brecha Quickspring, stands as a stark example of female insidiousness. The wicked wench even attempted to distract me, her king and yours, with foul temptations of fleshly rewards. It should bring relief to all our people to know that she has been removed from her seat at the council and, after being appropriately disfigured, has been confined to the dungeon of the Royal Fortress.

As presented as law in Edict Number Four, the king high thane shall, in due time, appoint her successor as thane of the Theiwar clan.

### Stonespringer Edict Number Eighty-one:
### Regarding the Corrupting Influence of Graven Images

Commencing immediately, all public images portraying the former leaders of Thorbardin, as well as those busts and statues of both historical and personal significance displayed within private dwellings, are to be destroyed. It is known to all that, as mandated by Edict Number Twenty-two, all images carved in stone to portray beings who are not dwarves—the most notable being the statue of the former elf king Kith-Kanan—have already been destroyed.

But Reorx has shown me that this destruction is insufficient. So long as we admire the graven visages of our former heroes, we are unable to move into the future of new might, new greatness, and new leaders.

The Public Guard enforcers of each clan will be responsible for tearing down any statuary on exhibit in public locations. Each property owner is required to destroy any privately held images. Such destruction must be accomplished by the end of the year; after that time, all such property that is discovered will be confiscated and its owners arrested for violation of this edict.

### *Stonespringer Edict Number Eighty-two: Regarding the Primacy of Reorx*

Reorx has long been the favored father of all dwarfkind, but he is displeased to see that small shrines dedicated to other gods—however secondary to his primacy—have various places of honor in Thorbardin. No such religious center, temple, shrine, or altar to any god other than Reorx shall now be tolerated.

Citizens coming upon such shrines shall immediately report their existence to the clan thane. It is the thane's obligation to see that the blasphemous site is shut down, the shrines to other gods destroyed.

Any dwarf caught worshiping at such a site or carrying any talisman or sign associated with any god other than Reorx shall be put to death by slow strangulation.

## Stonespringer Edict Number Eighty-three:
### Regarding the Elimination of the Aghar Race

Gully dwarves are a bane on the existence of the true dwarf races. For too long these "gullies" have been tolerated, working their mischief, spreading their diseases, and stealing our food, our goods, and, indeed, our honor. To the eyes of Reorx, a state of war has always existed between his hard-working, devoted children, the mountain dwarves, and these bastardized pests who have so long infested this nation.

To this end, the Aghar "gully" dwarves are banned from Thorbardin. Those who do not leave within one week are sentenced to death. Death may be administered by any male or female dwarf of clans Hylar, Daergar, Daewar, Theiwar, or Klar.

At the discretion of the clan thane, a bounty not to exceed five steel pieces may be paid for every Aghar head produced at the clan bounty house. The bounty is limited to adult gully dwarves; the little nits who survive, assuredly, will not be long for life.

It is hereby announced that the gully dwarf "thane," Grumple Nagfar, has already been put to death. His throne has been removed from the Council of Thanes, never to be restored.

Such edicts are written be decree of the king high thane, and to all Thorbardin they shall be known as law.

Signed

*King High Thane Jungor Stonespringer*

# ONE

## SCUM GUTTERS OF AGHARHOME

P*lop.*

Gus watched the globule of sludge fall from the ceiling, plummeting—as he had known it would—straight down onto Pap's bald, wrinkled pate. The ball of gooey liquid exploded noisily, spattering Mam and Birt. But most of the gunk ran down Pap's face or draped his very prominent ears like the draperies that used to ornament Thane Grumple Nagfar's palace. (Gus had seen the palace once when Thane Highbulp Nagfar, drunk, had fallen down outside the drain hole that was his palace entrance, and Gus, who also was drunk, had tripped over the thane and tumbled down the slick and slimy shaft.)

Just as he had anticipated the sludge's fall, Gus knew what would happen next.

"Move!" Pap snapped, roughly elbowing Mam from her small rock and sidling sideways to claim the newly vacated seat. His own perch, the largest rock in the entire Fishbiter household, he left unoccupied.

Mam kicked One Eye (Birt was his real name, but the family called him One Eye ever since that thing that happened when the brothers were fishing) over and took the space on the floor where he had been sitting. It was the only flat spot on the rocky, rubble-strewn floor of the lightless house, so she settled herself there with a stern look at Birt, Ooz, and Gus.

Gus sighed, watching the inevitable progression of nudges, punches, and kicks as Birt claimed the corner perch formerly occupied by Ooz (Ooz was his real name, but the family sometimes called him Hook Lip ever since that other thing that happened when the brothers were fishing), and Ooz knocked Gus out of his place in the doorway. Rubbing his sore ribs—Ooz punched him in the same place every time—Gus stood up and tried to decide what to do. He looked at the ceiling and saw that the ooze was only slowly beginning to bubble down below the crack; it would be at least two minutes before it fell again. Since his only other choice was to leave the crowded little house, he made his way to the rock that had been vacated by Pap.

He settled himself on the high seat, which was clean since Pap himself had intercepted the plunging sludge. For just a second, he relished the thrill of being high and dry, his rump nestled comfortably in the slight concavity atop the rock. It *was* nice up here!

"Hey! That my seat!"

Pap lunged to his feet, his face twisted into a grimace of ferocity, both of his teeth showing between his widespread lips. Gus sprang off the rock before the old Aghar's punch could land, allowing his father to reclaim his chair. Pap glowered menacingly at his youngest offspring until a louse in his beard compelled him to refocus his attention on scratching. Mam, meanwhile, wasted no time in reclaiming her place next to the rock, while Ooz and Birt likewise moved back to their previous roosts. Instead of sitting down himself, Gus looked at the ceiling, where another distended smear of viscous sludge was gathering underneath the wide place in the crack. Soon the mass was too heavy to cling and broke free to tumble straight down toward Pap's still-moist cranium.

*Plop.*

Gus decided not to stay around for the next step in the cycle, which was the usual after dinner routine of the Fishbiter clan. For one thing, dinner had taken place a very, very long time ago, and the shuffle and return was starting to get a little boring (though he never tired of watching the sludge spatter as it struck Pap's hairless scalp). And for another thing, Gus was starting to get very hungry again.

The previous dinner had been the bony carcass of a cave carp that Ooz had claimed from behind an inn in New Theibardin. Of course, all the usable meat had been picked off, but Theiwar cooks were notoriously wasteful. In this case, the head, all the fins, and the tail remained. Furthermore, there had been succulent little bits of flesh between the rib bones of the carp, meat that the cook had been too lazy or impatient to carve out.

As a result, there had been feasting in the Fishbiter household! Well, it was sort of feasting, anyway. At least Pap had eaten like a king; he got the whole head to himself. Mam had claimed the tail, greedily smacking her lips over each morsel. Ooz and Birt got the fins and ribs, and all four of them enjoyed something to eat.

Gus, unfortunately, had been left to scramble for the bits of bone, scale, and gristle that evaded the notice of his elders, though he grabbed one tasty morsel when he fooled Birt into dropping his fin to snatch at a tempting mouse that scrambled over his lap. Of course, the mouse had been only a puff of fuzz tangled at the end of a long thread dangled by Gus, but by the time Birt figured out the ruse, Gus was already smacking his lips, savoring the strong aftertaste of carp. Since Birt would have had to neglect the rest of his feast in order to pound his younger brother, he had to forgo any vengeance in order to protect the remainder of his share.

Even so, Gus's belly was rumbling, and as Pap, Mam, Birt, and Ooz rearranged the seating in the household once again, the youngest Fishbiter ducked his head and exited through the low tunnel that was the house's front door. He emerged into one of the dingy, filthy alleys of Agharhome, the largest "city" (though *nest* or *den* or *hive* or *warren* or *lair* might be more accurate terms) of gully dwarves in the whole of vast, subterranean Thorbardin.

The ceiling, a slanted slab of rock, pressed low over the narrow thoroughfare, which was one of a multitude of similar lightless, stinky, cramped enclosures in the city of the gully dwarves. Dozens of little circular holes led into the bedrock to either side of the alley. These were the doors of houses similar to the one in which Gus and his family lived. Some of them had residents, but a great deal were empty. Hunger, predators, and the deadly gangs of Klar thugs made for short life expectancy for the denizens of Agharhome.

Glumly, Gus started down the lane, descending the steep incline toward the lake, quickly emerging onto a narrow ledge above the water. He looked down to see where the dark waters of the Urkhan Sea lapped against many of the lower tunnels of Agharhome. These points of access were all crowded with hungry gullies, each seeking a lucky chance at a fish, and Gus considered whether he wanted to take his chances at shouldering through the crowd and trying his own fortunes.

Gus was neither unusually large nor unusually small by Aghar standards. He stood about three feet high, with a large nose the prominent feature of his round, weak-chinned face. A scraggly beard grew from that chin, but not thickly enough to mask its recession. His eyes were large and watery, his teeth jutted awkwardly forward from his mouth. He wore a surprisingly nice-looking red silk jacket (stolen from someone's laundry) but the elbows had worn away on it, and it didn't quite enclose his protruding belly.

His saggy pants were held up by a scrap of rope, and though he wore boots, the sole and the front were missing from one of them, so his large, dirty toes projected into view.

He spotted a throng of Aghar squeezed into the narrow mouth of the ravine directly below him. Only two could actually fit at the water's edge, where they crouched, hands extended, waiting for a fish. Behind them, the rest of the group pushed and jostled. "Move, you bluphsplunger goot!" one demanded.

"Back up, doofus wandwaver!" another replied, grappling the first. The two wrestlers tumbled down, pushing the two fishers into the water. One climbed out, crawling between the pair who had claimed the shore, shivering and dripping and again jostling for position.

Gus watched for two minutes before he turned around. His family was bad enough. He had no stomach for rough encounters with other Aghar who would invariably be bigger, rougher, and nastier. And the teeming numbers he encountered at every one of these ravines! He couldn't count very high, but a general guess suggested there were at least two, and two, and two more of them everywhere! Such throngs held no appeal for a loner such as Gus.

So instead of descending, he climbed. It was not too long before he emerged from the small tunnel of the alley into a loftier, though still narrow, passage. This was one of the dramatic clefts that scored the upper surface of Agharbardin, carved into the steep wall of the great cavern that surrounded the Urkhan Sea. As was ever true in Thorbardin, a rock ceiling vaulted overhead, but the ceiling was far above him, allowing a vista that carried far out across the black, still water.

This place was nearly lightless, only faintly illuminated from a few of the old sun shafts that still remained open; the others had long been filled in by debris. The pale beams diffused through the distance, glimmering over a few patches of still water.

It had not always been like this. A half century earlier, the whole shore of the Urkhan Sea would have been aglow with the spillage of light from the many forges, fireplaces, and other fires burning throughout the great dwarven kingdom. In those days the great cities along the lake shore rose up through many terraces on the steep cliffs rising from the water while the great Life-Tree of the Hylar, in the center of the lake, radiated light and warmth from thousands of windows, balconies, and overlooks.

All of those cities were abandoned—ravaged and at least partially destroyed by the depredations of the Chaos War. Vast sections had been hollowed out by mighty fire dragons that had burned tunnels right through the bedrock of the mountain, and in many places those scoured caverns had weakened the surrounding structures catastrophically.

In the center of the lake, where the Life-Tree once had dominated, loomed the most tragic wreckage of the Chaos War and its aftermath. The massive pillar had collapsed, leaving an irregular pile of rocks jutting from the surface. Most Thorbardin dwarves called that place the Isle of the Dead, though to the Aghar it was just the Dead Island. A stub of the great pillar still extended from the lofty roof of the cavern, but it terminated a long way above the top of the island. Every once in a while, new rocks would break free and plummet downward, an unpredictable barrage that ensured the island would not be reinhabited.

Indeed, all the environs of the Urkhan Sea were virtually abandoned; at least there were no proper cities or towns. There were dens of Aghar all around the lake, however, with the largest being Agharhome. Too, there were bands of feral Klar—the wild-eyed, often insane dwarves—who had rejected the new king's orderly city life to roam free in their vast undermountain realm. But the feral Klar were not interested in cities and only passed through the ruins periodically on their nomadic wanderings.

Even though there was virtually no illumination in the vast cavern, Gus could make out some details since light was not, strictly, necessary for deep-delving dwarves to see. The Aghar, like the Theiwar and Daergar, had eyes keenly attuned to the dim conditions of their stone-bordered world. As Gus looked out across the water, he could make out the motionless surface of chilly liquid, black as oil and still as ice. The ruined stub of the Life-Tree jutted from that surface, perhaps two miles away from him.

Beyond the Dead Island and much farther away—about two miles, Gus thought, the upper limit of his arithmetic ability—the vast front of Theibardin rose into view. From an array of docks and cavernous warehouses at the lake level, the great city of the Theiwar spread up the precipitous cliff of the lakeshore. It was dotted with villas, palaces, and temples, all carved from the bedrock of the mountain, each structure positioned to give its dwellers a grand view over the great underground lake at the heart of Thorbardin. Those facades were dark and lifeless as Gus stared, with irregular holes and great gaps showing where the war and its attendant erosion continued to tear away at Theibardin's foundations.

But everything that happened in ancient times (meaning more than two years ago) was beyond an Aghar's imagination. In any event, Gus's attention was directed closer to home. A rivulet of scummy liquid was flowing down the base of the ravine, and he sniffed at it without much hope. The vile brown sludge that flowed there was not, nor had it ever been, a source of food, but he sniffed again, just to be sure. Sighing, he stood and watched the flow go past, moving downward, fast where the ravine was steep, slower where the grade was shallower. It trickled right past the mouth of the tunnel/alley leading to the Fishbiter house. The floor of that side tunnel was about two inches above the flowing sludge. Gus remembered a time when the level of sludge had risen up to that tunnel mouth—it had been an unpleasantly wet and smelly time for the neighborhood.

Just beyond the tunnel mouth, Gus noted, the sludge stopped flowing. Gus knew that place, but he peered at the sight just to be sure. The viscous liquid was collecting in a large holding pond, held in place by a makeshift dam of loose rock that had spilled into the ravine some time about two years ago. Looking up at the cliff wall rising over his head and down at the steep ravine and the tunnel leading to his house, Gus suddenly realized that the sludge pond was poised right over his and his neighbor's houses.

Then he saw something else—there was someone down there, hunched over, studying something on the ground. Squinting, he discerned the hunched back; large, bare feet; and straggly strands of dirt-colored hair that suggested a female gully dwarf.

"Hey!" he called. "Who you?"

She raised her face, which was even dirtier than her feet. It was centered around a huge and not altogether unattractive nose. "Go away, bluphsplunger stoop!" she retorted.

Instead, Gus skidded down the slope to her side, which was right near the edge of the sewage pond. He saw that she was huddled protectively over the limp form of a skinny, bedraggled, and apparently very, very dead, rat.

"That my rat!" Gus declared boldly, hunkering down next to her.

"Go away!" she repeated, picking up the rat and holding it to her tattered dress. "I call you bluphsplunger stoop! You go away!"

"Who you?" Gus repeated, eyeing the rat.

"Slooshy," she replied, glaring at him.

"Why you call me stoop?"

She shrugged. "Not know. Bluphsplunger stoop—different one from you—push me down. But me lucky after all; found rat!" She brightened at the thought and held the grotesque rodent out in a filthy paw. "See?"

Gus was tempted to snatch the rat out of her hand,

but something gave him pause. "Share rat with me?" he suggested instead.

"No!" she snapped, pulling her hand away just as he made his grab. He got his stubby fingers around the hairless tail. But she had a grip on the body and jerked it away until it flew free from her grasp out over the sewage pond, where it landed with a dull plop. Despite the thickness of the liquid, it immediately vanished from sight, sending only a small ripple to the dam of rocks, allowing a small surge to slip over the barrier and spill toward the lake below.

"Now look! Bluphsplunger stoop! You big humpus maker, you!" she shouted, standing up and stomping her feet.

Gus sat on a rock, trying to ignore his empty stomach and the barrage of creative insults that emerged from Slooshy's mouth. She knew a number of interesting words, enhancing most with the "bluphsplunger" modifier as she called him a "doofa," a "goopar," and a "burfhoofing lumpus."

But he couldn't focus on her tirade and, inevitably, was distracted by other things, watching the ooze and the ravine and the barricade of rocks. Many random facts flitted, unbidden and mostly unannounced, through his little brain. He thought of the rat, the tempting morsel flying through the air, the plop in the sludge. The sludge . . .

The sludge was trying to go down, but it couldn't because of the dam.

This sludge was just like the stuff that dripped through the ceiling of his house.

All of his neighbors had sludge dripping through their ceilings as well.

The sludge was trying to go down, but it couldn't because of the dam.

A clatter of rock distracted him. He looked up just as Slooshy threw a small rock, one that had broken loose from high on the cliff. Her aim was good, and she stood right in front of him, so the jagged missile smacked him square in the right eye.

"Ow!" he cried, clapping a hand to his face. Through his other eye, he saw the stone had continued to roll, bouncing over the uneven ground and finally landing in the sludge pond with a smacking splash.

"Stoopy humpus bluphsplunger!" she cried, kneeling to look for another missile.

Still, Gus paid her no attention. He was *thinking*. The stone, like the sludge, was trying to go down. That idea, for some reason, struck Gus as vaguely important. He watched the ripples from the splash disappear as the rock finally vanished beneath the scummy surface. He didn't see Slooshy charging him until he felt the punch in his chest, which she landed with both fists. As the blow struck, his muddy boots slipped from the slick ledge he stood upon.

"Ow!" The pain came from his rump as he came down hard on the solid, slippery stone. His stubby fingers clutched for a handhold, but there was nothing to grab. Instead, he skidded off the ledge, bounced painfully off of a few boulders, and tumbled after the stone that she had flung against his face.

"Here! Grab me!" Slooshy demanded, holding out her hand. At the last moment, Gus did, and she yanked him to a stop, his feet and other hand braced against the slime-coated surfaces of the jagged rocks just above the edge of the pool.

Just like the stone, like the sludge, like everything, the gully dwarf had nearly tumbled down.

Everything goes down.

Then Slooshy let him go and squealed with delight as he did a face plant on the scummy rocks. He looked up at her, grinning in excitement.

"Everything falls!" he shouted.

The truth hit him as hard as the rock had, and he gaped at the amazing reality that was made even more obvious by the inexorable force tugging him down the slick stone surface. The girl laughed so hard, she had to sit down, even as Gus felt stunned by the universal truth of his realization. He clawed to hold his position until his nose started to itch. When he released his grip to scratch himself, his other hand lost purchase, and he skidded down again, down and down, bouncing and tumbling over the lip of the drop to splash heavily into the thick, scummy ooze of the drainage pond.

Gully dwarves tend to be natural swimmers, and Gus was no exception. He instantly popped to the surface and paddled over to the edge of the pond without really thinking about what was happening. Instead, he was still trying to grasp the intricacies, the beauty of the brainstorm that had dawned on him.

Everything goes down.

His hand brushed against something in the ooze, something limp and furry. In triumph he pulled it out to reveal the rat! Clutching his treasure, Gus climbed out of the sludge to find that he had unwittingly crossed the small pool and was perched on the loosely piled rubble left by the rockslide—the rubble that formed the dam that held back the sludge. To one side was the pond, the murky liquid lapping against the rim of the makeshift barrier. To the other side, Gus could see that the rocky slope tumbled steeply away. He recoiled from the edge, realizing that if he lost his balance, he would tumble all the way down to the dark hole where the sludgy stream disappeared into the ancient sewer extending under the Urkhan Sea.

Everything goes down, he knew, and that would include himself.

"Look! Got rat!" he crowed, hoisting the gamey morsel. Unfortunately his movement was too abrupt, and the slippery thing slid from his fingers, through the air, and back into the pond.

"You one funny bluphsplunger gully dwarf, you are!" Slooshy cried, still sitting on the ground, holding her sides from the force of her laughter.

Glumly, Gus looked at the place where the rat had vanished. He saw that more of the liquid, churned by his fall and subsequent swim, had spilled over the lip of the dam, running in gooey rivulets down the surface of tumbled stone.

Even as the thought possessed him, the loose pile of rocks underneath him shifted slightly. Gus scrambled to the side, kicking frantically to climb higher. He made it to safety with a single lunge, but his efforts knocked a couple of stones off the pile. They clattered downward, chased by a small spill of sludgy liquid as a bit of the pond scum trickled through the notch in the dam created by the falling rocks.

And in that instant, everything became really, really clear to the startled gully dwarf.

The sludge in the pond, like everything else in the world, wanted to go down. But the dam was stopping it from following the course of the stream. Instead, it sat there in the bowl of rock, and tried to go down a different way—the way that led through the ceilings of all the Aghar houses that happened to lie directly beneath.

"Hey!" he cried, hopping to his feet, quickly circling the small pond. Slooshy looked at him in confusion. "Hey! The sludge wants to go down!"

"That not so funny," she replied. "You fall in again?" she added hopefully.

"Everything falls down!" he shouted, throwing back his head.

A few Aghar were higher up on the sides of the ravine, climbing or descending within his view. They stared at him in surprise, startled by the outburst. Most of them simply ignored him, though one hefty, young fellow tossed a sharp rock in Gus's direction. He ducked, then shouted out in glee as the stone hit the liquid and, naturally, vanished.

"See! Everything goes down!"

"What? You crazy bluphsplunger now, you are!"

Slooshy said, backing away. "Go away!"

She started climbing up the sloping ground, stopping to throw a rock at him every few feet. He gleefully skipped out of the path of each missile. "See! Goes down!" he cried when each errant stone vanished into the pond.

"That crazy talk! Stoop humpus bluphsplunger Aghar, leave me alone!" Slooshy shouted back. She threw one more rock—another he easily avoided—from the top of the ridge before vanishing from his view.

He didn't care. He raced back up the ravine floor to the tunnel leading down to his neighborhood, skidding and sliding down the steep shaft. He almost couldn't control his momentum until he caught a flash of movement on the ground, something slithering along at the base of the wall.

It was a cavebug!

Gus stopped the only way that he could: he sat down on the hard stone ground. Ignoring the pain in his bruised rump, he reached down and grabbed the bug with his stubby thumb and forefinger. Hoisting it, feeling the hunger gnawing at his belly, he almost popped it right into his mouth.

Then he remembered: sting thumb, not tongue!

That axiom of cavebug dining had been passed down through generations of gully dwarves, and Gus remembered it just in time. The little, wormlike bug wriggled in his grasp, the numerous legs—at least two on each side—flailing for purchase. At the tail he spotted the sharp stinger, erect and thrashing. Squinting, carefully concentrating, Gus held up his thumb and let the wicked-looking barb plunge into the pad of flesh.

"Ow!" he shouted as fiery tendrils of pain shot through his thumb, his hand, and up his arm. The stinger itself detached from the bug to jut from the gully dwarf's skin. Knowing his prey was disarmed, Gus popped it into his mouth, breaking the segmented body with a crunch of his teeth and quickly swallowing the still-wriggling parts of the doomed creature. He smacked his lips and enjoyed the sensation of delicious food. If he was not exactly full, neither was he starving, and starving was a very pleasant thing not to be doing.

For a few moments, he inspected the floor of the alley, looking, hoping, seeking another one of the bugs. But he was lucky to have found the one creature and was unsurprised that no more were in view. He smacked his lips again, ignoring the searing pain in his thumb, wishing Slooshy would come along so he could brag about his precious discovery.

Only after two minutes did he remember that precious discovery, his mission, his crucial news. Then he hopped to his feet again and started down the steeply sloping alley toward his house, which was right around the next bend. Tumbling to a stop before the Fishbiter residence, he burst inside—fortunately, the Aghar family had no use for a front door—and immediately collided with Birt, who was lunging to outmaneuver Ooz to claim the rock that Pap, dripping with sludge, had once again vacated.

"Everything goes down!" Gus cried.

"Hey! That my rock!" Pap cried, knocking the momentarily triumphant Birt out of the way.

The patriarch resumed his place of honor, just as another dribble of goop gathered below the crack in the ceiling. Gus watched, waiting, knowing that it wouldn't be long. The globule grew heavy, distended, drooping ever further downward while Pap, once more king of his household, glared sternly at his wife and sons.

*Plop.*

# TWO

# WILLIM THE BLACK

The chamber was far beneath the summits of the
Kharolis, well below the reinforced bastion that
was the north gate, underneath, even, the teeming city
of Norbardin. In fact, the very lowest portion of that
city, the slum known as Anvil's Echo, was far above the
deep and isolated cavern, the large space that had been
excavated at great expense from the very solid bedrock
under the nation of Thorbardin.

That place had once been intended as the new Council
Hall of the Thanes, the seat of Thorbardin's government
in the wake of the Chaos War's devastation. It had been
designed at the commission of King Tarn Bellowgranite—
he who was called the Failed King—and many years of
labor, including complicated architecture and engineering,
had gone into its creation. Though it had never been used
for the purpose for which it had been intended, it had been
almost completely finished before being abandoned. Each
throne had a lofty dais that, even incomplete, overlooked
the circular floor of the chamber. Proud columns lined
the distant walls, and broad stairways provided access to
the upper rim that extended around the whole periphery
of the huge room.

Along one wall a broad ramp extended upward. At one time the ramp had connected to the environs of Norbardin, but no longer. Barely a quarter mile from the vast chamber, a solid wall of rock, tight-fitting stones installed by dwarf craftsmen, blocked all passage. The barrier was so well made that even air and water couldn't penetrate and so thick that the pounding of a hammer on one side of the barrier would be inaudible to a listener on the other.

To the rest of Thorbardin, the chamber was an ill-omened place, and most did not care to remember it or acknowledge its existence. Shortly before its intended completion, a rare earthquake had shaken the normally stable dwarven kingdom. Damage and injury had been minimal, except there, in the intended council hall. Along the base of the vast chamber, a great crack had scored the floor, opening up an apparently bottomless trench and releasing fires in the bowels of the world up into the realm of the dwarven kingdom.

When the new king had banished the Failed King, he had ordered that place sealed, closed off, and forgotten. The wall had been built, the roads above realigned to avoid even the dead-end passage, and the story of the grand hall was officially dismissed as just one more of the Failed King's unrealized dreams. According to the decree of the new king, the hall would remain forever unused, isolated, and forgotten.

But it was not.

Instead, one had come there who had no need to travel down roads, who found thick walls no barrier, who feared no fire, and who would be intimidated by no obstacle. He was a powerful wizard of the Theiwar—in his own mind he was *the* most powerful wizard of the Theiwar—and he had claimed that place as his own.

His name was Willim the Black, and he had been a powerful wizard for a very long time. He was ruthless and cruel. He delighted in the suffering of his enemies, so he had made many enemies indeed. When, decades earlier, the gods had taken leave of the world after the Chaos War, and the gods of magic departed with their other immortal kin, Willim—along with every other wizard of Krynn—had lost his magical prowess. His enemies had seized him and secured him in the deepest dungeon of the Theiwar quarter, gouging out his eyes as part of their punishment. He had languished in that prison, given only enough food and water to keep him, and his suffering, alive. And through all those dark years, his hatred had grown and grown, and his desire for vengeance had driven him to survive.

Until, finally, there came the summons he had awaited. The gods of magic returned! And when they did, the long-absent powers of their wizards had been awakened and revitalized. Willim had broken his bonds, killed his nearest and most dire enemies, and joined the rest of the wizardly orders in their fight to reclaim the Tower of High Sorcery at Wayreth Forest. Black, red, and white wizards had fought in unison to drive out the forces of wild magic and corruption that had claimed that sacred place. And finally, the true orders of magic had reclaimed their rightful status. The Wizards' Conclave was restored, and the practitioners of the magic arts had gone their separate ways.

Willim's path had brought him back to Thorbardin shortly after the Failed King had been banished and the new one installed. Such political realities were of little consequence to the Theiwar mage, who fostered his hatreds on a more personal basis. It just so happened that one of those hatreds, dating back to long before his imprisonment, was aimed at the new king, and it pleased Willim to know he worked toward his enemy's destruction in the very chamber that once had been intended as the seat of the king's power.

Willim the Black had much to do to effect his goals.

He sensed a stirring deep within the crack in the floor, and he knew that Gorathian was awake. The black-robed wizard perceived the movement of his pet, and he welcomed the presence as a more mortal dwarf would have welcomed a long-lost lover.

Willim had no need for lovers, however.

Gorathian was different. Gorathian was mighty— mightier even than Willim, in some ways—but Gorathian was also trapped, a creature bound by a stricture not of its own making. Willim held the key to Gorathian's trap, and Willim had promised that, someday, Gorathian would be set free. But that day was far in the future, and before then the beast had much to do to aid the wizard in achieving his ends.

The soft light of the beast's awakening was beginning to suffuse the dark lair, the deep place where, when Willim had magically come there, he had discovered Gorathian. It had occurred some years before, and the Theiwar mage had not been ready yet to employ an ally as powerful, but uncontrollable, as Gorathian. So Willim had ensured that Gorathian stayed down in its foul hole, lurking somewhere close to the very bowels of the world. Willim had taunted the creature, had fed it morsels to whet its appetite, had provoked it with tales of the evils done to the beast and its world. Gorathian had been roused to fury, but as yet William had kept it from emerging from the deep lair.

Willim wandered through the maze of his lab toward the deep, virtually bottomless, crevasse carved through the floor. The dwarf's eyelids were sewn shut, but he saw more clearly than any of the several Theiwar assistants who scuttled out of his way. Enlightened by a spell of true-seeing, Willim's mind perceived not just the variations of light, but heat, spiritual presence, objects masked by utter darkness—in short, everything there was to see and many things that could not be seen by ordinary beings. His powers were such that the spell was a permanent feature of his consciousness; the loss of his eyes was by then merely a long-ago unpleasantness, one that had been thoroughly avenged.

He wore the loose robe of black silk that was the symbol of his order. Though numerous runes of power had been woven into that material, the symbols were as dark as the silk itself and, thus, invisible to anyone who looked at him. His skin was almost albino pale, like many of his race, though his wiry beard bristled with gray. He wore soft boots that allowed him to walk silently even without the assistance of magic. His beard was long and black, tucked into the belt where he also wore a pair of short, needle-sharp daggers. He caressed the hilts of his weapons as he approached the great crack through the floor of his laboratory.

The deep fires burning in the pit where Gorathian lived warmed the place, and the radiant energy felt good on the dwarf's face and hands, the only parts of his body that were exposed around the enveloping cloak of his black wizard's robe. The heat grew more intense as he approached the crevasse until he had to murmur a magical word, conjuring a spell of protection against that infernal warmth. His flesh cooled slightly. His robe was immune to such temperatures, though a garment of normal cloth would have smoldered or worse as he stepped closer to the chasm.

Stopping at the very edge, he let the fiery embrace wash over him. The intensity there would sear normal flesh and kindle wood into instant flame, yet the wizard of the black robe was merely comfortably warm in the presence of the deep, subterranean inferno.

"Gorathian, my pet. The time will be soon," he whispered, lying and taunting as ever.

He sensed the movement deep within the pit, a writhing of serpentine coils, a shapeless body rearing, reaching, straining upward with limbs of pure fire. The end of a sinuous tendril, a slithering rope of flame, extended out of the pit and wrapped itself around the Theiwar dwarf's boot in an almost tender stroke. Willim smiled. He sensed the need, the hunger, in that incendiary touch, and he knew Gorathian's well-stoked frustration and fury would serve the dark dwarf very well indeed.

"Patience, my pretty one. But a morsel, for your pleasure."

He turned his eyeless face toward the far corner of his lair, where the cages were positioned. "Ochre," he called, attracting the attention of one of his apprentices. That Theiwar, a young male with bristling black hair, broad shoulders, glowering visage and very long arms, looked up immediately at his master's command.

"Fetch me . . ." Willim's voice trailed off as he inspected the occupants of the cages. The cells were solidly built, barred with steel, standing in a row of a half dozen along the floor a good distance away from the crevasse. He kept a variety of prisoners there since his work so often required fresh components, blood or tissues or organs drawn from living flesh. Currently the cages held a pair of elves, gaunt and hollow eyed, yet still projecting the stubborn dignity of that ancient race; a miserable goblin that, misunderstanding the wizard's attention, clawed at the bars and yelped in an effort to nominate himself; a filthy gully dwarf, sleeping as usual; and several Klar prisoners, feral dwarves who had been captured by the wizard personally, and stared sullenly at their vicious captor.

The elves were unique, too precious to waste. The goblin might be useful for something else, someday. Each of the Klar could be a valuable political pawn, each might find a place in the grand scheme of Willim's that drew ever closer to fruition.

"Fetch me the gully dwarf," the wizard said with a slight sigh.

"Up, you!" snarled Ochre, kicking the cage to awaken the filthy creature. The Aghar howled in fear, backing into the corner of his cell as Ochre opened the door. Seizing the gully dwarf in one meaty paw, the Theiwar apprentice dragged him from the cage and across the lair toward Willim the Black. Ochre threw a hand across his face to shield himself from the heat as he approached, but even so, he dared not come within twenty steps of the chasm. Instead, stopping as near as he could venture before the heat overcame him, he hurled the dwarf facedown onto the stone floor.

"You!" barked the mage, pointing a finger at the cringing Aghar. "Come!"

The word was not just a word, but a command of dark sorcery. The dimwitted creature could not have disobeyed even if he had been shrewd enough to sense the doom awaiting him.

So the Aghar numbly pushed himself to his feet and stumbled forward, into the aura of heat. His skin reddened from the blistering radiance, and his tattered shirt began to smoke. He howled miserably, but he endured the pain, compelled by the word of command.

Gorathian's fiery tentacle released its caressing hold upon Willim's foot, rearing like the head of a snake up from the floor. It waved and danced, almost as though it were sniffing the air, sensing the approach of its master's gift. When the Aghar was six or eight steps away, the tentacle lashed out, slapping the stone floor, stretching to wrap itself around the hapless creature's ankle. Flame seared the Aghar's dirty skin, and the tendril of fire pulled like a whip.

The gully dwarf toppled onto his back. He shrieked in terror as the effect of the command spell was broken. Twisting, clawing the floor with his dirty fingernails, the terrified Aghar tried to break away but to no avail. Gorathian tugged, and the gully dwarf vanished over the lip of the chasm, trailed by only the lingering echoes of his screams.

Ochre quickly retreated from the heat to return to his

daily task: crushing the coal that the wizard used to fuel his forge and ovens. The other apprentices—there were ten in all—had not even looked up from their labors. Willim nodded, pleased with their dedication, satisfied that they feared him and, more, feared him absolutely.

He glanced once more into the depths of the chasm. He could sense Gorathian seething down there. The morsel had not satisfied him, not at all. If anything, it had merely whetted his hunger.

Willim was pleased.

# THREE

## ROILING THE WATERS

Day and night were meaningless concepts in sunless Thorbardin, but an industrious society such as that of the dwarves required a method for keeping track of the passage of time. The typical convention among the Theiwar, Daergar, and other mountain dwarves involved counting intervals, each of which roughly approximated a twenty-four-hour cycle on the surface. That method allowed laborers to get paid for their time, rents to be charged, and other duration-specific matters to be calculated with remarkable accuracy.

The Aghar measured time in intervals as well, but it was fair to say they were a trifle less accurate than their more advanced cousins when it came to keeping track of the passage of hours, days, weeks, or years. To a gully dwarf, "one interval" was a short time, and "two intervals" was anything longer than a short time.

Thus, Gus calculated that it was two intervals later when he returned to the sludge pond and its dam in the ravine over his house. For once, he wasn't terribly hungry. Birt had snared a bat that carelessly flew into the family's house, and in the ensuing tug-of-war, Gus had claimed

33

not only one wing, but a good portion of the furry little body. He had gulped it down before either of his brothers or parents had been able to snatch it away.

In a sense, it was that satisfying repast that had propelled him back to the ravine. The rest of his family had been more than a little outraged by his success, and after a dozen cuffs about his face and ears, Gus decided that he might be a little more comfortable—or at least less bruised—if he hung about somewhere else for a while. So he had scampered out the front door, chased by a stream of pebbles and abuse. Almost without thinking about it, he had emerged from the alley and crossed around the sludge pond until he found himself standing on the loosely piled rocks of the dam.

He got around to the place where he had accidentally knocked a couple of rocks out of the way, where the modest rush of slimy water had been pouring out of the pond when he was last there. At the moment, however, there was only a tiny trickle passing through the gap. Gus stared, scratching his head. Was there a flaw in his understanding?

"Everything goes down," he reminded himself aloud, trying out the words. But there was not enough sludge in the pond to go down through the gap, for the simple reason that the surface of the liquid was two inches lower than it had been before. The muck couldn't go down because it would have to go up first to pour over the dam.

"Bluphsplunger!" he cursed, the sound of the nice expletive making him feel just a little better. He sat down on a rock and rested his chin in his hand, thinking.

It had been so promising, his idea. If the sludge pond went down, into the lake, it wouldn't keep going down into the Fishbiter house. But how could the sludge go down when it first had to go up to get over the top of the dam?

That was when the answer came to him in a flash: it was the *dam* that had to be lowered first! If the dam went down, then the sludge could go down again!

Eagerly Gus knelt on the crest of the dam. He tugged at a big rock, feeling it wobble slightly. Clawing at the edges, he dug at the gravel and sand, slowly excavating a narrow crack around the stone. His thumb still throbbed from the cavebug sting, and he momentarily stuck it in his mouth, thinking. Even by Aghar standards, his thumb didn't taste very good, so he decided to ignore the pain and go back to work. Soon the rock was wobbling freely, and Gus hopped to his feet and grabbed the top with both hands. Straining for leverage, he planted his feet and leaned back away from the pond, swaying over the steep face of the rock pile where it tumbled to the bottom of the ravine.

He knelt, ready to exert himself on the next rock, when suddenly he was distracted by screams and sounds of commotion from nearby. Quickly Gus scrambled up to the top of the ridge and peered out over the next steep, narrow valley, a ravine that ran parallel to his own, like all the others along the slope spilling down toward the dark waters of the Urkhan Sea. Several figures were bounding around in the narrow space, and at least two of them carried big, sharp swords.

"I got this one ... there goes another!" shouted a big dwarf—he sounded like a Theiwar—holding a squirming figure by the scruff of its neck. The captive, Gus saw at once, was a gully dwarf. Other Aghar had scuttled away, but at least one other was held down by the big dwarf's foot on his belly.

"You get the little bitch!" the Theiwar called to a companion. "I'll take care of these two."

Several Aghar squirmed up the base of the ravine, with a second Theiwar chasing after them. The two attackers were marked by the exceptionally pale skin that was a feature of their race. Possessing true darkvision, the Theiwar had no difficulty following after his desperately fleeing quarry. Still another gully dwarf started scrambling up the side of the narrow trench, heading toward Gus's vantage. He recognized her at once—Slooshy!—and was about to call out her name when his tongue froze in his throat. He could only stare, eyes bugging, at the scene in the bottom of the ravine.

The Theiwar was casually smacking the head of his captive on a rock, stunning him. Then he turned to the dwarf wriggling beneath his foot. Lifting his sword, he chopped down sharply, and the Aghar's head came sliding right off his body! Gus tried to turn his eyes away, but he couldn't, not before the Theiwar raised his bloody weapon a second time and decapitated the other helpless gully dwarf he had just knocked out.

Finally Slooshy was there, clawing frantically to climb up the last two feet, gratefully grabbing Gus's hand as he reached down to pull her over the steep crest. She was breathing hard and sobbing, and he quickly pulled her down, out of the line of sight of the murderers.

"Slooshy! It's me—Gus!" he whispered. Suddenly he felt terribly guilty for taking her rat and mocking her as she had thrown stones at him. "What happen?" he pressed.

"Big Theiwar! They come and grab my pop, cut him head off!" she wailed as Gus tried to muffle her mouth. Her terrible grief sent a cold shiver down his spine.

"Shh!" he urged. "We hide! Big Theiwar goofars go 'way soon!"

At least he fervently hoped they would. Slooshy sobbed against his chest, but she managed to stifle the noise of her grief, and Gus finally broke free, climbed to the crest, and peeked down into the neighboring ravine. The two dwarves were, in fact, heading away from them, descending toward the lake, where a large boat with one more Theiwar aboard had pulled up to the shore. The two killers carried their grisly trophies by the hair, and each bore several more small, lifeless heads dangling from each hand.

"Why the bluphsplunging Theiwar kill gullies?" he

wondered aloud as he slid back down to Slooshy. "Never do that yesterday!"

"They say 'kill for bunty,' " she said angrily, sniffing, wiping her large nose with the back of her hand. She glared at Gus accusingly. "What is 'bunty'?" she demanded.

"Not know," the Aghar had to reply. Whatever it was, "bunty" seemed a very frightening thing. "Come with me. We go hide."

She didn't argue, instead taking his hand as he carefully started to lead her down the slope. They avoided the sewage pond, instead dropping farther down, coming along the face of the rock pile that was holding back the gallons of sludge. They heard hoarse shouts coming from here and there along the shore, and he guessed that many more Theiwar were roaming about, seeking to kill Aghar in the service of the terrifying "bunty."

Gus had all but forgotten he had been trying to destroy that dam when he had been distracted by the Theiwar, but he was startled to see that the front of the dam was very wet. Maybe the sludge was coming down, after all; in fact, he didn't really care. Suddenly, the inside of the Fishbiter house—which was too small for any Theiwar to readily enter—seemed like the nicest, most welcome place in the world, leaky roof or not.

Staying low, Gus and Slooshy reached the base of the dam. He looked up at the next ridge, knowing they would have to scale it in order to reach the mouth of the tunnel leading to his house.

"When I tug, you run with me, really, really fast," he said. "Bluphsplunging Theiwar never catch us!"

"All right," she said softly, looking at him with an unfamiliar expression. (No one had ever regarded Gus with adoring eyes before.)

"Run!" he barked, jumping to his feet and sprinting around the curving base of the dam . . . and straight into the arms of a Theiwar dwarf who had been taking a break, sitting on a rock, slurping a drink from a flask that smelled like dwarf spirits.

"Hah!" cried the Theiwar, reaching out a big hand toward Gus's neck. "Gotcha!"

He spoke just a second too soon. Apparently reluctant to risk losing the precious contents of his flask, he had juggled the bottle and quickly stuffed a cork in the mouth before he made his move. By the time he reached out to grab the Aghar, Gus had dropped down prone and found that his face was right in front of the other dwarf's knee.

Gus did what instinct has always compelled gully dwarves to do in such dire circumstances: he bit his enemy as fiercely as he could.

Unfortunately, the knee did not prove a remarkably susceptible target for such an attack. The knobby joint was hard and resistant. The Theiwar jerked his leg forward, and Gus tasted blood—his own blood—as the dwarf's knee smashed his teeth and lips. He tumbled back and, looking up, saw stars twinkling in Thorbardin's roofed sky.

"Hey!" shrieked Slooshy, closing in and catching the unbalanced Theiwar by surprise. She chomped down on his fleshier thigh, provoking a howl of pain. The big dwarf stumbled backward, cursing as the glass bottle flew from his hands and shattered on the rocks of the hard ground.

"Damn you!" the Theiwar declared, reaching down and seizing Slooshy by her scraggly hair. Gus was sitting up by then, and he pounced to his feet and charged forward, driving the top of his head into his foe's solar plexus.

"Oof!" grunted the big dwarf, staggering backward and swinging a fist at Gus. The Aghar easily ducked the blow but looked for a chance to close in on the enemy who still held the wriggling female by her hair. "Gagger! Slice!" called the Theiwar loudly. "Help me out, here!"

He was immediately rewarded by cries of alarm and the sounds of boots scraping across the rocks of the ravine slope. They were coming from up the valley but closing fast.

Gus panicked. The tunnel to his house was only a short distance away, and he longingly thought of racing up the slope and diving through the narrow entrance like a cave rat running from pursuing lizard-wolves.

Then Slooshy cried out. Still squirming, she managed to deliver a kick to the Theiwar's groin that dropped the big dwarf like a toppled stone. Even as he fell, however, the fellow kept his fingers wrapped through the little Aghar's hair, pulling her down to the ground with him.

Gus knew he couldn't run away. "You bluphsplunger doofar!" he cursed, leaping on the fallen Theiwar, driving his fist into the fellow's nose hard enough to produce a spurt of blood. "You let go!" he shouted, drawing back his arm for another punch.

But by then Gagger and Slice were there, sliding down the ravine wall in a shower of rocks. One grabbed Gus by the neck and threw him to the ground with enough force to drive the air from his lungs. The other hoisted the squirming Slooshy, holding her at arm's length as she kicked and punched and flailed helplessly at the air.

"Let me do it," growled the first Theiwar, pushing himself to his feet, wiping the blood from his nose as he stared at Gus with cold hatred simmering in his black eyes. "This'll all be over in a minute," he sneered, pulling out a wicked-looking black blade.

Gus, still pressed to the ground, wasn't listening, though. Instead, he was thinking, wondering: why is the ground in front of the dam so wet? It seemed even wetter than it had been a minute earlier, when he and Slooshy had tried to make their escape. There came a sound added to the wetness, a groaning shift in the ground, wet rocks moving against each other, sliding, rearranging, everything going down.

"What in Reorx's name—?" the Theiwar swordsman demanded, looking up. "Run!" cried out another.

"From what?" demanded the third, who still held the wriggling Slooshy.

The answer came, quickly, with a swift collapse of stone, and a powerful gush of filthy water that, despite its effluent stench, Gus found strangely cleansing.

# FOUR

## SONS OF KAYOLIN

The body had decayed to the point where no flesh was visible on the death's-head skull, though the matted remnant of a once-lush beard lay in a tangle over the shattered breastplate. The right arm was missing, and the splinter of bone distending from the shoulder socket suggested the cut had not been clean—more like the limb had been torn from the warrior at some point in the unknown past. The left arm still wore a shield, but that protective plate was split in two, the wrist beneath broken. The helm, of good Kayolin steel, was dented deeply at the crest, indicating where the mortal wound had fallen.

Despite the signs of violence, the corpse seemed peaceful. As he studied the body that was seated against the cave wall, with its short legs—obviously a dwarf—extended outward, Brandon could imagine that the fellow had simply sat down there for a rest and had perished pleasantly during his deep delving, far under the Garnet range. He held his oil lamp high, letting the flickering illumination play over the grotesque corpse, but he couldn't suppress a shudder. His involuntary movement only increased the flickering garishness of the spectacle.

"How long d'you think he's been here?" Brandon asked Nailer, trying for a brawny, carefree tone that somehow turned into a nervous squeak.

"How in Reorx's name should I know?" His older brother scowled, glaring at Brandon as if irritated by the question, and Brandon knew Nailer had been as deeply spooked by the discovery as he had.

They had come upon the body by accident, almost stumbling over it as they pressed through the trackless caves with only the transient flicker of their precious wick to light their path. For many intervals they had explored with no sign of previous dwarf visitors. Then they had discovered that distinct sign, but it was not a good sign, not at all.

The elder shrugged and uttered a sound almost like a growl. "Let's get on with it."

"Shouldn't we . . . I don't know . . . bury him or something?" Brandon asked softly.

Nailer looked at him angrily but surprisingly did not make a contemptuous retort. Instead, he drew a breath, as if trying to be patient. "Look at his shield. Can you make out the sign?"

Brandon knelt and played the light over the shattered buckler. "No. Something black, some kind of shape. But it could be anything."

"So it's not the Bluestone Wedge, right? Right? He's not from our house?"

The younger brother shook his head as Nailer went on. "And he's got—he had—black hair. That marks him as maybe a Theiwar or Daergar, maybe a Klar. But he certainly wasn't a Hylar."

"No, not a Hylar," Brandon agreed.

"Then he's not even a dwarf of our clan. Let's leave him for his own kin to lay to rest. If it makes you feel better, we can report the finding to someone once we get back to Garnet Thax."

His brother was right, and in fact, Brandon only then reflected on how hard it would be to dig a grave in the solid bedrock. It could be done, of course—they were delving dwarves by nature—but it would take an awful lot of work. And the sounds of the digging would be sure to attract attention, he realized with a shudder.

"So do you think it's true? That these caves are haunted down here?" he asked tentatively.

"Does it look to you like he was done in by a ghost?" asked Nailer, back to his old sarcastic self.

Brandon winced, not wishing to consider the question. "I guess not. Anyway, we've come pretty far below the Zhaban Delvings. It seems like we might be in the right cave. At least there used to be something in here that discouraged exploration."

"*Used* to be?" Nailer snorted. "I'd give good odds that this poor fellow was done in by a cave troll and even better odds that the damned thing is still down here."

Brandon tightened the chin strap of his helmet and gripped the haft of his venerable axe in both hands, trying not to let his excitement show. He had battled goblins before and even—with Nailer and his father—taken on a bull ogre in its mountain lair. But a troll was fiercer, shrewder, and meaner than any of those foes. A troll would be very exciting. He sincerely hoped they'd have a chance to find it, kill it, and bring its head home as a trophy for the king. *That* would get his family noticed at the royal court!

"You're not so stupid that you *want* to meet a troll, are you?" Nailer asked in contempt, eyeing his brother warily.

Brandon bristled resentfully. "What if I am? We could take it, you and I." With his axe head, he indicated his brother's strong right arm, the hand that held the warhammer Nailer had recently purchased with its chiseled head of Kaylin steel. The length of that weapon's mighty hilt was impressive, half Nailer's height. Nailer had been carrying it in a sling across his back for most of the long weeks of their mission. Brandon saw his brother lift the hammer from its sling and hold it at the ready, easily balancing the heavy weapon in one hand.

"Wouldn't that just be the Bluestone luck?" Nailer snorted again. "Why not make it *three* cave trolls?"

He drew a breath, clearly trying hard to contain his exasperation as he fixed his younger brother with a stern glare. "Listen, you fool of a lad. We're down here because all the tests, every other cave we've explored, suggests there might be a true vein of gold in this rock. A real treasure, which would bring real rewards to mother and father—and to all of us. If we have to fight some cave troll to find it, so be it. But Reorx take my tongue if I'm going to go looking for the monster or let it distract us from our purpose."

"Yeah, I know," Brandon conceded. He adjusted the straps of his heavy pack and followed his brother as Nailer stepped past the decayed corpse and continued into the darkness. Still, the younger dwarf couldn't suppress another rush of excitement, and his knuckles whitened around his weapon as he stared into the shadowy niches to either side of the descending cavern. "But did you ever think that, just maybe, winning a fight with a troll might start to *change* the Bluestone luck?"

Nailer ignored him, and Brandon followed him along, feeling surprisingly cheerful. Exploration was a far cry from the grinding tedium of the king's court. He felt more at home exploring the dangerous passages with his brother than he ever did negotiating the banquets and ceremonies that attended the great throne room in Garnet Thax. There, he was keenly conscious of his role as a very insignificant member of a very insignificant, and notably unlucky, noble family, surrounded by swaggering wealthy merchants and captains, rich mine owners and shrewd traders.

Of course, his family had not always been insignificant, but if anything, that knowledge served only to aggravate his awareness of their current status. The Bluestone luck, dating back to the Cataclysm more than four centuries earlier, had ensured that the house had been unable to prosper.

And why should money matter so much, anyway? Well, in truth, it didn't, Brandon admitted to himself with a secret chuckle. Perhaps it made all the difference to the rich themselves and to the swaggering young men who dressed in finery and tried to impress the girls with family money. But it didn't matter all that much to the girls, really, not in his experience. He recalled very fondly the attentions of several noble young females. Buxom and blonde, always ready to enjoy a high-kicking dance or a tall mug of ale, those ladies seemed more than happy to spend time with Brandon and his brother rather than with the fancy-dressing, smug scions of the great merchant houses. One, a lass named Rona of House Darkwater, had been his regular lover for most of the past year. Their open romance had sparked more than one brawling encounter in which the Bluestone brothers were often outnumbered, occasionally taunted, and sometimes sucker-punched or jumped from behind by jealous rivals higher up the social scale of the elite.

The brothers won more fights then they lost, and even when they lost the fight, they usually won the girls. All in all, it wasn't a bad life. In truth, Nailer was a tall, handsome dwarf with flowing blond hair and a yellow beard. And Brandon, whether he knew it or not, was even taller, and more handsome. He had his brother's strapping shoulders, sturdy legs, and strong hands, but he also possessed a guileless face and a winning smile that had, all of his life, allowed him to make friends quickly.

"Hey, where are you? Back at the Cracked Mug?" Nailer asked, jolting him out of his reverie.

Brandon had, indeed, been recalling a certain barmaid who worked at that very tavern, the lovely Bondall. He blushed, realizing that his brother had halted a few paces ahead of him and was impatiently waiting for him to catch up.

"Sorry," he said, turning his attention back to their surroundings.

It was a natural cave created by the erosive action of flowing water, the two dwarves knew. The curves in the wall were rounded, and stalactites dangled from the ceiling above, pointing to stalagmites rising from below, in some cases merging into staunch columns that gave the cavern a sense of majesty, almost like the great hall of the king himself. The water had long vanished, leaving a floor that was strewn with rubble, rounded rocks that, like the walls, showed the smoothing effects of long erosion. In many places passageways, some narrow and others wide as a royal hallway, extended to the right or left. But the two brothers, long accustomed to the subterranean landscape, could see by the deep channel and the steadily descending grade that they were following the main branch of what was proving to be an exceptionally extensive cavern network.

The surrounding rock was limestone, typical of such a cave and not the type of rock that would normally contain a vein of any heavy metal, let alone gold. But their explorations had shown them that the stratum of limestone lay atop a much heavier, older layer of stone. That harder bedrock had already yielded indications of iron deposits and ore containing aluminum. Just a few intervals earlier, the brothers had located, between the stratum and the stream that flowed there, a shelf that bore definite traces of gold—flakes and tiny nuggets of exceptional purity. Making an estimate based half on long experience and half on an intangible hunch, Nailer had led them to that cavern, and—despite the old legends that the caves were haunted by some unnamed horror—they had been delving deep into the bedrock, seeking the source of the tantalizing bits of gold.

Until they had encountered the body of the long-dead dwarf, the place had looked promising. Every so often the tougher bedrock under the layer of limestone came into view, and the two dwarves nursed every hope that the next time that happened they would spot a vein of precious yellow metal intermingling with the dull stone. Conserving their precious supply of lamp oil by keeping the flame low, they took turns carrying the light and carefully probed their way deeper into the caverns.

But for the moment, everywhere was soft bedrock and shadows that gave it texture and mystery. It was Nailer's turn to carry the lamp, and he held it high in his left hand, keeping the hammer ready in his other. Brandon looked to the right, where the cavern ceiling sloped into the darkness, meeting the rubble and dust of the floor in a crease that might have ended in a foot's drop or continued for a hundred miles. To the left was a series of columns, arrayed almost like a drapery, with rippling edges and articulated spires—still, eternal, and almost lifelike.

Then one of those columns moved.

It had appeared as immobile as a cliff, a tower of pale gray, until a great club of an arm shot out, a mighty fist driving toward Nailer's shoulder.

"Look out!" Brandon cried. Even before he finished the shout, he reacted, unconsciously. He hoisted his axe and brought it down, backed by all the strength of his broad shoulders and sturdy, muscular arms, directly into that striking limb.

The fist was attached to a monstrous creature, he saw, recognizing the beast as a cave troll. The hulking monster, as cold and gray as the very bedrock, had been virtually invisible standing there among the natural columns of the cave. It seemed to move as swiftly as a striking snake, lunging with that punch that could have smashed Nailer's shoulder or, if it landed against the side of his head, break his neck.

But Brandon had moved even faster. His axe blade, of ancient steel, struck the troll's arm at the elbow and sliced cleanly through the grotesque, stony flesh. The severed limb knocked Nailer to the side, still, though it was a blow interrupted. The elder dwarf dropped the lantern, which cracked on the stone floor. The spilling oil ignited, offering welcome extra illumination for at least a brief moment. The monster howled and spun around to face Brand, swinging its left hand in a sweeping punch while the flaring light cast its shadow as a gargantuan outline on the cavern wall and ceiling.

The young dwarf ducked, and the troll's fist only grazed the top of his helmet—yet even that glancing blow stunned Brandon and threw him onto his tail. Knocked breathless, he strained for air and gaped at the troll as it leaped toward him. His nerveless fingers strained to grasp, much less lift, his axe. Brandon's vision was filled with a ghastly face: slate-gray skin, as jagged as a craggy bluff; two eyes as lightless and deep as cave mouths; a nose that jutted like a spur of rock; and a mouth gaping wide, lined with rows of sharp stalactites and stalagmites.

A heavy hand, cold and hard as granite, pressed against Brandon's chest, the pressure choking him, and that maw flashed close, foul breath coiling like miasma around the terrified dwarf's head. Before the fatal bite landed, however, Nailer charged in, landing a blow with his hammer on the troll's shoulder and knocking the monster to the side. Howling again, a screech that grated on dwarf ears, the beast backed away.

It loomed over the brothers, with its left arm dangling limply from its shattered shoulder. The severed stump of its right arm flailed, but as Nailer swung his hammer again, the troll continued to retreat, backing into a niche between two of the graceful columns masking that side of the cave. Brandon finally caught his breath and jerked to his feet. The two dwarves closed in, but the troll sprang away, the stone-shaped beast again moving with incongruous agility.

"Where in Reorx's name did it go?" demanded Nailer, following the monster through the gap, halting and peering into the consuming darkness. "There's all kinds of places to hide back here."

"We hurt it bad; let's get after it!" Brandon urged, charging forward, trying to shoulder his way past his brother. He looked at the rocky floor, seeking blood or any other trail sign. There was only the slab of the cave bed, slanting gradually up and away from them. There were at least three dark alcoves in view, any of which could have been a shallow niche or the start of a long side cavern.

"This way!" he guessed, charging toward the middle until Nailer's strong hand on his shoulder yanked him to a halt.

"Careful," counseled the older dwarf. "We go together. Get the spare lamp."

"All right," Brandon agreed, realizing that the light from the broken lantern was quickly fading as the spilled oil burned away. Quickly he removed the second one, poured some oil from their flask into it, and touched off the wick with the last of the dying flame.

Side by side, the brothers warily advanced up the sloping shelf of rock. Quickly they saw the right-side passage was a mere hollow in the cavern wall, too shallow to conceal a creature the size of the troll. Nevertheless, Nailer insisted they check it out thoroughly, reminding Brandon of the monster's uncanny concealment prior to the ambush.

That niche proved empty, and the middle passage was only a little deeper and also unoccupied. Still shoulder to shoulder, they advanced into the third opening and quickly found themselves climbing up the winding floor of an ancient dry riverbed. Loose rocks scraped and slipped underfoot, making it impossible to move stealthily. At least the space was wide enough to give them fighting space if they encountered their quarry. Brandon took heart from knowing the troll's arms were virtually useless.

"By Reorx!" gasped Nailer, suddenly leaping back and bracing his brother with a halting hand. "Is that *another* one?"

Brandon stared as a looming cave troll, both arms extended, emerged from the shadows before them, charging fast. The two dwarves raised their weapons, and the troll halted, eyeing them with those lightless sockets. They could hear the rasping growl in its chest, smell that familiar stench of its breath. Both hands, tipped with sturdy, flexing claws that looked like flint blades, stretched forward menacingly.

"Look!" Brandon hissed, staring at the creature's right arm. The limb was extending, the claws growing longer as they stared. "It *is* the same troll, but its arm grew back!"

"How in the name of the Forge did it do that?" Nailer demanded, backing up a step as the monster loomed closer.

Brandon was worried about more immediate concerns. As the troll sprang, he slashed his axe at its grotesque face, driving the beast back. Nailer closed in, swinging his hammer, but the nimble monster skipped to one side and came at Brandon from another direction, while Nailer was blocked by his brother from bringing his weapon to bear.

Shouting the name of Reorx in the ancient dwarf battle cry, Brandon swung his axe in an overhand blow, the keen blade slicing into that wicked nose. The troll feinted a recoil, and brought its regenerated, powerful right arm around in a wild swing. Claws ripped into the dwarf's biceps, but he twisted away, using the haft of his weapon to partially parry the blow. He sidestepped so the two brothers could stand side by side, and the troll retreated, leaning forward to brace itself on its hands and long arms.

Abruptly it pounced again, its agile moves reminding Brandon of a feline—a very large, monstrously heavy cat.

The troll smashed into the two dwarves, and Brandon went down onto his back. He kicked both feet just as Nailer shouted an agonized cry of pain. The double kick drove hard into the monster's legs, drawing the troll's attention back to Brandon and allowing Nailer to push himself along the floor, putting some distance between himself and the beast.

Once more the troll loomed above him, and Brandon held his axe in front of him, trying to ward off the coming blow. Still prone, he didn't have room to swing the weapon with any force, but the monster hesitated, seeming wary of the keen steel.

"For Reorx and Kayolin!" Nailer's battle cry echoed through the cave as Brandon's older brother, limping slightly, lunged to the attack. His hammer smashed into the troll's back, bringing the creature slashing around to face the new attacker. In that instant Brandon scrambled to his feet.

Finally, he had some room! He brought the axe up, pulled it back, and made a sweeping roundhouse swing into the monster's side. The blade bit deep, and the troll howled, twisting reflexively. Brandon clutched the haft of his axe and stepped sideways as the troll spun.

The monster's spin gave Nailer another opening, and he leaped forward, swinging his hammer over his head and smashing the heavy steel weapon into the base of the troll's skull. Again the beast roared, but then it swayed groggily, trying in vain to strike at either of its tormentors.

Brandon finally pulled his axe free and immediately pounded a lumberjack swing against the troll's leg. The blade bit deep, and the monster went down to one knee.

Nailer brought his hammer around, bashing the troll's good knee, and the hulking beast stumbled forward, braced on its hands, its head swaying dazedly. Already the wound in its side, where Brandon's blade had bitten so deeply, was starting to close up, healing before the dwarves' horrified eyes.

But Brandon didn't let up. He raised his axe again and chopped down hard, slicing halfway through the creature's neck. The monster went down, thrashing, and the dwarf made a second chop. Then the troll's head tumbled free, rolling like a rock until it came to a rest on the stump of its neck. The soulless eyes gaped as dark and as wickedly as they had in life, but the great body at last lay still.

"Nice chopping," Nailer grunted, clapping a hand on his brother's shoulder.

Brandon felt the older dwarf's weight, remembering that he'd been limping. "Are you all right?"

Nailer grinned at the troll's head and nodded. "Never better," he said cheerfully.

"What are you so happy about?" Brandon sputtered. "We could have died! Did that thing conk your brains around in your skull?"

The younger Bluestone followed his brother's gaze and let out a whoop of joy. "I see what you mean!" he said, stepping forward and moving around the decapitated head. He was staring down at a thick vein of bright yellow metal, a line of gold running like a seam through the bedrock of the deep cave. He said the words he knew his brother was thinking.

"Maybe the Bluestone luck is about to improve."

# FIVE

# DOWN THE DRAIN

Gus's hard labor paid off. The rocks he had loosened fell away from the barrier, and the releasing flow immediately widened the gap, allowing the contents of the pond to plunge downward in a single, frothing wave. The whole dam sagged away, and everything—Gus, Slooshy, and the three Theiwar killers included—went down.

"Me did it!" Gus crowed, though his voice was swallowed in the churning froth.

A great gout of syrupy goo enveloped the gully dwarf as the contents of the pond poured through the hole where the dam had been. Gus flailed his feet and hands, but for two seconds there was only that ooze and a sensation in his belly that was very similar to falling. Rocks crashed and tumbled around him—there seemed to be as much sliding stone as there was liquid in the spilling slide—and his flesh was bruised and battered by the crushing pressure.

"Gus!" he heard Slooshy call, and he reached out toward the sound.

Before he found her, he smacked into a rock and bounced out of the spilling debris, tumbling lazily through a somersault. Wiping his eyes, he saw a steady plume of liquid sludge bursting through the gap, carrying two rocks with it. Slooshy tumbled past, trying pathetically to swim. Then Gus bounced off the rocky ground again, and since he had landed on his head, he was a little groggy as he spiraled, tumbled, slid, and careened down the steep face of the rockslide.

As he slid on his back toward the bottom, he found himself looking up at the ceiling of Thorbardin. Something was wrong with his lungs, and he found it impossible to draw a breath. However, his limbs seemed to function. Gus lifted up his arms and kicked his legs just in time to see one of the Theiwar tumble past. The dwarf's face was a mask of terror as he bounced out from the steep trough and hit the waters of the Urkhan Sea, where he promptly disappeared.

More rocks and debris spilled into the lake, pummeling the large boat that had drawn close to shore. Gus whooped in delight as one end of the boat, battered by rocks, slipped under water. Several terrified Theiwar leaped toward shore, but lacking the Aghar's instinctive swimming skills, most of them vanished beneath the surface.

"Help!" Slooshy was clinging to a nearby rock as the slide, more liquid than rock, spilled around her. Gus slid down and held out his hand, which she took gratefully. Since he had neglected to hold on to anything with the other hand, however, his firm grip simply pulled him into the slide with her. Another wave of sludge washed into them, carrying them both down the slope.

His gaze shifted and he saw they were tumbling toward a big hole in the ground. It was a drain at the side of the lake, where the sludge from the Daergar sewers vanished into the bedrock—a drain installed hundreds of years ago so the effluent of the sewage pond did not pollute the pristine waters of the Urkhan Sea. At one time the drain hole had been protected by an iron grate, but the vagaries of time and the disruption of the Chaos War had done away with that barrier.

The gurgling and splashing and roaring got louder and louder all the time. Gus kept his hand tightly wrapped around Slooshy's as he tumbled and whirled, trying to look up toward the ceiling, but all he could see was a churning froth of brown murk. It was all around them. Abruptly, Gus's lungs started to work, and he drew a deep breath. Some instinct for survival (such instincts are second nature to the Aghar) caused him to close his eyes and hold that deep breath. Beside him, he sensed Slooshy doing the same thing.

In two seconds the flood reached the bottom of the ravine, the rush from the ruptured dam sweeping the two Aghars' stubby little bodies right down the drain. Once again there came the sensation of falling, and it lasted for a very long time—two seconds, at least. Gus was surrounded by noise and propelled along by a gout of foul sludge. Occasionally he skidded against the side of the drainpipe, which only confirmed that he was indeed going down very fast. Still the Aghar pair clung to each other, somehow drawing close enough to clasp each other in their arms, holding their breath, a single bundle of terror as they plunged ever more swiftly downward.

Abruptly the sludge started to churn, and Gus plunged through it, his own momentum carrying him still deeper even as the sudden flood down the drainpipe started to back up. He panicked as the wrenching movement tore Slooshy from his arms. Then he rolled and felt the wave push him this way and that.

Suddenly he popped up to the surface, banging his head against a very low ceiling of smooth rock but discovering a narrow air space, a gap barely high enough to allow him to draw a breath. Slooshy was there too, her mouth open and eyes squeezed shut as she gulped precious breaths. For two minutes the liquid swept them along. It was more like dirty water than sludge, and Gus and Slooshy kicked and splashed and paddled with all the swimming strength a frenzied gully dwarf could employ.

The force of the flow pummeled and punished them. Gus's head banged against low rocks on the ceiling. His shins and knees collided with jutting obstacles on the sides and bottom of what seemed to be some kind of pipe hewn from the bedrock of the mountains. He found Slooshy nearby during any chance he had to open his eyes, but the current was too violent for them to hold on to each other.

Occasionally the pipe narrowed and the water filled the entire circumference of the shaft, but each time, Gus managed to gulp air before he was submerged again, and fortunately none of the bottlenecks was more than about two feet long, so he was able to get his head out of the water now and then. And always he saw Slooshy there as well, swimming frantically along near him. His heart soared when he heard her curse the bluphsplunging water; he knew she was doing all right.

Abruptly the shaft turned downward again, and the two gully dwarves rode the gushing water through another drain hole. Once more they were dumped into a subterranean pipe, but it was much larger. Blinking, Gus spied an arched ceiling far over his head, and he was aware that the water flowed more quietly, more slowly there than it had in the narrow pipe. Even so, it was still moving along at a fair rush and carrying the soaked Aghar deeper and deeper under Thorbardin.

"Where we go in this goofar place?" demanded Slooshy, splashing at the water.

"Down!" he replied, before another surge of water splashed into his face.

*Everything goes down.*

Gus remembered the drain where they first plummeted under the ground and realized with some shock that the tunnels were actually *beneath* the Urkhan Sea. Yet they still plunged deeper and deeper, farther away from his home than he could ever have imagined. When he looked around for his companion, he could see no sign of her.

"Slooshy!" he cried. There might have been an answering cry from somewhere upstream, but he couldn't be sure.

Where was she? He struggled through water and surged and rolled with a powerful current, but the surface was relatively smooth, without the white churning froth that had choked him before. Keeping his head out of the water was easy, and he peered anxiously upstream and down, looking for a strand of scraggly hair, a flailing hand, any sign of Slooshy.

For two minutes he floated along, peering despairingly across the smoothing waters. The current was fast but no longer as crushing, and he started looking around for some way to pull himself out of the flow. A narrow ledge appeared along one side and quickly vanished behind him, and he realized that he was looking the wrong way. Turning around, he faced the direction in which he was being borne by the current.

Two seconds later another ledge came into view on the left side, and Gus kicked his way toward it—but the current shoved him past before he could grab the lip. Still, he was close to the side of the huge shaft, and when the next dry perch hove into view, he was ready. His strong fingers grabbed the edge, slipping along but finally grasping tight.

With a strong kick, Gus pulled himself up and out of the water, collapsing on the surprisingly wide shelf of flat stone, just about two inches above the level of the still-surging water. For two long minutes, he lay there, quaking first in fear then from the cold, keeping his eyes open as he studied the water for some sign of Slooshy floating past.

But there was only that cold, flowing water.

Shivering, he sat up and took a look around. Almost immediately he spotted an opening in the side of the water cavern. It was a corridor leading away from there! The ceiling was just high enough for Gus to step along without stooping, and the passageway was wide enough for him to stretch out his arms and just barely touch the—thankfully dry!—walls to either side.

He strolled along jauntily, rather pleased to have survived such an adventure. He recalled Slooshy with a pang but knew she must be dead by then. And he was still alive! Though sodden and chilly, he could walk, and he even allowed himself a glimmer of enthusiasm as he wondered if he might not discover some food somewhere along the dark pathway. Things were indeed looking up! In fact, although it might have been his imagination, he grew cheerful at the vague sense that the air around him was getting warmer.

Gus wandered along the dark corridor, not sure if he was climbing or descending, for at least two minutes. He realized he had been right about one thing: it was definitely getting warmer! His sodden garments gradually dried, and he no longer squished and splashed with every step. The narrow escape from a watery tomb and the loss of his companion left no lingering trauma, forgetfulness being one of the finely tuned coping mechanisms of the Aghar race. Indeed, he pursed his lips and whistled a merry tune as he trekked along, feeling as though suddenly he didn't have a care in all Krynn.

Then he remembered Slooshy again with a sudden hollow feeling in his middle. The sound of her voice calling "Help!" left a weird echo in his head, and though he tried to knock it out, all of his beating against his temples only seemed to make his head hurt more. And there was that continuing strange pain in his belly every time he recalled her, remembering the feeling of her arms around him, her hand clutched in his.

Thinking of the pain in his belly, he realized he was pretty hungry. He didn't know if he was walking in the right direction toward food or any place safe, but he wasn't about to go back and jump in the river, so he was doing the only thing he could think to do which was to keep walking along the underground passage.

If he had taken a little more time to inspect his surroundings, he might have noticed that the corridor was straight and level with stone arches at regular intervals. That was clear proof that he wasn't in a natural cave, but rather was following a route carved by dwarves at some point in the unknown past. Gus's nose was paying more attention than his brain, sniffing at the air, seeking low and high, right and left, for any morsel of food.

A cave grub, exuding the characteristic musty stink of its species, could not elude his notice. He dug the plump creature out of a narrow crevice in the cavern wall and popped it into his mouth, smacking his lips delightedly as he savored the gooey juice and chewy membrane. Recalling his thrilling ride down the subterranean flume and finding that surprising delicacy, Gus beamed. It was looking like his lucky day!

As a result, the pudgy Aghar had a certain spring in his step as he continued along his way. He almost swaggered as he savored the last creamy swallow of slug. His big eyes, attuned to perfect darkness, took in the smooth walls, the perfectly level floor, the arrow-straight course of the passage before him, and he felt as though he could walk that nice path across the whole of Thorbardin. There was nothing to stop him.

As was his wont, his mind wandered. What would it be like to be highbulp of all the Aghar, master of the under-dwellers, a gully dwarf so important that he held a great seat at the council of thanes? But why stop there, at mere highbulp? What if he, Gus, were to become high king of all the dwarves? Now *that* was a dream worth imagining!

What would his house be like? Splendid, of course. What would he wear? Why, anything he wanted. He'd have a full closet of at least two nice outfits. What would he—he gasped at the possibilities—what would he *eat*?

The question was full of such boundless appeal, such unlimited possibility, that it took his breath away. What, indeed, would he eat, if he had all the power of the high kingship? Well, he would probably start with fish eggs, the roe of the cave salmon that he had sampled once or twice, when he had dared to root through the garbage outside of an upscale Theiwar inn. After that, he would have . . . well, why not have two more salmon eggs? Why, as high king, he could live on salmon eggs, and nobody could tell him otherwise!

But a king needed a queen, didn't he? He sniffled suddenly, remembering Slooshy again. Too bad she wasn't alive. He would have kind of liked the chance to offer her a seat on the throne of the dwarves . . . and also a dish of salmon eggs, all her own to eat.

His thoughts meandered through a menu of other treats as he swung along the corridor. His imagination was so active, he could practically smell the delicate salmon eggs, feel them bursting on his tongue, taste the salty nectar within. Thus it was he didn't notice the dark figures lurking in the corridor until he almost walked right into then.

Then he had to notice. He froze, one foot in the air in the middle of a step. There were three of them, big and burly dwarves, dressed in black cloaks that masked their facial features and concealed their limbs and torsos. They stood side by side, blocking the corridor completely, motionless and silent as they regarded the approaching gully dwarf.

Immediately, a lifetime of survival instincts took over Gus's mind and body. He gulped loudly even as he spun around on his planted foot. The mysterious figures had offered no ominous sound, no gestures indicating menace, but any Aghar who lasted to adulthood did so by not taking chances. Any nongully dwarf encountered anywhere in Thorbardin, at any time, under any circumstances, as likely as not possessed murderous intentions. At least, that's what the survival-minded Aghar was forced to assume.

Before Gus had even completed his gulp of alarm, he was sprinting in the opposite direction at full speed. His heart pounded against his ribs as loudly as his boots drummed along the stone floor. The walls to either side passed in a blur as the terrified gully dwarf heard swords unsheathe and the footsteps of pursuers echo in his mind, his thoughts a cacophony of fear. His eyes blurred, tearing from the frantic speed of his flight, and he vividly imagined cold, steel blades or mailed hands reaching for his vulnerable back.

He ran headlong into a net that had somehow deployed across the corridor, blocking the path he had just traversed. The coils of webbing closed around him, cocooning him, hoisting him from the floor to dangle helplessly, swinging through a slow spiral.

Eyes bugging, he stared helplessly as he swung around toward the direction of the shadowy pursuers. He saw with astonishment that the trio of dark figures remained exactly where he had first glimpsed them. Slowly they shimmered then faded from view.

Magic! Gus gulped again, the maneuver complicated by the fact he was hanging upside down. Coughing and sputtering, he shivered in terror as he continued to pivot until he faced the direction in which he had been fleeing.

Two dwarves were strolling lazily toward him. One of them was coiling a long rope that led through a hook in the ceiling down to the net where Gus was imprisoned. He noted their milky, pale eyes and their bristling beards and recognized the pair as Theiwar.

"Well, we caught us a prize, eh?" said the one holding the rope. He released his grip, dropping Gus head-first onto the floor.

"Aye. The master will be pleased," said the other. He reached down and grabbed a corner of the net. When he pulled, the gully dwarf—still stunned from the head blow—tumbled free of the webbing to lie shivering on the floor.

"Up, you," said the first Theiwar. He prodded Gus none too gently in the thigh with a short sword. "You're coming with us."

Still trembling, the Aghar climbed to his feet. He glanced once more at the empty corridor ahead, where the apparition of a threat had propelled him into their real trap.

"A bit of the master's magic, that," chuckled the sword-bearing Theiwar. "We likes to catch youz without havin' to break a sweat."

His head throbbing, Gus could only shuffle along, guarded by the watchful captors. He didn't know who the "master" was, but he guessed he would soon find out.

———DH———

The powder of the amanita mushroom, as deadly a toxin as existed in the world, was fine-grained and completely dry. Willim carefully stoppered the vial containing the poisonous stuff; his spell of true-seeing allowed him to determine the cork had no imperfections and fit so tightly that no air could enter or leave the container. Carefully setting the glass onto a metal ring, he touched the stone underneath the ring and muttered a word of magic.

Immediately, that stone surface began to glow, radiating a warmth the Theiwar mage could feel against the skin of his face. Satisfied, he turned to another process, using a black steel knife to stir a bowl containing a viscous mix of carrion-crawler ichor and a sludge of oily mud. He counted a hundred spirals of the blade, his mind relishing his focus on the precise tasks.

Around him, the laboratory was still. Many of his attendants were gone, hunting subjects in the dark caverns beneath Thorbardin; the rest were currently resting or gambling in their garrison quarters. His captives, the elves and Klar dwarves and goblin, sat silent and sullen in their cages; none of them wished to make any sound or disturbance that might attract the attention of their sadistic captor, so they made themselves as invisible as possible behind the bare steel bars of their cells.

When the hundredth stroke was completed, Willim put down his blade and returned to the vial containing the amanita powder, which had become hot. Long years of torture had destroyed the nerves in his stubby fingers, so he picked up the glass container without discomfort. Indeed, the faint whiff of burned flesh smelled pleasant in his nostrils.

He shook the vial, pleased to see the powder was suspended in the air within the container, swirling as a murky—and very lethal—gas. He set the vial on a shelf beside a wide variety of similar containers. Some of them contained liquids, while others appeared empty—an appearance belied by the dwarf wizard's keen senses; his magical vision knew the lurking toxin or enchantment was masked by the clean air in the apparently-empty bottles.

For a moment Willim the Black allowed himself the luxury of relaxation. He breathed in his sulfurous air, expelling the warmth in an easy sigh while he strolled to the edge of the deep chasm, the pit where Gorathian lurked. He could feel the beast down there, waiting, hungry as always. In his mind's eye, the wizard envisioned the creature's powerful coils, its grotesque body and burning, hate-filled eyes. As if sensing his thoughts, Gorathian stirred, a billow of warmth, tinged with black smoke, rising from the depths.

"He fears me, you know," he murmured as if Gorathian could understand his words. Or perhaps the beast did; at least, the sound of the wizard's voice provoked a warm surge of energy, a glow of liquid fire that brightened the interior of the crevasse, casting a pale mirror of that shape on the lofty ceiling of the chamber once destined to be the council hall of the thanes.

"That one-eyed fool . . . he even named me in one of his edicts!" Willim actually giggled as he recalled his amusement.

On one of his many magical journeys into Norbardin, he had spotted the king's new edicts. Moving invisibly, his flesh rendered into a gaseous form so he would not have to endure any physical contact, the black-robed wizard had traveled the streets and alleys and even the shops and homes of the great underground city. The dwarves appeared busy as ever, he had observed, but to him the masses also looked even more chagrined and depressed than ever before. Most walked with their heads down, avoiding contact with each other and studiously avoiding the swaggering enforcers, mostly Hylar and Daergar, who wandered about in groups seemingly everywhere, seeking any violations of the king's increasingly long list of proscriptions and prohibitions.

Willim had been surprised to observe very few females in public, and those he observed were always escorted by a male and seemed in an unusual hurry to reach their destinations. There were none of the bands of young dwarf maids, formerly ubiquitous, who used to laugh and carouse together on the streets.

When, finally, the wizard had drifted up to the edicts posted in the city's great central plaza, he had understood why the women and girls had become scarce. And he had read with delight that the king had specifically listed Willim the Black as a dangerous outlaw.

"If only he knew *how* dangerous." The mage chuckled. Imagine if the king had known the wizard's laboratory was right under his city, in the very grand chamber that had been excavated by order of the previous king! Oh, the irony of it all!

"I could kill him today if I wanted to," the wizard continued, speaking aloud. "Perhaps he knows that.

Perhaps that is why he names me in his edict—because he fears me, as he should."

He giggled again, an oddly high-pitched sound emitting from his whiskered face with its sewn-shut eye sockets pinched like scars. "But I will not kill him. Certainly not yet. No, I have something special in mind for the one-eyed king. He will learn—they *all* will learn—in due time."

Willim's meditations were abruptly interrupted as magic shimmered in the upper alcove of the great chamber. It ws a spell of teleportation, but the wizard immediately realized there was no threat here. Instead, the door to his laboratory opened. Two of his apprentices returned from their hunting expedition, prodding a miserable-looking gully dwarf before them.

The mage sniffed disdainfully. A gully dwarf wasn't much of a prize. For a moment Willim thought about Gorathian, ever hungry, ever burning, and he thought he ought to toss the empty-headed gully dwarf right into the chasm.

Then he sighed. Even gully dwarves could be useful, he knew, remembering several new potions he needed to have tested. And his Aghar cage was currently empty, the last hapless captive having been awarded to the beast several cycles earlier.

"Put him in the cage," the black-robed wizard commanded. Already he was making a new plan, concocting an experimental recipe. "I will have something for him to do very soon."

Without another look at their shivering captive, who gaped in awe at his new surroundings as his captors thrust him into a vacant cage, Willim returned to his workbench, warmed another section of the stone slab, and got to work with his ingredients and his plans.

# SIX

# A BROTHER'S BLOOD

This could be bigger than the Haxx Delving!"
Brandon declared, referring to one of the famous
long-standing gold mines in the Kayolin caverns. "Let
them try to ignore the Bluestone clan once we start to
produce that gold!"

He and his brother were striding upward through the
long dark tunnels they had so recently explored. The lamp,
with the last bit of their carefully conserved oil, was burning
low, but it still offered enough light that they could make
good time as they wended their way back to the city.

The connecting passages to the Zhaban Delving were
just ahead when the elder dwarf stopped and looked at his
brother seriously.

"Remember, Brandon," Nailer said solemnly. "We
haven't brought an ingot of gold out of this place yet.
We haven't even filed our claim in the king's court."

"Governor's court, you mean," Brandon corrected.
"The only true dwarf king dwells in Thorbardin."

Nailer chuckled grimly. "Well, that's what tradition
says. But if Regar Smashfingers wants to call himself the
King of Kayolin, I suggest you don't argue the point with
him while we're trying to establish our claim."

"Right," the younger dwarf agreed. "But between you and me, he's claimed more than his due."

"You'll get no argument from me," Nailer declared. "But you must be discreet with such opinions."

"By Reorx, Nail!" Brandon protested. "This is the best thing that's happened to our clan since . . . well, since before the Cataclysm! We've just changed a run of bad luck that's lasted four hundred years! I have a right to be excited."

"Sure you do. I am too, whether you want to believe that or not. I keep picturing father's face when I tell him we've discovered enough wealth to get the Bluestones a seat on the Kayolin council again. Just between you and me, there's nothing I'd like better than to make that old dwarf proud."

Brandon felt a flush of shame. He'd been thinking about dazzling the dwarf maids by wearing jeweled rings, ornate platinum breastplates, and exotic feathered plumes on his steel helmet. He had already mapped out the floor plan of the new house he was going to commission, a dwelling that would be excavated from the virgin bedrock of the Garnet range. The parties he would host! The cream of Kayolin society would rub elbows with him!

But Nailer was right. Their discovery, a new delving of tremendous prospective value, meant much more than mere trivial wealth. It would provide for the restoration of one of the great clans of Kayolin's history. The Bluestones had produced great miners, generals, even a governor, in the long centuries before the Cataclysm. The dwarf nation in the Garnet range had been mostly immune to that violent act of cosmic revenge, but when the gods hurled the mountain down upon Krynn, there had been several cave-ins and collapses in Kayolin. The most destructive of those had destroyed the Bluestone Delving, and in that instant the clan had been reduced to a minor player in the nation's power and politics.

For more than four hundred years, the Bluestones had struggled along, managing small mines, branching into trade and manufacturing, but never attaining a status that gave them a regular presence at court. Always they were plagued by ill fortune: a mine tapped into a submountain aquifer, drowning the workers and submerging a small treasure in silver ore; a marriage that had produced two impotent offspring, narrowing the line to Brandon's father's and one distant cousin's families. One enterprising great uncle had thought to display a captured ogre for the edification of Garnet Thax's citizenry and had been unlucky enough to use cast-iron brackets, rather than steel, to contain the beast. Although the only fatal casualty of the incident had been the uncle himself, it had been a spectacularly public example of House Bluestone's ill-starred history.

Other newcomers, epitomized by the wealthy and ruthless Heelspur clan, had long eclipsed the Bluestones. A small smelting venture had practically bankrupted Brandon's father, Garren Bluestone, when the Heelspurs had erected a larger and more modern factory on the same level of the undercity. With the claim that Brandon and Nailer Bluestone intended to file in the governor's court, that long decline would be reversed.

"Do you think the new mine might be as rich as the Third Delve?" asked the younger brother, remembering the tales of the mine that had brought the Bluestone family its first epoch of glory, some seven hundred years earlier. Indeed, it had been a bedrock strata of sapphire-infused rock that had caused their ancestors to adopt Bluestone as the family name.

"How in Reorx's name should I know?" Nailer snapped. But then he paused to consider the question and shrugged. "Maybe. It just might be, you know!"

"Yes, I know!" Brandon exulted. "Just imagine it! We could start a whole new house!"

"And what's wrong with the House of Bluestone?" demanded the elder, glowering.

"Well, nothing." Brandon cheerfully waved away

his brother's concern. "I mean, I'm just talking. I don't want to start a new house, anyway. Especially if this means that our luck is changing. But if we were that rich, we could!"

"And if I had wings, I could fly to the Lords of Doom," Nailer retorted. "That doesn't mean I would."

"I would!" Brandon replied delightedly. "I mean, don't you want to try some new things, go new places? Maybe places dwarves have never gone before?"

"My home under the mountain is all the place I'll ever need. And if you know what's good for you, you'll come to the same conclusion. You remember old Balric Bluestone, don't you? How he just had to climb that mountain?"

"Sure I do." It was a story that every scion of the Bluestone family learned as a lesson in youth. "And I always loved his sense of adventure. I mean, not too many dwarves set out to climb *any* mountains, much less Garnet Peak."

"And he was the *only* one who happened to be doing it when the Cataclysm struck!" Nailer reminded his brother. "They never even found his body. Just his axe, the one you're carrying right now. Now come on. Let's get out of here. We've got a lot of work to do before this gets settled."

"Should we go see father first when we get back to Garnet Thax?" Brandon wondered. Indeed, once he thought about it, winning approval from crusty old Garren Bluestone would bring him a flush of pleasure deeper, more significant, than any that could be aroused by the building of new houses or collection of gem-studded jewelry.

"I'd like to," Nailer replied. "But I really think we should go right to court. Once the claim is recorded, there'll be plenty of time for celebration."

"Right," Brandon agreed. "Let's go to the palace first."

Another ten minutes of climbing brought them to a narrow passage almost blocked by tumbled rocks. The gap forced them into single file, Nailer leading the way as he used his hands to pull himself up. At the top the passage became almost a chimney. "Here, take the lamp and hold it up for me," the elder dwarf requested.

"Sure." Brandon held the flickering lantern high, watching as his brother wedged himself into the chimney. After a few moments, the sturdy dwarf braced his hobnailed boots against the stone walls and started pushing himself up and through the crack connecting to the massive Zhaban Delving.

Above them sprawled an ancient network of mines that had produced silver, lead, and some gold for the wealthy Heelspur clan over the past six hundred years. Their access point was in a shaft that had been long abandoned—and, in fact, was vigorously avoided by sensible dwarves since there had been many unexplained and fatal encounters there over the years. The cave troll, the brothers knew, had been the reason behind the "hauntings," and they were rightfully proud of the courage that had led them to challenge the beast and earn the spoils of their hard-fought victory.

At the top of the chimney, Nailer turned and reached a hand down. Brandon passed him the lantern, which he set on the floor at the edge of the gap, then reached down again to help Brandon up the last stretch. With a last kick and a pull from his brother's strong arm, the second dwarf rose up from the gap and set his boots, once again, on a stone floor that was plotted and mapped in the official surveys of Kayolin.

For a moment the two dwarves stood, breathing heavily, resting for the long walk back to Garnet Thax, Kayolin's great capital city.

Then the shadows moved.

Brandon opened his mouth to cry out a warning, but a black-cloaked figure behind his brother was already lunging, wielding a black steel blade. Nailer grunted, sounding surprised, and Brandon saw the blade emerge from his brother's chest and felt drops of liquid spatter his face.

"Nailer!" the younger Bluestone shouted. He pulled

his axe from its belt sling even as he caught the slumping dwarf and felt his brother's warm blood soaking through his shirt.

Already there were more shadows moving, dark-cloaked dwarves attacking from his left, and he was forced to let Nailer fall while he defended himself, his axe clashing into a pair of thrusting blades, snapping one off at the hilt and deflecting the other.

The attackers were strangely silent, breathing harshly as they closed in. Brandon counted five of them and quickly dropped one, splitting his skull with an overhand blow. He parried attacks from both sides, standing over Nailer's bleeding form. When the four dark dwarves pulled back for a moment, he rushed forward two steps, swinging his axe through a half circle.

The two to his right backed away, a clear attempt to get him to charge and expose his back, and it almost worked. A red haze of battle seemed to film Brandon's vision, and he lowered his head, ready to charge. Only as he started to lunge did he realize the danger, halting then spinning around to parry the double stabbing blades slicing toward his back. With a resounding clang, he knocked the blades away.

"Assassins!" he cried at the top of his lungs, his voice ringing out even louder than the dueling steel weapons. "Help!"

It was a futile plea in those abandoned passages, and he knew this fight would come down to his own prowess. He charged the two dwarves to his right, but they fell back, and Brandon was forced to pivot again to avoid exposing his back. One of those black blades sliced into his arm, and he grunted in pain, at the same time swinging his axe hard, severing the swordsman's arm at the elbow. With a shriek of pain, the stricken attacker dropped away.

But the three who remained were skilled, and they worked together to push Brandon back. He stepped across Nailer's motionless form, his heart breaking even as he struggled not to slip on his brother's slick, rapidly expanding pool of blood. His boot stopped at the edge of the chimney as he used the niche as some measure of flank protection. The attackers pressed hard, blades slashing in high and low, and Brandon's elbows banged against the walls of the narrow confines as he tried to swing his axe.

He teetered at the brink; then his boot slipped. He felt himself falling backward as three black blades lunged for him. The tumble into the chimney was the only thing that saved him, even though he bashed painfully into a protruding rock and dropped his axe as he clawed to arrest his fall. The precious weapon, a family heirloom more than four hundred years old, clattered into the darkness below, while Brandon clung precariously to a ledge of rock in the narrow vertical passage.

A large stone, thrown from above, bashed into his head, and he slipped, skidding another dozen feet downward. More rocks followed, a punishing barrage, and before he could wriggle out of the gap at the bottom of the niche, a heavy boulder clanged off his helmet, knocking him into a blackness that was even darker than the lightless caverns under the world.

———DH———

Brandon gradually became aware of a consuming, pounding pain in his skull, and it was that agony that finally told him he was still alive. He lay still for a very long time and gradually reconstructed the events that had brought him to that place. Groaning as he remembered his brother, stricken in the corridor a few dozen feet overhead, he tried at last to move and cried out as a searing pain stabbed through his shoulder.

Gritting his teeth, cursing his attackers, pleading for strength from the great god Reorx, he pushed himself up to his hands and knees. He tried to open his eyes, but they would not respond, and he was terrified at the thought that he had been blinded. It was only when he had finally pushed himself to a sitting position, freeing his hands, that he was able to touch his face and find that his forehead was crusted with dried blood. That sticky fluid had dribbled over his eyes, and his lids were sealed shut.

Each scrape was agony, each probing finger brought renewed stabs through his skull, but he slowly clawed the dried blood away until he could open his eyes. Though it was pitch dark in the deep delving, he tried looking around in the murk and was almost pathetically relieved to see the blurry silver glow of his axe blade—the weapon that had once been Balric Bluestone's axe. He pounced on it and picked it up, ignoring the pain provoked by the sudden movement, and he began to feel a little better.

He felt better, at least, in that anger was beginning to supplant grief in his churning emotions. He slung the axe onto his back and stood, shakily at first but with growing strength. The chimney was full of rocks, blocking his escape, but he set to work pulling them away. Dragging and clawing until his fingers were raw, he cleared away the blockage, aided by gravity as the last of the stones finally rolled free into the deep cavern. Hand by hand, his boots jamming against the walls for traction, he pulled himself upward, finally emerging into the upper corridor, the ancient connection to the Zhaban Delving.

As his head reached the floor level, he found himself staring directly into Nailer's lifeless eyes. He groaned a choking cry of grief. Pulling himself out of the shaft, he collapsed on his brother's body, cradling Nailer's motionless form and sobbing uncontrollably. The lamp still flickered, and he angrily knocked it away, as if the darkness could block him from acknowledging the stark truth of his brother's death . . .

The truth that the Bluestone luck remained as bad as ever.

Only after several minutes of grieving did he start to

consider the potential danger to himself. Belatedly, he looked around, but there was no sign of the mysterious assassins. He remembered the arm he had severed, but even that limb was gone, the wound marked by only a smear of dried blood on the floor. Also removed was the body of the slain attacker.

Brandon slowly rose to his feet, resolute and grimly determined. He reached down and hoisted his brother's body into his strong arms. Staggering under the weight, gritting his teeth against the pain that still wracked his body, he began to walk home.

For many long hours, he trudged through the abandoned passages, making his way ever upward. He had to stop frequently to rest, and in these intervals he thought of his mother and father, his heart nearly breaking at the thought of their grief when they heard his news. All of their hopes, the whole future of the clan, had been vested in the two brothers and their bold exploration.

Remembering the goal of their mission while he caught his breath, Brandon wondered if that vein of gold, somehow, had led to his attack. He didn't see how it was possible. But then, who had killed his brother and why? He growled deep in his chest as he pondered the question and vowed that, when he had the answer, that person would die a miserable death. Then he hoisted his brother's body in his arms and once more started trudging upward.

Eventually he came to a rail tram used for hauling ore out of the still-working parts of the delving and two kindly miners allowed him to place Nailer's body on top of their cargo of ore. Brandon trotted along beside the cart, still moving upward, until they reached the large smelting plant at the summit of the extensive Zhaban Delving. There were a number of dwarves around, and several who were just getting off work offered to help him cart his brother's body toward Bluestone Manor, on one of Garnet Thax's midlevels.

"Thanks, friends. I'll do it myself," Brandon said. He did gratefully accept the loan of a two-wheeled wagon, and with that simple machine bearing Nailer's corpse, he began the last long climb.

Stairways linked the city's levels for foot traffic, but several wide, spiraling ramps facilitated the ascent, or descent, for wheeled vehicles. It was as Brandon trudged up the first of those, a road that climbed through all ten of the deep-levels, that he looked up to see one of his father's friends hurriedly approaching, his bearded face marked by an expression of grave concern.

Harn Poleaxe was a foreigner, a Neidar hill dwarf who had been a long-time visitor to the mountain dwarf city. That in itself was not unusual—there were clans of Neidar in several parts of the Garnet range—but Poleaxe was also a dwarf from south of the Newsea. In fact, he was a Neidar who hailed from the hills around great Thorbardin itself. Brandon didn't know him well, but the visitor was a regular guest at his father's house, and the son knew Poleaxe and his father had been discussing business dealings for more than a year. Poleaxe was an inherently likable fellow, always quick with a story or to flip a coin to the bartender to buy the next round.

As he hurried toward Brandon, however, his face was gray, and he blanched as he saw the bloody bundle in Brandon's cart.

"Word was spreading through the bazaar just a half hour ago. I came down as soon as I heard." Poleaxe was a big, handsome dwarf. His breath, as he leaned close, was sweet with the aroma of dwarf spirits, which was no surprise to Brandon as Poleaxe and his father were both fond of the strong drink.

The Neidar didn't seem the least bit drink-addled right then, however. Instead, he was stern and commanding, planting his hands on his hips and glaring about at the nearby dwarves—mostly gritty miners climbing from the delvings to their inns and living quarters—as if he expected to locate Nailer's murderer among them. "How did it—?" He grimaced. "Never mind, there'll be time enough for the tale. You!"

He pointed at a sturdy blacksmith who was watching them curiously. "Take word to Garren Bluestone! Tell him his eldest son is slain, and we are bearing his body home!"

Brandon was impressed by the visiting hill dwarf's sense of command and so, apparently, was the blacksmith. "Yes, sir!" he declared, hastening off at a sprint.

"Now let me give you a hand with that sad burden," declared Poleaxe. Brandon finally felt his weariness and allowed the Neidar to help him pull on the yoke. He barely noticed as the burly dwarf took more and more of the weight, and the young Bluestone was left to stumble along beside the wagon, numbed by a mixture of grief and exhaustion.

Others were taking note, and a small crowd began to collect, trailing along with them on the curving section of ramp. Brandon didn't even notice when one dwarf then another offered him a shoulder, but soon he was assisted along by the pair of sturdy helpers. Before he knew it, they had climbed to the fifth midlevel, the section of the city where the current Bluestone manor was.

"Thanks, all," said Poleaxe with obvious sincerity, addressing the dozen or so dwarves who had formed their small procession. "Now let's give the family their privacy, eh?"

"Right you are, Harn," said one of the dwarves who'd been supporting Brandon. "You take care, lad," he added as the numb Hylar nodded his thanks. The group quickly dispersed, leaving the Neidar and Brandon to haul the cart down the narrow street toward the stone door of the house.

Garren Bluestone himself opened the front door, and

from the stricken look on his father's face, Brandon knew that word of the vile murder had already reached the house. For some reason, the stern visage of the family patriarch steeled the young dwarf's soul, and he suppressed the tears that felt like they wanted to burst forth.

"They killed him, Father. Five dwarves, assassins, came out of the darkness."

"Bring him in." The elder's dwarf's face was a stony mask, utterly devoid of emotion. He stared at Brandon, and suddenly his eyes showed their deep pain, a window of grief. "Are you hurt?" he asked hoarsely, his eyes going to his surviving son's arm.

Brandon looked down and was surprised to see the dried blood crusted there—he had all but forgotten the slice of the assassin's sword. But then the pain flared anew, together with the throbbing in his head and back, where the boulders had rained down on him. "I—I don't know," he said. "Maybe a little. It's nothing."

He looked at his brother's body and couldn't suppress a sob.

"Your sons were in the delvings," Harn Poleaxe offered softly. "Brandon carried Nailer up to the deep-levels, and from there word spread through the stalls in the bazaar. I met him on the ramp."

"I thank you for your help," Garren declared, his voice choking as he clasped Poleaxe's arm. Only for a moment did his expression harden again. "But you must know, my decision is final."

"Of course," Poleaxe said, bowing humbly. "Though, with respect, old friend, this"—he gestured to Nailer's body—"makes it all that much more important that we reach an agreement."

"Now is not the time!" snapped Garren sternly.

"Certainly. I understand. My deepest apologies and regrets. I merely wished to help a friend in his hour of need. I shall leave you to your grief in privacy."

The hill dwarf quickly backed away as Karine Bluestone, Brandon's mother, rushed up to the cart and, sobbing, embraced the body of her son.

"Tell me how it happened," demanded Garren, leading Brandon into his study as Karine and several family attendants wept over the body and gingerly carried Nailer toward the room where he would be prepared for burial.

Starting with the discovery of the "haunted" passage, Brandon recounted the fight with the cave troll, the search that led them to the fabulous vein of gold ore, and the treacherous attack as the two brothers had returned to the known passages of Kayolin.

"You say you made the connection through the Zhaban Delving?" Garren pressed grimly.

"Yes, down some of the deeper passages that were tapped out a hundred years ago. There was nobody there to witness."

"This smacks of the Heelspurs," declared the elder dwarf. His eyes were moist with grief-inspired tears, but his voice growled with an undercurrent of rage. "And there is one way to find out."

"Tell me, Father!" pleaded Brandon. "I will avenge my brother."

"Wait, and be patient," said Garren. "We must be very careful. Come with me now to the king's atrium."

"You mean the governor's atrium," Brandon corrected, immediately recalling the conversation he and his brother had shared.

"I fear that may be only memory," Garren suggested grimly. "But we may know more when we arrive at court."

# SEVEN

# THE LABORATORY

The newest potion was done, and as Willim the Black admired the ink-black liquid, the consistency of fatty cream, he was pleased. The bottle contained barely enough of the stuff to fill up half of a dwarven drinking mug, yet if the black-robed wizard's calculations were correct, the poison would be strong enough to kill a hundred men or more.

He set the bottle on his granite-slab table, next to another potion, the product of his previous day's work. Where the first poison was black and rested in a clear bottle, the second elixir was clear, and as a matter of humorous conceit, he was storing it in a bottle that was labeled as *Midwarren Pale,* a well-known and especially potent distillation of dwarf spirits. Behind him, his heating surface had cooled, and he had used a few brief cantrip spells to clean his mixing bowls, his steel knives, and his other utensils. Willim was done working for a while; it was finally time to test.

"Apprentices, come to me," he barked. He spoke softly, but even though more than half of his students were in corners of the cavern well removed from the laboratory, the magically enhanced power of his voice was enough to ensure that all of them heard his words. Fear of their master, as he well knew, was enough to ensure they all obeyed promptly.

Within a minute the ten young Theiwar males had gathered before their master. Willim looked the group up and down and was not displeased. Each of the dwarves had demonstrated keen intelligence and the kind of ruthless purposefulness that indicated the clear potential for the Order of the Black Robes. They were young, but they were learning.

Tarot, the most experienced of the group, stood erectly at attention at the end of the line. He had already mastered the spell of the lightning bolt and was a natural at finding the subterranean-based components—including fungi, mineral, and animal—that were necessary for developing the most potent toxins. Beside him stood Ochre, not as clever as Tarot but big, strong as an ox, and utterly loyal. A stolid, if plodding, researcher, Ochre had demonstrated a dedication to his master that Willim had rarely encountered.

Of course, the others of the group of ten had shown similar, if less advanced, dedication. It was a good class, he reflected, realizing with some surprise that it had been more than a year since he had been forced to put one of his apprentices to death.

"You have labored well for me this past year," the wizard began, clearly surprising the young dwarves with his praise. "I have asked much of you, and you have responded. You know I expect all of you to serve me well, but you will be well rewarded when we are ready to strike at the new king and all of his fanatical fools on his council of thanes."

"Thank you, Master," Tarot said, replying for the group. "We ache with eagerness for the day we may assist you in claiming that lofty throne."

"I know you do," Willim said. "But patience. That day remains well in the future. Of course, we could kill him in a moment, if that was our only goal, but you should know that my aspirations are higher. We must do more than merely assassinate the king; we must prepare the dwarves of Thorbardin for a new king, so that they will accept, even embrace, a Theiwar wizard on the high throne. For that to happen, they must learn to hate and fear their current ruler."

Willim turned to his table and snatched up the bottle labeled *Midwarren Pale*. Holding it reverently, he turned back to his apprentices.

"This is a new creation," he said, watching without surprise as their eyes widened in appreciation. "It is a potion, but a transformative, not a magical spell. It will embed in the one who drinks it new powers, advantages that will, I suspect, be not only permanent, but will continue to grow with the passage of time. I would like one of you to volunteer to test it."

"I will, Master!" came the reply from ten throats, each apprentice immediately taking a step forward then turning to glare warily at his rival colleagues.

Willim held up his hand. "I knew you would all reply in the affirmative, and I am grateful for your zeal. Tarot, you have earned the right to test this, by your performance. But you are my best and brightest pupil, and I do not care to risk losing you."

That apprentice, who had brightened at the sound of his name, looked suitably crestfallen—even to Willim's power of true-sight, which had been watching for any carefully concealed sign of relief that the apprentice was relieved of the dangerous test. The wizard was pleased to note that Tarot's disappointment was genuine.

"Ochre," he continued smoothly. "I have chosen you to test my elixir. You have proved your allegiance many times, but you will never be the spellcaster that Tarot is expected to be. Therefore, it might prove useful to enhance your power in other ways."

"Thank you, Master!" cried Ochre, lumbering forward with his long arms swinging at his sides. If he felt any slight by his teacher's assessment, Ochre gave no sign. Instead, the apprentice bowed before the wizard then watched excitedly as Willim poured a small amount of the potion—about the equivalent of a shot of rotgut—into a small glass. When the Black Robe extended the vessel, the apprentice took it from his hands and, upon seeing the mage's gesture of encouragement, drank it down in one swallow.

Immediately he began to cough. The glass fell from his nerveless fingers, shattering unnoticed on the floor. Rigid, Ochre leaned back, quivering in all his limbs.

"Catch him—quickly!" Willim snapped, and two apprentices stepped forward to break Ochre's fall as he toppled over backward. "Lay him on the floor, and do not be concerned. The magic is working as I anticipated."

His apprentices did as they were told, though several looked askance at the quivering Ochre, who by all appearances seemed to be suffering the effects of a powerful seizure. His jaws clenched, his eyes rolled back into their sockets so only the whites showed, and a froth of foam appeared at his lips. All the while his limbs trembled uncontrollably.

But that was the price of magic, and Willim silently watched those who appeared unduly worried; their lack of faith would be remembered.

Then his eyeless face turned from right to left, looking beyond the robed apprentices, noting the cages in the back of the laboratory where the miserable elves and dwarves huddled in silent misery. His magical vision fell upon the newcomer, the pathetic gully dwarf all alone in his large cage, and the Theiwar's mouth wrinkled into a cruel caricature of a smile.

He gestured casually to the bottle of black liquid, the new toxin he had just created. "This is a poison, I believe, that will allow us to fell a great number of our enemies with a single blow. It, too, remains to be tested, of course."

"With Reorx's blessing, you will smite all of our foes," Tarot pledged zestfully.

"Precisely," Willim replied. He turned to the table and picked up the vial. "Now bring me the Aghar, and let us watch to see if the poison does its work."

Tarot and another apprentice hastened over to the cage, while Willim cradled the precious bottle of elixir in both of his hands. He could actually *feel* the poisonous power of the concoction. Not only was it crafted to be lethal, even in the dose of a single drop, but it had been tailored to create fiendishly cruel effects the Theiwar wizard was certain to enjoy.

If his calculations were right, the first effect would be to completely paralyze the victim, leaving him incapable of action or speech even as he remained completely aware of all that was going on around him. The second effect would be to heighten the stricken target's sensations, so that every sound, every spark of light, would flare with excruciating intensity through every one of the stricken fellow's nerve endings. Thus, the dying victim would not only understand what was happening to him, but would experience all taunts and tortures, the slightest prick of his skin, with searing agony. Willim could picture his ultimate victim one day—the new king, helpless at his feet—imagining the delight he would take with the application of a small dagger or perhaps a tiny spark of flame to the paralyzed king's hypersensitive flesh. Of course the king's remaining eye would have to be plucked out very slowly.

Then, after perhaps an hour of helplessness—Willim hadn't settled on the duration, which depended partly on the poison—the victim's flesh would begin to dissolve. It was his intent that the dissolution would begin at the tips of the extremities, and take an extremely long time to reach the vital organs, and only when the heart or lungs failed, finally, would death provide the doomed king with blessed relief.

His thoughts blissful, the black-robed wizard uttered a high-pitched giggle. The poison augured a truly inventive way to kill, and he had hopes of masking the potion in a keg of stout bitters, allowing it to be consumed by a banquet room full of his enemies. But just as he didn't know the details of the agony's duration, he was not certain how long it would take for the initial symptom, the paralysis, to manifest itself. It could not be too quick, or some of the targets would observe the effects in their comrades before they had quaffed their own drinks.

Hence, the test.

Willim watched as the two apprentices dragged the quivering Aghar from his cage. The abject wretch bawled and struggled. Then in the space of an instant, both apprentices were hurled backward, Tarot crying out in pain as he fell to the floor.

The black bolts were thin, almost invisible, but the mage's spell of true-seeing allowed him to observe them clearly. Unseen attackers must have fired the missiles from the other side of the laboratory, and each bolt had struck its target unerringly in the heart. Even as he spun, seeking the intrepid intruders, Willim was aware of the last breath expelled through the lips of his slain students. He winced at the loss of Tarot; he had invested many years in the training of that unique pupil! But there was no time for regret.

"We're attacked!" he cried. "Find the enemy! Kill them!"

The apprentices turned and raced around the workbench, charging across the laboratory. Several brandished daggers while one, another fairly advanced student, paused and began to cast a magic-missile spell. Ochre, still on the floor, grew still, blinking his eyes and trying to turn his head. A large bulge, like a blood-red wart, had appeared on his left cheek. His hand flailed up and scratched at the growth.

Willim watched in disbelief as his missile-spellcasting apprentice was shot down as soundlessly and certainly as the first two. He roared his rage and cast a spell of illumination. Bright light spilled across the vast chamber, clearly marking a company of assailants, at least twenty strong, rushing toward them from the banished darkness. They burst from the shadows behind the tall columns lining the upper rim of the bowl-shaped floor of his laboratory. The lingering effects of the mass teleportation spell, like sparks lingering but slowly dying in the air, faded behind them, and the mage understood that, somehow, his lair had been discovered and the murderers magically transported there.

The attackers carried small crossbows. Each dwarf was concealed by a mask, and all were dressed entirely in black. They wore no armor, instead moving quickly and stealthily in soft boots and fitted shirts and trousers. And they displayed a military discipline as they stopped, raised their weapons, and fired a volley of lethal darts.

Willim cursed, instinctively waving his hands and barking out a powerful word. Immediately a shield, magically conjured, shimmered in the air before him. Fully half the bolts had targeted the mighty Black Robe, and those struck the shield and were obliterated into harmless dust.

His apprentices were not so lucky—nor could his magical barrier extend to them. Four more went down, fatally pierced, while the remainder dived for shelter behind the benches, chests, and casks that cluttered the wizard's cavernous workspace. Furious, Willim called forth a fireball, a tiny bubble of flame that erupted from his finger and sailed, like a propulsive, glowing marble, toward the enemy. The Black Robe could only snarl in disbelief as one of the foes leaped at the globe, snatching it in his hands and holding it to his breast. The fireball exploded, but somehow, inexplicably, the blast was absorbed by the brave assassin. That unfortunate fellow blossomed into yellow flame, vanishing into a cloud of ashes and charred flesh, yet his sacrifice had saved his fellows.

"Impossible!" hissed Willim, even as he knew the word to be a lie. It was all too possible. The mage turned, wondering how many of his apprentices survived, and was surprised to notice that the Aghar prisoner had, foolishly, scrambled back into his cage—as if that could provide him with safe shelter! There was Ochre, forcing himself up into a sitting position but staring around in confusion. Before Willim could say anything to the dazed apprentice, the wizard's full attention shifted back to the deadly troop of killers.

Another of his apprentices managed to cast a magic-missile spell, the sparkling arrows driving into the chest of one of the trespassers and felling him at once, but two of his fellows shot the spellcaster, and that apprentice, too, dropped with a bolt through his heart.

"Die!" spat Willim, casting another spell, which sent a cloud of green gas spewing from his fingers, billowing through the cavern.

The cloudkill was an imprecise, even desperate tactic, but the Black Robe was in a desperate situation. The first to die were his own two remaining apprentices, for the cloud swept over them and they couldn't help inhaling the green death. But the gas continued to flow, sweeping across the room, enveloping at least half of the attacking force, while also drifting through the cage containing the two precious elf prisoners. They died as miserably as they had lived, but so, too, did at least ten of the intruders, Willim noted with satisfaction.

The remainder pressed the assault, dispersing to minimize the impact of another area-effect spell but charging as aggressively before. They fired another volley, and once more Willim was forced to raise a shield spell, distracted from the counterattacks he would have preferred to launch. He did spit off a magic-missile spell of his own, greater than any his apprentices could summon, spraying the conjured arrows in a wide arc that bloodily cut down another of the attackers, but then he was forced to ignominiously dive for cover as a burst of magic exploded from the finger of one of the masked killers.

Ochre was shaking his head, pushing himself to one knee. He locked eyes with Willim, and something in the Theiwar's eyes convinced the wizard that, indeed, his potion was at work. "Master?" he croaked, clearly confused.

"We're attacked," the Black Robe explained curtly. He gestured to the far side of the laboratory. "Kill them—but wait! Let them come to us."

"I shall obey," Ochre said, bowing his head, quivering in his eagerness. He stood shakily, once again scratching at the strange wart that swelled even larger on his cheek.

The pair was, for the moment, blocked by the large, overturned table. Willim snapped out a spell of invisibility, touching first his apprentice—who immediately vanished—then absorbing the effects himself. As soon as he had disappeared from sight, the mage scuttled across the laboratory to a cabinet where he kept a variety of potions. The attackers were momentarily disoriented and converged toward the table, behind which the invisible Ochre waited for them. From his cabinet of potions, Willim snatched a certain bottle—a potion of teleportation—but did not drink it immediately. As a last resort, he could use the magic to escape, but he was not about to leave his treasures in the hands of the assassins unless it was absolutely necessary to his survival.

"He's gone!" one of the attackers shouted, the first to come around the table where Willim and Ochre had been hiding. The dwarf wielded a short sword, but the wizard was more interested to diagnose the accent in the fellow's voice: a Daergar!

The treacherous Daergar were prime allies of the Hylar

king, he knew. The monarch was inclined to employ them as agents for all manner of dirty tasks for which his Hylar minions were temperamentally unsuited—tasks such as espionage and attack expeditions and murder. The first of the Daergar was grabbed by the invisible Ochre, however.

The Daergar screamed as he died, and the veil of invisibility fell away from the Theiwar apprentice, who turned and roared at the others closing in on him. Ochre picked up another assassin as if the dwarf were a toy, tossing him high in the air so he smashed against a stone column and tumbled limply to the floor, his back broken.

An assassin fired a crossbow bolt directly at the apprentice, but Ochre snatched it out of the air with a gesture too swift for the eye to follow. Even in the midst of the precarious fight, Willim couldn't help but be pleased at the clear demonstration of the potion's power. The young Theiwar sprang forward, more like a panther than a dwarf, and bore the shooter to the floor where, with a quick twist, he broke the Daergar's neck.

Willim spit the command word for another spell, even though the casting caused his own perfect invisibility to shimmer, revealing himself as a hazy outline. But the attackers had their backs to him, and he didn't care; he was not going to flee his place after all.

He and Ochre were going to kill the Daergar.

His spell took effect as a coil of magic swirling outward, looping about the neck of the nearest Daergar. Willim clenched his fist, and the magic cord snapped tight. The stricken dwarf clawed and clutched as his neck was constricted. The doomed villain even tore away his mask in a desperate effort to breathe. He lurched against the bench and stumbled to his knees, his pale face purpling as the magic slowly strangled him.

Meanwhile, Ochre had grabbed another of the black-clad Daergar, spinning him around with a grip on his ankle and letting go to cast the fellow across the laboratory, right into the crack of Gorathian's lair. Immediately, the flames percolating there flared high, followed by a rumble that shook the floor of the place as the Daergar toppled, shrieking, into the depths. The burgeoning illumination brightened the vast chamber, and the noises of the dying assassin and awakening monster shook the stone foundations and the air.

Two Daergar were rushing at Ochre with blades extended, but he parried the blows with a swipe of his fist, knocking one of the swords out of the attacker's hand and forcing the other back to the wielder's face. That Daergar retreated two steps, overwhelmed by the apprentice's enhanced physical strength, ferocity, and fearlessness.

One of the remaining Daergar boldly tried to distract the wizard, hurling himself at Willim with an upraised sword. The Black Robe struck him down with a simple gesture, a paralyzing stab that rendered the dwarf's limbs weak and caused him to crumple on the spot.

Only two were left alive. Those two skirted the edge of the chasm, battling Ochre, trying to maneuver him into a mistake. The apprentice, growing more powerful by the minute thanks to the experimental potion, punched to the side, knocking one assassin down with a single blow of his fist, then wheeled to glare at the other. That Daergar, not unsurprisingly, hesitated. But his real enemy did not stand before him, for Gorathian, as ever, lurked in the pit.

The beast had been following the progress of the battle, its flaming tendrils lashing upward, seeking, probing, snapping like whips over the rim of the chasm. Two of those flame fingers wrapped themselves around the ankles of the two remaining Daergar, constricting like a snake and pulling with inexorable force. The two dwarves buckled, one of them losing his sword as he clawed futilely, sliding across the unforgiving stone. The other kept his grip on his blade and tried to hack at the tendril, as thick around as a dwarf's arm. However, his keen steel melted away as it made contact with that otherworldly flame.

Willim saw, to his horror, that a third tendril had wrapped itself around Ochre's waist, searing the apprentice while dragging him toward the chasm.

"No! Stop!" cried the wizard, rushing forward. "Not that one! Release him!"

But the beast was determined to have its prey, and Willim's command had no effect. The three victims were pulled slowly toward the rim. The dwarves shrieked and screamed, the fools even begging mercy from Willim. But the wizard could only stand and watch as the doomed assassins and his own loyal assistant were inexorably drawn to the edge. There Gorathian seemed to toy with its prey, even loosening the grip of its tentacles slightly, giving the dwarves the brief illusion of hope. They clawed and tried to crawl away.

But there was no hope. Again those powerful fire-limbs constricted, and the beast did not stop until the three dwarves had vanished over the lip of his prison, their screams echoing for a very long time as the trio plunged into the depths.

Willim found himself trembling with barely suppressed rage. He counted the bodies of his nine apprentices, all dead, and thought of the immense amount of work he had invested in their training—all work wasted.

Stalking angrily but purposefully through his laboratory, he came to the Daergar he had stricken with the choking spell. The dwarf's tongue and eyes bulged from his head, but he still clawed at the invisible noose, still clung to life. With a snap of his fingers, Willim dispelled the enchantment, watching with contempt as the would-be assassin drew a ragged breath then coughed the air back out. For long seconds the wretch struggled to breathe, his bloodshot eyes gradually focusing on the eyeless Theiwar who stood over him.

"Please . . ." croaked the attacker, raising a beseeching hand.

"Surely you don't expect mercy?" demanded the wizard.

"No . . . I beg you . . ."

Willim placed his boot on the dwarf's chest and stepped down, snapping bones and driving the air from his lungs. Then the wizard released the pressure of his weight and watched impassively as the Daergar was racked by another fit of painful coughing.

"Who sent you?" demanded the Black Robe when the other dwarf finally drew a breath.

"It . . . it was the council of thanes—and the king himself! He fears you!" croaked the doomed one.

"As well he should," Willim answered dryly. "But how did you find me?"

"A traitor . . . one of your apprentices. He revealed the location of this place for payment in gold and the promise of high office when you are dead."

"Liar!" snapped the wizard, once again stomping down on the dwarf's chest, in his fury grinding his heel into the rib cage. Yet even as he accused the fellow of lying, he was analyzing, thinking, contemplating.

And he knew that the enemy dwarf must have spoken the truth. He was appalled, sickened at the notion that one of his trusted students would have betrayed him, but there was too much fear and despair in the dwarf's eyes for him to be lying. Who had it been? He couldn't know, couldn't even begin to imagine, as he pondered that cruel revelation.

Willim would have to be more careful in the future. For the moment there was one last puny act of vengeance. He reached down and seized the Daergar by the beard, his deceptively powerful arm pulling the wretch to a sitting position and finally to his feet.

"Your master has made many mistakes—this is but the latest—and he will make more in the short time left to him. For you should know, Daergar, know before you die, that the reign of Jungor Stonespringer will soon come to a terrible end. *I* will end it, as *I* will end him, and place myself on the throne. The next high king of Thorbardin will be the greatest, and he will be Theiwar, and he will be a mage of the black robes!"

With that, Willim hurled the would-be assassin aside, sending him tumbling across the floor to the rim of the pit. He halted there at the edge, blubbering, frantically trying to move away.

Then Gorathian's tentacle touched him, and he was gone.

# EIGHT

# THE THRONE OF KAYOLIN

W hat are we going to do, Father?" Brandon asked.
He felt like a young, wide-eyed lad again,
helpless against the chaotic events of the "grown-up"
world. Garren Bluestone had ever been his anchor in
that world, and even as an adult dwarf warrior with a
number of successful fights under his belt, he needed
his father's strength and advice as never before.

"We're going to put on our formal garb and go to the
king's palace. There, we will file your claim."

Brandon nodded, for once not even bothering to correct
the improper use of the governor's title. "What about
Nailer's murder?" he asked.

Garren's eyes shone with rage and grief, but he placed a
cautioning hand on his son's shoulders. "Listen, Brandon,"
his father said finally with a sigh. "Nailer must be—will
be—avenged. But we don't know enough to embark on a
vendetta—not yet, anyway," he added grimly. "So we will
work on the first task we should accomplish and endeavor
to learn more before we act on the other. Now I suggest
you go talk to your mother for a few minutes while I have
the servants assemble our garments."

Brandon nodded, wondering if it was his own exhaustion

or his father's clear rationality that had knocked the stuffing out of him. Numbly, he went into the next room, where Nailer's body had been laid out on the bed. His mother and several of the servants were tenderly combing his hair and beard, weeping softly. When her younger son entered, Karine swept him into an embrace, clinging to him, sobbing into his beard. Her grief, somehow, made Brandon feel stronger, and he wrapped his arms around her and pulled her close, letting her anguish slowly drain away.

"I—I'm sorry, Mother," he said when her tears had dried.

"I know," she whispered. "We all are. Now go with your father. Make us proud."

He saw Garren was standing in the doorway of the room, waiting for him. Gently disengaging, he followed his father to the anteroom, where the servants had laid out formal capes trimmed with bear fur and a fresh tunic to replace Brandon's torn and bloodstained shirt. He sat down and exchanged his miner's boots for the formal black footwear preferred at court, and they were ready to go.

A small crowd of neighbors and friends was waiting quietly in the street when they emerged from the front door, and one by one those gruff dwarves and teary-eyed dwarf maids offered condolences as the two Bluestones started down the street.

"Terrible," one muttered sadly.

"Our condolences," said a pair, husband and wife, holding hands.

"It's that old Bluestone luck," whispered an old dwarf to his nearly deaf companion, the words carrying clearly to Brandon's ears.

"I'm so sorry, Brandon," said Bondall, the barmaid who ran the Cracked Mug—the level's most popular tavern. She gave him a long, shuddering hug, and he held her tenderly, feeling his own eyes grow wet. Finally, sensing his father's growing impatience, Brandon thanked her and broke away to enter the great stairwell.

They climbed the long, spiraling stairway connecting the city's levels in grim silence, the air of foreboding surrounding them clearing any dwarves they encountered out of their path. At many places the stairwell gave out onto wide plazas, popular gathering places with inns and gaming floors and fungus gardens, but the two Bluestones took no note of those popular diversions as they climbed ever higher.

Garnet Thax was the capital city of Kayolin and the one great city in that nation. It was aligned vertically, with levels and half-levels and terraces and tunnels all arrayed around the wide, virtually bottomless pit called the atrium. The deep-levels were the lowest of those, centers of manufacturing, smelting, and refining. Those were the smoky neighborhoods that Brandon had passed through while bringing Nailer's body up and out of the delvings, which were the vast mining networks extending far out and below the city. The midlevels, where the Bluestones dwelled, were numerous terraces of houses, shops, inns, and other places of business, where the majority of Kayolin's population resided. They were the heart of the city.

As they climbed through the upper-levels, they approached the nerve center where the important decisions in Kayolin society were made. The inns at the landings became more exclusive, the crowds less teeming, the dwarves behaving more quietly and wearing better clothes. Brandon knew his family's house once had been located on those exalted floors, but as he looked at the aloof dwarves—mostly Hylar—seated in their comfortable chairs near the atrium, he was happy he had lived his life in a more humble place.

All dwarfkind could be found in Kayolin. Unlike the Thorbardin of lore, wherein each clan maintained its own separate city, Garnet Thax was host to all types and clans. True, there was a Theiwar quarter on a number of the deep-levels, and the hapless Aghar maintained their miserable warrens wherever they could dig enough living space out of the rock. But for the most part the Daergar, Daewar, Hylar, and Klar lived beard by jowl with each other, pervasively in the midlevels. Of course, as was ever the case among dwarves, some of the Hylar considered themselves better than the rest of their kin and maintained their own exclusive lodgings in the best, and highest, levels.

Brandon thought briefly and ruefully of his grandfather, who had been the last patriarch of the Bluestones to live up there. Then a question started percolating in his brain. He gave voice to the query as he and his father continued on the long climb.

"Father, what did Harn Poleaxe mean when he said that 'now was the time to do it' or something like that? What does he want you to do?"

Garren looked sideways at his son, even as he continued his measured, ascending steps. For a time the elder dwarf said nothing, but Brandon got the impression he was considering his reply.

"You've heard the history: how our family was named for the sapphire infused rock strata that led to the Third Delve?" his father began.

"Yes, of course," Brandon replied. "That's why we're called House Bluestone." He saw that Garren was looking at him strangely. "Isn't that true?" he asked.

"No, it isn't—at least, not entirely," replied the elder dwarf, startling his son with the revelation. "In fact, we possess an actual wedge of bright blue rock, an artifact that our ancestor Galric Axeblade discovered, and brought back to the city with him. He knew it was valuable, and unique, and so he invented the tale of the sapphire strata to keep the existence of the real Bluestone a secret.

"But the story is partly true, as well, insofar as Galric Galric Axeblade discovered it when he was exploring the mine that would become the Third Delve. He changed his named to Galric Bluestone and founded our house with the wealth he gained from those mines."

"I never heard that," Brandon declared. "I always believed the story of the official history—that the sapphires, and the rich mines, were the source of our house's foundation, and fortune."

Garren shook his head. "It wasn't just the Third Delve that made Galric a wealthy dwarf. It was the stone itself. It's a powerful talisman in its own right. Now it's all we have left of the wealth that once exalted our family; the rest was lost in the Cataclysm and its aftermath as my father tried to stay in business, to pay his workers and his loyal clients even after his mines had been destroyed." There was something in Garren's tone that showed he approved of his own father's decision, and Brandon felt a stab of fierce family pride.

"Harn Poleaxe wants to buy the Bluestone from me," Garren said quietly, his steps still steady as they spiraled up the wide, stone stairs. "He is offering me a tremendous amount of money; he's been raising the offer for more than year, every time he sees me."

Brandon knew Poleaxe had visited his father at least every five or ten intervals over that time. He struggled to digest the information. "Why does he want it so badly?" he asked finally.

"He says it's part of a hill dwarf legacy, one the Neidar have only recently uncovered. There are several of these stones, all of them dating back to the days of the Graygem. His clan, the Neidar, already possess the green one, which he calls the Greenstone. He assures me if he could return home with the Bluestone, his status among his people would be permanently cemented. He would become a virtual lord."

"And how much is he offering you for the stone?"

Garren stopped climbing for the first time and looked straight into his son's eyes. "Enough money for me to move our house up to the highest levels again. It would make me a force in Kayolin, not quite with the clout of, say, the Heelspurs, but very nearly. It would change our luck for the better in a way that the whole nation would see."

Brandon whistled aloud. "All that—for a single stone?" he asked quietly.

"Yes, for the stone that is our family's legacy," Garren replied, shaking his head. "For the stone that is all we have left of our ancestors, of the good fortune that made us a family house in the first place."

"I can see why you won't make the deal," the son said. "I wouldn't either, not ever."

Garren smiled somewhat wistfully. "I can't say I won't make the deal—not ever. But the deal isn't right, not yet. Plus, there's something . . ." His voice trailed away.

"What? What is it?" pressed Brandon.

"Something about Harn himself. I like him well enough; he's good company, generous, helpful."

"He likes his dwarf spirits," the younger Bluestone suggested.

"If fondness for strong drink was a fatal flaw, I daresay none of us would survive to old age," Garren said mildly. "But you're right, he does seem to have a bit more of a weakness for the stuff than you'd like to see in a mature person."

The elder dwarf shook his head, his gray hair cascading around the ursine fur fringing his cloak. "Anyway, this discovery of yours and Nailer's might have made the whole issue irrelevant. Let's get to the top so we can file your claim, and then we'll see."

They started but after a few steps, Garren stopped again. "But remember: Regar Smashfingers calls himself a king. So *we* call him a king. Understand?"

"Yes, I do," Brandon replied, taking his father's point.

The king/governor's palace was fully a thousand feet above the midlevel city quarter inhabited by the Bluestones, but neither of the dwarves was the slightest bit out of breath when at last they arrived at the regal caverns that formed Garnet Thax's uppermost level. Immediately to the side of the stairwell was the pit known as the Governor's Atrium. Only recently, Regar Smashfingers had rechristened the shaft as the King's Atrium, signaling to his subjects his intent to claim the high title that had so long been limited to the ruler of Thorbardin.

The atrium was a deep shaft that connected with all of the city's levels. Illuminated by a glow of magma far below, it was the source of a constant updraft of warm air that seeped through the city, providing its passages, levels, homes, and shops with a more comfortable temperature than could typically be expected underground. Rings of balconies, many of them containing the tables and chairs of popular inns, surrounded the pit, and throughout the ages skilled carvers had worked images of dwarf heroes into the very bedrock of the mountain. Legend had it that the statues of those heroes watched over Kayolin and that—if the nation found itself in perilous need—those graven images would spring to life and fight in the land's defense.

Brandon wasted scarcely a glance at the hero images. All his attention was directed to the wide-open doors, flanked by pillars as thick around as a giant's torso, that marked the entrance to the governor's palace.

As they approached, a female voice cried out. "Brandon Bluestone!"

It was Rona Darkwater, a Hylar dwarf maid from one of the city's elite families. She had been in the audience watching Brandon win a wrestling tournament a year or so ago, and they'd enjoyed a casual, but passionate, romance in the time since.

"Hi, Rona," he said, somewhat sheepishly as his father raised an eyebrow.

She was a stunningly beautiful female with golden hair extending in a sweep as far as her knees, a trim waist, and a swelling bodice that she flattered at that moment with a filmy, low-cut top of red silk.

"What brings you to the nosebleed levels?" she asked mischievously before taking note of his stern, solemn manner. "Is something wrong?"

"My brother was murdered a short time ago. Our family is grieving. Now I have come with my father to see the gov—the king," he amended.

"Oh! I'm so sorry," she said with obvious sincerity. "Please, let me know if there's anything I can do."

"Thanks," he mumbled, following his father toward the palace.

"Rona Darkwater?" Garren said quietly. "Maybe you're already starting to move your way up the levels?"

Glowering, Brandon didn't reply. Instead, he strode determinedly beside his father toward the royal entrance. A score of armored dwarves, elite members of the King's Guard, stood to attention at either side of the entry. Each was a brawny Daergar with long, black hair and beards all combed and oiled to slick perfection. They wore shiny black boots and plate mail breastplates of the same color. On each of their chests was emblazoned the sigil of House Smashfingers: a golden fist atop a black anvil. The guards held spears with tips upraised but merely watched the flow of interested citizenry who entered and exited the palace without interference.

Brandon had been there many times before, but in the past he had been merely a curious onlooker. This was the first time he had come into the palace with a goal to set before the governor (no, the king, he reminded himself), and the memory of his brother's death—he could still feel Nailer's blood spattering against his skin—fueled his resolve. As if sensing his passion, his father reached out a hand, laying a touch that appeared to be gentle but was in fact a steely grip, on his youngest son's arm.

"Remember: patience," Garren whispered. "We are here

to stake a claim, not to gain vengeance."

The court was meeting in a large, circular chamber, a dozen feet below the level of the gallery where the Bluestones and other onlookers were ushered. The gallery formed a ring around the entire court, an expanse some two hundred feet in diameter. The crowd was sparse, so Brandon and his father had no difficulty pushing their way to the front of the gallery, where they could look down directly on the governor and his court.

Regar Smashfingers sat in a grand chair, raised on a dais so, even when he was seated, his head rose a foot or two higher than the tallest dwarf standing before him. Courtiers and dwarf maids, dressed in the silken finery that had recently become the style of Kayolin's wealthy, stood attentively to either side, leaving the space directly before the throne open to the petitioner.

That petitioner, Brandon recognized with a flash of anger, was none other than Lord Alakar Heelspur, head of the wealthiest clan in all Kayolin and long a toadying adherent of the king/governor's policies.

Heelspur was a tall, brawny dwarf. His hair and beard had gone to gray, but his posture presented a picture of robust health and aggressive manner. He was gesturing with his hands outspread, speaking in a formal, polite tone.

"This new delving, Your Majesty, promises to expand the worth of the royal treasury by a virtually unprecedented amount. My assessors have not yet completed the formal survey, but they confirm there is enough gold in this vein to keep a thousand miners busy for a dozen years, and that is only to excavate the ore that is already patently visible. As Your Majesty well knows, past experience indicates that the total value of the claim will likely exceed this estimate by a figure tenfold or even a hundredfold greater."

"It sounds impressive, very impressive indeed," declared Regar, who was sitting up straight and paying very close attention to his subject and loyal lord. The king stroked his fingers through his beard. "And your men discovered it only recently?"

"Yes, majesty. It is an adjunct of our old Zhaban Delving, long thought to be haunted. But we Heelspurs are nothing if not intrepid, and it was my own son who led the expedition force that discovered the vein."

Brandon stared in amazement. He couldn't believe his ears. He immediately understood who had attacked him and slain his brother. "That's our claim!" he whispered to his father, more loudly than he had intended, provoking looks and muttered reactions from some of the other onlookers. Garren's eyes flared, but he laid a restraining hand on his son's shoulder.

"In fact," Heelspur continued, puffing out his chest, preening for the crowd. "My son single-handedly slew the cave troll that was guarding the new delving."

The gathered courtiers oohed and aahed at his impressive claim, which was too much for Brandon.

"Fiend! Liar!" the young Bluestone shouted impulsively, his words booming from the balcony. "That vein was discovered by Nailer Bluestone and myself—and my brother was murdered by your dark servants and I was left for dead as we returned to Garnet Thax to file our claim!"

That declaration was met by gasps and grumbles from the gallery and, at first, stony silence on the floor. Still, the king and Lord Heelspur both looked up to see who voiced the angry challenge.

"Silence!" hissed Garren, squeezing his son's arm again, but the words were already spoken, and they had been clearly heard.

"Who speaks?" demanded Regar Smashfingers after a long pause.

"I am Brandon Bluestone, Sire. And I speak the truth!" he declared defiantly.

"You interrupt this lord to make a Bluestone claim?" Regar Smashfingers growled. "This is an unacceptable, even intolerable violation of decorum!"

"Not only is it a false claim, my liege!" cried Lord Heelspur, his voice choking with wounded pride. "He levies a slanderous worse charge—of murder! Must I put up with this insult, this dishonor, here in open court?"

Brandon was ready with a reply, but his father was already pulling him away from the gallery. "It's true!" he shouted, but the words were muffled by Garren's hand planted firmly across his mouth.

"Don't be a fool!" snapped the elder Bluestone, dragging Brandon back between the guards flanking the palace gate. Garren propelled his son toward the stairways spiraling back down to the city's midlevels. "Now move! Get out of here before you do more damage!"

"But, father, he was claiming our find! The find that cost Nailer his life!" spit Brandon, finally breaking free from the patriarch's steely grasp. "He is behind Nailer's murder!'

"*I* know that!" retorted Garren. "But we must present our case to the king—and now you have humiliated his ally in public court! Quickly, down the stairs."

"But—" Brandon was forced to obey, propelled by his father's stern push. "What are you—we—going to do?"

"We?" growled Garren Bluestone, pushing even harder. Behind his father's anger, Brandon realized, was a very powerful undercurrent of fear. "It's you I'm worried about now. *We* are going to do the only thing we can! We are going to try to save your life!"

# NINE

# WINGS OF MAGIC

With his hands pressed tightly over his face, Gus peered through the gaps between his fingers. He watched in terror as the deadly bolts flew through the wizard's lair, cringed as one dwarf after another was killed by weaponry or magic. The green cloud of lethal gas drifted near to his cage, and he couldn't help coughing and gagging as he drew small, painful breaths, but the bulk of the poison gas passed over his head. He could only stare in horror as the two elves in the next cage writhed and puked and, ever so slowly, died. The gully dwarf tried looking away, but the male elf was staring at him, and he couldn't help staring back, watching those ancient eyes until they slowly glazed over and finally went dark and still.

He gaped in awe when the wizard vanished from sight, then watched him reappear. He saw the bottle that the Theiwar pulled from his cabinet and watched as the mage set that bottle down on the bench, near to the bottle of black liquid and the other of dwarf spirits that the Black Robe had seemed to cherish so much. Gus cowered at the sight of a young Theiwar, one of the wizard's helpers, who seemed to fight like a crazed monster—throwing his foes around the room and leaping after them with a speed and agility unlike any dwarf's.

When at last the fiery tentacles emerged from the deep pit, he yelped in abject horror and pressed his face to the floor. He heard terrible screaming and felt the heat of infernal fires warming his skin. Only as the sounds of battle slowly faded and the intense warmth waned did he risk looking again through the stubby fingers that offered so little protection.

He listened to the talk between the wizard and the doomed assassin, not entirely understanding what they were talking about—though even a miserable Aghar knew that Jungor Stonespringer was the high king of all dwarves, the mightiest and most lofty ruler in all the world. And the black-robed wizard sought to supplant him!

He must be very mighty indeed, and that thought made Gus even more afraid.

That last prisoner died, and the terrible, powerful usurper was looking around his lair again. The Aghar tried to make himself very small . . . to no avail.

"You!" snapped the wizard, pointing at Gus. "Come out of there."

The words were more than just an audible command. They were a summoning spell, and Gus could no more have disobeyed than he could have turned himself into a cave bat and winged away. His knees knocked as he forced himself to his feet and stumbled forward, clumping like an automaton as he emerged from the still-open door to his cell. Once outside he stopped, for the wizard had made no further immediate command.

"I mean, come over here, to this bench," said the Black Robe in irritation.

The wizard was horrible to gaze upon. His eyelids were sewn shut, sealed with ghastly scars. His beard was filthy, matted with bits of food and possibly drool—though when he spotted a bit of mushroom tangled in the drool, Gus's stomach momentarily growled. But terror quickly pulled his attention back to the magic-user's commands.

Gus, unable to resist the magical compulsion, did as told. His eyes widened as he saw the sinister black liquid. He could sense the evil power there, and it made him very afraid. Beside that bottle was another, of dwarf spirits, which Gus recognized as something that would make him very sick—he had tasted the liquor once before, when he had claimed a nearly empty bottle off the body of a dead Klar. And there was a third bottle too, the one that the wizard had taken out of his cabinet while the fight was raging in the laboratory.

"Now listen carefully, you miserable little dimwit," snapped the Theiwar wizard. He gestured to the bench where the black liquid and the other two bottles rested. "I want you to take a very small sip of this tasty potion. You must drink now."

Again, the compelling spell of command allowed no disobedience. Gus's hand shook uncontrollably as the little dwarf reached upward—the top of the bench being as high as his chin.

"Be careful! Don't drop it!" snapped the dwarf wizard.

At his words a burst of fire erupted from the crack in the floor, the flame and smoke billowing into the cavern as the great beast that lurked there seethed and burned. The mage turned his face, momentarily grinning at the horrific display of fiery power.

Gus was reaching up, compelled to grab the bottle, to drink a small drop. The wizard's command was insistent, magical, irresistible. But that black liquid terrified him so! His hand hesitated, terrified by the dark swirl of the bottle's creamy contents. Even so, his fingers started to close around it, curling shut despite every effort he made to balk.

Some tiny corner of his brain raised a good, pertinent

point. The wizard had not specified *which* liquid he was required to drink. He said to drink "this," but maybe he meant one of the other bottles. He moved his hand ever so slightly in that direction, pleased that the spell didn't keep him from doing so. And the wizard didn't notice. Gus quickly snatched up the bottle that looked like dwarf spirits, but then remembered the retching, the pounding headache, that had resulted last time he drank something like that. Nope, better not, he told himself at the last moment. So he let go of the dwarf spirits bottle, which dropped into the sagging pouch of his front pocket.

The wizard was still distracted, admiring the glowing aura of his pet monster, but just then he started to turn back toward the gully dwarf.

Eagerly, like a drowning swimmer snatching for a lifeline in a stormy sea, Gus grabbed the third bottle, the one the wizard had brought out of his cabinet. He raised it to his lips and took a small sip even as the Theiwar returned his stare to him and the potions.

"No, you fool!" shrieked the mage. "Not that one!"

But the liquid was already trickling down his gullet, a strangely bubbly sensation that tasted like water but was not. The wizard reached furiously for him, his eyeless face contorted, and Gus instinctively flinched away, wishing he was somewhere, *anywhere,* besides that horrible place. Besides terror and hunger, he felt the bottle of dwarf spirits flopping around in his deep pocket.

Then suddenly, miraculously, the dread wizard was gone. His whole laboratory was gone. It was dark but not dark like the dark of a deep cave. Gus felt very cold, as air moved past his skin, a sensation he had never experienced before. Instinctively he looked up, seeking the ceiling, the upper wall of whatever chamber he was in.

Instead, he saw a speckling of tiny lights, impossibly distant, and uncountably numerous. Around him were great mounds of rock, some of them dusted with a curious whiteness. Most of all, there was an undeniable sense of vast distances, of space above him and to either side, a feeling that he had never experienced before. Only gradually did the truth dawn:

He wasn't in Thorbardin anymore.

——DH——

Willim trembled with uncontainable rage. He shouted and shrieked, and fire flew from his tongue, searing through a cask of charcoal and filling the entire cavern with thick, acrid smoke. He stamped his foot, and a crack shivered across the stone floor, the jagged scar extending all the way to the edge of Gorathian's chasm. He pounded his fist upon the massive stone workbench, and the granite slab shuddered and groaned before snapping in half.

Only at the last second did Willim come to his senses. As the table gave way, he remembered the two precious bottles of potion: the deadly poison that the Aghar was supposed to have tested and the elixir that had proved so effective in enhancing Ochre's abilities. He must not destroy them. But where were they? His hand lashed out as the table fell and he tried to catch the vials before they came to harm. He snatched the black poison out of the air but couldn't find the elixir in the bottle labeled as the dwarf spirits.

The pieces of the stone surface thundered to the floor, raising clouds of dust, scattering a spray of gravel-sized debris, and Willim frantically dug through the rubble. But there was no sign of the bottle. Nor, thankfully, did he see any broken glass or the *Midwarren Pale* label.

He drew deep breaths through his nose, forcing himself to grow calm. Despite his recent setbacks, he had splendid powers of control—one did not command the high art of the black robes without extraordinary discipline. Slowly, methodically, he reflected on all that had transpired, tried to reconstruct what had just happened to top his very bad day.

His spell of command had worked to perfection. The miserable little gully had been compelled to obey Willim by that enchantment, and thus, he had advanced to the table, had been reaching for the bottle and getting ready to drink the potion.

Then Gorathian had flared, and the wizard had turned away for a fleeting moment. When he had turned back, the Aghar was picking up the bottle—only it was a different bottle. The bloody fool gully dwarf had gulped the potion of teleportation instead!

Then, out of sheer terror no doubt, the wretch had blinked himself away. The wizard hissed an inarticulate shiver of rage, hoping that the worthless creature had blinked himself into the fiery depths of the Abyss or perhaps popped into sight in the middle of the ocean—or, even better, right into the bedrock of the earth, where he would be instantly crushed.

Good riddance to him. But where was the elixir?

Willim forced himself to concentrate, and he recalled the images of his spell of true-seeing almost as if they were playing like pictures in his mind, only slowed down, one after the other in a series. And that was when he saw: he saw the bottle fall into the gully dwarf's pocket, then he saw the wretched creature disappear.

Blasted gully dwarf!

Suddenly, the question of the Aghar's whereabouts assumed a whole new significance. The elixir represented a year of work and had consumed components that were, for all intents and purposes, irreplaceable (especially with so many apprentices out of commission). It was an innovative new recipe of alchemy, one that Ochre had proved worked as Willim had anticipated. And it was the key to his entire plan, the means by which he would create a company of undefeatable warriors for the master attack that would destroy Jungor Stonespringer and all his lords, allies, and guards in one blow.

All right. He knew what he had to do: the teleported gully dwarf would have to be found. It was with a steady hand and a cold, clear purpose that Willim the Black pulled down a spellbook and, ignoring the inconvenience of his eyeless sockets, began to read.

Several hours passed before he set the book down, having absorbed and memorized the ritual required to cast a very potent spell. He rose and stretched, ready to get to work—until he looked around, reminded of the chaos in the laboratory. The wreckage, the debris, the shattered crates and table would need to be cleaned up, but in due time.

The laboratory would have to wait. Indeed, Willim wondered if he might have to rebuild and move his laboratory to a new location. It seemed that the king had learned of his whereabouts, and it wouldn't do to be continually bothered by raids and assassination attempts and other nuisances. But that decision, too, could wait.

The bodies needed tending, however. They already reeked and would soon begin to rot. With a grimace of disgust, he cast a spell and used his fingertip to whisk, one by one, the corpses of the company of Daergar attackers, as well as those of his slain apprentices, over to the crack leading to Gorathian's lair. He let them drop into the depths, and with each additional bit of flesh, the monster flared and growled.

Willim knew that Gorathian preferred living flesh to carrion. Even so, the beast seemed content with the bonus feeding. Perhaps it even regretted the earlier impetuous hunger that had caused it to sweep Ochre, along with Willim's enemies, to death. At least, Willim would like to think that the beast was capable of that kind of remorse. In any event, the fire in the deep pit was banked low, a dim crimson radiating like embers from the depths of the world. And the wizard was free to turn to his task.

He had a spell to cast. He found a large ceramic bowl and

filled it with clear water. He removed a pinch of charcoal from the bottom of his storage cask—the part that hadn't been incinerated by his blast of rage after the Aghar's escape—and dropped it in the water.

He considered the next component he desired and cursed. If he had retained even a drop of the magical elixir, he could have cast his spell with guaranteed accuracy. Instead he would have to settle for an approximation. Using a small pinch of mushroom powder, he added fungus to the water, stirring the liquid with precise strokes of an ivory paddle. When the contents were mixed and swirling smoothly, he concentrated on the look, the smell, the feel of his missing potion, and cast the words to the spell of location.

Immediately the components in the swirling liquid came together in a snakelike mass, writhing against the direction of the water's flow. A black image took on a solid aspect, first as a coil but gradually straightening itself into an arrow. The arrow spun like the needle of a deranged compass, but as the water's swirl gradually settled, the arrow grew still. The tail dropped to the bottom of the bowl, and the tip pointed almost straight up.

For several seconds it remained fixed until the water ceased its movement and the arrow dissolved, leaving a pale-brown mixture, completely still, in the bowl.

And Willim had all the information he needed—at least, all he could gain from his imperfect components.

Thoughtfully he leaned his head back, turning his eyeless face toward the ceiling of the lofty cavern. So the idiot Aghar had teleported himself—and the potion he unwittingly carried in his pocket—almost straight up. That would simplify matters. Since the imperfect spell revealed the direction of the object sought but not the distance, a compass bearing such as north or south could have meant that the wretched thief had teleported one or even one thousand miles in that direction. However, since the direction was primarily upward, it seemed likely that the gully dwarf was somewhere high in the peaks of the Kharolis Mountains, the lofty summits towering over all of vast Thorbardin.

"Good," Willim declared.

For a moment he considered teleporting after the Aghar himself, but he quickly discarded the tempting thought. No, it would take some searching, perhaps a lot of searching, before the fool was discovered. Much as Willim would have relished making that discovery himself, he had too many other things to do back there in his lair.

So he would have to cast another spell.

That one required heat, and again he grimaced, remembering that in his rage he had smashed his favorite granite worktable. He would have to use a bench that had been carved from the bedrock of the mountain, a stone cube near one wall of the laboratory that had once been intended as the dais for a thane's throne. He touched it with his hand and murmured the spell, and immediately the stone glowed red. As Willim concentrated on the magic, the illumination gradually faded to yellow, and finally the stone was white hot. So intense was its radiance that the wizard, generally immune to such discomfort, was forced to take a step back.

Quickly he went about assembling the rest of his components, gathering them in a medium-sized iron cauldron. Scales and dried blood were tossed in, as well as the eyes of insects and other, even less pleasant, ingredients. When he came to the final, and most vital, ingredient, he cursed aloud, remembering the dwarf corpses he had fed to Gorathian. If he had only remembered to save *one* of them!

Searching around, he surveyed his chamber, his eyeless face turning this way and that as his spell of true-seeing swept the half-destroyed room. It came to the cage where the two elves had died, slain by the cloudkill spell, and immediately the dark dwarf nodded to himself: an elf corpse would work just as well as a dwarf.

With a flick of his finger and a muttered word, he lifted the rigid body of the male elf and brought it over to the cauldron. A few more manipulations placed the heart and the brain of the corpse into the vat; the rest of the drying flesh was discarded. Finally, he set the metal kettle on the white-hot stone of his workbench and stepped back to work another incantation.

The raising of a minion was not something to be done casually or quickly. For more than an hour, Willim stood before the cauldron, working the spell, sweat pouring from the Theiwar's face, trickling through his beard, causing his robe to stick to his skin. Never, however, did his intense concentration waver, and finally the kettle began to smoke then to burn. Flames shot upward, at first yellow and bright, then gradually fading to pale blue flickers barely extending over the rim, and at last fading away.

The cauldron continued to smoke, however, and that smoke grew thick, black, and strangely opaque. It rose in a column, but instead of dispersing through the chamber, it held together, coalesced, and in fact seemed to concentrate in on itself as more and more churning vapor surged into the cloud. Very slowly, the smoke emerging from the cauldron diminished as all of the components were consumed. Finally, there was nothing left save for the tall, amorphous pillar of black murk lingering in the air over the black kettle.

"Minion—awaken!" Willim commanded, his voice booming through the chamber. At the same time, he clenched both fists, and the smoke column contracted, writhing and, increasingly, wailing as the magic wove it into a physical presence. It floated to the side, then settled down onto the floor of the chamber. Two slender legs, ending in taloned feet, extended downward to support its weight. A pair of black, batlike wings extended from its shoulders. Finally eyes appeared:

almond shaped and wide set, like the eyes of an elf.

But those eyes were red and glowing with hellish heat like the blazing coal within a hot forge.

Willim concentrated his thoughts; then, without speaking, he conveyed to his minion a mental image of the gully dwarf and instructed it to follow in the direction the Aghar had gone away from there. Only then did the Black Robe give voice to his command.

"Pursue the gully dwarf until you catch him. When you do, kill him and bring me everything he carries."

The minion bowed deeply, those eerie elf eyes pressing all the way to the floor, in obeisance. Then the black wings spread and the horrid creature, taller than a tall man, took flight. It rose, met the stone ceiling of the vast cavern, and continued on through the bedrock of the world.

# TEN

# HEADING SOUTH

Garren Bluestone, pushing Brandon before him, rushed through the front door of his family's manor. "Send for Harn Poleaxe," he ordered his doorman. The young dwarf, a lanky Daewar, departed at once.

"Father!" complained Brand. "I was telling the truth; I deserved to be heard!"

"You deserved to be heard, maybe. But your actions were more likely to get you arrested, even killed!" declared the elder in exasperation. "Don't you understand who wields the power in this nation? The power, whether you want to believe it or not, of life and *death?*"

"I saw the death part," growled the son.

His father's face fell, looking as though he had been struck a physical blow, and Brandon immediately regretted his tone. But Garren's voice when next he spoke was steady, almost calm.

"I only have one son left. We have to get you out of Kayolin," he said bluntly. "As soon as possible."

"Do you think the governor will try to kill me right here in Kayolin? First they'll have to arrest me, give me a trial!" Brandon blurted in disbelief.

His father glared sternly at him. "The king, I keep telling you, can do anything he prefers to do. And if it can't be done legal and nice, Lord Heelspur has plenty more of his thugs to throw at you. One will pick a fight; others will be lurking. Your temper is not without some renown." Garren looked wistful as he regarded his youngest son. "And everyone knows about the Bluestone luck. Whatever your fate, many people will say that you provoked it and you got what you deserved. Others will say it's simply the curse that follows our house. We are in a real pickle here. My son, I would like to fight them too, but we have to keep you safe while we build up our case, muster allies and supporters."

"But—*leave?* You tell me I must leave Kayolin?" Like most of the nation's mountain dwarves, he had done his share of exploring the peaks and valleys of the Garnet Range. But the land beyond those lofty summits was completely unknown to him. "Where would I go?" he asked, finally.

"That's where Poleaxe comes in. Now collect a few traveling things—just the essentials—and be here the moment he arrives. I'll have a purse of about eighty steel coins for you; you'll have to use it pay expenses, book passage on a ship, and so forth. We have no time to waste. And Brandon—"

"Yes, what?" he asked, numbly.

"Take your axe, and remember your house. It has not always been a legacy of bad luck, you know. Balric Bluestone was carrying that weapon when he set off to climb Garnet Peak. He was lost in the Cataclysm, but his axe was returned to us—the rescuers found it immediately, as soon as they went to look for him."

"I . . . I know the story," Brandon replied, confused.

"The point is, I've always felt that discovery meant something to us, to our family. It's a symbol of hope, a sign that if we look toward the future, there is a promise of better things ahead. Bear it proudly, and find that future. Now go."

Brandon's heart was pounding as he went to his rooms and looked at the tunics, trousers, cloaks, boots, and belts that made up his wardrobe. Buy passage on ship? He couldn't even imagine floating on an ocean! He had a chest of tools, another of weapons, each containing implements he had used during the nearly five decades of his life as he grew to adulthood. How could he shrink it down to the few items he could carry on his back?

He was standing there, feeling helpless, when his mother came in. Karine walked up to him, and he put an arm around her, drawing her against him, surprised by how frail, how small, she felt.

"I understand I am losing *two* sons today," she said sadly.

He frowned. In his own wallowing, he had forgotten how his actions would affect the rest of his family. "I'm sorry," he said awkwardly. "I didn't mean to—I don't want to—that is, Father insists—"

"And he's right," she said firmly. "He told me what happened in the court. You won't be safe here, but you should know, Brandon, that I am *so* proud of you."

"But—why? I haven't done anything to make you proud!"

"Shh," she said quietly, touching a finger to his lips. "I know what you and your brother found. And I know what you did, carrying him out of the delvings by yourself. You are a credit to yourself and to our house."

He couldn't speak for a moment, just held her close. Finally he waved his free hand at his wardrobe and chests. "I don't even know what to take," he admitted.

"Let me help," she said practically, bustling over to the chests, throwing the lids open, and clucking her tongue at the mess she saw in each. Yet somehow, in the space of a few short minutes, she had helped him gather together a compact traveling kit. He donned his most durable clothes, wrapped a knife, a waterskin, gloves, and a rope into a spare robe, and strapped his axe to the sheath on his back. The cook brought in some bread and cheese wrapped in dried lambskin that Brandon could carry in his belt pouch. At his mother's advice, he put on his most comfortable walking boots, leaving both his hobnailed climbing boots and the ceremonial footwear he had worn to the palace behind.

He said a dignified good-bye to his mother, though her courageously dry eyes made him want to cry. "Go," she whispered into his ear, and the anguish in her voice made him understand her grief and steeled his own resolve. He emerged to find that Harn Poleaxe had come quickly and was being ushered into his father's study.

"I have reconsidered," Garren Bluestone said to the hill dwarf when the Neidar and the patriarch were comfortably seated. Brandon stood inside the doorway, watching and listening as his father spoke. "I accept your terms, on two additional conditions."

"Excellent!" rejoiced Poleaxe before narrowing his eyes. "Conditions?" he said warily. "My offer is on the table: a hundred times a thousand steel pieces for the Bluestone."

Brandon tried to listen, though his head was whirling with the fast pace of events. He couldn't even imagine a hundred times a thousand pieces of steel. And what were the new conditions? He had a feeling they involved himself, and his departure.

"The terms don't change," Garren declared. "But the conditions are these: I want you to take my son with you when you return to Hillhome. And you must leave immediately."

Poleaxe blinked, looking Brandon up and down in blunt appraisal. "To the first, I agree," he said. "Your young son is a hale companion, and of course I will welcome his company. But why the second?" he asked, perplexed. "Is the lad in some trouble?"

"Precisely," Garren replied. "He can tell you about it when you are on your way. Time's a-wasting. Can you do it?"

Poleaxe shrugged, the simple gesture seeming somehow grandiose, almost kingly. "I will need an hour or two to settle my affairs. And, of course, I don't have those steel pieces readily at my disposal. It will take some time to arrange for a moneylender's draft to be sent up here from the south. You understand, after all this time, I did not anticipate having to conclude our arrangement in the matter of a few minutes."

"I do understand. Brandon will carry the stone until you have the draft sent. Will that be adequate?"

Harn Poleaxe stroked his beard, his handsome features marked by a pensive expression. "Yes, I agree. We can leave as soon as I've settled my affairs; I travel light, and I have nothing that I can't leave behind for another trip." He looked at Brandon then rested a hand—a hand that thumped down with the force of a felled tree—on the younger dwarf's shoulder. "What about you, young Bluestone? Are you prepared for an arduous journey?"

Brandon, speechless, could only nod his head in the affirmative.

Garren cleared his throat then rose to his feet. He removed a key from beneath his tunic, one that he wore on a chain around his neck, and inserted it into a niche in the wall that Brandon had never before recognized as a lock. With a quick turn, he released the catch then pulled open the heavy stone door to reveal a large safe. Within was a single object, wrapped in soft leather, that looked to Brandon to be about the size of a hammer's head. He set the thing on his desk and slowly, reverently, unfolded the wrapping.

Though, throughout his life, Brandon had seen the Bluestone Wedge depicted on tapestries and shields, on the family's front door and on his father's ornate breastplate, but he had always thought it to be an abstract symbol. He had never laid eyes on the precious artifact itself. He was moved by the sight of the actual heirloom. It was just as portrayed: a simple wedge, wide and blunt at one end, while tapered and narrow, though not sharp like an axe blade, at the other. As he had surmised, it was about the size of a regular hammerhead, smaller than the head of a warhammer.

But it was not the shape nor the size of the object that took his breath away. Rather, it was the color. It was not just a turquoise or bluegranite, but nearly the infinite, perfect azure of a sapphire. He imagined he could stare into that stone for hours and never see the same image twice, as if there were countless facets and unique features, dazzling details that would compel him to keep seeking, confound him with wonder at each new discovery.

He shook his head, and it was almost like breaking out of a trance. Harn Poleaxe, he saw too, was similarly transfixed. Garren Bluestone was ignoring the Neidar, watching his son with an expression, Brandon hoped with a pang, that indicated he was proud and satisfied with the object of his scrutiny.

Finally, with a curt gesture, his father pulled the wrapping over the stone again, and the spell was broken.

"Here you go," he said, hoisting the bundle and handing it to Brandon. "It's time you two were on your way.

———DH———

"Now this will be Caergoth, coming up," Harn Poleaxe said ten days later, gesturing expansively to the large community ringed by fortified walls and towers and crowned by a massive castle, that had been gradually materializing before the two dwarves during their past three hours riding along the road. "Greatest port in southern Solamnia—though they say it's no match for Palanthas, way up in the north."

Brandon looked up, startled out of a reverie that had involved both the barmaid Bondall and the heiress Rona Darkwater. He was relieved to see the Neidar hadn't noticed his inattention.

"So this is where we hire a ship to take us south, across the Newsea?" he asked.

It had been a long, hard ten days. His rump was so sore, he thought he'd never want to sit down again. How could a horse be so damned uncomfortable? And wobbly? And just plain cantankerous? As if to mock him, the animal underneath him shivered and lurched a bit, sending new jolts of pain through his buttocks and lower back.

He squinted, impressed in spite of himself with the vista of the great, fortified city ahead. But it was so confounded bright out there on the plains; he had a constant headache, it seemed, just from trying to cope with the sunlight and the wide vista of sky. Of course, he'd been outside of Kayolin before, exploring the mountains of the Garnet Range, but most of his forays had been through the lush pine forests, and even when he'd been up on the rocky ridges, there always seemed to be stone and cliff and frowning overlook looming over him, intermittently blocking out the blistering rays. For four days they had been out in the wide open, and it seemed as if the clouds had decided to stay permanently out of sight. For four days he had suffered the full blazing glory of the sun.

"So we're going right to the docks when we get there?" he asked hopefully.

"Nah," Harn said breezily. "There's an inn I know in the castle district. Friendly folk, even some dwarves. Like as not we'll be able to rustle up a game or two of knucklebones. You know, a little social activity before we head out on the water."

Harn gave an involuntary shiver at the word *water,* and Brandon sympathized. The idea of travel by sea held little appeal for any dwarf. They were traveling by ship because there was no other way to get back to Harn's hill country, in the rugged foothills of the Kharolis Mountains, which wasn't too far from fabled Thorbardin itself.

Yet despite his reluctance to leave dry land behind, Brandon was even more reluctant to stay in the Solamnic city any longer than was strictly necessary.

"Remember what happened in Garnet?" he prodded, noticing that Harn had produced his flask of dwarf spirits and was leaning back to swizzle a long gulp. Brandon glumly shook his head when his companion generously extended the bottle toward him.

"Of course I do," the Neidar declared irritably. "I told you, it was vital that we buy horses! And it was. Sore as your ass is right now, trust me, you didn't want to walk that long road on foot. We'd still be coming up on the Kingsbridge, fifty miles back!"

"It took two hours to buy horses," Brandon pointed out. "We were in Garnet for four days!"

Although he was complaining, Brandon had to admit that the days—and, especially, the nights—in the bustling city at the foot of the Garnet range had been an eye-opening experience and not without its share of good times. Three days after walking out of Kayolin's main gate, the two dwarves had emerged from the foothills and entered the first city, other than Garnet Thax, that Brandon had ever visited in his life.

The sights and sounds and smells had been overwhelming—tantalizing and thrilling, even. The population was mostly human, but the people were very amenable to dwarves—and dwarven coin. Harn had led his young companion immediately to his favorite inn, where the Neidar had proceeded to get drunk and make friends with everyone in the place. Brandon had been preoccupied taking in the sights, talking to the first humans he had ever met—the women, in particular, seemed taken by his broad shoulders and friendly, easygoing grin—and sampling some of the meat and bread and cheese that wasn't available in sunless Kayolin. Besides he couldn't keep up with Poleaxe on a drink-for-drink basis.

That was just as well because the Neidar overdrank and needed Brandon's help just to walk from the first inn to another of his favorite places, where Harn got even drunker. In his third favorite inn, Brandon had pulled his companion out just before a fight erupted, and in the fourth, when the fisticuffs inevitably commenced, Brandon had simply joined in the fun, and the two dwarves had triumphed over all comers in an exhilarating brawl.

But when the same pattern repeated itself the following night, and the night after that, Brandon began to feel a little concerned and restless. Harn kept assuring him he was shopping for the right horses, but the young dwarf grew increasingly skeptical, mainly because they never visited any stables or farms. Finally, on the fourth morning, he had let Harn sleep it off in their boardinghouse room, and Brandon himself had gone in search of a livery stable. Since there seemed to be one on about every other block of Garnet, his search hadn't taken long. He had purchased a pair of serviceable, if not spectacular mounts, and tipped the stable boy enough that the lad cheerfully showed him how to saddle and bridle the horses, how to stay balanced on said saddle, plus a few tips on food and water requirements for the mounts. The transaction cost him ten of the eighty coins his father had sent with him, but he deemed the investment worth it. By the time Harn had woken up, groggy and hungover, Brandon was waiting outside their lodgings with the horses raring to go and all their possessions packed into their saddlebags—except for the Bluestone, which Brandon always kept wrapped and bound in a secret bundle he tucked into the small of his back.

Brandon shrugged and decided not to argue the point. If truth be told, he was hungry and thirsty, and the inn below Caergoth Castle proved to be a convivial place. Brandon was pleased to get a hot meal into his companion before Harn started on his second bottle of dwarf spirits. The young Hylar, by comparison, decided that he would stick with beer, which—much to his surprise—the humans had proved capable of brewing with commendable quality.

As Caergoth was the second human city he had visited, Brandon felt almost like a sophisticate as they wolfed down a hearty meal and listened to a pair of minstrels playing their exotic lutes over in a corner. The two dwarves struck up a conversation with a quartet of pikemen, in uniform but unarmed, who were eating and drinking at the next table.

"Do you serve in the army of the king of Solamnia?" asked Brandon. He was buzzing enough with the effects of his beers that he took no offense when the men reacted with laughter.

"We have no king in Solamnia," one scoffed. "Haven't for years."

"Yeah that's right, Bennett," said his companion. "We got something better: an emperor!"

"Guess you ain't heard," the one called Bennett said to the dwarves. "We're an empire again! Why, me and my blokes here, we helped to make it so. Didn't, we boys?"

"Aye," said another. "We fought the horde of Ankhar the half-giant when Jaymes Markham was our lord marshal, and we fought him again after he was made emperor! If Ankhar wasn't dead, I'd be ready to go to war with him and fight with the emperor a third time tomorrow."

"Aye, and me too," pledged the fourth pikeman, who looked morosely into his empty glass. "There's not been a merry war for nigh on a year now!"

"Here, let me buy you lads a round," said Harn Poleaxe, waving a barmaid over and securing a pitcher of beer for each table. Brandon was quietly glad his companion was eschewing the stronger dwarf spirits, at least for the time being. "Tell us about this war."

Brandon knew a little something about the campaigns of the Solamnics against the barbarian horde of the half-giant, Ankhar. Regar Smashfingers had sent several companies of dwarves to the emperor's aid, and his forgers made quite a profit, so it was said, selling strong spring steel to the humans so they could build some newfangled kind of weapon, a bombard it was called, that had proved a decisive factor in the wars. Of course, that highly profitable activity had been limited to the king's inner circle; the Bluestones hadn't been involved. Still, since many of the goblins and ogres of Ankhar's army had been drawn from the valleys of the Garnet Range and had perished in the war, the outcome of the conflict had had a beneficial effect on the dwarven kingdom.

"So how big is this empire?" Brandon wondered, thinking about how much ground he and Poleaxe had covered since they left home. It was a big world, he was beginning to realize, but it was startling to think they had been traveling in one nation that whole time.

"Why, Garnet and Caergoth are just the far south," Bennett explained. "We got Solanthus and Vingaard and Thelgaard. The empire goes all the way to Palanthas, way in the north. That's where the emperor has his palace."

"Say, you fellows wouldn't be interested in a little wagering, would you?" Harn said casually, pulling out the small bag holding his knucklebones. He rolled the shaped ivories onto the table, smiling as each settled with three points turned up. "I have a few steel coins been burning a hole in my money pouch."

Before Brandon knew what was happening, the two tables had been pushed together and each of the four men and two dwarves had a small pile of coins stacked before him. Ever mindful of his family's luck, the young mountain dwarf decided to limit his gambling to twenty steel pieces. They took turns rolling the bones, making bets, passing their steel pieces back and forth, and drinking from the never-ending stream of pitchers that Harn Poleaxe kept ordering.

Brandon was having a great time, even though he was down to his last two coins after a couple of hours. He noticed, vaguely, that the four soldiers were also short on coins, while Harn Poleaxe had somehow amassed a rather impressive pile of the valuable steel pieces. Perhaps Brandon was aware that the emperor's men were not having as much fun as he was, but he was still surprised when the fight erupted.

For some reason, Bennett broke his mug over Harn's head, an act that did little more than get the big Neidar to freeze, raise his eyebrows irritably, and rise to his feet with a grin and a roar—somehow sliding his coin stack into his purse at the same time. Poleaxe swung a wild punch at the pikeman. The blow failed to connect with its intended target while knocking out the soldier sitting directly to Bennett's left.

Another of the men lunged at Brandon, who defended himself instinctively, first breaking the fellow's hold around his neck then clocking him with a punch that smashed his nose into a flat purple bruise. Harn, meanwhile, grasped the necks of both Bennett and the fourth man and pulled, crunching the two heads together and letting the men flop, unconscious, onto the table.

Somehow, however, the two dwarves had failed to notice that the bar was heavily crowded with other humans who were all wearing the same blue tunics as their gambling companions. Those soldiers wasted no time in joining in, lunging after the dwarves, and for a lively ten minutes, the two traveling companions stood back to back, enjoyably defending themselves against thrown chairs and bottles, punches and kicks.

Then a bugle suddenly sounded, and the whole bar cleared out, seemingly in the space of an instant, leaving only the two dwarves and about a dozen pikemen who were unconscious, injured, or simply too stunned to scramble away. The front door—none of the fleeing soldiers had departed that way—burst open, and three tall knights came striding in. Their heavy armor was decorated with the image of a white crown on their chests. The largest marched forward, looming over the dwarves, and glared down at them with his hands on his chest. Brandon, no stranger to facial hair, couldn't help but be impressed by the fellow's long, feathered mustaches.

"What in the name of all the gods is going on here?" he demanded.

"Who wants to know?" shot back Harn Poleaxe, trying to step forward and being quickly restrained by Brandon's strong arm.

"We were fairly defending ourselves, your lordship," the Hylar said politely.

The knight looked in contempt at the scattered soldiers, some of whom, groaning, were trying to sit up or push themselves to their feet. "Against this rabble?" he asked.

"We were led to believe they were honorable soldiers," Brandon explained. "But they didn't take kindly to my companion's success at knucklebones."

"What kind of success?" the knight demanded, looming closer.

"None of your—oof!" Harn's retort was interrupted by Brandon's elbow to his guts.

"Show him," the mountain dwarf encouraged in a conversational tone.

Grudgingly, the Neidar pulled out his money purse and displayed the steel coins. The knight reached in and helped himself to a handful, eyeing Poleaxe sternly, while Brandon kept a tight grip on his companion's arm—partly to hold him back and partly to hold him up, for the Neidar was starting to sway alarmingly.

"How long are you planning to stay in town?" the knight asked when he had taken his share, glaring at them.

"Do I need to clear space in my dungeon for you?"

"We're leaving first thing in the morning," Brandon said at once.

"Yeah. First thing," Harn agreed sullenly.

"Very well," the knight replied, smiling tightly. "We can escort you to a nice room by the waterfront. You don't want to be late for the morning tide."

# ELEVEN

# WORKING WITHOUT A ROOF

The High Kharolis is the loftiest, most extensive mountain range upon the continent of Ansalon. The summits are grand and numerous, and while they are not so craggy as some of the Khalkist Mountains and they are not fiery volcanoes like the Lords of Doom, their majesty is apparent to anyone within fifty miles of the foothills of the range. They cap the great subterranean city of Thorbardin and have long been a fastness of the dwarf race. The mountain dwarves preferred to live under the mountains themselves, while the hill dwarves populated the outer valleys, their towns and villages too numerous to count, spreading out over nearly all of the habitable space below the range's timberline.

Late at night those communities mostly slumbered. Here and there sounds of raucous celebration—punches landing on noses, curses exchanged, crockery smashed over heads, kicks bouncing off kneecaps—indicated not all the hill dwarves had turned in for the night. Mostly those revelries were confined to the village inns and taverns, though in a few cases the sounds arose from private homes, part of the sweet togetherness that was the typical dwarf marriage. In most of the houses, a fire ebbed on the hearth or a candle glimmered in a window, giving a pastoral illumination to the simple villages in the Kharolis valleys.

Of course, in the great undermountain realm, there was no night, no day. Forges smoked and smiths banged away throughout the great city of Norbardin. Farmers worked the great food warrens, some using the mighty Urkhan worms to pull their implements through the moist loam, others harvesting fungus in a hundred varieties or fish from their breeding ponds for hauling the next morning to the city's famed market. But those activities occurred out of sight of the world and, for most, out of awareness.

The highest summit of the Kharolis was the mountain known as Cloudseeker. Eternally shrouded in snow and glacier, it was a massive peak made even more monumental by the fact it was not completely surrounded by cliffs. Instead, it rose from the bedrock with broad shoulders, long, sinuous ridges connecting to the lower summits, and slopes leading down to the valleys with their forests and lakes. It was one of the loftiest mountains in the world, but because of those long, gradual slopes, it was not impossible to climb. Still, the thin air, cold temperatures, and constant winds made the climb inhospitable.

Right then the summit was occupied by a very solitary, very frightened, and very confused gully dwarf.

Gus huddled on the ground, clutching his knees to his chest, shivering and getting colder by the second. He tried to worm his way deeper into the soft surface, but that didn't seem to be warming him up. His rump and legs were not only cold, he realized, but wet! With a yelp, he bounced to his feet and took a closer look at the surface under his feet.

"What kind of bluphsplunging rock *are* you?" he demanded of that surface.

It was not stone, he realized (almost) at once. It was

soft and, yes, wet and oddly pale in color, like a cave carp's belly. He had seen white stone before, but that was just like the black or gray or any other color of stone—hard and bruising. The white stuff under his feet was slushy, more like extremely cold mud, which he sank in up to his knees. He could kick through it, though when it clumped in through the holes in his boots, it made his feet very cold. When he picked some up, it packed into a solid sphere in his hand, cold and wet.

Maybe it was some kind of food, he thought, as his belly rumbled. He tasted it and was surprised when it seemed to turn to water in his mouth.

All in all, the stuff was not very promising. Still, it was more comforting to look down than to look up. When he did turn his face toward the top of the world, he saw those countless specks of light and nothing else. It was as if a multitude of candles burned in the loftiest reaches of that place, but even their light was not enough for him to make out whatever kind of ceiling it was that vaulted over his head. How the many candles could simply float in the air and not light up the roof was a riddle beyond his comprehension.

When he looked to the sides, he saw massive piles of rock, many of them covered with the same whiteness that was currently numbing his feet and legs. They were countless, those monstrous mounds, and seemed to stretch into a distance that was so vast he couldn't even begin to comprehend it. He could count well for an Aghar—all the way up to two—and as regarding distance, he knew two miles was a vast length of space. However, his best guess was that the neighboring pile of rock was at least two miles away, and there were many other such obelisks beyond that, by extension another two miles away.

The one he was standing on, he reckoned, was the biggest one of them all. His mind whirled. Where was he? And how could the place be so large that he couldn't even make out the ceiling over his head?

Another bout of shivering wracked him, and despite his many questions, Gus was forced to accept one unpleasant truth: if he stayed there, he would die. But where should he go? In every direction, the ground sloped downward, so it didn't seem to make much difference except that, when he started walking, he noticed the ground in front of him seemed to drop away steeper and steeper until, with frightening abruptness, it just seemed to vanish.

He stood at the lip of a precipice. Far below he could see the faint outlines of lakes, and those, at last, were features that looked familiar to him. In his experience, lakes were a promising source of food, so he decided to go down there. But he couldn't take a straight path unless he wanted to fall all the way to his destination. So he started along the edge of the cliff, slipping and shivering in the cold, white slush, looking for some way down. He walked for a long two minutes until he saw a ridge descending from this auspicious height. That, at least, seemed to promise a possible route, so he made his way onto that ramp and, still slipping occasionally, started to climb down off the massive pile of rock.

He had not gone very far when some sixth sense prickled the hairs on his neck. Gulping, he turned around, looking back toward the summit he had just vacated. A shadow stretched black across the whiteness, hampering his view. He shrank down and tried to make himself invisible as he stared, eyes agog, at that shadow that had such an air of menace.

It was not merely a shadow, but some sort of creature: something terrible that was lurking there. He made out the shape of a being with large black wings and a gaunt, nearly skeletal body. It turned its face this way and that, and when that visage swiveled in the gully dwarf's direction, Gus froze, caught by a pair of fiery, crimson eyes.

Immediately those eyes seemed to bore into him, and the mighty wings pulsed, giving flight to the ghastly shape.

Shrieking, Gus turned and ran, quickly falling on his face as his feet got caught in the slushy white stuff. Clawing his way upright again, he cast a glance over his shoulder and saw that the flying beast had already covered half the distance to him and, as he feared, the gully dwarf was clearly its quarry.

Gus trudged and tromped and struggled through the clinging whiteness, which seemed to be much deeper on the steep-sided ridge than it had been near the top of the rock pile. He didn't squander another look behind him, but he could *feel* the creature coming closer, and when that feeling became terrifyingly imminent, he darted to the side, plunging face-first into the icy material and burrowing into the chill wetness.

He felt a terrible pain in his shoulder as one talon dragged across his body, tearing through his ragged shirt. But his face-down plunge had saved him, at least for the moment, as the flying monster couldn't quite get a grip on him and, thus, swept past, spreading those wings again as it came around to make a long, banking turn. Those red eyes sought, and found, the hapless gully dwarf, and the flying creature dived close again.

On his knees, Gus quaked and trembled. He was too exhausted to rise to his feet, to try to flee farther. There was something hypnotic in that evil gaze; a compulsion seemed to root him to the spot. Wide-eyed, blubbering in terror, he could feel the creature's awful presence as it swept closer. When it was almost upon him, he threw himself facedown again onto the chilly whiteness, burrowing like a grub into the soft material.

Once again, his last-minute plunge caused the monster to miss its grab. Gus scrambled to his feet, feeling his doom descending. He tried to run in two directions at once, but that only caused him to stumble again. In its rage, the monster opened a beaklike maw and uttered a harsh, penetrating screech as it dived once more.

But when that sound struck the white-crested ridge, all of that whiteness—and the gully dwarf clawing his way into it—suddenly broke free and began to crumble. Gus was immediately swallowed in the churning, frosty mix that was not rock and not mud. There were infinite grains of it, like powder, flooding against his skin, and the sensation of falling was muted by the fact he was trapped within a great, thundering avalanche; he was falling as part of a big slide, not like a pebble bouncing down an otherwise solid slope.

Down became up, and up became down. He inhaled and coughed out bits of whiteness. Those bits he didn't cough out became water in his mouth. He was thirsty, Gus realized as he tumbled through a succession of somersaults, and the water felt cold and refreshing. Still, it was hard to drink while falling. Come to think of it, it was hard to do much while falling—except fall.

He flailed with his hands and feet but couldn't make contact with anything solid. Once, he bounced to the very top of the avalanche and saw that the whole mountainside seemed to be sliding toward the valley. The Aghar whirled crazily atop it for a moment, thinking, Whee! This is not so bad. He spied the black flyer in the sky, hunting for him. It was far away, for the moment.

Then the whiteness swallowed him again, and he could see nothing. The sense of movement rumbled and grew into an implacable force, gaining momentum, carrying the little Aghar along in its irresistible sweep. Once Gus smacked into something that felt like a *real* rock, not the soft, white, wet kind, and that blow stunned him. Still he kept falling.

Gradually, the momentum of the avalanche faded away. He was sliding a little; then he was still. He tried to move his arms and legs, but they were immobile, trapped by the white stuff packed tightly all around him. Gus's head throbbed, but he couldn't see the flying monster—he couldn't see anything, truth be told—and that, at least, was a relief.

In fact, his recent adventures had drained him more than he had realized. It felt strangely safe there in his icy prison, and he was very, very tired.

It seemed only natural to simply go to sleep.

——DH——

Gus could *feel* the talons reaching, scratching for him. It was that terrible sensation that woke him up, at which time he quickly realized he was still imprisoned in the icy pack of white stuff. He felt numb from the cold and utterly helpless. He heard terrible clawing, relentlessly scraping away at the surface above his face, the sounds of the talons coming closer, increasingly closer. He struggled, gasped, groaned, and kicked, but he might as well have been encased in stone for all the movement he could manage.

Still the noise came closer. He saw a burning brightness—he was lying on his back—and he presumed he was experiencing the fiery fury of the winged monster's eyes. Even so, those eyes seemed impossibly brilliant, as if the creature's eyes were a mighty bonfire, the kind of pyre that could light up the whole of the Urkhan Sea.

Then one talon penetrated all the way through the white slush, scraping painfully across Gus's face, and the light swelled to a truly excruciating brightness. It was as though a huge fire had surged right in front of the Aghar's eyes, and he was virtually blinded. In that, Gus actually found some comfort since he was utterly helpless to escape, at least his blindness would spare him the horror of watching the monster devour him. Again, those talons clawed across his face, and he shuddered at the thought that his flesh was being ripped away, perhaps his eyes torn out, his bulbous nose severed.

Yet those claws did not seem so sharp as before—nor did the monster seem intent on savagely rending his flesh. No, it seemed more like it was merely tormenting him.

The blindness began to ease slightly as his eyes adjusted to the brightness. He could make out a few details—most prominent, a set of white, curving fangs, drooling eagerly between widespread jaws. Again those talons raked at him, but he realized they were clawing at the icy stuff imprisoning Gus, not at the Aghar himself. Probably, he thought, the monster wanted to have a snack of white stuff before getting down to the main meal.

The mouth above him gaped wide, and Gus tried to recoil, deciding that the creature had unleashed some form of foul breath weapon. He held his breath as long as he could; then he had no choice but to inhale the stench of its fetid exhalation, and he almost snorted in derision. As a gully dwarf, he had smelled many vile odors; it would take more than the creature's stale breath to choke and kill him.

But his elation was short lived. The jaws spread wide again, fangs yawning to either side of his face as that horrible maw, still panting its tainted breath, lowered to his face.

Yet what he felt wasn't sharp teeth, but a long, coarse, and surprisingly warm tongue. He felt the tongue slurp across his face, clearing away the icy bits that coated his skin, bringing a sweet tingling back to the flesh that had been all but frozen. Gus coughed and sputtered and tried to move, and the creature set to work digging again, raking those powerful paws around the Aghar's arms. When one arm finally jerked free, Gus reached up to ward off the horrible attacker, but instead of a skeletal, chill minion of darkness, his hand came into contact with a shaggy coat of hair.

Gradually, Gus understood that, despite the talons and fangs and fetid breath, it was not the creature that had chased him on the mountaintop. Nor was it the source of that blinding brightness, the intense light that had all but robbed him of vision. Blinking, the gully dwarf saw that the fiery brilliance came from much farther away, from a yellow spot somewhere high above on the lofty ceiling of that place. Somehow, that ceiling, which previously had been a black expanse speckled with tiny lights, had turned a pale blue in color. One single, incredibly brilliant, orange-yellow light shined down upon him.

"Kondike? What did you find there?"

Gus heard the words, spoken in a female voice that didn't sound terribly menacing, and he wondered how the monster had learned to speak such expert Dwarvish. Only when the fanged head, with its drooping jowls and incredible tongue, lifted away and the creature uttered a deep, guttural "woof," did he realize that the speaker was not the shaggy beast, but some other individual off in the near distance that he couldn't see.

Realizing that even melodious and gentle female dwarves had been known to pound the stuffing out of hapless Aghar, he struggled to rise and flee. Turning his head, Gus saw the female dwarf, approaching through the snow, carrying a stout staff in one hand, marching straight toward him with a curious expression on her face.

She looked like a dwarf, but Gus knew he was—he *must* be—in the presence of a goddess.

Her hair was as bright yellow as spun gold and cascaded around a full-cheeked, wide-mouthed face. She wore a fur cape, open in the front to reveal a blue tunic flowing over a pair of perfect, swelling breasts. Her leggings were blue as well, tight-fitting like the tunic, and her boots were white fur and came as high as her knees. When she looked down at Gus, he saw that her eyes were as blue as the ceiling of that place, and when she smiled her lovely smile, he knew that he was in the presence of immortal grace.

"Well, what happened to you, little fellow?" she asked cheerily. She raised her face, looking up the mountain-side toward the lofty ridge, and she whistled as her eyes followed the path of the thunderous avalanche. "Looks like, whatever your problems, Reorx was looking out for you. And Kondike, of course."

"G—G—Gus!" he croaked worshipfully. "I'm Gus!"

"What a nice name," she said sweetly. "I am called Gretchan Pax, and I am very pleased to make your acquaintance. Now let's see about getting you out of there. Then perhaps you'd like a bowl of hot soup?"

She knelt down beside him and, with the monster Kondike energetically assisting, quickly freed him from the white stuff. Gus, however, did not even realize when he was free.

In fact, he had completely swooned away.

——DH——

The soup was the most exquisite food Gus had ever tasted, up to and including cave grubs. There were bits of red things and green things and white things in it, and the liquid itself was a pleasant brown color, aromatic and comforting. Gretchan had led Gus to the edge of the white ground—she called it "snow"—and effortlessly kindled a fire from some sticks and twigs she scooped up right off the ground. Now the Aghar's teeth had finally stopped chattering, and he slurped down a second bowl as soon as he finished the first.

"Good!" he declared, licking out the metal dish. "What kind food?"

The brightness was still painfully intense, but his eyes had become accustomed to the constant glare enough that his headache was waning. She had explained to him that the blue ceiling was called the "sky," and the fiery orb was the "sun." Gretchan leaned back, puffing on a small pipe she had loaded with some kind of dried plant. The smoke that emerged from her nose was pleasantly aromatic, though when Gus leaned in to take a big sniff, he had been unable to suppress a wet sneeze that spattered her pretty thoroughly. With a grimace of distaste, she blotted off her face and bodice.

"Stay away from my pipe . . . and my face," she chided him. "This stuff isn't good for you."

She was a genius besides a beauty, Gus thought. When she frowned, he wanted to do whatever he could to obey her, to cheer her up. And when she laughed, that jolly sound made his heart pound with delight. "I take it you've never been on the surface before," she said. "Those are vegetables—carrots, peppers, onions. They're fairly common up here. Did you come from under the mountain?"

"No!" Gus declared. "I come from Thorbardin!"

With his words, he was assaulted by memories of that sunless place: the terrifying wizard and his cave, the drain-plunge where Slooshy had lost her life, the Theiwar bunty hunters who cut off gully dwarf heads, his prisoner cage, all that. He sniffled miserably. "Not go back, though. Not ever!"

"Well, I don't think they grow vegetables in Thorbardin." She grew serious for a moment, looking into the distance. "Someday, I'd like to find out for myself," she admitted.

"Thorbardin? I can tell you all about Thorbardin!" Gus boasted, eager to impress his rescuer. "It's big!"

She laughed again. "So I've heard," Gretchan replied. "And how does a little fellow like you get *out* of Thorbardin? Surely you know that the gates have long been sealed?"

"Get out?" Gus hadn't really processed that idea yet. He shrugged, trying to think; then he remembered. "I took drink from bad wizard's bottle. Strong drink, fizz my throat. Then I was out!"

Thinking more, he reached into his pocket, and pulled out Willim's bottle of elixir, the bottle from the Midwarren Pale spirits distillery. "Bottle kind of like this. But drink different."

Gretchan looked rather alarmed. She reached for the

bottle, and Gus let her take it in her hands, noticing that she shivered as she touched it. Holding it up to the light, she studied the bottle, shook it so the potion swirled around inside, and set it down while she cradled her perfect chin in her graceful, surprisingly long-fingered hands.

"Good thing, if you ask me, that you didn't drink from that bottle," she said softly. Turning those blue eyes to the gully dwarf, she asked, "Would you mind if I carried it for you?"

Gus would have given her his right arm, or any portion of his body, if she had asked him, and he didn't want any dwarf spirits anyway. So he nodded his assent. She wrapped the bottle very carefully in some sort of cloth and gingerly set it into her backpack.

"Hmm. It is a mystery how you got here," she said. "A mystery worth pondering. But now what am I going to do with you?" she added pensively. "I can't very well send you home—of course, if I knew how to enter Thorbardin, I'd take you there myself!"

The thought of going home to Agharbardin suddenly seemed like a bleak and hopeless prospect to the forlorn gully dwarf. "Maybe I stay with you? Here in snow place?" he asked eagerly. "Gus big help! Finds lotsa food! Fight bad dwarves!"

She smiled gently, and his heart melted. "Well, I guess you can come along for now. I have some work to do, but I don't think you'll get in the way. And sooner or later we'll meet some other gully dwarves. There are plenty of them out here in the real world too, you know. I bet you'll be quite a hero to them, with all you've gone through."

"Yes! Me hero gully dwarf. Spit in eye of him say not!" Gus crowed.

Delightedly, he hopped to his feet as Gretchan turned to go, striding beside the female dwarf and Kondike, who was not a monster but a "dog," he had learned.

Kondike was a very big dog: his head was higher off the

ground than Gus's, and even underneath the heavy coat of shaggy black hair, there was a body of powerful sinew and long, graceful legs. Gus was grateful that Kondike seemed to consider him a friend.

Only once, as they crested a snowy ridge and started into the next valley, did Gus have a shuddering memory of the horrible minion that had stalked him the night before. He wondered where it had gone and whether it would be coming back to chase him.

But he decided it was better not to say anything about the ghastly fiend to his new friend. After all, he didn't want to worry her.

# TWELVE

# INTO THE KHAROLIS

Brandon staggered off the single-masted sailboat, down the rickety wooden pier, and onto the hard-packed dirt of the anonymous little fishing village. There, he dropped to his hands and knees, where he gazed lovingly at the solid, unmoving ground.

"Never again," he groaned as Harn Poleaxe sauntered merrily after him.

"What?" asked the hill dwarf innocently. "It was just a little fresh breeze and some sprinkles—nothing like when I sailed north. Then we went through some real storms!"

"We had water pouring over the deck! Half the sails tore away! If that wasn't a storm, I'll eat my axe!"

"At least it's all overland from here—down the coast of the Newsea and into the hills of home." Chuckling, Harn helped Brandon to his feet, and they looked around the village.

The place was a far cry from the bustling port of Caergoth. In that Solamnic city, ships with masts and galleys with oars had steadily made their way in and out of the broad, deep channel. A long curve of waterfront had included docks, warehouses, markets, and an extensive shipyard, where three new hulls were busily being constructed.

In contrast, the seashore village was a cluster of huts with one long rickety building that seemed to be a smoke-house for fish. A couple of small fishing dhows were pulled up on shore, and another, larger boat rested at anchor in the small bay.

"Doesn't look like there's an inn worthy of the name," the hill dwarf said in disgust.

"But there is a stable," Brandon noted happily. After all that time rolling and rocking on the waves, the prospect of a long stretch in a saddle didn't seem so bad.

Two hours later they were on the road. Brandon's head was clear, and his lungs relished the taste of dry air, free of the taint of salt. Bouncing on his horse, he felt almost comfortable. He even allowed himself to hope that, there on the dry land of the south, away from Kayolin, his luck might be about to improve.

Though he was acutely conscious of the treasure he bore, still wrapped in the pouch he wore at the small of his back. The Bluestone Wedge was heavier than just a stone. To Brandon, it was the weight of the legacy of his father and his grandfather and the whole of his family's house.

——DH——

After an hour of contemplation and analysis, Willim decided he would not move his laboratory, even though the king and his agents knew where it was located. He inspected the seal of the original tunnel, found it to be as air and water tight as ever. Detection spells, with wafts of smoke as his feelers, determined that no holes had been drilled or otherwise established that would allow access to the underground chamber from any other direction. Let the king teleport in more toadies if he would; Willim could defeat an army of dwarves! And if hard pressed, well, he could always resort to a teleportation escape, a magical flight that would be impossible for his enemies to pursue.

Only after making his decision did he allow himself

the luxury of cleaning up the debris from the battle and its aftermath. Casting a spell of levitation, Willim rose from the floor until he floated in the air, high above the floor of his laboratory. From there, he could see better what needed to be done. Wielding his magic as if it were a team of laborers, he slid a heavy bench across the room and righted several shelves and bins that had been upset during the melee. He repaired boxes and barrels that were damaged, plucked stray arrows from his wooden table and benches. Finally, he repaired his granite table, using the gesture of a finger to weld a seam through the crack his tantrum had wrought in the hard, smooth stone.

Then he drifted around the great vault of the chamber, mindful of security. He set spells of alarm to create noise and light if any intruders appeared or if any sound of digging or boring was detected through the walls. He installed traps he could activate by a simple command word, devices that would send granite columns and great shards of stone shooting through the chamber if they were triggered. He rigged the entire vast hall with a powerful spell of stone-shattering, ensuring that, if he were forced to retreat from a fresh army of attackers, he could bring the roof down on their heads even as he made his instant escape.

Just he was settling back to the floor, he felt a tingle of alarm and sensed the presence of another. But the newcomer was no threat: his minion dropped through the ceiling, spreading its black wings as it came to rest before him. The gaunt minion, with its Abyss-red eyes, pressed itself obsequiously to the floor, paying homage to its lord.

"Where is it?" hissed the Black Robe. "The flask!"

"The Aghar is destroyed," replied the minion. "But his body was lost, frozen in an avalanche. I searched and searched but could not discover him in the cold vastness before the sunrise drove me underground."

"Fool!" snarled Willim, raising his fist. He twitched

irritably; whatever blow he delivered would make little difference to the soulless being. "I don't care if you spend the entire year up there, you must go back as soon as it is night and look harder and find his body. Most importantly of all, bring me the thing that he carries!"

"As you wish, lord," replied the creature, spreading its wings as it prepared for departure.

"Wait," declared the wizard, holding up his hand. "Let me seek him again—that way, I might be able to confirm that he is dead and where his body may be found."

Once more he went through the spell to locate an object, swirling the liquid in the bowl, watching the position of the enchanted arrow. His eyeless face creased into a frown as the indicator took shape, marking a line that pointed more toward the northeast than before.

"See! He is not dead. He has moved, fool! You have been tricked and eluded by a gully dwarf! Now hunt him down—destroy him!"

"As you wish, lord." His minion took flight, its ghastly shape rising through the cavern, vanishing into the bedrock of the Kharolis Mountains as it pursued its prey.

Willim went back to work, muttering to himself about stupid minions.

He had a long list of things to do. He would need new apprentices, more components for spells and potions, new test subjects to lock in his empty cages. The Aghar didn't matter at the moment, for he had an army to raise and a king to destroy.

———DH———

Days and weeks on the trail had introduced Brandon to a host of new, and for the most part fascinating, experiences. After the constant nausea of the sea crossing, Brandon welcomed firm land as though it were a long-lost relative, enjoying the glimpses of wildlife, the earthy smells, the ever-changing landscape. They journeyed from village to village down the coastline of Abanasinia, staying on a simple dirt road that meandered along about ten miles from the coast—the terrain along the shore being for the most part marshy and impassable. Each night they stayed at an inn if the village had one, or they paid a copper coin for the right to sleep on the floor of a cottage or in the haystack of a local's barn.

The people who dwelled along the coast were humans for the most part, though occasionally they encountered a hill dwarf working as a carpenter, bartender, or blacksmith among the humans. Apparently the social life of village taverns didn't appeal to Harn quite as much as did the lively establishments in the cities up north. Though they quaffed a few ales when the opportunity afforded, the big hill dwarf avoided drinking marathons and fights and was ready to resume their journey each morning with the dawn.

They trekked down the western shore of the Newsea. Brandon quickly realized that the world was drier down there than it was in the Garnet Mountains or even in the part of Solamnia they had traversed on their way to the port on the Newsea. Harn told him that that was nothing, and he described the Plains of Dust. That, Poleaxe said, was a desert that swept off to the south for hundreds of miles. Brandon was amazed to think of such a vast expanse, barely moistened by rain, crossed only by a very few streams and one river.

He found himself fascinated by the variety of birds, especially the great raptors, the eagles and the vultures, that drifted on currents so high overhead, covering great distances without any appearance of effort. Only carrion birds were common in the Garnet Range; others were rare and precious. Antelopes and great wild buffalo, long of leg and fearsome of countenance, commonly regarded them from the forest thickets beside the road.

They camped for one night at the great ruins of Xak

Tsaroth, where Brandon was barely able to sleep. Instead, he stayed up nearly until dawn, admiring the sketchy outlines of ancient walls, imagining the towers and battlements that once must have dominated that place. It startled him to think about how those ancient glories had been eroded by the effects of wind and rain and other natural forces—effects that were virtually unknown underground, where an abandoned battlement might look pretty much the same after a thousand years of neglect as it did when the last dwarf marched away from it.

Following the coastline past the beginning of the Kharolis Mountains, they turned inland as they neared the southern end of the Newsea. There they entered more rugged country and slowly began to climb. Brand's heart gladdened to the faint suggestion of lofty mountains rising before them, and he swelled with dwarf pride when Poleaxe confirmed that, yes, they were in fact the summits of the High Kharolis.

"Ah, smell that air—the breath of home," Poleaxe declared finally after some five weeks of steady travel. "The first hills, at least. It will take us a few more days to get to Hillhome, to be precise—finest town in all the Neidar lands in my opinion."

"Are we that near, then?" Brandon asked, swinging easily along in the saddle that had seemingly become comfortably attached to his anatomy.

"Less than a week, anyway," the hill dwarf informed him.

The next village they encountered, as the landscape rose around them, was Flatrock, and it was the first community where the population was primarily hill dwarves—though a scattering of human families lived there as well. Harn had friends—many friends—in Flatrock, and they welcomed their long-lost comrade with a long night of celebration. Brandon seemed as popular as Harn and enjoyed the festivities immensely, though he was puzzled that the Neidar had introduced him as a clan cousin.

"Ah, but you don't understand," Harn said the next day when the two were back on the road after a late start. "Hill dwarves and mountain dwarves: where you come from, they may not be the best of friends, but they're rivals, not enemies. Down here, around Thorbardin, you have to remember there's a blood feud that has lasted more than four hundred years, since those treacherous mountain dwellers locked my ancestors out during the Cataclysm."

"Well, but like you said," Brandon pointed out, "that was four centuries ago. There aren't any dwarves around who were even *alive* back then!"

"No, but there are plenty who heard the tales from their folks and grandfolks—those who actually did remember. And it's a scar that runs deep—hasn't even begun to scab over yet."

"But you live right next to each other!"

Harn shrugged, eyes narrowing as he regarded Brandon thoughtfully. "Thorbardin might as well not be there, as far as we Neidar are concerned. The gates are sealed and have been for these past ten years. The only mountain dwarves we concern ourselves with are the refugees in Pax Tharkas."

"What about them?" Brandon wondered, surprised at the news of a settlement of mountain dwarves living in exile aboveground.

"Well, they got huffy and left after some kind of civil war. They're a bad lot—their thane is a Hylar, Tarn Bellowgranite, and he used to be king of the whole place. When they kicked him out, he brought some real ruffians. He's got a company of Klar who like nothing more than raiding Neidar towns."

"But if it's just a small band of exiles, how can they stand against all the Neidar?"

"You don't know Pax Tharkas," Harn said in disgust.

"Thane Bellowgranite has maybe a thousand dwarves in there, but half that many could hold it against twenty thousand attackers. It's a stronghold and they're crazy fighters."

"So that's why you told your friends I was your cousin?" Brandon concluded, feeling a new trepidation about his sojourn to the south.

"Yeah. And come to think of it, maybe we should stick to the back roads for a while until we draw closer to Hillhome."

For the next three days, the two dwarves followed rugged paths, avoiding the many small villages, making discrete camps near streams or in glades in secluded valleys. When they stopped to make camp on the fourth night, however, Poleaxe announced that they were, at last, on his home territory.

As if to prove his point, that night the Neidar dwarf built a large campfire, clearly abandoning the caution that had limited them to small, well-contained cookfires over the long march. With an air of sly celebration, he produced a flask from his saddlebags, and when he shared it with Brandon, the Kayolin exile was pleasantly surprised to discover that it contained top-shelf dwarf spirits, the bitter but potent brew that was barely tolerable to humans, elves, or kender but represented the nectar of Reorx himself to a thirsty dwarf. Poleaxe must have been saving it for that occasion. The brew was better than any they had had on the road.

"Now that hits the spot," Brandon remarked after drinking deep, leaning back against the saddlebag that served as his pillow. The fire was warm against his face, comforting in those southern climes where the air was undeniably chillier than in the more equatorial north. The liquor was even warmer in his belly, and he felt a languorous pleasure as the effects seeped through his bloodstream into every part of his body.

"I thought you'd like it," Poleaxe said. "Help yourself to more, and then pass the bottle back."

Brandon followed his companion's advice, looking up to watch the stars come into view against the slowly darkening sky. "How long has it been since you've been home?" he asked.

"More than two years, now," Poleaxe said wistfully. "That's how long it took to settle my affairs in Kayolin."

"All that time to buy a stone?" Brandon mused.

"Ah, but it had to be the *right* stone. That's why I was so pleased your father finally decided as he did."

Poleaxe handed the bottle back and Brand, obligingly, took another slug. He reminded himself to be careful, however—it wouldn't do to drink too much and wake up the next morning groggy, having to cling to a saddle and ride through the rugged hills.

"What is it about the Bluestone that makes it so valuable to you?" Brandon asked finally, a question that had been hovering in his mind during the whole journey.

"Ah, there's a reason, and you'll find out soon enough. But it's too long a tale to be telling now," the hill dwarf said breezily. He gestured to the bottle again. "Help yourself," he said encouragingly.

"No, thanks. I think I've had enough for now."

"Suit yourself." Harn held the bottle himself for a long time, and by the time he offered it again, Brandon didn't need his arm twisted; the dwarf spirits had thoroughly warmed his belly and soothed away every worry, every concern that might ever have bothered him. His distant home, the loss of his older brother, his parent's grief and fear . . . all of those melted away in the soothing pleasure of the moment and the strong drink.

He didn't think he'd taken that many sips from the bottle, but he was surprised by how his head was starting to spin. Like most dwarves, he had a strong tolerance for the strongest dwarf spirits, and he felt a little embarrassed when he realized that his tongue was growing thick, his speech slowing and slurring.

"Had 'nuf," he said, passing the flask to his companion, but Poleaxe simply passed it back. It never seemed to grow any emptier, though as the stars began to spin over his head, Brandon was well aware that he had had an awful lot to drink.

"Gonna be a tough day 'morrow," he muttered finally, his head drooping near to his chest. He knew from experience that his head would hurt and his stomach churn in the morning and probably, considering how much he'd imbibed, well into the afternoon and evening.

"No more," he blurted when Poleaxe tried to pass him the flask again.

"Are you sure?" asked the hill dwarf, standing over him. How was it possible that the fellow didn't seem the least bit drunk? They had been sharing the potent liquor for hours!

"Sure," Brandon declared with some difficulty. "No more."

Then something struck him, very hard, on the side of his head. He was more mystified than angry as he fell over in slow motion, lying on the ground, gaping up at the sky. The stars were no longer pinpoints of lights, but instead had become a mere whirling blur. Against that blurry backdrop loomed a familiar figure: Harn Poleaxe.

"Hey!" Brandon mumbled. "Wha . . . ?" The question trailed away as he couldn't articulate the rest of the word.

Then it didn't matter because Poleaxe hit him again, and everything went black.

# Thirteen

# Visitor in the Night

Gus experienced a myriad of wonders on that, the most splendid day of his life. With the beautiful dwarf maid beside him and the dog Kondike bounding ahead, he strode through a deep valley of the Kharolis. Lofty peaks, mostly covered with snow but occasionally revealing crags of sheer, towering rock, pushed up on either side. On the lower ground in the valley floor, they were able to walk between the snowfields on ground that varied from hard and rocky to marshy mud that squished entertainingly around his boots—and his toes where they poked through the worn material of his ancient footwear.

He stared in amazement as they skirted a deep lake, the water as blue as the turquoise gems that ornamented so many Daergar nobles. Fish darted through those waters, moving with a speed and grace that was very different from the blind cavefish that meandered through the Urkhan Sea. In places the blue sky turned white, marked by what Gretchan called "clouds," and Gus gaped at the myriad of shapes assumed by those cottony blobs.

"Clouds good to eat?" the gully dwarf wondered as his belly rumbled.

"Well, I don't think anyone's tried," Gretchan replied.

"I try!" he boasted. "I eat *two* clouds!"

"Good luck," she said with a laugh. "Are you going to climb back to the top of the mountain? Or can you fly?"

Gus pondered the problem. He looked back to see some of the clouds were, indeed, brushing the summit of Cloudseeker. At the same time, he could see the mountain-top was a very long way away, and the clouds were also a very great distance over their heads.

"Try clouds later," he conceded, privately resolving not to get more than two steps away from his new, best, very smart, and beautiful friend.

His belly rumbled again and he belched, and she showed her appreciation for his company with an interesting grimace on her lovely face before she quickly turned away. It seemed to Gus as though she walked a little faster when she started back down the valley.

As they descended farther, he discovered "bushes" and "trees." The latter were not like anything he had seen in Thorbardin; they were fragrant and impressive, rising far over their heads, waving branches laden with feathered green needles. He saw birds that rose in squawking flocks from the smooth surface of a sheltered pond and beavers that swam through the waters, slapping their tails in a loud smack when Kondike bounded near to them. The dog didn't seem to mind the creatures' eluding him; he delighted in springing through the shallows, throwing curtains of spray that shimmered like diamonds. When his long black coat was thoroughly soaked, he trotted back to his dwarf companions, braced himself, and shook mightily. Gretchan laughed, stepping behind a tree just in time, but Gus was showered with cool water and laughed himself at the dog's obvious delight.

"Get fish here?" the Aghar asked hopefully as his belly helpfully reminded him to think of food. He licked his lips at the prospect.

"No," she said. "I'd like to make a few more miles before we make camp."

"Those vejables there?" he asked about two minutes later as they passed a field dotted with waving blossoms.

"No," Gretchan replied before pausing to think. "Well, maybe they are. You can go look if you want, but I'm going to keep walking. You can catch up."

"No," he said firmly, pulling his finger out of his nose to inspect the impressive results of his digital probe. "Me stick with you!" he declared loyally.

She muttered under her breath what Gus took to be appreciation for his excellent nose-picking; he didn't catch her exact words because he was loudly belching again. That time, when she started to walk, he was certain she had picked up the pace. He had to huff and puff as he trotted along, and unfortunately for Gretchan, he was breathing too heavily to continue entertaining her with his endless thoughts and ideas.

At least the shadows beneath the trees were easier on his eyes, which had been strained by the morning spent between snowfields under the open sky. He stared into the shade and relished the sight of spring flowers. When the sun dipped behind the western mountain ridge, the cool evening air and the muted illumination were wonderful to behold. They came upon a deer in a clearing, and the Aghar gaped, awestruck, until Kondike took off like a shot, moving with amazing speed through the long grass as the antlered herbivore sprinted, even faster, into the woods. It was a long time later that the dog, his tongue hanging low and his flanks heaving, padded back to the two dwarves.

"Did he kill it?" Gus asked, eyeing those long white teeth.

"Only in his dreams," Gretchan assured him, patting the dog affectionately. "He's fast, but a deer is faster."

Soon the dwarf maid announced it was time to bed down for the night. Gus suddenly felt his weariness and greeted the news with relief. He plopped down between two outstretched pine roots, pulled his ratty cloak over his head, and prepared to slumber.

"Not so fast, bub," Gretchan chided him, prodding him with her toe. "You go get some firewood, and I'll make us a fire."

"Who Bub?" he demanded, looking around belligerently. "*I* get you firing wood!"

The process took longer than necessary because Gus wasn't clear on exactly what constituted firewood. His first few expeditions into the wood were ruled out; no rocks, moss, or any of the soggy driftwood that he pulled from the stream with no small effort. Eventually, the patient Gretchan showed him the dry branches to be found low on the big pine trunks, and when he found a deadfall, limbs intact but dry and brittle, she praised his diligence enough that his chest puffed out in sheer pleasure. Soon she had a hot fire going, and Gus eagerly filled her small kettle with water from a nearby stream.

"Gonna make some more vejables?" he asked and was delighted with her affirmative answer.

Kondike, meanwhile, stalked back and forth along the bank of that stream. Gus was amazed to see him plunge his face into the water once or twice before emerging with a wriggling trout in his jaws. Several times the dog repeated that remarkable procedure, feasting on two catches as Gretchan and Gus enjoyed a warm, filling vegetable stew.

After their feast, Gus was truly drowsy. With a belly more comfortably full than it had ever been in his life and the companionship of the most wonderful person he had ever met, he sighed in contentment and leaned back against a tree trunk, gazing through drooping lids at the warm embers of the flameless fire. Gretchan pulled a cloak around herself and, using her pack as a pillow, settled herself on the far side of the glowing coals. She put more of the crushed leaf into the bowl of her pipe and puffed quietly.

Gus enjoyed the aroma but remembered her caution, so he remained on his own side of the fire, drifting off to sleep.

Abruptly, a deep, menacing growl echoed through the camp, and Gus's eyes snapped open, his heart pounding. Kondike stood beside the dwarf maid as she sat up. The dog's fur bristled and he growled again, the sound like the deep rumble of a rockslide.

"What is it?" Gretchan asked, her hand wrapping around the haft of her walking stick.

Two spots of red glowed at them out of the darkness, and immediately Gus knew why the dog had warned them.

"It—it—it—" He tried but he couldn't quite articulate what he intended to say.

The embers of the fire suddenly whooshed into a blaze, crackling high, casting bright light through the wooded campsite and illuminating the horrifying image of the creature that had attacked Gus. Its great wings, batlike and widespread, seemed to reach out toward them like encompassing limbs. Eyes blazing with infernal heat, the monster opened its mouth and uttered a screech that sent a paralyzing tingle of fear down Gus's spine. Those crimson orbs remained fixed upon the gully dwarf as the monster took a long, sinuous step forward.

The little Aghar sat up, rigid with terror, his back pressed against the rough bole of a pine. Knees knocking, hands trembling, he wanted to flee into the darkness, but he couldn't make himself climb to his feet. His mouth opened, closed, and opened again, but somehow he couldn't even muster the control to shriek his fright out loud.

Kondike lunged forward, jaws wide, fangs bared, barking furiously—a snarling sound totally unlike the friendly "woof" Gus had become accustomed to. The creature raised a taloned paw. Unafraid, the dog stood its ground, barring the path into the campsite as the apparition took another step closer.

"Kondike—come!" ordered Gretchan. Still growling,

the dog took a spring backward just as the minion swiped a hand that could have torn the animal's head away. Kondike bristled and snarled, stiff legged, but slowly retreated toward his mistress.

Awestruck, the Aghar saw that the dwarf maid had risen to her feet and was holding her staff before her in both hands, the butt of the thick shaft planted on the ground. Bravely she faced the approaching horror. Kondike stood before her, forelegs widespread, the thick fur on his back bristling, making the big dog look even larger than he was.

"Halt, beast!" cried Gretchan, and the metal image of an anvil atop her staff abruptly glowed with a pure, golden light—like a tiny burst of sunlight penetrating the gloom of the forest night.

Gus gaped, forgetting the monster, the wizard, Thorbardin, everything. He really, really knew he was in the presence of a goddess. How else could she turn night into day?

With a shriek suggesting raw, physical pain, the monster recoiled. One of its wings closed over its face, as if to block its face from that harsh illumination. Arms flailing, talons slashing, the thing backed away. It seemed diminished, no longer towering like the great trees. Roaring and howling, it stepped back, under the fringe of the trees surrounding the campsite. There it crouched and, abruptly, lunged toward the gully dwarf.

Or, at least, it faked a lunge. Gus yelped and fled around the fire pit to cower behind Gretchan, and the monster hesitated, again shielding itself with its wings, as the dwarf maid challenged it. "Go!" she commanded, her voice ringing like a trumpet. "Leave us!"

To Gus's astonishment, Gretchan took a step toward the monster, the anvil glowing brighter than ever. She raised the staff from the ground and brandished it like a spear, thrusting the glowing head toward the creature, forcing the monster away from the fire. It uttered another unworldly wail, and its red eyes blazed more brightly then ever as it stared at Gus with palpable hatred. The gully dwarf's knees collapsed, and he dropped to the ground, pressing his face into the dirt, throwing his arms over the top of his head.

Kondike barked even more frenziedly, his loud woofs echoing through the woods. The big dog bluffed a charge, but firmly held his position close beside his mistress. The monster stepped to the side, and the dog moved to block it, bristling and snapping, nimbly ducking back again when a taloned claw lashed out.

"Go!" Gretchan cried again, striding steadily forward, forcing the monster to scrabble back. She broke into a run, and those great wings spread as the thing leaped into the air, clawing for altitude as she swung the staff viciously at it. When the anvil struck the beast's foot, it shrieked even louder and quickly vanished into the dark, night sky.

Gretchan, her face slick with sweat, gasped for breath as she retreated back to the dying fire. Kondike kept pacing, stiff legged, around the perimeter of the little camp as Gus slowly stemmed his trembling and, with considerable effort, lifted his head from the ground, sat up, and pushed himself to his feet.

He found himself looking up at the dwarf maid's staring face. It was still a beautiful, round-cheeked, and sweet face, but there was a new appraising expression in her eyes and furrows across her forehead. She cast another look upward to make sure the monster had gone then stepped up to the gully dwarf to kneel before him.

The pure blue of her eyes had turned to ice, and there was a sternness in her voice Gus had never heard before as she addressed him.

"Well, little fellow," she said softly. "You're more interesting than first appearances might suggest. What is it that you haven't told me?"

——DH——

True to form, Brandon's skull throbbed painfully when he woke up. It was the worst headache he had ever experienced, and for a few minutes, all he could do was grit his teeth and fight the pain. He was vaguely aware that full daylight had brightened the camp, while a cold breeze chilled his sweaty garments and made him shiver. His tongue was swollen in his mouth, and when the throbbing in his head rose to an almost unendurable level, he rolled onto his side and retched the contents of his stomach onto the ground.

He felt terrible, but even so, he was surprised that the hangover afflicted him so severely that he couldn't even move his arms, which seemed to be awkwardly pinned behind him. Where was he? What in the name of Reorx had he been drinking?

Gradually, a few answers came to him from deep inside his foggy mind. He had been in a campsite, traveling with Harn Poleaxe. They'd been sharing a flask of dwarf spirits . . . but then everything got confusing. What had happened to them?

Only gradually, as he continued to struggle to form his thoughts, did he realize the bitter truth: he was bound! He struggled against the tight cords that restrained his wrists, speared by pain as he forced himself into a sitting position. He looked around for Poleaxe, wondering if his companion, too, had been taken captive by unknown foes. But how? Hadn't Harn told him that, at long last, they were back on his own, friendly territory?

Even when he saw his Neidar companion, sitting across the smoldering remnant of the great bonfire, grinning cheerfully at him, he didn't remember what had happened. Only when he took in the other dwarves, a full dozen of them, armed and armored as if for battle, did he begin to comprehend the betrayal. The newcomers were casually seated around Poleaxe, clearly no threat to him. Two of them sipped mugs of steaming tea, while several more leaned against tree trunks, their booted feet propped casually on rocks near the fire.

The Bluestone luck! He'd been betrayed and captured. Complete understanding dawned when he recognized the hollow belt pouch, the sleeve containing the venerable Bluestone, held casually in Harn Poleaxe's hands.

With an inarticulate cry of rage, Brandon tried to hurl himself across the camp. His futile effort ended in a pathetic thump onto his face when he couldn't free his hands and, at the same time, discovered that his legs were tightly bound together at the calves and ankles.

"Here now, son," Poleaxe said genially. "Take care you don't pull a muscle or plant your face in the fire. Those coals are still plenty hot, you know."

"Filthy thieving bastard!" Brandon spit, wrestling himself around, once again sitting up clumsily. He was trembling with rage, furious at his own impotence.

"Now watch your tongue, or I might just have to hit you again. Harder this time." Poleaxe patted the hammer he wore at his belt, and Brandon understood why his head was throbbing so badly. Poleaxe addressed one of the others, who—the prisoner guessed—were obviously his fellow hill dwarves. "I tell you, these Hylar can't handle strong drink. They should stick to lemon water or iced beer."

His witty remark was greeted by chuckles but aroused Brandon to fresh, and fruitless, struggles against his painful bonds. "You tricked me!" he declared. "That was more than dwarf spirits in that bottle."

Harn Poleaxe laughed and gave a mocking little half bow of thanks, as if he had just been complimented. "I wouldn't have had to if you'd just drunk it like a dwarf. But instead, you sipped it like an elf maid so, yeah, I had to doctor the recipe a little."

"You brought me all this way just to rob me?" Brandon asked, astounded at the treachery and mystified as to his former companion's behavior.

"In a word, yes," Poleaxe said. He was clearly enjoying himself. "But you should know that this is much, much more than a simple robbery. Do you know how hard it was to follow you and your brother through the caves under Garnet Thax? I had to track you all the way! Then, after you fought the troll and found the vein of gold, I knew that your father would never sell the stone—he had no need of my payment, not if you could file your claim."

"No!" Brandon protested in disbelief. "It was *you*? You were there—"

"Ah, comes the dawn," said the Niedar with a wicked chuckle. "I hastened to get word to Lord Heelspur, so that his fellows could meet you and Nailer. Of course, I had to make sure that one of you survived, and that Heelspur got to claim the new vein. All in all, I put in a lot of work to make this happen."

"But—*why*?" demanded the Kayolin dwarf.

"You see, we're going to make a war, and you—or your family's stone, more properly—is going to help us."

"A war? Against who?" demanded the Kayolin dwarf.

For the first time, the Neidar's genial front cracked. "Against your own cousins down here!" he spat. "The mountain dwarves who've been the bane of my people's existence since before the Cataclysm. No longer content to cower behind the gates of Thorbardin, they dare to battle us on the surface." He hefted the beautiful blue wedge. "This is part—one part—of the head of a hammer that will smash the gate of Thorbardin wide open. It will be like pulling off the top of an anthill. Just imagine the mountain dwarves' consternation as the Neidar army pours in. We'll send them on their final march to Reorx!"

Brandon sat back, stunned and focused. So many bad things had happened to him recently, he had thought he was over the worst. But the full scope of the disaster that was striking his family began to dawn on him, and his throat tightened with a mixture of self-pity and despair.

First, Nailer Bluestone had been murdered at the moment of hope and possible redemption. Then he, himself, had been forced into exile, carrying the last hope of the clan represented by the stone that rested in Poleaxe's possession. He saw that Harn had even stolen his axe—the axe Balric Bluestone had carried on the surface when the Cataclysm stuck. The weapon had been strapped into Brandon's pack, but it lay on the ground beside the arrogant Neidar.

All hope was gone, finished.

"What are you going to do with me?" he demanded with as much bluster as he could fake.

"That's an interesting, but a tough, question," Harn replied. He pushed himself to his feet and strode back and forth, glancing at his new companions. Brandon studied them too and didn't like what he saw. They were a lot of ruffians and outlaws, he guessed. One wore an eye patch, while several proudly displayed the scars of battle on their faces or bare arms. An older Neidar spit ostentatiously, his eyes never leaving the prisoner's.

"I know for a fact this one's a spy," Poleaxe declared loudly for everyone's benefit. "He's here to scout our towns and report back on our preparations. Why, at Flatrock, he claimed to be one of my own clan-mates. He's a scoundrel, I tell you."

"You lying bastard!" protested Brandon, flailing uselessly. "You know as well as I do why I came here . . . and why I claimed to be a Neidar in Flatrock!"

"A confession!" Harn crowed triumphantly. "See!"

Poleaxe stopped pacing. He pointed to a pair of the hill dwarves, burly fellows with bristling beards and stout shields. Each wore a short sword at his waist and, as if understanding the treacherous Neidar's command, they drew their weapons at his gesture.

"Kill him," Poleaxe ordered, and the two dwarves raised their blades and stepped forward. Brandon, though he knew it was useless, continued to strain and struggle against his bonds, feeling the leather cords cut into his wrists, the blood flowing down onto his hands.

"Now wait a moment, Poleaxe," declared another dwarf, a grizzled warrior with his own heavy shield and a war axe tucked into his belt. "That's mebbe going a little too far. We can take his treasure; we need it, and I know that as well as you do. But he represents no threat to us now. And perhaps he doesn't deserve death in cold blood."

"Who are you to say that, Fireforge?" growled Poleaxe, clearly irritated at the challenge. "I brought him here. I know the darkness in his soul."

"It's cold-blooded murder!" retorted the one called Fireforge.

"Not murder. Merely execution of a criminal."

"Then what's his crime?" demanded the stubborn advocate.

Poleaxe looked at Brandon with a sneer of contempt. "He's a mountain dwarf spy!" he declared. "I told you, and you yourself heard him admit it. Ain't that crime enough?"

"That's a lie!" shouted Brandon. "You know it is!"

"You think I don't know about your secret mission? The maps you were supposed to make for your mountain dwarf king?"

The captive struggled vainly for a second, his tongue as tied as his arms and legs, fury dropping a red haze across his vision. The two executioners looked at Poleaxe expectantly, though one of them cast an uneasy glance at Fireforge.

Brandon understood that the latter, for whatever reason he was defending him, represented his only chance at survival. "He stole my father's life-fortune with his treachery," he protested desperately. "I come from Kayolin. Why would my governor, who is no king, have interest in provoking an attack on the hill dwarves of Kharolis?"

"Good questions," Fireforge noted. His hand still rested

on his axe, though he had made no move to draw the weapon. "At the very least, they deserve to be settled in trial. You might be the clan chief, Harn, and we all know your reputation and your courage in battle, but I won't stand for a cold-blooded execution, not here and now."

Poleaxe flushed, grinding his teeth behind the tangle of his beard. He took a step toward Fireforge, towering over the other dwarf, as he did every one of the other members of the band.

But there was something in the grim determination of his opponent's steady, and eerily calm, gaze that held his hand. Poleaxe turned and spit in Brandon's direction, the spittle hitting the mountain dwarf's outstretched boot. Finally he shrugged, a gesture of casual, if insincere, acquiescence.

"Have it your way," he said sullenly. He glared at the two dwarves he had ordered to kill Brandon. "Untie his feet and pick him up. But watch him carefully. He's a snake, that one."

Then he turned to the prisoner, and again his face was transformed by that mocking smile. "You've got a lot of walking to do," he declared before turning and mounting his horse.

# FOURTEEN

# THE DWARF WHO ONCE WAS THANE

The Kharolis mountain range sprawled over an immense distance beyond the lofty ground of the High Kharolis, from its center around Cloudseeker. The prominent ridges ran generally north to south, with a slight lean toward the east in the north and the west in the south. Some of the escarpments extended into Abanasinia, reaching almost to the Newsea at the northern end of the range, while others, in the south, formed frowning bluffs overlooking Ice Mountain Bay and the cold waters of the southern ocean. In their whole extent, the mountains of the Kharolis presented a formidable barrier between south central Ansalon and southwest Ansalon.

In between those great ridges existed many different types of terrain. A wide lowland, generally flat but scored with gullies and ravines and steep, rocky ridges, extended for dozens of miles north of Thorbardin. Called the Plains of Dergoth, the lowland was flooded extensively during the depredations of dragon overlords and the forces of chaos. The southern portion of the former desert was called, simply, the "Bog" and was crossable by only a single, narrow track, and even that during only the dry season.

The ancient fortress of Zhaman, ruined during the Dwarfgate War of the post-Cataclysm dark age, dominated the plain, with its high bluff, scarred into the eerie image of a death's-head. The humans, and many dwarves, called the place Skullcap, and most avoided it completely under the not-unbelievable impression that it was dangerously haunted.

North of Skullcap and the plain, another great tangle of mountains arose. These summits were not so high as Cloudseeker, but they were manifold and featured extremely steep crags and sheer ridges. Trees and streams marked the valleys, which could often be traversed—to a certain extent. Eventually, even the most promising routes terminated against the impassable barrier of the sheer wall. Those heights were so formidable, they could be crossed only on foot, and even then the precipitous paths were limited to the hardiest of climbers, traveling light.

The one exception was the Tharkadan Pass, a long and winding vale that cut generally southeast to northwest through the mountain barrier. A good road followed the pass, and for years it was the lone land route connecting not just Qualinesti and Thorbardin, but the two large sections of the continent wherein those two nations coexisted.

Firmly astride that road, right in the middle of the long pass, stood the fortress known as Pax Tharkas.

Built as an impervious barricade across the pass, the fortress was essentially a great wall flanked by two massive towers. Oriented to defend primarily against attack from the north, two additional curtain walls barred approach from that direction. Each of the curtain walls was pierced by a single gate, and the roadway approached each gate via a long, utterly exposed upward ramp. An attacker would have to penetrate both of those lesser defenses just to reach the formidable bastion itself, and the whole route was exposed to view—and to barrage with arrows, rocks, flaming oil, or even garbage—from the heights of the walls and towers.

Despite its strong orientation against northern attack, the fortress was no easy objective to an attacker coming from the south. Though it lacked the two curtain walls to delay an approach, both the main wall and the two towers loomed high over the floor of the pass, and any army coming from that direction would likewise be exposed to a ruthless barrage as it set to work against the massive stone gates that allowed access to the interior of the Tharkadan Wall.

The twin spires of Pax Tharkas, immense and blocky, mountainlike in their appearance, rose to either side of the long, broad battlement that connected the pair of lofty eminences. The Tharkadan Wall itself was a defensive battlement unmatched anywhere on Krynn. The two towers that flanked it to the right and left were joined, at their bases, to the sheer cliffs that flanked the valley, ensuring that anyone who was not a mountain goat had to pass through the fortress to travel north or south along the road.

Each of those square-walled spires was a fortress in its own right, with walls forty feet thick formed of tightly wedged stone blocks. They were divided into levels and contained the living quarters for, at that time, some one thousand inhabitants. The interior of the Tharkadan Wall, while also a huge and enclosed space, was not used for anything except as a training room for the military garrison.

Despite its appearance, so square and blocky, so suggestive of dwarven stolidity, the fortress was in fact a cooperative work of both the dwarf and elf peoples. Constructed shortly after the great elf king Kith-Kanan had formed his new nation of Qualinesti, Pax Tharkas had become a testament to the long peace between those two ancient peoples and the nations of Thorbardin and Qualinesti. It was only during later years, after the Cataclysm had set dwarf against dwarf and elf against human, that the fortress had fulfilled its promise as a bastion of war. Even when—due to the utter obliteration of the elven realm—the race war was a far distant memory, Pax Tharkas stood as a monument to dwarf implacability.

Tarn Bellowgranite knew the exalted history of the place, and he thought of those stories often as he walked the top of the Tharkadan Wall alone, as he did at the start of every day. He had read the tales of the builders who had labored so hard and so diligently to create Pax Tharkas. The staunch masonry was a testament to dwarf skill, but the location and the design had been the work of elves. The two races had worked together to create the mighty fortress, and all had regarded it as a symbol of amity. For a millennium and a half, the two nations had garrisoned Pax Tharkas together, elf and dwarf soldiers rubbing shoulders as they manned the battlements and watched the pass, ready to meet any potential enemy, sharing the belief that a foe to one race was a foe to both.

Then the gods had hurled their wrath upon the world in the form of the Cataclysm. The elves had fled to the depths of their forest home, and Pax Tharkas had become the gateway—very stoutly barred—to Thorbardin. Internecine warfare had rocked the dwarf world as the mountain dwarves refused to shelter their hill dwarf cousins under their mountain. Pax Tharkas was manned by the mountain dwarves, but it had been carried by storm when the wizard Fistandantilus and his army had attacked Thorbardin during the Dwarfgate War. That war had ended in disaster for both sides and left the two kin clans of dwarfkind licking deep wounds and nursing even deeper grudges.

Two centuries later, during the War of the Lance, the dwarves, mainly Neidar, had held Pax Tharkas against the onslaught of the dragonarmies, allowing many thousands of refugees, including humans and elves in great numbers, to escape southward, evading certain and horrible death. Following that war, the Neidar had for the most part returned to their villages, leaving Pax Tharkas, again, to the mountain dwarves of Thorbardin.

Key to the fortress's imperviousness was the ingenious defense mechanism that had closed the gates against Verminaard's dragonarmy: the interior of the Tharkadan Wall was hollow, penetrated by only a single massive gate in the north face of the wall and an equally large, lonely gate in the south. The space within the wall, and above the two gates, had been filled with many tons—a small mountain's worth—of heavy boulders. When the enemy had threatened to breach the defenses, those rocks had been released and fell into the gap between the gates, forming a solid and intractable barrier.

That fill thwarted the attackers, and it had remained in place for many decades, blocking passage from north to south, a sturdy reminder of the darkness that had befallen the world with the coming of the Dark Queen's legions. Nearly a century after the War of the Lance, the world had finally changed enough for a reopening to be considered.

The lone dwarf on the rampart felt a thudding through his boots and knew that the important work never ended. Another ton of rocks had been cleared from inside the gates and carted upward to arm the great trap again. His workers, those of the day shift, were already busy after relieving their colleagues who had labored through the night, for it was a task that continued, under the orders of Thane Bellowgranite, around the clock.

Tarn Bellowgranite felt the vibration, heard the rumble of rock, and he was pleased. His was a life that had been occupied with many vital tasks, but he had convinced himself that none of them were so crucial as that, the job that he would see completed in the twilight of his days. The road through Pax Tharkas would reopen, and it would be Tarn—well, the dwarves of Tarn's clan, more accurately— who would make it happen.

They called him the Tharkadan Thane, his loyal dwarves did, even though the title was vaguely embarrassing. He had once been a true thane, leader of the Hylar clan in Thorbardin—an unusual and exalted post for him because he was an exotic blend, descendent of a Hylar father and a Daergar mother. Both of his parents were long gone, killed during the Chaos War. For a time, the son who bore their legacy had seemed to have exceeded even the promise of his twice-noble birth: indeed he ascended to become the high king of Thorbardin, the highest-ranking noble in all dwarvendom.

But that seemed a lifetime ago, even though it had been only a decade. Jungor Stonespringer's revolt had overthrown him, and he was exiled. At first he had come with merely three hundred others, including his pregnant wife and their infant son. A mixture of Hylar and Klar dwarves and a few Daewar—those who had not journeyed east with the Mad Prophet—joined him. In the following years, other mountain dwarves had come along until he ruled a population of a thousand or so able-bodied adults, together with their young and elderly dependents. They called themselves a clan, though they were really refugees from three true clans, and they called him their thane, though he was really just the leader of a band of refugees.

Still, he was a sort of leader, and they were a sort of clan, and their home was important: Pax Tharkas. It was their position in that great fortress, more than anything else, that gave them a sense of identity and continuity in dwarf history. Even more, it provided them all with a purpose, for Tarn had vowed to see the Tharkadan Pass reopened before he died. He deemed the task of reopening the pass so important that many nearby fields lay fallow since the farmers who would have tended them were otherwise busy in fulfilling their thane's commands. That goal gave him the strength to rise and face each new day.

To be sure, he very much wished to see his children grow to adulthood and prosper, but his years suggested that might not happen. He had married late, to a much younger dwarf maid, and though she had borne him two wonderful offspring, his age made him feel more like their grandfather. He was glad they were there with him, but as he often reflected privately, he often acted as father to a nation more than father to his two children.

Long had he spurned trade with the hill dwarves, the Neidar whose settlements dotted all of the surrounding lands. His intransigence had not sat well with his wife, who was of Neidar blood, but he understood the ancient rivalries of his people better than he had when he was younger, and he knew that a mingling of populations would inevitably hurt the mountain dwarves in Pax Tharkas. He nursed the idea that his "clan" would one day return to Thorbardin to oppose and defeat Jungor Stonespringer and his fanatical followers. That narrow-minded despot represented everything Tarn hated about dwarf stubbornness, rigid thinking, and mindless obedience to authority.

Tarn Bellowgranite's life had already been marked by too much disappointment and tragedy. He had known love only once; his true beloved—a Hylar warrior named Belicia Slateshoulders—had died in the residual destruction of the Chaos War, and after that he had thought himself destined for a life of loneliness.

His marriage to Crystal Heathstone had been a political arrangement, but even as they took their vows, he had hoped that it might signal a thaw in the long enmity between the dwarves of the hills and the mountains. He and Crystal had become fond of each other, even learned to love each other in a limited way, but at the same time the fractures between their two peoples had seemed to grow deeper. Eternal wars, betrayal under the mountain, and lingering clan hatreds had all cast their pall over the life of the thane and his wife. Only in their two children had they found a focus, and a hope, for the future.

Tarn completed his circuit of the wall, looking up as he approached the east tower. The sky was clear, but the sun had not yet risen high enough for its rays to penetrate the steep-walled valley. Even so, he could detect the first signs of bright daylight limning the crest of the ridge overhead, and he paused to admire the daybreak for a minute before approaching the door to the tower. A Hylar guard snapped to attention, holding his battle axe at port arms as the thane approached then quickly opening the door for his thane.

Tarn nodded his thanks and entered the large, open room that served as a rallying point and ready room for garrison troops. It was currently empty of dwarves, but the rows of benches and the racks of weapons and shields lining the walls gave proof of its martial purpose. A single stairwell spiraled through the center of the room, leading both up and down.

The thane would soon descend to his living quarters, but there was another part of his morning ritual that he needed to complete first. Climbing the steps to the next level, he reached the fortress's command center. The level was divided into four large rooms, connected by a central hallway, and he headed to the farthest of those rooms. The door was open, and he strolled into the office of the garrison commander, Captain Mason Axeblade.

Axeblade was seated at his desk, talking to his former commander, retired general Otaxx Shortbeard. The two Daewar started to get to their feet as Tarn entered, but the thane waved them back to their chairs and took a seat for himself.

"No incidents reported overnight, my thane," Axeblade replied. He had been one of Tarn's loyal captains during the civil war, and Bellowgranite had welcomed his choice to follow him into exile. "The night workers lifted twelve tons of rock by the time their shift was over."

"Good," Tarn replied. "Looks quiet out there this morning as well."

"I almost wish something would happen around here!"

huffed Otaxx. Ever a man of action, he chafed as the long, empty years passed by.

But there was more to his glum nature. Both of the dwarves bore a burden Tarn couldn't fully appreciate, as they were among the few Daewar who had remained behind in Thorbardin when Severus Stonehand, the Mad Prophet, had marched away with the bulk of the clan on his mad quest to regain ancient Thoradin. None of those dwarves had ever been heard from again, and they had long been given up for lost by those they had left behind.

Axeblade's parents had gone with Stonehand, but Otaxx had suffered an even more grievous loss. His wife of twenty years, pregnant with their first child, had also departed on the quixotic quest for the lost kingdom. Ever true to his duty—which he vested toward the whole kingdom, not just his Daewar clan—Otaxx Shortbeard had been unable to follow his pregnant wife, for to do so would have betrayed the oath he had sworn to his king, Tarn Bellowgranite. Even though Tarn had given him leave to go, Otaxx had elected to remain behind; he had been a source of great strength to Tarn and all Thorbardin during the dark years after the Chaos War. But Otaxx sorely missed his wife, and pined for the child he had never known—the child that might not even have made it to birth.

He was too old to fight anymore, however, and Tarn knew he spent his days remembering his bride and second-guessing his path in life. Always gruff, Otaxx had become more irascible and more depressed as the years passed. He always hoped to hear word of Severus Stonehand's fate, but no word ever came. Still, he was one of the few who clung to some hope the Mad Prophet's expedition might not have met complete disaster.

"Any word from Garn Bloodfist?" the thane asked with some trepidation.

"I sent him another message two days ago; he's on

campaign in the hill country, but I haven't heard back," Axeblade said.

Tarn nodded, not surprised. Garn was the captain of the Klar contingent of the Tharkadan garrison. Some three hundred strong, the dwarves of that impetuous, high-strung clan were unsuited to the steady labor of rock-hauling required for work on Pax Tharkas. They craved action, and Tarn had found it impossible to keep them immobile in the fortress; the inevitable fights and fits and brawls were too disruptive to the rest of his band.

So every so often the Klar marched out of Pax Tharkas to raid the hill dwarves who lived in countless small towns throughout the vast foothills of the mountain range. Sometimes they killed some Neidar, and sometimes they lost some Klar. Almost always they returned with plunder and food, which they shared willingly enough with the rest of the garrison. Though Tarn didn't condone their dubious activities, he knew that the Klar kept the hill dwarves off balance and probably prevented them from marshalling their forces all at once to lay siege to his fortress. Still, Garn Bloodfist was a bit of a loose catapult, and the thane could never be sure exactly what kind of trouble he would make.

"Well, let me know if you get a message," Tarn said not very hopefully.

"Aye, my thane. I will."

He left the two Daewar and headed down the stairs, past the ready room, into the many levels of living quarters that filled the lower half of the east tower. On the fourth of those, he left the stairs, walked down a short hall, and opened the door to his open, private treasure room.

"Papa!" Tor cried. The robust ten-year-old raced over to his father, proudly holding up a wooden sword. "Look what I made! Otaxx Shortbeard promised to teach me how to parry once I have a sword! Look what I can do!" He waved the sword wildly.

Tarn chuckled, leaning down to embrace his son. "Why don't you go show Otaxx; I'm sure he can teach you a trick or two."

Next he hugged Tara, two years younger than her brother. He let her nuzzle his beard, as she loved to do; then he carried her around the playroom on his shoulders, her whoops and shrieks brightening his day like nothing else. Only when he was out of breath did he put her down, promising to return in a few minutes.

He went into the bedroom, then, and found his wife, Crystal Heathstone, standing at the window, as she often did, as he had known she would be doing. She turned to look at him, the anguish on her face tearing at his heart. She would always be a hill dwarf, daughter of a former clan leader, and her life as the wife of a mountain dwarf ruler had not been easy, he knew.

"Garn Bloodfist has taken the Klar out again, hasn't he?" she said, and he knew it wasn't really a question.

He merely nodded.

She sighed and shrugged off his touch when he went over to her. "One of these days, he's going to stir up a hornet's nest, and that could be the end for us all," she declared.

"The hornets are always buzzing," Tarn pointed out. "Sometimes Garn swats them away."

"Why can he only do it through war?" she demanded.

He shrugged, wishing they weren't having that conversation. "It's always been that way," he pointed out.

"Not always!" she retorted. "It had a beginning: the Cataclysm. Why can't there be an end? Why can't *we* end it?"

"We're dwarves," he replied, not knowing what else to say. "War is in our nature. You might as well try to stop the sun from moving through the sky."

She looked at him with a strange expression, a look that, to Tarn, was more scathing even than a glare of contempt. When she spoke, it was almost to herself. "Once, I thought you might be the kind of dwarf who would try to do just that, and to the Abyss with the consequences."

He turned on his heel and went to the door, tense and angry. He would not slam it, not when his daughter was so near, but he looked at Crystal as if he didn't recognize her.

"Maybe I was that dwarf, once. But I've seen too much. I'm not him now. I'm not that Tarn Bellowgranite anyway, not anymore."

# FIFTEEN

# HOMES OF THE NEIDAR

Brandon's mouth felt as dry as a bale of cotton and still tasted of bile. His head throbbed inside because of the lingering residue of the dwarf spirits, and it throbbed outside, where it had been bruised by Harn Poleaxe's powerful blows. Yet for all his physical aches, he felt emotionally worse. It seemed clear that his family's poor luck had at last found its nadir. For he had allowed the Bluestone, the symbol and the reality of his family's legacy, to fall into the hands of a treacherous hill dwarf.

And the Neidar *were* treacherous, Brandon realized—almost incomprehensibly so! His mind reeled as he recalled Harn Poleaxe's cheerful camaraderie, his friendly advice as he'd escorted the young Hylar across half of Ansalon. By Reorx, he'd been using his victim to carry the treasure that was his true quarry! And all the while, Poleaxe had been responsible for Nailer's murder—even if he had not actually wielded the fatal sword—and for the betrayal of Brandon's and Nailer's claim to the ruthless and avaricious Heelspurs.

The bitterness of the reality made Brandon sick to his

stomach. What a cruel irony: the hill dwarf who drank so freely, and so carelessly, had used alcohol—apparently enhanced with some kind of soporific drug—to immobilize his victim.

"Move it!" One of the Neidar prodded him with his own axe, and he stumbled as he tried to balance on feet and legs that were numbed from their bonds. Angrily he shook off the push. Shaking his head, gritting his teeth, he started to walk.

The hill dwarves and their captive moved under a slate-gray sky, which occasionally spit at them with rain showers; the sky perfectly mirrored Brandon's mood. They trekked away from the campsite but remained on the rugged crest of the ridge instead of moving into the more easily passable valley floor. They descended a bit to avoid a lofty, open promontory, but then quickly climbed back to resume the trek on the ridge crest.

When they came to a steep-sided ravine, his captors pushed him roughly, and he skidded down to land on his hip, sliding roughly to the bottom, unable to use his bound hands for any help. Grimly he plodded up the winding trail on the opposite side, resolving that he would not give the Neidar the satisfaction of hearing him complain or seeing him suffer. Nor would he give them an excuse to beat or, worse, ridicule and mock him.

All the while he was nursing his anger, which had already flared into hatred. They were not like any dwarves he had ever imagined; they were not worthy of Reorx's chosen! They were worse than the lowest gully dwarves, he finally decided.

It was many hours later before the troop of hill dwarves finally marched down off the rocky ridges onto a smooth road. The pair who had originally been charged with Brandon's execution had been marching grimly behind the prisoner all day, never hesitating to poke him between the shoulders, in the area of his kidneys, or right in the buttocks with the sharp tips of their short swords. He had noted that one of those two was also carrying Brandon's axe, clearly displaying his enjoyment at the feel and heft of his new weapon. The dwarf's chuckles of amusement proved, to Brandon, that he considered the dishonorable torment to be fine sport.

The captive barely felt those small annoyances, however, so deep was the gloom that had settled around him. The whole day he trudged along, mourning the loss of his father's treasure, cursing himself for the foolishness that had led to his capture without even a respectable show of self-defense. All was lost, and it seemed only a matter of time until Poleaxe staged his charade of a trial and executed the Kayolin dwarf as a spy.

It wasn't until near sunset that Brandon finally, forcefully, reminded himself that he wasn't dead yet. And, he told himself, if all he did was wallow in self-pity, his life may as well end in an ignominious whimper. He could not, *would* not, give up! If he was to perish here, he would make sure the Neidar bastards paid dearly for the privilege of killing him.

But his wrists were still securely bound, and his captors numbered a full dozen, so there was no release for his anger—at least, not in his present circumstances. He vowed to Reorx, to his father, and to the memory of his slain brother that someday, somehow, he would find the means to claim vengeance. For the moment, he would stay alert, nursing his anger.

His eyes, when he raised them, sought Harn Poleaxe, who strode at the head of the little column, swaggering along, regaling his companions with tales of Kayolin hubris and wealth.

"Their governor has decided to call himself a king," Poleaxe declared in an incredulous tone. "Even though he doesn't have half the holdings of Thorbardin. Believe it or not, he does most of his trading with humans!"

"Ah, you're making that up!" said one of Harn's ruffians.

"I swear on the Forge of Reorx!" Harn declared with an air of wounded dignity. "He sells steel to the emperor of Solamnia, and in return, the humans protect Kayolin from the goblins."

That was a lie, Brandon knew—Kayolin was in no danger from even the most numerous and aggressive bands of goblins—but the prisoner wasn't about to waste his breath rebuking Poleaxe, not when his own life was hanging in the balance.

The other Neidar, all except the one called Fireforge, laughed heartily at Harn's anecdotes while Brandon's rage simmered. He watched that hill dwarf, whose full name was Slate Fireforge, for any signs he might be able to appeal to him for help. Despite the fact he had objected to Harn's plan to summarily execute the captive, however, Fireforge gave no sign that he was willing to extend him any other unusual sympathy.

As his mind cleared—from both the effects of Poleaxe's blows and the lingering hangover—he reflected on the events that had led him to his sorry state. For there was more than just bad luck involved. Clearly, Poleaxe had planned the theft carefully; he had sent word to his cronies, and the band had waited in hiding for the travelers, moving in to assist when the treacherous Neidar acted.

That itself was an interesting fact, Brandon realized. Why had the big hill dwarf felt that he needed help? After all, he stood a half head taller than the mountain dwarf, who himself was a bigger-than-average specimen. And Poleaxe outweighed Brandon by a good two stone. Yet even with his victim extremely drunk, he had not struck until backed up by significant reinforcements. Perhaps Poleaxe was not as fearless as he pretended.

And why had he made his move out in the wilds? Poleaxe just as easily could have had Brandon surrounded or captured in town at an inn or in a tavern. Instead, he'd arranged for his handpicked men to effect the betrayal away from eyewitnesses.

The more Brandon thought about it, the more he wondered whether Harn's behavior might not meet with the approval of every citizen of Hillhome. Perhaps he might be able to find, if not outright allies, a few decent dwarves once they got to the town.

The road they were following meandered along a valley surrounded not by mountains, but by forested ridges. Soon they passed a dam—made of stones set so perfectly it could only be the work of dwarves—and a millhouse, where a large wheel turned with the flow of the stream. Brandon began to spot stone houses in the woods to either side, and when the road passed around another bend, they came upon a bustling village, filling the valley before him from wall to wall.

"Welcome to Hillhome!" gloated Poleaxe, calling back to his captive. "Now you can have a taste of Neidar hospitality."

"False hospitality, you mean," Brandon retorted. "Not like my father's, when he fed you and gave you drink at his own table."

"All the more fool him," Harn shot back, though he glowered unpleasantly. Was it possible? Did he feel some guilt over his foul treachery?

"Take him to the brig behind the smelting plant. Then come and report to me; I'll be at Moldoon's place," Poleaxe added, instructing the two guards who had tortured Brandon during the long march.

The prisoner, determined not to miss any chance at escape, looked around carefully as the guards escorted him through the town. He saw immediately that Hillhome consisted of two parts: a small central section of neat stone buildings, and an outer ring of wooden buildings and shacks. The houses in the town center were mostly modest, though a few boasted several rooms and outbuildings. Sturdy slate roofs and ornate rock gardens gave those structures a sense of permanence, as though they were every bit as old as the hills themselves. The inns—he spotted several—were large but similarly neat, as were the mill, smithy, and a few other shops they passed.

Brandon got a good look at both parts of the town, as he was marched down a curving lane that seemed to serve as a boundary between the two districts. The outer ring contained more buildings, and covered more area, than the rock-solid center. Those structures looked more temporary and seemed more crowded. He saw lines of laundry stringing between many of the buildings, and as his captors led him past a large inn, called Snarky's Place, a band of swarthy dwarves called down to them from the long porch.

"Hey, Rune! What's that garbage you're dragging into our town?" shouted a burly, black-bearded Neidar with a bulging belly and a patch over one eye.

"Ah, he's a mountain dwarf," called the captor, the one who was carrying Brandon's axe. "Harn Poleaxe is back, and he brought this fellow with him as a souvenir."

"Mountain dwarf?" screeched a female hill dwarf, a toothless crone sitting on the steps of the inn. She hawked and spit a gob of saliva that Brandon nimbly sidestepped. Eyes forward, he kept plodding on, and his guards hurried beside him, quickly leaving the belligerent drinkers behind.

"In here, mate," Rune said abruptly, grabbing Brandon by the shoulder and propelling him to the left, toward a wooden structure that looked more sturdy than most.

A burly guard stood at the front door, which consisted of heavy logs strapped together with iron bands. The hinges were as stout as a dwarf's arm. There was not a window in the whole structure.

"Got a mountain dwarf, needs a room—at least for a

day or two," Rune said with an evil chuckle.

"Got just the spot," said the jailer. He was a repulsive-looking hill dwarf with a filthy beard and dirty leather pants and shirt. He spit a messy gob onto the plank floor, and from within his tunic, he fished out a massive key, worn on a thong around his neck, and unlocked the door. He needed the weight of his shoulder to push it open, but it gradually yielded to his efforts.

Prodded by his tormentors, Brandon clumped up the two steps to the brig and stepped inside. His nostrils were assailed by the stink of overflowing gutters and unwashed bodies. As his eyes adjusted, he was being pushed down a corridor between two banks of cells. The little cages had solid walls and doors of heavy iron bars. Most of them were empty but a pair was occupied by hill dwarves who barely looked up as the new arrival passed. Each of them stank of whiskey and vomit, and the smell—which called to mind his own recent excesses—almost made Brandon gag. Their leather tunics were stained, torn, and patched, and the normal Neidar complexion, brown and weather scoured, had faded on their faces to an unhealthy pale.

Just beyond was another cell. That one held two dwarves who did not look like Neidar. Their skin was pale too, but more naturally so, and their stout boots were cobbled with metal cleats. With some surprise, Brandon guessed they were a pair of mountain dwarves. Like their hill dwarf cousins, they looked up listlessly as the new prisoner was pushed past.

In another two steps, they came to the cell at the end of the corridor, a little closet-sized room barely half the space of the others. The door stood open, but Brandon wasn't prepared for the shove that sent him stumbling through. He dropped to his knees and, with his hands still bound behind him, couldn't prevent his face from smashing into the slimy wall. He squirmed around, bouncing to his feet in fury, only to see the door slam in his face.

"I'm locked in good here; at least untie me!" he demanded, glaring through the grid of iron bars.

"You're fine for now," Rune taunted, hoisting Brandon's axe so the prisoner would be sure to see it. "We'll let you know tomorrow if we're going to untie you and feed you or cut your head off!"

All three Neidar laughed raucously as they passed out of the brig, slamming and locking the outer door, leaving Brandon in the darkness and the stink and the despair.

——DH——

"So the black dwarf locked you in a cage and was trying to kill you for some reason, and then, after this attack you have described, he sent that creature after you because you escaped?" Gretchan's tone was patient but terribly serious.

Gus nodded miserably after finishing his long, long story—at least two minutes' worth. His stubby fingers wove through Kondike's shaggy coat, scratching the dog between his massive shoulders. The Aghar couldn't look the dwarf maid in the eye.

"Monster come kill me on top mountain," he admitted dolefully. "But snow kill me even better. I think him gone away."

"The black minion failed to kill you ... and you escaped?" Gretchan said, her eyes widening. "Well, that's a formidable achievement. Reorx must be fond of you."

"I very formable! I run fastester than him can ever chase!" the Aghar declared, suddenly boastful. "Him bluphsplunging claws not even grab me!"

"And then the snow fell down, and Kondike found you," the dwarf maid said. "Hmm. Well, you're certainly lucky if you're not fast."

She was right, Gus knew, once more feeling a little guilty for having dragged the beautiful goddess into his troubles. "I lucky sure. But I thought him gone," he said, sniffling.

"I never thought him come for you and Kondike."

"Well, lucky thing for you we were here," she said, not unkindly. "That minion fears me now, but that doesn't mean it will never be back. Still, I think we're safe for the time being. We can afford to get some rest; my dog is a very light sleeper."

"I should go 'way," Gus said, shaking his head, though he wanted very much to stay right there. "It's not fair you get killed for me."

Gretchan reached out and patted him on the knee. "None of us are going to get killed. At least, not by that thing. Indeed, I think you should stick with us for a while." She stared at him, and he felt that her eyes were peeling back his skin, looking right through him.

"Is there anything else you ought to tell me?" she asked sternly.

Gus tried to think. "Uh. Mebbe. You know 'bout bunty hunters?"

"Bunty hunters? No. What are they?" she asked.

"Big, nasty Theiwar. Kill gully dwarf, cut him head off. Say for 'bunty.' "

"That was back in Thorbardin?" she asked and Gus nodded.

"I can't believe it!" Gretchan snapped. She suddenly seemed to be very angry. She stood up and stomped away then spun around and pointed a finger right at Gus's face, making him a little bit afraid. "You wouldn't be lying to me, would you?" she demanded very seriously.

"Gus no lie! Bluphsplunging doofar bunty hunters kill Aghar! Cut off heads!"

"How in the name of Reorx is that possible?" the dwarf maid cried, smacking one fist into the palm of her other hand. She raised her hands and shouted at the sky. "Are you even paying attention?" she shouted. "Dwarves have been killing each other for centuries; it seems we don't even need an excuse! Wars and gates and pride and clans give cause enough! But now, for one clan to charge a bounty for the heads of another? For gully dwarves!"

She stomped on the ground and planted her fists on her hips, glaring downward. "And you, down there—you claim to be the descendents of the great mountain dwarf clans! You're a bunch of frightened little rats, hiding in your holes! Why, if I could reach you, I'd pull your beards out by the roots!"

Gretchan stalked back and forth in the little clearing. Gus stayed very still, hoping she would forget about him. He didn't understand who she was yelling at, but he was pretty certain it wasn't him, and he was determined to leave it that way. Finally, after two long, loud minutes, she came back to the stump by the fire and sat down with a heavy sigh.

"I'll be damned," Gretchan said, looking far away into the night. Her tone was sad, but not so loud anymore. She looked at him and shook her head. "You tell a very interesting story. It sounds as though things have soured under the mountain these days."

Gus didn't know what 'soured' meant, but he was inclined to agree. He would have said so too except Gretchan didn't seem to want to talk anymore. She went back to her sleeping roll and, with her staff nearby, bundled herself up in her blanket. Her eyes were open, staring past the gully dwarf and the fire, peering into the darkness of the woods. She filled her pipe, lit it with a stick she drew from the fire, and puffed furiously as she glared at the night.

Wracked by guilty feelings, Gus nonetheless needed only about two minutes to fall asleep. His dreams were untroubled, and when he woke up, the forest floor was dappled with sunlight, and Gretchan already had a fire going and a pot of tea on to brew.

His ability to forget meant that Gus's mood had brightened, his fear—and guilty twinges—vanquished to some distant, cobwebbed portion of his brain. He cheerfully warmed his belly with the tea and filled it with a hearty slice of dried bread. Soon they were up and striding through the woods.

"What we do today?" he asked as they set out. "More walking?"

"Some," Gretchan replied with a laugh. "Actually, I'm on a working expedition."

"Work? Extra-mission?"

"Yes, like an 'extra-mission.' I'm a writer. A historian, I guess you could say. At least, I'd like to be. I travel around and talk to dwarves and write down their stories. I've been working on a book for a very long time." She sounded a little wistful as she concluded her statement.

"Writing" was a concept as foreign to the gully dwarf as "reading." He didn't really understand what the dwarf maid was talking about, so he settled for a more pertinent question.

"Where we walking to?"

"I'm on my way to have a very interesting talk with a dwarf woman," Gretchan replied. "I've heard many things about her, and I think it's time I meet her for myself."

"Where dwarf lady?" wondered the Aghar.

Gretchan chuckled, the sound as musical as ever, and Gus felt a fresh bounce in his step.

"She lives with a tribe of Neidar," she said. "They live pretty close to here—in a sleepy little village called Hillhome. It won't be long and we'll be there."

# SIXTEEN

# THE ORACLE

Harn Poleaxe approached the small hut with a measure of trepidation. He hadn't seen the oracle for more than two years, but he well remembered the frisson of mingled terror and excitement that his last encounter with the old Neidar crone had provoked.

Yet he was returning in triumph, he told himself. He held the Bluestone wedge in his left hand as he raised his right and knocked, hesitantly, at the flimsy door.

"Enter, Harn Poleaxe!" came the command from within the hut.

Grimacing, the big Neidar tried to suppress the trembling that shook his hand as he pressed against the door. He ducked his head to pass underneath the low frame. The interior of the one-room house, not surprisingly, was dark, for the one who lived there had no need of illumination.

"I have returned, Mother Oracle," Harn said, bowing humbly. "I take it you have been informed of my arrival?"

The old dwarf woman who sat in the shadowy room uttered a dry bark of laughter. "No one spoke to me," she said. "But I knew you had come to Hillhome. And I know, too, that you bring the Bluestone from Kayolin."

Harn shuddered at the evidence of the oracle's far-seeing powers then quickly extended the heavy wedge of stone. As his eyes adjusted to the murk, he watched as she reached out her arthritic hands to take the talisman, lifting it easily into her lap.

The oracle had been a very old woman when she first came to Hillhome, some ten years earlier. To Harn, who had not seen her since he had departed for Kayolin two years ago, she looked the very same as when he had left, which was the same as when she had first wandered up the hill road into the town. Her hair was white and thin, hanging in a scraggly tangle around her round, wrinkled face. Her eyes were open but milky white, proof of the blindness that had long afflicted her. Her shoulders were rounded, and her posture, as she sat in a small rocking chair, stooped and frail looking. She wore a worn cloak of pale brown, patched in many places. Her feet were encased in soft moccasins.

But her voice was strong, and so were her hands. He watched as she hefted the heavy Bluestone, feeling the smoothness along both sides. She raised the artifact to her face and smelled the stone, running it along her wrinkled cheek, holding it to her ear as if she expected it to speak to her. For all Harn knew, she did hear something there. In any event, she issued a cackle of laughter and lowered the object into her lap.

"You have done well," she said. "I believed in you, but even so, when I sent you to gain this stone, I knew you would face many obstacles. I was not certain you would succeed."

Harn lowered his face, pleased by her praise and her acknowledgment of the severity of his challenge. "I had to live among the mountain dwarves for a long time," he admitted. "But in the end, I was able to win their trust and gain the stone."

"Go to the chest, over there by the window," she said, handing him the Bluestone. He saw a small strongbox, protected by a solid steel lock, but when he crossed to the container, the lid turned out to be unsecured. He lifted it, looking down in amazement at another stone, the perfect image of the one he held in his hands except it was as green as emerald, albeit impossibly large for any such gemstone. He had known about the other stone's existence, but it was moving, even awe inspiring, to see them together.

"Put that one in there, with the Greenstone," the oracle said. He did as she asked, noting that the two stones nestled easily together to form a sharp-pointed, broad-based wedge.

"Close the lid and lock it. Bring me the key," she instructed, and again he did as requested. "There is one more. When we obtain it, we will be ready to act," she said.

"Huh. Where is this third stone?"

"I am not certain. It is moving now. I will need to study, consult my auguries, before I can pinpoint the exact location."

Harn shuddered. Like most dwarves, he had a strong distrust of magic, and her suggestion of auguries, not to mention her inexplicable knowledge about matters unearthly, smelled too much like sorcery for his taste. Still, her information had always proven accurate, and her arcane knowledge made her his most important ally.

"Go to the stove," she ordered suddenly. "And kindle a fire there."

She had a small pot-bellied iron cook stove in one corner of the hut, and Harn did as she instructed. He found some dry straw for tinder as well as small sticks of firewood and a piece of flint. He struck the stone against the blade of his knife to drop sparks into the straw, and soon a small blaze ignited. The oracle was tapping her feet impatiently, so he blew on the fire to hasten it along then added more sticks until it was crackling enthusiastically.

"Ah, good," she said at length. "Now take my teapot

and fill it from the water cistern outside; you must use rainwater, not well water."

"Aye, Mother Oracle," Harn replied. He found the teapot, a battered old ceramic vessel, and went outside to see that the barrel poised under her downspout was nearly full. A few neighborhood youngsters were playing tag nearby, and they snickered to see him performing such woman's work, but they quickly scampered away when he glared at them. With the teapot full, he reentered the hut.

"Now put it on the stove. Keep the fire going; make it boil!" she snapped.

Again he did as he was told, feeding more wood into the stove, wondering about the purpose of the tedious ritual. Still, he wasn't inclined to ask questions and, fortunately, the water was boiling a few minutes later.

"Bring me my tea," the oracle commanded, pointing a bony finger toward a cluttered table near the stove. Amid a cheese crock and a box of small spice bottles, he found a container, heavy and glazed, that held a bundle of bitter-smelling brown leaves. He took it over to her and watched as she worked by feel, counting ten leaves into the palm of her hand.

"Put these in a mug, and cover them with the hot water," was her next instruction, which he duly followed. He was surprised to see the brew foam and bubble when the boiling liquid contacted the leaves. The smell was truly vile, and he wondered what it must taste like.

But she had no intention of drinking it. After he handed her the mug, he had to jump backward to avoid the scalding spray as she unceremoniously upended the container and dumped the water and leaves right onto the wooden floor at her feet. With a surprisingly fluid gesture, she pushed herself out of the chair and dropped to her knees. Gingerly reaching out her gnarled hands, she traced her fingers over the hot leaves, taking care not to move them, but using touch, she carefully studied their positions on the floor.

She spent a long time in that slow activity, several times clucking her tongue in apparent displeasure. Harn didn't dare interrupt her scrutiny, and he was startled when she looked up suddenly, fixing those blind eyes upon him as if they could read his thoughts.

"You did not return alone from the dwarven nation in the north," she said, her voice suddenly sharp.

"No," he admitted warily. "I came with a Kayolin dwarf. It was his family, an ancestor, that uncovered the stone, and his father bade me bring the son along. It was the only way I could get the stone."

"That was a mistake," she said, sitting on her haunches and shaking her head dismally as if she could not believe the scope of Harn's incompetence.

"What do you want me to do?" Poleaxe asked, suddenly—he couldn't say why—chagrined.

"The Kayolin dwarf must never leave Hillhome," replied the oracle. "He must be eliminated."

"Well, I intend to do just that," Harn said defensively. Suddenly his throat felt terribly parched, but he wasn't about to ask for a drink, not from the Mother Oracle. He gulped. "He's locked up right now, and I have arranged for him to be charged as a spy. If the trial goes as planned, he will be executed shortly."

"Make sure, then, that the trial does go as planned," she said. "For this Kayolin outsider is a great danger to us if he lives. Remember, he must never leave Hillhome."

"I will make it so, Mother Oracle," pledged the Neidar stoutly. "Is . . . is there anything else you need from me?" he added, silently hoping the answer would be "no."

"Yes," she said immediately. She leaned forward for a moment, touching the leaves again, even bending down to loudly sniff at them.

"Another stranger, a female, approaches Hillhome—a dwarf maid. She interests me. I want you to meet her, study her, see what her purpose is."

"Why is she coming here?" Harn asked worriedly.

"She comes to seek me. But I will not allow her into my presence. You must make sure she stays away."

"How can I do that?"

"For now, tell her that I am very unwell. Sick, even dying, in my bed. I will accept no visitors."

"I will," Harn said. "But what if that doesn't work?"

"Then," she said sharply. "Think of something else."

——DH——

Gus gazed into the valley as the road crested a gentle rise and began to wind again toward the lowland. He saw a collection of brown shapes, apparently made of wood, sprawling through the fields, along the roads, up and down the banks of the narrow stream, and scattered all around a wide, central square.

"Those are buildings, and this is a town," Gretchan explained. "Hillhome, to be precise."

"Hill home," repeated the Aghar in awe.

The dwarf maid, together with the Aghar and the big, black dog, ambled down the road toward the place. Gretchan puffed easily on her pipe as she walked along, while Gus looked around at new wonders as they approached: fenced pastures where cattle, pigs, sheep, and horses grazed; wooden houses with flower gardens; neatly tended ponds where fish jumped and splashed. He was particularly taken by the sight of a lumber crew, Neidar dwarves using axes to fell tall trees while massive horses hauled the logs toward a pile of timber next to the road. He gawked so long, he had to race to catch up to his companion, who had kept walking and was already at the edge of town.

"We'll stop at an inn first," Gretchan said. "I learned years ago that that's the best way to find out what's happening in a community—especially a town of dwarves!"

"I like inn!" Gus agreed. He had never actually been

inside of such an establishment—the dwarves of Norbardin were notoriously strict about keeping the Aghar out—but he had sniffed around the edges and sorted through the garbage of many eating and drinking inns. Maybe, with his new friend Gretchan at his side, the Neidar would actually let him inside the door.

Gretchan was busy looking around the town that crowded the valley before them. She frowned. "I really can't believe Hillhome is *this* big."

"Never been here before?" Gus asked.

She shook her head. "I've been doing my work for a number of years," she admitted. "Traveling. But I've really only scratched the surface of the vast dwarven nations."

"You can scratch my surface," the Aghar offered helpfully, doffing his cap in case she needed access to his scalp.

The dwarf maid recoiled with a grimace, which to Gus's eyes was a mighty beautiful expression. "Listen, Gus," she said in a low, gentle voice. "Sometimes people aren't always nice to . . . um, your kind. You just stick with me, and I'll do the talking, all right?"

"All right! You do talking!" he agreed. Strutting proudly along on the right side of Gretchan, with Kondike pacing on her left, Gus marched purposefully into his first hill dwarf community. Several dwarves, maids filling buckets at a well, looked at him scornfully, but he ignored their hostile glances—they were nothing he hadn't experienced every time he dared to skirt the edges of Norbardin. He was more concerned with the hill dwarf males who, to a man, ignored the gully dwarf in favor of ogling the pretty Gretchan. He wanted to rebuke them—challenge them to a fight—but he remembered the dwarf maid's instructions and decided that he would indeed let her do the talking.

So he tried to communicate his displeasure by glaring at the dwarves who took such a lascivious interest in his companion, but when one fellow uttered a long, low whistle, Gus lost his temper.

"You stop it, you big bluphsplunging doofar!" he barked, taking a step toward the hill dwarf, but Gretchan snatched him back by his collar.

"Keep quiet!" she snapped, and he vowed he would really, really try.

They wandered down a street that was busy with pedestrians and cart traffic. Gus spied vaguely familiar sights: a smith pounding iron beside his hot forge; a baker pulling loaves from an oven; a fishmonger standing at a cart full of a fresh catch, calling for business, exchanging his wares for silver or copper coin. But much of Hillhome was utterly unprecedented in his narrow experience. He yelped and jumped out of the way as a team of oxen, lumbering like giants over his head, rumbled past, pulling a wagon full of beer kegs. He gawked at horses and ponies in the street, and goats and chickens in the yards of some of the houses. They passed carts full of vegetables, for sale like the fish, but more brightly colored and fresh smelling than any food in all of sunless Thorbardin.

He reached for one of the things Gretchan called "carrots" but flinched back when she cuffed him on the head. "Hands to yourself," she told him, then sighed at his crestfallen expression.

"Listen, we'll stock up on food before we leave town, I promise," Gretchen said as he stared forlornly at the endless baskets of produce. "While we're here, though, don't touch anything, and don't take anything. Besides, we'll let others do our cooking for us."

"Others *cook* for us?" declared Gus in wonder. He was starting to think that he would like Hillhome very much indeed.

"This looks like a good place; it's called Moldoon's," the dwarf maid explained, helpfully pointing to the name above the inn door. "It's been here a long time; it shows up in some of the old stories of this place. Rich in history. Perfect for my work."

Gus followed her and Kondike up the few steps to enter the cool, smoky inn. The Aghar's nose was assailed by many strange smells, nearly all of them enticing. A few dwarves sitting around tables in the great common room turned to look over at the newcomers. Gus froze as he heard a loud challenge coming from the red-bearded dwarf behind the bar.

"Hey! You can't bring that big dog in here!" he declared.

Gretchan gave him her sweetest smile. "Oh, that's all right," she chirped. "He goes with me everywhere!"

The bartender blushed, stammering and staring into the dwarf maid's blue eyes then running his eyes approvingly up and down the outline of her tunic. Resenting the bold inspection, Gus planted his fists on his hips and stepped in front of Gretchen, glaring furiously at the dwarf innkeeper. The hill dwarf's eyes widened in surprise at the sight of the small, smelly gully dwarf, and he looked as if he were about to raise another objection when something caused him to clamp his mouth shut. Instead, he gave Gretchan a broad smile and wink and, when she sat at a table—with Gus on an adjacent chair and Kondike flopping onto the floor at her feet—he came bustling over to her.

"And what might the little lady want?" he said merrily with an effusive manner that Gus found very irritating.

"I'll take a mug of your finest ale. And bring a smaller glass for my friend here, if you please."

"Hmm." Once again the bartender frowned at Gus but then overcame his unspoken objections to quickly fetch the two drinks. "And what brings a pretty stranger such as yourself to our humble village?" he asked, plopping a small glass down in front of Gus before wiping the table and gently placing a foaming mug before Gretchan.

"Well, I'm a historian by avocation, and I'm traveling the lands of the hill and mountain dwarves, writing down as much as I can learn. I'm trying to visit every town from the old days that I can find. Hillhome is more legendary than most, of course."

"Of course it is!" boasted the bartender.

"Are you Moldoon, himself?" Gretchan asked.

"Yes! Well, no. I mean, I'm the current owner, Web Breezefallow. Moldoon—the original Moldoon—was my wife's grandfather. He's not around anymore. So I'm a Moldoon by marriage."

"That is very interesting," the dwarf maid replied, daintily sipping from her mug then slurping the foam from her lip with a flick of her pink tongue. She took some parchment out of her knapsack and scribbled a note on it, much to the awe of the bartender and Gus.

"Excuse me, miss," said another dwarf, walking—swaggering, it looked to Gus—over to the table. "Did I hear you say you're interested in our town?"

"That I am," she said. "My name is Gretchan Pax."

The newcomer whistled and, without waiting for an invitation, sat down at the table, rather rudely nudging Gus to the side. He was a very tall and sturdy dwarf, a little thick around the middle, but his girth suggested strength more than sloth.

"And you are . . . ?" She left the question hanging in the air as she pointedly put her notepaper away.

The big dwarf straightened abruptly. "Sorry. I'm Harn. Harn Poleaxe."

"What a coincidence," Gretchen replied. "I've wanted to make your acquaintance, having heard your name on my travels."

"All lies, I assure you!" Poleaxe protested good-naturedly. "And I was never near that woman's house!"

His loud comments drew raucous laughter from the group of dwarves at the table he had recently vacated. Gus glared stonily at the rude dwarves, but they didn't pay any attention—all seemed to be casting admiring looks that shifted between Poleaxe and Gretchan.

The two did make a rather attractive pair, Gus thought sulkily. Gretchan's beauty was unsurpassed, and Poleaxe had an easy confidence, buttressed by his impressive size, that seemed certain to attract the admiration, even obedience, of lesser dwarves. Gus tried to sit taller, puff out his chest, hold his chin up.

"Ah, be quiet, you rock-scrubbers!" Poleaxe called out before leaning in and taking Gretchan's hand in both of his big paws. "And who," he said, looking dubiously at Gus and slightly wrinkling his nose, "is this, uh, little whippet?"

Whip it! thought Gus angrily.

"Oh he's my, uh, assistant," answered Gretchan smoothly with a slight wink.

Sisstant, thought Gus proudly.

"What say you and I get out of here and find some place we can get better acquainted?"

She smiled sweetly, somehow extracting her hand without Poleaxe's noticing. "What a charming invitation," she commented. She pulled her pipe and pouch of dried leaves from her tunic, slowly filling it. "But after this drink, my assistant and I must get busy. First we will have to find a place to stay while we're in town."

"I know just the place! I'll walk you over and show it to you when you're ready."

Again Gretchan smiled sweetly. She took a candle from the table and lit her pipe, the pleasant smoke swirling around her as the two dwarves chattered on and on about many things that Gus didn't understand: touching on the Neidar, the Dwarfgate War, the wandering elves, and some hideous monster they called the Green Wyrm. About the only thing the Aghar could extract from the long, boring conversation (at least two minutes' worth) was some monster called the Green Wyrm had died some time ago, destroying most of a city, Quali-something, in the process. He shuddered, glad the creature was gone.

After a while his eyes were feeling a little bleary.

"So what do you want to see in Hillhome, besides me?" Harn asked at one point with a chuckle. "I warn you, though, it'll all be downhill after Harn Poleaxe."

Gretchan laughed good-naturedly. "Actually, there's an elderly woman I'd really like to meet. I've heard she lives in these parts. I don't know her name, but people call her Mother Oracle, I believe. You wouldn't know where I could find her, would you?"

"Know her? Why, I was just there myself; she's an old friend of mine!" Poleaxe declared. Then his demeanor grew solemn and sorrowful. "Sadly, she's not well. Wouldn't even see me after I returned from two years' traveling. Told me to come back in ten days and see if she was feeling any better. I could ask her then if she'll see you."

"Ten days?" the dwarf maid replied, looking disappointed. "Oh. I don't know if I can stay here that long. I have work to do, so many other places to go."

"Well, that's unfortunate," Harn said. "But I hope you'll be here for a little while longer. I'd like a chance to get to know you better," he added slyly.

Gus bristled, but Gretchan, strangely, acted as if she found the hill dwarf kind of beguiling. She gave the Aghar a warning look whenever he opened his mouth to voice his opinion. He settled for clamping his jaws shut and glowering his most menacing glower at Harn's back.

"There's a lot of history in these old hills," the Neidar boasted. "Of course, my people have lived in these lands for better than two thousand years. Lots of it prosperous too until the damned mountain dwarves locked their gates during the Cataclysm. That's a cause we're still settling!" he concluded, thumping his chest.

"Why is there always some cause to be settled?" Gretchan snapped back, her vehemence taking the hill dwarf by surprise. "I mean, the Cataclysm was more than four hundred years ago! How long can you people hold a grudge?"

"It's more than a grudge!" Harn protested, holding up his hands. "Why, the Dwarfgate War—"

"Who do you think started the Dwarfgate War?" she cried, smacking her fist onto the table so hard that the mugs bounced. Her voice was rising, and the gully dwarf sensed that everyone in Moldoon's was looking at them. Gus slowly slipped down in his chair until just his eyes were above the edge of the table.

"Well, I mean, Fistandantilus—" Poleaxe stammered.

"Fistandantilus used the dwarves as his tool!" the dwarf maid shot back. She rose to her feet, both fists planted on the table as she stared into the big dwarf's face. "The dwarves were fools! You Neidar are always so happy to bring him up; I should think you'd be ashamed by the memory! Your ancestors fought and died for a foolish war and a foolish cause based on a foolish grudge. Oh, *why* can't you understand!"

She sat back down suddenly as if exhausted. Harn looked at the surrounding dwarves, many of whom were gaping at the female with expressions ranging from awe to fright. Poleaxe shrugged and looked at her as if thinking about edging away.

"What's the use?" Gretchan asked with a sigh as if all the anger had blown out of her. She shook her head. "I'm tired."

"Um, well, then, maybe I can show you a place to stay," Harn said. "You know, clean rooms, good beds. Just for sleeping, of course!" he added hastily.

"Fine. Please do that," she replied.

When Gretchan had finished her beer—Poleaxe had consumed three mugs in the same interval—they rose and left the place. The big dwarf walked right beside the maid, who seemed to be her usual cheerful self again. Still, when Harn placed his arm around her shoulders, she smoothly shrugged herself free. Gus and Kondike lagged a short distance behind. The Aghar continued to glare at the hill dwarf's back, and he had the comforting feeling that the dog shared his distaste. He continued to watch suspiciously as Gretchan stopped at several stands in the market, purchasing some vegetables and, from a butcher, a large joint of bone with bits of meat on it.

True to his word, Poleaxe led them to a clean, comfortable boardinghouse, waiting while Gretchan paid, in advance, for two rooms for the next week. When the big Neidar tried to follow them up the hall, she turned and spoke gently but with a firm undercurrent.

"You've done too much already. I just thank you so much for your helpfulness and hospitality," she said, dazzling him with her smile. "I can find my way from here. But I do hope I'll see you tomorrow! Perhaps at Moldoon's again?"

Poleaxe looked as though he were going to argue. Before he spoke, Kondike pushed past him, stopped before his mistress, and dropped to the floor with a heavy sigh. The big, black dog simply lay there, head raised, brown eyes fixed upon the hill dwarf.

"Well, all right, then," Poleaxe said, his eyes narrowing a bit. "Tomorrow it is."

——DH——

The sun was an excruciating, intolerable blaze against the blackness of the minion's ghostly flesh. The harbinger of dawn crested the eastern horizon with surprising alacrity, stabbing forth those hateful rays while the creature was still licking its wounds from the scorching presence of the dwarf maid's blazing staff.

Hissing in fury and discomfort, the monster sank through the ground with the coming of dawn and spent the long, warm day nestled directly in the bedrock of the hills, a hundred feet or more below the surface of the world. Time was no matter of concern for it as it dwelled easily among the ancient rocks and absorbed the cool power at the base of the world. The minion had a purpose to serve, a task to accomplish, but it had to wait until nightfall.

Only when the sun had fully set and cool night was lord of the world did it again emerge. Seeping upward, it emerged from the ground like smoke rising from a buried fire. At first immaterial, it coalesced in a woodland glade, taking shape, extending its great limbs, flexing talons and bringing the fires of the Abyss to those hateful, glowing eyes.

Spreading black wings, it finally took to the air, gliding silently through the night sky. The red and white moons were waning, setting low in the west, but the black moon was high and full. Unseen by most, that orb of black magic, named for the god Nuitari, cast its full measure across the widespread wings of the minion. The minion relished the cool wash of magic, a balm greater than warm sunlight on the flesh of a shivering dwarf or human.

When its red eyes fixed upon the ground, the creatures of the woodland sprang anxiously toward their dens or cowered under rocks or beneath steep riverbanks. Even hunting owls took to sheltered limbs, and wolves, lips curled against the unseen but dangerous flyer, cringed in the shadows and hoped for the monster to fly past. And always the minion did just that, for the moment. Its wide nostrils flared, it tasted the breeze and picked up the scent it sought.

Pressing forward with powerful wing strokes, the monster soared over ridges, flying in a straight line above a course of winding valleys that would have forced any land-bound traveler to meander wastefully. Soon the minion spotted the twinkling lights and the multitude of buildings that were proof of a sizable town, one that completely filled the bottom of a valley between two steep ridges. Many sounds of voices, some clamorous, some drunk, some singing, some angry, reached its sensitive ears. A smith was working late into the night at his forge, the pounding rings of his hammer marking a cadence that seemed to underscore the energy of the whole town. Cattle lowed and pigs squealed when the minion flew above their pens, sending the animals scurrying for their barns and sheds.

Circling back above the town, the minion flew low, trying—for the time being—to remain unseen by the denizens. Any one of them might look up to see the gaunt form of the monster silhouetted against the stars, and the beast did not want to take that chance. The memory of that searing light, the charring of the dwarf maid's staff, caused its lips to draw back in an unconscious snarl. She had powers that the monster feared and must avoid.

But at the same time, her presence was a beacon.

The minion knew beyond a doubt that the maid and her staff were down in the town somewhere, and it would have to avoid her terrible talisman. At the same time, the minion understood that, near to the dwarf maid, it would find the gully dwarf that was its prey.

# SEVENTEEN

# A NIGHT IN HILLHOME

Gretchan watched Harn Poleaxe swagger down the hall and through the inn's entryway. She frowned, trying to decide what it was about the big Neidar that bothered her. She disliked him—he seemed an unusually stubborn and boastful example of his kind—and she suspected that he had not been telling her the whole truth about the Mother Oracle. What was his game? She knew she would probably have to talk to him again, employing all her considerable persuasive skills, to get to the bottom of the story. For the moment, however, she was glad to be rid of him.

"You and Kondike take this room," Gretchan suggested, opening the first of the two she had rented. "I'll take the other one."

The little Aghar's face grew pale. "Where is other one?" he asked nervously.

She laughed. "I keep forgetting how strange this all is to you. Don't worry; I'll be right next door."

"*Where* next door?" he pressed.

"Right here." She touched the neighboring door. "But I'm going to go out for a while. I'd like you to stay here and keep an eye on Kondike for me."

"Keep eye on him?" Gus looked skeptical. "My eyes on *me!* Two eyes for me!"

She sighed, shaking her head in exasperation. "Now don't be silly. Of course you keep your own eyes, but just watch Kondike for me, all right? 'Keep an eye on him' means to pay attention to him. Don't let him get into any trouble."

In fact, Gretchan was perfectly comfortable leaving her dog alone in a room while she went about town; she had done so in many communities in the course of her travels. She was more worried about the gully dwarf getting curious and bumbling into trouble, so she had invented the little job to make sure he stayed put until she returned.

"I watch him," Gus declared. "I keep eye on him! And two eyes on me!"

"Thank you. Here . . . these are for both of you." She removed the packages she had purchased in the food market. The Aghar's eyes lit up as she handed him a small wedge of cheese as well as a few carrots and radishes. Kondike welcomed the soup bone and immediately started gnawing away on the scraps of meat still clinging to the large joint.

But Gus was scowling again. "Where you go? You not eat food? You go see big Poleaxe dwarf?" he asked suspiciously.

She blinked in surprise, suddenly realizing that he must be jealous. Touched, she didn't mock him. "No, actually. I thought he was a bit of a pain—I mean," she added, "I think he talked too much. But I have some research to do that I must do on my own. I'd like to meet some other Neidar and speak with them. I want to get to know this town, and I suspect there's a lot more to it than Harn Poleaxe."

Five minutes later, the Aghar and dog were secure in their room, happily munching their food. Gretchan got settled in her own room, opening the window and pulling back the curtains to air out the somewhat stuffy chamber.

Opening her backpack, she found her hairbrush and ran it through her hair a few times.

She was putting it back when she noticed the strange bottle that the Aghar had brought out of the wizard's lair. She reached for the bottle, looking it over carefully. The label, *Midwarren Pale,* suggested a brand of dwarf spirits from Thorbardin, but her senses tingled as she held the flask, and she knew that it held something stranger and far more powerful than even the most potent alcoholic beverage. She removed the stopper and sniffed at it, wincing at the smell—which *was* very reminiscent of dwarf spirits.

Shrugging, she decided that mystery would have to wait. She set the bottle on the stand next to her bed and closed up her pack. Then she strolled out the inn's front door and into the lamplit streets of Hillhome. She turned away from Moldoon's, heading instead toward the newer parts of town, the wooden neighborhoods on the outskirts. Soon she found another amiable inn—the dwarven town was full of them—and seated herself at an outside table, watching passersby: loggers returning from the woods, soot-stained coal-diggers coming from the smithies; teamsters bringing their horses, mules, and oxen into their corrals.

She quickly struck up a conversation with a young dwarf who had stopped by to wet his whistle. Garrin Hammerstrike was his name, and he seemed to know a lot about the town.

"Well, the mayor has been running things while Harn Poleaxe was gone, but now that's bound to change," Garrin said before taking a big gulp from his mug.

"Oh? How long was Mr. Poleaxe gone?"

"About two years, give or take. Went all the way to Kayolin, he did."

"Kayolin?" Gretchan was impressed. Perhaps she had underestimated Poleaxe; few travelers from those parts made it as far as the northern kingdom, and she would be interested in Harn's observations. She thought it odd that, for all of his boasting, Poleaxe hadn't mentioned his trip to that distant place.

Her eyebrows raised as Hammerstrike continued. "Yep. Word is the Mother Oracle asked him to go."

"Really?" She was intrigued by the connection. "I've heard of her. I understand that she's not well?"

Hammerstrike shrugged. "Couldn't say, myself. We never see much of her; she stays inside that little hut, right up at the end of that road, there."

Gretchan saw the little side street, extending toward the wooded ridge that flanked the edge of Hillhome. She made a mental note of the location, then turned back to the talkative local.

"So Harn Poleaxe returned from Kayolin just a few days ago?"

"Only yesterday, it was. Even brought a Kayolin dwarf back with him, they say. Turned out to be a spy—they got him locked in the brig right now."

"You say there's a dwarf from Kayolin right here in Hillhome?"

"Aye-uh. Big fellow too, I hear. But he got the stuffing knocked out of him by Harn, of course. My friend Slate Fireforge helped to bring him in, just today."

"Where is this brig?" she asked.

Garrin chuckled. "Well, it's right around the corner there. But you won't be able to get in. Old Shriff Keenstrike guards the door like a hawk morning, noon, and night."

"Well, I might give it a try. Thanks for the information," she said. She called over a barmaid and handed her a copper. "Give my friend here another drink when he's ready."

A few minutes later, she was approaching the brig, a sturdy building with narrow, barred windows. She guessed that the armed dwarf standing vigilantly at the door must be the reputed Shriff Keenstrike. He was a disreputable-looking fellow with about a week's worth of spare food stored in the tangled mat of his brown beard who watched warily as she neared.

"Hi there," she said, sauntering up the steps and offering him her most dazzling smile.

"Well, uh, hi there, yourself," Shriff stammered, blushing. "What kin I do for you?"

"I'd like to talk to one of your prisoners," she said, leaning close. "Do you think that would be all right?"

"Well, really . . . um, no one's supposed to go in there. Them's the rules. I don't make the rules up; I just enforce 'em."

"Oh, I *promise* not to disturb anything," she breathed. "And it will just be for a few minutes. Surely a big, brave fellow like you can make sure that nothing bad happens. I mean, you look like you really know how to use that sword."

"Well, yes, of course, I do know how to look out for myself," Shriff said. "I suppose it wouldn't do any harm for a few minutes or so." He hesitated, frowning. "What's your business, ma'am?"

"I'm a historian," she said proudly, batting her eyelashes. "I'm here in town to learn about the area, and I always like to take a look at the important government buildings. Who knows, a handsome guy like you, you may end up in my report."

Shriff stared at his shoes, blushing again. He looked up and down the street then turned back to Gretchan. She smiled again, and he was unlocking the door a second later.

Men, she thought. They are so predictable.

She hesitated slightly when the stench of the place reached her nostrils but quickly gathered her determination and marched into the brig. She had certainly smelled worse in the course of her research!

As soon as her eyes adjusted to the gloom, she picked out the mountain dwarf. The other prisoners—she counted four, in two separate cells—were listless and filthy, while the prisoner from Kayolin didn't look quite as abject. Indeed, he glared fiercely at her from his cell at the end of the hall. She advanced purposefully, stopping just outside the barred door.

The prisoner said nothing but stared at her suspiciously. He was unusually tall, and quite handsome under the dirt and bruises. When she smiled her most pleasant smile at him, his expression didn't change. He glowered even more.

"Hi there. I'm told you're from Kayolin," she said. "Is that true?"

"Who wants to know?" he growled. "And what are you doing here?" The Kayolin prisoner was squeezed into the small space, his knees bent, his back against the wall. She realized his hands were behind him and that they were probably bound. His cell was the smallest unit in the place, with barely room enough for him to stand or turn around.

"I'm sorry to intrude," she said sympathetically. "My name is Gretchan Pax. I've been compiling stories, histories, anecdotes about the dwarves of Krynn for some time now, with the goal in mind of writing a book about my travels and observations. I've never had the chance to interview someone from Kayolin, though. I talked my way past the jailer."

"What makes you think I'd want to talk to *you?*" he snapped.

"Well, I don't think there's anything special about me, particularly," she replied, taken aback by his rudeness. After all, *every* male dwarf wanted to talk to her! "I mean, just, you know . . . I'd like to hear about your nation, anything you'd care to tell—I mean, talk about."

Damn, she was stammering like a child!

"Looks like you made someone pretty mad," she said, changing course. "That's quite a bruise under your eye. The word is that you're accused of being a spy. Is that true?"

"True that I'm accused, not true that I'm a spy," he replied stonily. "But why should it matter to you anyway?"

She tried to catch his eye and put some of her usually reliable flirting ability to use, but his head was slightly downcast so his eyes were partly masked by strands of brown hair that hung across his forehead.

"I see your hands are tied," she said, shifting tactics. "I don't see why I shouldn't untie them. You're not dangerous, are you?" She tried to say that last as a joke, but he snorted contemptuously at her feeble humor.

She hesitated. There was something undeniably dangerous about him.

Then, with a shrug, he pushed himself awkwardly to his feet. He turned his back and presented his bound wrists to her, pressing his hands between two of the bars on his cell door.

"What's your name?" she asked as she fumbled with the knots. The cord was a leather thong, twisted tightly. She winced as she saw how it had already cut into his skin. The knot was tight, and she had difficulty, even though her fingers were strong and nimble.

"Don't you have a knife?" he asked impatiently as she strained at the knot.

That remark—and the fact he had mocked her courtesies thus far—irritated her. "No!" she snapped. "But I do have a hammer. Maybe you want me to conk you on the head instead."

For some reason he laughed at that remark, which just made her angrier. She furiously pulled at the leather thong, knowing the line was cutting into his flesh, but the stubborn fellow didn't even give her the satisfaction of reacting to the pain. Finally, she released the knot, and the cord tumbled free. He pulled away from the grate— grabbing up the cord, she noted—and turned to face her, rubbing his wrists.

"Thank you," he said in a subdued tone. "My name is Brandon Bluestone."

"Ah," she replied, her anger melting into sympathy at his introduction. She tried to come up with a pleasant and relevant reply but realized that when she learned the name of a Neidar hill dwarf, or any mountain dwarf of a Thorbardin clan, that name invariably gave her an insight into the subject's clan and background, not to mention all his likely friends or enemies stretching for generations. Yet all her information about Kayolin dated back more than four hundred years. She was at a disadvantage with such a rare specimen.

"I'd like to learn more about Kayolin. Can you tell me, for example, who is the governor there nowadays? Do you know the names of his predecessors?"

"Governor or king?" demanded the prisoner brusquely. He crossed his arms over his chest and leaned against the wall, glaring at some point over her shoulder.

"Will you talk to me politely?" she asked. When he made no reply, she grew angry again. "You said you'd talk to me if I untied your hands!" Gretchan accused.

He snorted and she scowled, remembering that she hadn't actually elicited such a pledge from him. "Look, tell me your story," she said, gesturing to the cage, to the whole sturdy building that was the brig. "Why were you arrested? How did you get here?"

"In the course of the last day, I've been cheated, assaulted, robbed, and locked up," he said coldly. "Why should I talk to you? Why should I trust you? How do I know you even are a historian? You don't look like a historian to me. Maybe you're the spy!"

Unconsciously, Brandon had struck her where she was vulnerable. Some days she wondered if she really was a historian, whether she ever would truly write the book she boasted about. Momentarily speechless, she glared at him.

Brandon glared right back, and she could see his brown eyes smoldering through the tangle of hair that still hung over his forehead. Intriguing eyes, they were, compelling even. Were the eyes of all Kayolin dwarves brown? She made a show of whipping out her notebook and scribbling something down before tossing her head angrily.

"You know, you seem just as stubborn and cantankerous as any other kind of dwarf!" she snapped. "You're always happier in a fight than a conversation. Well, Reorx take you, then! I don't have to put up with this! Not from a hill dwarf and *certainly* not from a mountain dwarf from Kayolin!"

"And what about you?" he shot back. "A hill dwarf, I suppose, like all the other fools around here? I can tell by your tan; no self-respecting mountain dwarf would let herself spend so much time in the sun!"

"You've gotten pretty brown yourself!" she shot back. "Or is that all part of your disguise?"

"Damn you—this is no disguise, and I'm who I claim to be! Can I help it if every one of you ignorant Neidar is too stupid, too stubborn, too all-fired *blind* to see the truth in front of your nose?" he shouted.

"Well, I hope you rot in here, then. I've obviously learned all there is to know about the likes of you!" Gretchan spun and stomped back to the outer door, which Shriff opened at her first knock. She was so irritated that she forgot to thank him and didn't even try to charm him with a smile. Instead, she stomped through the street, thinking of a dozen things she wished she'd said to the stubborn Kayolin dwarf.

She had visited imprisoned dwarves before, and for the most part, they were like any others but usually bored with their imprisonment and eager to tell their stories. But Brandon Bluestone had somehow thrown her off balance. Damn it, it was those eyes! He'd been beaten and robbed and jailed—she found herself believing everything about the few words he'd spoken—and yet he was rude and defiant, even challenging the one person who had offered him some sympathy.

She realized he didn't want sympathy; he wanted freedom and, most likely, vengeance. Maybe he wasn't a spy, but he certainly was dangerous. "Well, let him find vengeance on his own, then!" she grumbled to herself, stomping along the street. "He certainly will get no further help from me!"

The night was young, but she had no stomach for further research or interviews. She wandered around the town for a little while, finally making her way back to the boardinghouse and stopping outside the door of the room where she had left Gus and Kondike. The loud snoring brought a slight smile to her lips; only a gully dwarf could saw lumber like that!

But her irritation returned when she entered her own room. There was no lock, so she pushed the door open and stepped inside. She was surprised to find it utterly dark— she was certain she had left the window curtains open, and there was plenty of lamplight on the street outside. Remembering where the bed was, she stepped gingerly, making her way toward the window.

A tremor of alarm ran down her spine; something was wrong! In the next second, a strong hand clamped over her mouth and someone with a bearded face leaned his mouth close to her ear.

"Now just be quiet, lass, and this will be nice and enjoyable for both of us," he whispered.

She recognized Harn Poleaxe by his voice, but before she could speak, he was pressing her down onto the bed.

——DH——

"Gimme that bottle!" snarled Tufa Rockslinger, lunging for his fellow Klar warrior.

"Get yer own!" snapped Roc Billingstone, punching his comrade in the nose, crunching a few bones and bringing forth a surging gout of blood.

Garn Bloodfist had sensed the simmering tension between the two dwarves and was quick to act.

"Hey, you louts!" shouted the company captain, lunging between the pair as they squared off beside their cookfire. Already the rest of the mountain dwarves were starting to gather around, cheering Tufa and Roc, placing bets, shouldering their way close to the impending fight. The two combatants closed in, and the captain clocked Roc hard on the ear. Tufa retreated when Garn feinted another punch to his already-bleeding nose.

"Stop it!" ordered Garn. His stern tone and commanding presence forced the two combatants to back away from each other. Roc sneered and ostentatiously raised his flask to his lips, while Tufa used his cloak to try to stem the flow of blood from his broken nose.

"Why, I have a mind to report you both to General Shortbeard when we get back to Pax Tharkas!" the captain growled. Otaxx Shortbeard, grizzled veteran of many a campaign, was famous for his intolerance of Klar malcontents. But the troops knew it was an empty threat: the only thing General Shortbeard disliked more than unruly Klar warriors was a certain aggressive—and ambitious—subordinate named Garn Bloodfist. Roc even made the mistake of snickering contemptuously in the face of his officer's threat.

Garn reached out and snatched the bottle from Roc's hand, raising it to his own lips and taking a sip of the searing dwarf spirits. His soldier glared at him but knew better than to challenge his captain on his own turf. After a long pause, Garn handed the bottle back. When he spoke, he made an effort to make his tone calm and reasonable.

"Look, men. I know you're ready for action. I feel the same way. We've been marching through these Reorx-forsaken hills for two weeks now, and we're a long way from Pax Tharkas.

But I can tell you, we'll be swinging our swords before tomorrow night—and not at each other!" he added pointedly.

"Where, then?" demanded one of the Klar warriors. "Another hill dwarf hovel? A couple of huts and a mill? Last time we raided one of them crap holes, all we got was a keg of stale beer and two pigs!"

"So? That bacon was mighty tasty, wasn't it?" retorted Garn. Then he shook his head. "Anyway, that won't happen on this expedition. This time we strike a target worthy of us—all three hundred of us! It's a real thriving town, and it's got wealth. There's a vault, and a smelter where they purify real gold. It has a market and a brewery, and we might even dally a bit with the ladies," he added with a lewd chuckle. "After we take care of their men!"

"What town is that?" asked the questioner with slightly less hostility.

"It's right over these ridges," Garn replied. "It's called Hillhome. After we're done with it," he added with a chuckle, "maybe they'll call it Hellhome."

His troops settled in to their bedrolls with his assurances of imminent action. But Garn, as always when battle loomed, couldn't sleep. He stalked around the periphery of the camp, checking on the status of his sentries. All were awake and bristled and glared at his approach, proving their watchfulness.

Beyond the ring of guards, Garn Bloodfist was alone in the night. But as always when he was by himself, he keenly felt the presence of another.

"Give me strength, my father," he said softly. "Allow me to prepare for my vengeance! Keep my blade keen, my wits sharp, on the morrow! Trip and confound and blind my enemies, so that they will fall before my charge!"

With each word, his voice grew louder. He didn't realize the sentries were watching nervously, hearing his voice rise from the hillside and ring through the night. Garn's fists clenched and he raised them to the sky, holding his pose, allowing his father's resolute strength and unbending will to flow through him.

Then Dashard Bloodfist was before him, his father's bloody face staring down at him from the night sky. That was the exultant truth that brought Garn Bloodfist, so often, under the open skies of the world: the chance to, again, see his father, stare at the gaping wounds that marred his face and neck, that ended his life. Dashard Bloodfist had been killed by dwarves—the rebelling Daergar and Hylar of Jungor Stonespringer's war. He had been betrayed by the troops of his own company because he had trusted soldiers who were not his fellow Klar.

"Revenge!" Garn Bloodfist cried in a voice that was nearly a howl.

In his mind he pictured the houses and shops of Hillhome, imagined his shivering joy as those structures were destroyed, as the hill dwarves perished under the sudden onslaught of his ruthless Klar.

Only it wasn't the Neidar who were the target of his vengeance. They were merely a target of convenience, an enemy that gave him cause to fight, to raid, and to kill. They were capable enough, the hill dwarves, and over the past ten years, they had learned to fear Garn Bloodfist and his Klar. After the next day, they would have still greater cause to be afraid.

But he would fight and kill them only because the real enemy was beyond his reach. The vicious Hylar, the fanatics who followed Jungor Stonespringer in his determination to seal Thorbardin against the world—they were his true enemies. They had killed his father during their civil war and would have killed Garn as well if he hadn't gone into exile with the Failed King.

And Tarn Bellowgranite might be a failure, but for the time being, he provided the Klar with a place to live and a fortress wherein they could keep their battle skills sharp. Tomorrow those skills would come into play again.

But soon, Garn Bloodfist vowed, the Klar would find a way to attack their true enemies. They would shatter the gates of Thorbardin and carry the war, an orgy of killing, into the world under the mountain.

# EIGHTEEN

## DREAMS AND FLIGHT

**B**randon glared through the darkness of the brig. For many long minutes, he didn't move, keeping his eyes fixed upon the door where Gretchan Pax had departed. Her unannounced visit had jarred and unsettled him. He had been steeling himself for a confrontation with Harn Poleaxe or one of the Neidar's agents, and instead the strange dwarf maid came to converse with him, as if he were some kind of tour guide or research subject.

Who did she think she was? Some sort of dwarf queen, apparently!

Still, Brandon acknowledged as he cooled down, she wasn't the person with whom he was really angry; she just happened to be the one who came along while he was stewing. In point of fact, Gretchan had been really something to look at. Her smile, her hair, the pronounced swell in the front of her tunic ... she would have turned heads even amid the loveliest dwarf maids in all Kayolin. Thinking it over, Brandon began to feel a glimmer of gratitude; she had, after all, untied his wrists willingly enough. Though why in Reorx's name didn't she carry a knife, as virtually every other self-respecting dwarf, male or female, did?

Bah! Why was he wasting time thinking about another damn fool hill dwarf? He'd had enough of the Neidar to last him the rest of his lifetime! He slumped against the cool, damp wall of his cell, crossing his arms over his chest and closing his eyes.

"Psst! Hey, you. Brandon, right? Is it true, what she said?"

Brandon looked up in surprise. He was being addressed in a hoarse whisper by one of the two dwarf prisoners closest to his cell, both of whom he had guessed to be mountain dwarves. The fellow's beard bristled, and his hair sprouted from far down on his forehead. His eyes were pale and milky, but his expression was genuinely curious.

"What about what she said?" Brandon replied warily.

"That you're a mountain dwarf? That you come from Kayolin? Up north, across the Newsea?"

"Yeah, that part's true," he acknowledged. He studied the bristle-haired mountain dwarf. "I take it you're no hill dwarf either?"

The other dwarf scowled and spit. "I like to keep as much space as I can between me and the filthy Neidar." He chuckled grimly. "Seems like they want to keep company with me, though."

"Tough luck, that. Are you from Thorbardin?" Brandon asked curiously.

The other dwarf shook his head. "You really are from out of town, aren't you. There's no dwarf gone into or out of Thorbardin in many years. The new thane sealed the place right after Tarn Bellowgranite was exiled."

"But there are mountain dwarves living outside of Thorbardin, then?"

The other dwarf shrugged. "In a few places. Pax Tharkas, mainly. That's where Bellowgranite ended up with his exiles. They're the ones stirring up most of the trouble between the clans—his Klar captain, Bloodfist, is a real butcher. Likes to make war and leaves it for the rest of us to live with the consequences."

"So there is still warring between mountain and hill dwarf?" Brandon pressed. Maybe that explained a little about Poleaxe, who had talked with hatred about the mountain dwarves, Brandon remembered, and appeared to be some kind of leader among his own kind.

"The feuding and fighting never really ended," said his informer. "Take us. We're simple Theiwar miners, working our claims on the far side of the Kharolis. "Of course, we can't trade with our own nation anymore, not since the kingdom was sealed. But we try to make an honest living; there's a few towns and delvings of our kind in the mountains. We were unlucky enough to get swept up by the Neidar when they was marching against Tarn Bellowgranite and his men."

"When was this?" Brandon asked.

The Theiwar shrugged. "Maybe a year ago. Hard to keep track of time in this place."

"What happened? Were the Neidar attacking Pax Tharkas?" asked the dwarf from Kayolin. "I heard that place was practically impregnable."

"Well, maybe it is. I don't think the Neidar was trying to take the fortress, though. They just made an ambush for when the Klar came out and tried to wipe 'em out on the trail."

"But they didn't succeed?" Brandon guessed.

"Nope," the Theiwar said with evident satisfaction. "Say what you will about those wild-ass Klar; they're damn fine fighters. I think the hill dwarves lost a couple dozen of their men, and the rest went running for home. We were one of the lucky ones, I suppose, prisoners."

"Yeah," the speaker's companion said bitterly. "Our mine just happened to be right on their way."

"I know a thing or two about bad luck," Brandon agreed. "Mine hasn't exactly been gold-plated either these last few days."

"I hear you, mate," said the Theiwar.

"What were you charged with?" asked Brandon. "Did you get a fair trial?"

"Fair trial?" asked the Theiwar, poking his friend in the ribs. Both sat back, roaring with laughter. "Who's been telling you fairy tales?"

Brandon slumped back into the darkness, thinking about the sad twists and turns his life had taken—a life, he was forced to conclude, that might not last more than another day or two. The darkness, the silence, the stench of the place surrounded him.

But when he finally slept, he dreamed of a golden-haired dwarf maid. He smiled at her, rather than scowling, and once again, he felt her nimble fingers working to release his bonds.

———DH———

Gus wandered through a field of glorious, colorful vegetables. He picked and ate them as he strolled, but he never seemed to get full. He came to a stream, and a fish jumped right into his hands. It was so delicious, he halted on the bank and waited for another one, which jumped out of the water two seconds later. Everywhere he looked, he saw food, a natural banquet practically begging to be eaten—by him!

And he did his best. He rooted around on the ground, pulling up carrots, chomping contentedly on the orange crispness. He saw other vegetables hanging off trees, and though they hung on branches high above the ground, when he approached, the limbs of the trees dipped low and he plucked and ate the bounty of the forest. When he was finished eating, for a little while at least, he ran through the meadow, and nobody chased him.

Life had never been better. He was warm, happy, well fed, safe . . .

Until he heard the ominous, rumbling growl. The sound

was deep, obviously made by a very large creature, deep and menacing.

"Kondike?" he called, looking through the trees, across the nearby meadow. But there was no sign of the big dog.

The Aghar spun through a full circle, but all he saw was the meadow, the meandering stream. He saw no dog, no threat.

But when the growl sounded again, the surrounding trees seemed to move in closer, loom higher and darker. Soon they towered over his head, casting him in chilly shade. He flinched and looked up at the sky, suddenly remembering the creature that was stalking him.

But the sky, though dark and gray, was empty of fearsome creatures, or even birds.

The third time he heard the growl, it was right beside him, and he awakened.

Heart pounding, he realized he was in a dark room, and in a flash he remembered Hillhome. Gretchen was in another room, but Kondike was right beside him and growling fiercely at something.

Gus squealed in terror and burrowed under the blanket that had somehow gotten all twisted and tangled while he was sleeping. Even as he dived for cover, his face popped out the other end. He put his hands over his eyes to hide himself, daring to split his fingers slightly and look around.

The big dog stood beside the bed, facing the door, growling deep within his barrel chest. That augured danger, but Gus quickly thought of someone else who he ought to protect.

Gretchan! He sprang out of bed—or would have if he weren't entangled by the unaccustomed luxury of a blanket, which tripped him onto his face. As soon as he scrambled to his feet, he raced to the door and pushed it open. Kondike knocked him aside, the big dog lunging into the hallway, still growling. Nothing was in the hallway.

Teeth bared, Kondike moved to stand stiff legged outside of the neighboring room.

Gus heard sounds in the dwarf maid's room. His hand was trembling, his knees knocking together, but he reached for the latch, ready to open the door.

——DH——

"Wait! Stop!" hissed Gretchan, intentionally keeping her voice low. Poleaxe had overpowered her physically; she had to use her wits to save herself.

"I've been waiting all night while you cavorted around Hillhome. How dare you tell me you're going to bed and then leave! You're a teasing, lying wench, you are!"

She was astounded at the sheer animosity, the malevolence, betrayed in the big dwarf's voice. She struggled in growing panic, trying to reach the small hammer she wore at her belt. She gasped at Poleaxe's strength as, with one hand, he pinned both of hers over her head. His other hand reached for the buckle of her belt and snapped it free. The belt, with her only weapon attached to it, tumbled to the floor.

"Let's talk this over!" she urged, trying not to panic. "Let me go!"

"We did enough talking to about wear out my tonsils," growled the hill dwarf. "I'm ready for some different fun." He grasped her breast, roughly squeezing, laughing at her struggles.

"Ouch—you're hurting me!" she protested.

"Well, don't resist me, then," he replied, taunting. "I'll be gentle if *you* will."

Then the door to the room burst open, and Kondike was there, a snarling missile tipped with sharp, white teeth smashing into Poleaxe, knocking him right off the bed and onto the floor. Dog and dwarf rolled across the tiny room, smashing into the table, twisting and grappling on the worn rug. Gus came charging in right after the dog, grabbing one of the Neidar's feet—Harn had removed his boots already—and biting him on the big toe.

"Ouch, damn you!" snapped the hill dwarf, trying to kick at the gully dwarf while he held the dog's head at bay. Despite the feet that flailed at him, Gus held on tenaciously, even as his little body was thumped and kicked against the wall.

Breathing hard, Gretchan scrambled to her feet. Poleaxe lay on his back, grunting curses as, with both hands, he held Kondike's head away from his face. The dog was snarling viciously as Gus bit down a second time, and again the hill dwarf howled in pain. The struggling Neidar bashed into the wall of the small room and rolled back across the floor, nearly knocking Gretchan over. She stepped back, looking for an opening, as Kondike pressed in, snapping his jaws, his teeth just inches from the hill dwarf's nose.

Where was her belt? There—she spotted it as the combatants rolled around on the floor. Gretchan reached down and snatched up the hammer that was suspended by a little sling. It was a small tool, light and silvery, but its looks were deceiving. She brought it down heavily against Poleaxe's skull, and with another grunt, the hill dwarf collapsed limply.

"All right, boys, thanks," she said, gently touching her big dog's shoulder. Kondike relaxed slightly, allowing her to ease him off the dwarf's still form. "You can stop biting him now," she told Gus, who was leaving bloody teeth marks on a third toe.

"What this bluphsplunging doofar do?" demanded the gully dwarf, removing Poleaxe's foot from his mouth but holding it close enough that he could resume his attack at a moment's notice. Kondike, hackles up, growled at the unconscious hill dwarf.

"He was waiting for me; he attacked me," Gretchan said, feeling a queasy sickness as the full reality of the awful situation sank in. "I don't know what would have happened if the two of you hadn't rushed in to help. Thank you, again."

"He not dead yet. Want me kill him?" suggested Gus with a little too much enthusiasm for the dwarf maid's comfort. She regarded the motionless hill dwarf with revulsion, but killing him was not even a remote possibility; it would have been a betrayal of everything she stood for: decency, honor, civilized behavior. Perhaps she ought to have him arrested, but then, thinking of her encounter with the Kayolin prisoner, who had professed his innocence yet was stuck in jail, she didn't have much faith in the local justice.

"No, we can't—we won't," she said immediately. She looked around the bare room, at her backpack—it had tumbled open somehow, scattering her few possessions— and suddenly knew they had to get out of that place. Hillhome had proved inhospitable.

"We're going to leave," she announced. "Tonight. After I go talk to one more person."

She quickly gathered up her possessions and strapped them into her pack. Kondike and Gus hurried to keep up as she left the inn at a trot and made her way to the shadowy street where Garrin Hammerstrike had pointed to the oracle's hut. A few minutes later, she stood in the darkness of an overhanging barn roof, studying her objective. The house of the Mother Oracle was obvious: it stood at the end of the narrow lane, dilapidated and dark. There were no other houses, barns, or other structures nearby.

"You two wait here," she ordered sternly, worrying more about disobedience from the gully dwarf than from the dog.

Her staff in her hand, she started down the street. She strained for some sensory suggestion—sight or sound, smell, or even something on a more subconscious level— that would help her prepare to enter the small house. She felt nothing at all, and that fact disturbed her deeply. It was as if some kind of protective screen surrounded the house, like the building itself was prepared to resist her.

She approached the battered, shabby front door and she felt the resistance more directly. It took an extra effort of will to take the last two steps to bring her up to the portal. Gretchan, always confident and serene in the face of danger, felt a surprising unease and hesitated to touch the door. Uncertain whether she would knock or just push it open, she started and gasped when she her a sharp voice from within.

"Go away!"

The speaker was an old woman, she discerned, but if she were weak or invalid, that frailty did not transfer into her voice: the words were vibrant, thrumming with a sense of power that almost forced Gretchan backward. It took all of her resolve to reply.

"I want to talk to you. Will you let me in?" she asked directly.

"I said, go away!" The words were tinged with clear anger.

"I will not!" Gretchan shot back. "I've come to Hillhome, traveled hundreds of miles, to meet you. You are known in places far beyond the Kharolis range. Now will you open this door, or must I shout at you from the front step?"

Surprisingly, the door creaked open, and the Mother Oracle stood in the entryway, confronting the dwarf maid. She was shorter than Gretchan, thin, and wrapped in a threadbare shawl. Her face was creased with wrinkles and her eyes were milky pale, seemingly blind—except that the dwarf maid felt those useless eyes examining her very carefully. Gretchan sensed the power in her, and her hand tightened around her staff. The anvil at the head of the pole glimmered slightly, and the oracle snorted in contempt.

"Do you think the light of the Forge can protect you here? Hillhome is lost to you—and soon, so will be the rest of the Kharolis!"

"Who are you?" demanded Gretchan, clinging to her staff even more tightly than before.

"You may learn someday, but that day will be your last!" sneered the old crone. She waved a hand, and abruptly fire crackled around the door of her house, searing yellow flames surging into the night. The heat forced Gretchan to recoil.

"Help!" screamed the old woman, and she did sound feeble, weak, and terrified. "I am being attacked!"

A second later Gretchan heard doors bang open farther down the street. The old woman screamed again, and other dwarves, swarming out of their houses, shouted in alarm and surged toward the flames.

"It's Mother Oracle!" someone cried.

Gretchan backed up farther, throwing up her hands to screen her face from the searing heat. She glanced over her shoulder and saw a half dozen or more hill dwarves charging toward her. Some carried buckets, but at least a few bore pitchforks or axes. She turned back to the hut and saw that the oracle had slammed the door—with herself inside. The flames surged higher, but the dwarf maid discerned that they were not consuming, not even charring, the dry planking on the outside of the building.

"Hey, you! Get away from there!" came another shout, undeniably hostile.

"You old fox," Gretchan declared, shaking her head in dismay. With no good choice in front of her, she clutched her staff, put down her head, and ran into the darkness. It took her ten minutes to circle around to find Gus and Kondike where she had left them. By then, she saw that the flames were out, and she was not surprised to observe that the oracle's house was none the worse for the experience. A number of agitated hill dwarves milled about in the narrow land in front of the hut.

"Come on," she said in disgust to her two relieved companions. "We're getting out of here."

——DH——

Harn Poleaxe came to with a throbbing headache. His mind was foggy, but when he remembered what had happened—he had had the wench on her bed, was holding her down, when that ferocious dog and stupid gully dwarf had interrupted them—his fury wiped away his pain. He stood, staggering slightly. He limped on a sore foot and looked down at his bloody toes, cursing the damned little Aghar that had dared to chomp him.

A quick look around was enough to show him that the beautiful dwarf maid had taken her possessions and gone. How dare she! A low growl rumbled in his chest. Then he sagged onto the bed, too tired to pursue her—she was probably long gone, anyway—his rage fading away. Holding his throbbing head in his hand, he just felt weary.

A momentary thought flashed though his mind: had she taken *everything*?

Quickly he reached into his boot, still on the floor behind the door where he had left it as he prepared for his encounter with the voluptuous maid. He felt weak with relief as he touched the cold glass and pulled out the bottle of dwarf spirits, the one that she had left on her night table. The one he had quickly stolen for his own.

He'd been pleasantly surprised to discover it—she didn't seem the type to be carrying strong drink around—but he'd snatched it up right after he broke into her room, having the foresight to set it aside for later. She hadn't taken everything with her, and if she were going to leave something, he was glad it was that bottle of strong drink. Just what he wanted and needed right at the moment. It was all he needed. Poleaxe gazed fondly at that perfect blend of distilled spirits, swirling like liquid treasure in the flask.

"Midwarren Pale." he read. It sounded like a mountain dwarf vintage but not one he was familiar with; that didn't matter; he had broad tastes when it came to strong drink.

He could resist no longer. Pulling out the cork, he placed

the bottle to his lips and tilted it upward. The first drops of the liquid touched his lips, and he experienced an exquisite agony, a pain pure and piercing that rapidly became an overwhelming pleasure. It was not dwarf spirits, not even a foul and sour version of that splendid drink.

The elixir trickled down his throat, flowing from his belly into his limbs, invigorating him, thrilling him. He gulped down the contents of the bottle in one long guzzle, feeling a liquid fire surging in his chest. He trembled, feeling the rush all over his body, black and smothering but at the same time comforting and protecting.

Suddenly convulsing, the hill dwarf fell onto the floor, the empty bottle tumbling from his nerveless fingers. His body quivered as the essence of the elixir seeped through every fiber of his being. Shivering, he lay helpless on the floor, surrendering to wave after wave of ecstasy. He felt vibrantly, fully, sensually alive in a way he had never been before.

He couldn't move, could barely breathe. But his mind was filled with powerful images, scenes of conquest and triumph.

Lying there, almost peacefully, he recalled the command of the Mother Oracle and knew the Kayolin prisoner must die. He, Harn Poleaxe, would make it happen, and the people of his village would hail him as a hero for doing the deed.

Then he stared into the haze of the distance, and it was as though his vision were more keen than it had ever been before. He swept closer until he stood in the middle of a battle, untouched by enemy blade, laying waste to all sides. He saw a host of foes, dead and dying all around him. He saw an army of Neidar, charging at his command, sweeping toward a high fortress.

Yes, he, Harn Poleaxe, was a great leader of dwarves!

He recognized the fortress even as his consciousness slipping away: the two towers, the long connecting wall, and the gate—the gate standing open to admit him, to admit his army.

Finally, the towers and walls came crashing down, and Harn Poleaxe stood victorious upon the wreckage of Pax Tharkas.

——DH——

The minion soared over the town of hill dwarves, flying low since the lights were dimmed with most of the citizens retired for the night. The red and white moons had set, leaving the black moon master of the skies—for those, like the minion, who could sense its presence. The creature watched from the air as the dwarf maid who had burned it with her horrible staff stalked into the street, accompanied by her dog and the gully dwarf that was the creature's quarry. But she still walked with that pole in her hand, swinging it easily at her side, and the minion dared not approach, for fear of that searing brightness.

Snarling like a rasp of wind through dry branches, the monster banked, hovering above the two dwarves and the dog. Its nostrils flared and its red eyes glowed as it sought the spoor of the treasure that the gully dwarf carried, the flask of potion that he had stolen from the wizard in Thorbardin. The minion's keen senses probed, seeking, looking, smelling. Its master had commanded it to retrieve that elixir, and it had to find it.

But to its great surprise, its senses told it that the potion was no longer carried by either the gully dwarf or the female.

Once again the gaunt creature veered, curling through the skies over the town, circling, roaming, seeking. It found itself in a quandary, one of conflicting goals: the wizard had charged it with killing the Aghar and returning to Thorbardin with the missing potion. No longer was the potion in the possession of the gully dwarf, though.

The minion stared at the dwarves as they strode rapidly

down the road and out of town, thinking of that tall, magical staff.

The dwarves could go, for the time being. The minion would circle in the skies over the town and try to figure out what had happened to the potion.

# NINETEEN

# ON TRIAL

**B**randon awakened with the loud opening of the brig's door. Several dwarves entered the building and stood near the entrance while the jailer, together with the bullying Neidar called Rune, came swaggering all the way back to the mountain dwarf's cell. Rune flourished a sword while the turnkey unlocked the barrier and pulled it open. Brandon wondered what the bullying Neidar had done with his venerable axe.

"Time to come out and play," Rune sneered. "You get to be the center of attention!"

Pushing himself to his feet, Brandon emerged from the cell. But they didn't know his hands were no longer tied. He owed the dwarf maid historian a favor, he reckoned.

Abruptly he jabbed his elbow into the jailer so hard, he knocked the dwarf into one of the barred doors. With a curse and a clatter of metal, the filthy turnkey tumbled to the floor.

"Watch yourself!" Rune declared, jabbing the tip of his sword against Brandon's side until the prisoner swiftly twisted out of the way and grabbed the hill dwarf by the wrist, pinning his sword hand against the bars of an adjacent cell.

"Hey—how'd you get your hands untied?" Rune demanded, squirming. The jailer scrambled to his feet and moved toward Brandon, but he froze at the glare from the burly Hylar.

The other dwarves at the door, swords drawn, edged closer, and Brandon could see there was no escape. Releasing Rune's wrist and brushing past the jailer, Brandon shrugged and continued toward the outer door and the painfully bright daylight outside.

"Good luck," he heard the Theiwar prisoner say loudly, and he grunted an acknowledgment.

It was morning, he saw as he emerged, and Hillhome was bustling with pedestrians. At first he guessed that the moderately crowded street was busy with hill dwarves making their way to work. Only most of them weren't going to jobs. They were going to his trial.

Rune prodded him down the steps and toward the middle of town. The gathered hill dwarves watched him with barely concealed hostility, and the bulk of the crowd followed along as the Neidar led his prisoner toward a small square in the center of Hillhome.

A raised platform occupied one end of the open area. A pair of hill dwarf guards, each carrying a long-hafted battle axe, stood to either side of a large, thronelike chair—which was unoccupied. To the left, a wooden rack had been erected, and judging from the manacles attached to the upper and lower supports, Brandon deduced that the contraption was a means of immobilizing, while undoubtedly torturing, a spread-eagled prisoner. He felt a twinge of fear but resolved not to give his captors the satisfaction of seeing him squirm. Instead, he swaggered into the plaza with all the bravado he could muster.

The edges of the square were crowded with muttering hill dwarves, mostly males conspicuously armed with a variety of weapons. They glared at Brandon as he was pushed into the center of the square. Rune stood right behind the prisoner, his sharp blade prodding the mountain dwarf at intervals. The dwarf from Kayolin tried to scan the crowd, looking for a glimpse of blonde hair, of that pretty, oval face with the small, upturned nose. He felt surprisingly dejected when he realized Gretchan Pax wasn't here to record his fate.

"All set for the festivities, are you?"

He turned to see Slate Fireforge eyeing him. The hill dwarf had ambled up behind him, and while his expression wasn't exactly friendly, nor was it as hostile as so many others in the crowd.

"Don't see that I have much choice," Brandon replied with a shrug, trying to appear nonchalant. He squinted at Fireforge. "Why'd you stop him from killing me that morning up in the hills? You don't believe him, do you? You know I'm not really a spy, don't you?"

Fireforge made a face, half bemused, half grimace. "Can't say one way or the other, to tell the truth. But I believe there's a proper way to do things, and slicing your head off on a rock up there just didn't seem, well, proper. And Harn Poleaxe knew that too, or he wouldn't have listened to me."

"He seems to be a pretty important fellow around here. Why is everyone so anxious to do anything he says?"

The hill dwarf pondered the question for a while but finally answered. "He comes from money—his father was the richest goldsmith in the north hills. And he's always been a leader. Quite handy with a sword . . . and with the ladies."

"And with a bottle," Brandon noted, his bitterness showing.

"Aye-uh, that too. But mainly it was when that old woman, whom they call the Mother Oracle, came to town, 'bout ten years ago. She took him under her wing, so to speak, and he's been on a run of good luck and prosperity since then. I hear it was her sent him to Kayolin, to look for that stone you brought down here."

"Who's this Mother Oracle?" Brandon asked.

"An old, blind dwarf woman, is all," Fireforge replied. "Claims to have some mystical powers. I guess she's given Harn Poleaxe some good advice, though." He nodded at the other side of the plaza, where the crowd was starting to stir. "Looks like the show's about to start. Good luck to you," he said, apparently sincere.

"I'll need it," Brandon muttered. "But I don't think I'm going to get it."

He stared at the platform with its lofty chair, a veritable throne, and was not surprised to see Harn Poleaxe swagger into view, pushing his way through the crowd that parted for him. He was dressed in a fur cape and shiny black boots, looking for all the world as if he were the lord of the place.

But a closer look at the hill dwarf leader did surprise him—just as it apparently surprised the others in the crowd, who whispered to each other or simply stared at the hulking figure of the Neidar.

For Harn Poleaxe had changed considerably from the last time Brandon had laid eyes on him. His already oversized body seemed to have grown bigger, so that he towered over the biggest Neidar of his bodyguards. His head, in particular, looked huge and swollen, with his eyes receding into deep, almost cavernous, sockets. Several warts had sprouted on his cheeks, and the hill dwarf scratched at one of them as if it gave him great pleasure. He twitched in a sudden nervous gesture, looking behind him and glaring. Then, as Poleaxe neared the chair on the platform, those eyes turned menacingly at the Kayolin dwarf. He was a new, strangely transformed, frighteningly different Poleaxe.

Brandon met that glare even as he felt its power. A wickedness lurked in Poleaxe's presence, an abiding evil that, somehow, hadn't been obvious before, during his long journey with the hill dwarf. Poleaxe puffed out his barrel chest and strutted back and forth on the raised platform, and some in the crowd audibly gasped at his remarkably strapping presence. His arms, too, seemed to have grown in size and length, and his muscular limbs swung easily, his fists seemingly reaching to his knees.

"We are here to usher in a new dawn of Neidar pride," Poleaxe proclaimed, even his voice louder and more fearsome than before. "And to rid ourselves of the symbol of an old enemy." With a flourish, he lifted a leather pouch that Brandon recognized—for he himself had worn it around his waist on the long journey southward from Kayolin. Harn pulled the Bluestone out of that pouch, holding it up so all in the plaza could see.

"This is the stone that the Mother Oracle sent me all the way to Kayolin to find. I return with it now, in triumph!" he declared.

Most of the crowd watched silently, though a few of Poleaxe's personal guard shouted hurrahs for their leader. With another broad gesture, Harn raised another stone, one he plucked from another pouch at his side. Brandon stared in surprise, realizing the object was nearly identical in shape and size to the Bluestone, except that it was a deep and shimmering green color.

"And this is the stone that our beloved Mother Oracle herself brought to Hillhome, nearly ten years ago," Harn declared loudly. "She told us then that we needed both of them to work the will of Reorx. See how they match and complement each other! Now we have them both!"

The loud cheers came from all around, all quarters of the Neidar crowd. The big hill dwarf then set the two colored stones down on a small table beside his chair and waved his hand, a gesture for silence that the citizens of Hillhome quickly heeded. It was then that Brandon saw his axe, the weapon of Balric Bluestone, sitting on that same table—it was like a display of Harn's prizes, all stolen from a betrayed companion. Poleaxe glared about the square, scratching at the wart on his cheek, then abruptly raised his hands in the air, fists clenched. With a sudden twitch, he dropped his right hand, finger extended, to point at Brandon.

"But it is not only good news that I bring you, my friends and fellows," Poleaxe said, his voice ominously lowered. "Here today we have an enemy in our midst, and he presents a danger not just to our hopes and ambitions, but to our very survival."

Suddenly, Brandon, seething inside, was keenly aware of hundreds of Neidar eyes turning to regard him with a mingling of accusation, distrust, and anger.

Finally Harn took his seat on the large throne. "I recognize the prisoner," he cried, his voice booming through the suddenly silent square. "He is a son of the mountain dwarves and came all the way from Kayolin to Hillhome. Who will recite the charges against him?"

"He is accused of being a mountain dwarf spy!" grandiosely declared Rune, stepping forward and turning to regard Brandon with a sneer. "He came hither to infiltrate our lands, to gain intelligence and to purchase agents of sedition!"

"That's a lie!" Brandon shouted. "I came—"

Rune's backhand blow caught him across the mouth, knocking him staggering backward.

"Silence!" roared Poleaxe. "How dare you address this court? Gag the prisoner!"

Immediately rough hands pulled on Brandon's hair, yanking his head back while a cloth was wound across his face. Only when the muzzle was wrapped tight and knotted behind his head was the prisoner allowed to stand again on his own.

"Now what proof can you offer?" demanded Poleaxe of Rune.

"He was taken in the night, on the very border of Hillhome's lands, captured as he tried to sneak into town!" shouted one of the dwarves Brandon recognized as one of Poleaxe's gang.

"Yes, he was traveling off the known roads," cried another, pointing a stubby, accusing finger. "Truly, he was determined to arrive at Hillhome unnoticed."

"And there is word from Flatrock: there, he pretended to be a hill dwarf, so he could pass in our midst without anyone knowing his true nature," called a third. "A lie!" the Neidar spit. "What more proof do we need that he is a spy!"

The onlookers shouted and jeered.

Brandon twisted in the grip of his captors, struggling to speak, but the crowd of hill dwarves only laughed at his inarticulate squawking. The gag dug into his cheeks, and he felt his eyes bugging out as he strained. He caught a glimpse of Slate Fireforge, but even that hill dwarf, who had insisted on his trial, turned away, unwilling to meet the prisoner's eyes. It seemed that whatever vestige of fortune he'd ever possessed had deserted him entirely. He heard his doom as Harn continued to rant.

"Dwarves of Hillhome! My fellow Neidar. We have been blessed by the guidance of the Mother Oracle, who has kept us from disaster these many years. Her wisdom sent me on my quest. We have seen the evidence in the shape of this blue stone that is our destiny. And we have heard how the prisoner tried to deceive and sneak his way into our midst. I suspect his true mission was to steal and abscond with these precious stones!"

He let the charge hang in the air then stood with his fists planted on his hips. "This court has seen enough!" declared Poleaxe, his eyes sweeping the crowd, meeting only nods and muttered encouragement from all present. "We sentence him to death by burning! Secure him to the rack! Bring tinder! And let us watch the spy die!"

"I should kill bad dwarf!" Gus repeated for the hundredth time, as he and Gretchan trudged through the darkness across the rugged landscape away from Hillhome. They encountered neither friend nor foe; no one was about at that hour. The dwarf maid maintained a vigorous pace, and the Aghar had to trot along breathlessly in order to keep up.

"Why you not let me kill him?" he asked forlornly, catching up and tugging on her sleeve.

Gretchan stopped momentarily. She was still shaken by the confrontation with the Mother Oracle and by the aftermath of Harn's attack. She shook her head, heaving a sigh. "I confess—if there was ever a time I felt inclined to resort to violence, that was the time. But there's always too much killing among dwarves. I refuse to be a part of it." She smiled and patted Gus's head. "Or to let my protectors be a part of it. Still, thank you. You were very brave, rescuing me."

"I rescue you!" the Aghar said proudly. "*Next* time I kill!" he added, smacking his fist into his palm.

The dwarf maid patted his head again. "Oh dear, I trust there won't *be* a next time. Come on," she said. "I want to make it to the top of this ridge before it's full daylight. We don't want anyone in Hillhome to spot us and know where we are . . . or where we're going."

"Good deal. Where are we going?" asked Gus as Kondike bounded up a steep cluster of rocks. The big, black dog paused, his short tail wagging, as he looked back at the two dwarves and impatiently waited for the two to catch up.

"Well now that you mention it, I don't really know," Gretchan replied, sitting down on a big rock as she caught her breath. They had been climbing for more than an hour, making their way from the valley to high ground. She decided it was time for a break and pulled out her pipe.

Carefully she started to fill the bowl. "Away from here, for sure. There are lots of other towns I have yet to visit," the dwarf maid noted. "And, too, there's Pax Tharkas."

"What Patharkas?" Gus asked, his eyes narrowing suspiciously. It must have sounded like the name of a dark mage or a dragon, to his ears.

Before Gretchan could reply, they heard a low growl from Kondike. They looked up to see the dog springing down from the ridge top toward them. The dog crouched in the rocks nearby. His hackles bristled as he stared and growled into the dawn light to the east.

"Get down," Gretchan whispered, quickly tucking her unlit pipe away. Gus immediately hunkered down beside her. Heart pounding, the gully dwarf stared across the rocky ground, wondering what terrible danger would befall them next.

They saw a file of dwarves walking along, just below the crest of the ridge, heading directly toward their hiding place. Each of the dwarves wore a metal breastplate and a helmet. They were armed with an assortment of weapons, including axes, hammers, swords, and spears, and they marched along in a narrow formation. Beards bristling, they looked this way and that with wide, intensely staring eyes.

Gus huddled in the shadows between the rocks as the dwarves marched past, barely a stone's throw away from them. "Klar!" he whispered in Gretchan's ear, obviously recognizing them.

She nodded, touching a finger to his lips and silencing him.

The company finally passed them by and continued on down the slope. By the time the sun was up, they had disappeared into a small grove of trees at the bottom of the valley.

"I fear you are right. They are Klar, and they're on their way to attack Hillhome," Gretchan said with a heavy heart.

"Why sad? Hillhome bad place!" Gus declared.

"No, it isn't so bad, really," she said. "Even if there's a bad dwarf here and there, or more than a few for that matter, there are many more that live normal lives and try to stay out of trouble. Anyway it just means more killing—dwarves killing dwarves."

"Where from those killer Klar?" asked Gus, growing more brave once the heavily armed band had disappeared from sight. "Thorbardin?"

"I don't think so. I don't see how they can be from under the mountain. Unless things have changed, the gates of Thorbardin are still sealed," Gretchan explained. "That's what really bothers me. I think they must have come from Pax Tharkas."

"Patharkas!" echoed Gus worriedly.

Gretchan sighed heavily, putting her head in her hands. She pushed herself to her feet, her face dry, her expression stony.

"Come on," she said. "Let's get going."

———DH———

The hill dwarves wasted no time. As soon as Poleaxe pronounced Brandon's death sentence, a number of burly Neidar grabbed hold of the Kayolin dwarf and carried him over to a square-framed rack. The prisoner struggled but was easily overpowered by the half dozen captors competing for who would punch and drag him. His arms were hoisted so that cuffs could be snapped around his wrists. Next, his legs were pulled apart, each ankle secured by a manacle, until he was helplessly spread-eagled in the middle of the stout, wooden frame. His captors, on a grunted count of *one, two, three,* hoisted the rack to a vertical position, so the condemned dwarf had a good view of the entire crowd.

No sooner were the braces snapped shut on his limbs than other hill dwarves rushed forward with tinder—bits of twigs and some dry straw—that they hastily spread on the ground around him. More wood was passed forward, stout logs that would burn long and hot. Brandon tugged desperately at his manacles and tried to kick his legs free, but he was firmly trapped. Struggling to speak despite the gag that still choked him, he vowed not to let the barbarous hill dwarves witness his fear. He wished he would die swiftly.

So engrossed was he in his own miserable drama that he didn't immediately notice the commotion erupting on the other side of the square. The hill dwarves who had been carrying logs toward the rack abruptly dropped their loads and sprinted away from the platform. Neidar began to shout, drawing weapons, surging away from Brandon. Only then did he hear the clash of steel and realize some sort of battle was under way.

A phalanx of armed and armored dwarves was streaming into the plaza, charging in tight lines down the city's main street. The hill dwarves, utterly taken by surprise, fell back initially before the disciplined attackers. Brandon cheered mutely as he saw the bully Rune go down, felled by an attacker's hammer blow to the head. The newcomers were wild eyed, Brandon noted, with long beards tucked into their belts. They wore black armor and carried shields of the same color and were armed with a mixture of axes and swords—and a few crossbows too, Brandon saw, as a rank of archers raised their weapons and fired a volley of bolts into the hill dwarves still gathered around the central platform.

"Rally to me, Neidar!" Harn Poleaxe cried, leaping down into their midst. He waved a mighty sword over his head, his roaring voice cutting through the chaos. Hill dwarves cheered, and those who had weapons readied them, coalescing around the big warrior.

"Charge!" Poleaxe cried, and immediately the hill dwarves followed his lead as he rushed toward the armored dwarves who had swarmed into town.

The two forces came together in the middle of the square, blades clanging against breastplates, boots pounding on the pavement. Shouts invoking the name of Reorx rose from throats on both sides. Screaming maids and children fled, while more hill dwarves, some strapping on helmets or breastplates, rushed toward the fight from the surrounding streets.

The attackers maintained their steady advance with impressive discipline, Brandon noted. Shoulder to shoulder, they formed a wedge and used their heavy shields to push the defenders back, sometimes sweeping them right off their feet. They came on with full-throated, almost joyous battle cries, staring with crazed, bulging eyes, swinging their weapons with brutal fury. Brandon recognized the newcomers as members of the clan Klar, but they were more disciplined, more organized, than any Klar he knew of.

The fallen were trampled as the attacking dwarves gradually steamrolled their way across the square. Their shields edge to edge formed a wall of steel that allowed only slight gaps wide enough for a sword or axe to come stabbing out from the phalanx. Many Neidar fell, wounded or killed, and the rest were slowly forced back. Soon the attacking force reached the raised platform, and the last fighting swirled around the dais, hill dwarves standing their ground around Poleaxe's great chair. Swords and axes bashed against armor, and the cries of the wounded and dying mingled with shouted commands and hoarse battle cries.

On that chair, Brandon remembered with a jolt of excitement—and trepidation—lay the Bluestone and its emerald twin. Desperately he resumed his struggle to move, but the chains fastened to the manacles only allowed him to thrash impotently. Who were those attackers, he wondered? Fellow mountain dwarves, of course. But where did they come from, and why?

He could do nothing to free himself. The battle surrounded the immobilized prisoner, who was ignored by combatants on both sides. A pair of hill dwarves, wielding short swords, fell back until they were planted right in front of him, staunchly contesting a trio of attackers who bashed their sword blades with heavy axes. One Neidar made a lunge, momentarily forcing the trio to retreat, but when the other Neidar tried to slip past Brandon, the captive was able to stretch out his foot a little and trip the hill dwarf into the pile of tinder under the rack.

An attacking dwarf brought his axe down hard, and the fallen Neidar's head rolled from his shoulders. That Klar suddenly noticed Brandon and pulled off his gag.

"Who are you?" he asked.

"An enemy of your enemy!" gasped Brandon. "How about a chop against these brackets?"

With a wicked grin, the mountain dwarf brought his bloody axe blade down, splitting the beam holding his ankle bracelets. Another sideways whack broke the side support, and the square rack tumbled apart, falling to the ground and taking Brandon with it.

"All right. But now you're on your own, pal," cried his rescuer, joining his companions as the attack moved on, spreading across the plaza.

Despite being burdened with armor and shields, the Klar moved swiftly. The Neidar had fallen back but were once again rallying around Harn Poleaxe. However, they were scattered by the Klar's charge, and even their hulking commander stumbled back—though not before Poleaxe felled a pair of Klar with crushing, well-aimed blows.

Meanwhile Brandon was kicking his feet, sliding the loop of chain free from the splintered board. Twisting and pulling with his muscular arms, he broke the rest of the frame apart. He was still secured by four manacles, each with a thick chain attached, but no longer were those cuffs anchored by heavy wood. He jumped free of the pile of debris and firewood, albeit hung with chains and attached brackets and manacles on his wrists and ankles.

He couldn't get very far that way, he realized. He needed the key.

Rune! He remembered that his old tormentor had locked him into those brackets, and perhaps the hill dwarf still possessed the key. Stumbling forward, dragging his chains, Brandon lunged across the square toward where his foe had fallen. Rune was still there, bleeding from the hard blow to his head but struggling to rise, pushing himself to his hands and knees.

Brandon fell on him with the full pent-up fury of his betrayal. He swung his arm, heavily smacking the hill dwarf on the side of the head with a wildly lashing length of heavy chain. When Rune went down again, Brandon climbed on top of him, reaching under his tunic for the key he wore on the thong around his neck. The Neidar barely twitched, groaning and resisting only feebly as Brandon pulled the key out.

Twisting around and sitting on the immobilized Rune, Brandon quickly worked the bit of metal into the locks on his right and left wrists, freeing his hands. Next came the locks on his ankles, and finally he was able to shed all of his trappings and stand on his feet, once again a free dwarf. Maybe, finally, his luck was changing for the better! Almost as an afterthought, he reached down and smacked Rune one more time. Then he snatched Rune's sword off the ground, looking to take his place in the fight.

But he quickly saw that, while he had been busily freeing himself, the tide had turned. More and more hill dwarves, some fully equipped with battle gear, had continued to pour into the square, and the reinforcements outnumbered the attackers by at least two to one. The mountain dwarves were gradually falling back, following with discipline the lead of their commander, whom

Brandon spotted in the thick of the action shouting out orders—a handsome, blond male with exotic eyes and long, free-flowing hair.

Brandon groaned as the blond Klar, passing the platform where he had just undergone his "trial," stopped and stared at something. Eyes widening, the Klar leader snatched up the pouches containing the two stones. He opened one, and his teeth flashed a grin.

"Fall back!" the Klar captain brayed. "Tight ranks! Retreat!"

"No!" shouted Brandon, but his voice was drowned out in the melee.

The Klar had secured the pouch around his waist. The mountain dwarves, forming a tight rank, backed out of the square and down the street from which the attack had burst. The Neidar pursued them, but the Klar force was like a bristling hedgehog, spears and swords pointing out from behind shields, lethal to any pursuer who dared to draw close.

"They take the stones! Fall on them! Kill them!" Harn Poleaxe cried, cursing frenziedly. Spittle flew from his lips and his face, distorted by rage, seemed to erupt in several more grotesque warts. Brandon could only stare as the Neidar mob, led by his nemesis, raced past him, mere yards away, without taking the slightest notice of one dwarf rooted in place.

Behind the Neidar fighters, villagers were swiftly moving through the suddenly quiet, abandoned areas, tending to the wounded, pulling cloaks over the faces of the dead. Several Neidar approached Rune, and Brandon stepped quietly away, averting his face. He was not dressed in black armor, so the hill dwarves paid him little attention. He took one longing glance at his axe, where it lay on the table beside Harn's throne, but there were at least a dozen hill dwarves up there. He didn't dare try to retrieve it at that moment.

So he watched the diminishing battle as it moved away

from him and realized with a surge of emotion that he was alive, no worse for the wear; he had been unusually lucky, even if the Bluestone was once again gone from his hands. He thrust his captured sword through his belt, trotted down a side street, and made his way down a lane up and away from town.

From there, he would follow the progress of the retreating mountain dwarves and, Reorx willing, recover his family stone.

# TWENTY

# CAPTAINS OF DWARVES

Harn Poleaxe led his hill dwarves in another frantic charge, but again and again the Neidar hurled themselves against a solid shield wall of Klar. Poleaxe himself cut down his share of the enemy dwarves, stabbing one laggard then splintering another Klar's shield, helmet, and skull with a single downward smash of his great sword. Unfortunately, that last blow also snapped off the blade of his weapon, and the huge Neidar finally had to drop back.

Gasping for breath, he felt as demoralized as his town mates. They had pursued the Klar for more than a mile out of town, at first along the road, then into the narrow side valley. Here and there the mountain dwarves had paused to form up a rearguard. The enemy captain was, cleverly, leading the retreating company through a narrow niche in a rocky ridge. The mountain dwarves were able to bar the entrance to the pass with just ten or a dozen of their number while the rest of the column made good their escape.

The number of pursuing Neidar had swelled to more than five hundred, but they were defeated finally by the narrow confines. At least two dozen of Poleaxe's followers had fallen, and the shoulder-to-shoulder press of mountain dwarves holding the gap showed no signs of weakening. Whenever they found an opportunity, the manic Klar even lunged forward, cutting down a couple of hill dwarves who were too slow to jump out of the way.

The panting, exhausted Neidar were nearing the end of their endurance. Several burly warriors looked at Poleaxe nervously, fingering their weapons and eyeing the impermeable barrier of Klar shields. The dwarves of Hillhome, though they had successfully driven the enemy from their town, were not as well equipped, nor mentally prepared, for a pitched battle on such a steep and rocky slope.

Rage seethed through Poleaxe's veins, muscles, flesh, but he understood that rage alone would not carry the day.

"Fall back," Harn ordered, his voice tight through clenched jaws. "We'll take the war to them soon enough."

Slowly the Neidar backed away from the line of Klar, ignoring the taunts—"Run away, old women! Go back to your nursemaids' teats!"—hurled by the victorious raiders. Most infuriating of all, to Harn, was the knowledge that the mountain dwarves had borne away not just the Bluestone, but the Greenstone as well, from the town.

He blamed himself for forgetting all about the precious artifacts when the fight started. The stupid Klar probably didn't even know what they had in their possession. The Mother Oracle would be very angry. And Harn was suffering from an almost unbearable thirst. His parched throat seemed barely to allow the passage of breath, and his tongue felt swollen in his mouth.

For their aggression, the Klar would be repaid with death and destruction, Poleaxe vowed silently. And he would—he must—regain the Bluestone and Greenstone.

But that vengeance would have to wait.

He led the dejected Neidar down off the ridge, with the Klar watching them warily until they started on the road back into town. Their taunts against the retreating hill dwarves echoed down from the surrounding ridges as, finally, the rearguard of mountain dwarves broke their shield wall and followed their companions through the rocky niche, disappearing from view as they started on their way back to Pax Tharkas.

The mood was bitter as the warriors trudged back into the main square of Hillhome with humiliated expressions. Harn went immediately into Moldoon's and snatched a large jug of dwarf spirits, quaffing a long swallow as he stalked back out into the street. The liquor seared his tongue but seemed, at least a little, to quench his paralyzing thirst.

Bodies of the slain, discreetly covered with blankets or cloaks, lined one side of the plaza. More than a dozen Neidar had died there, and several times that many had fallen during the failed pursuit. Nobody, not even Poleaxe, felt triumphant that they had driven the attackers away. All of the survivors were painfully chagrined by the knowledge they had been taken by surprise and nearly overcome.

They all had been too focused on the execution of the mountain dwarf outsider—busy assembling the pile of tinder, with the fire poised to burn, to consume, the wretched prisoner, even as the attack began. Brandon had been shackled and strapped to the rack. Although the condemned spy had been putting on a stoic front, Harn had been looking forward to the moment when his victim's flesh began to char, his eyes boiling in their sockets. He knew Brandon would have broken down and wept as he died.

Strange, Poleaxe thought—the thought dawning as a sudden inspiration—how the Klar raiders arrived just at the very moment of the Kayolin dwarf's doom.

Abruptly Poleaxe looked around for the prisoner, having forgotten him almost as completely as the vaunted gemstones. He jumped up on the platform and stared, seeing the pile of wood on the ground nearby, but it took a moment for him to recognize the splintered timber as the square rack where Brandon had been suspended, waiting to die.

And he howled aloud when he realized that the prisoner had escaped.

"What treachery—where did the Kayolin go?" he demanded, springing down from the platform, striding across the plaza with spittle foaming his beard.

The Neidar shrank away from the infuriated warrior. Two of Poleaxe's personal guards, an armored pair carrying massive axes, exchanged looks as their leader stalked to the broken rack and kicked through the debris as if he expected to find the prisoner crouching down among the itty-bitty twigs and pieces of straw.

"Where did he go?" he roared again.

A hundred dwarves milled about the plaza, and every one of them was utterly silent in response to Poleaxe's demand. Thus, when one dwarf groaned softly, all eyes turned to him.

"It's Rune!" cried a maid, kneeling beside the warrior and dabbing at his bloody forehead with her apron.

Poleaxe stomped over to his lieutenant and glared down at the stricken, dazed Neidar. The huge dwarf leader kicked contemptuously at the empty manacles that lay on the ground around Rune.

"Tell me, fool. How did he get the key?" growled Harn.

"I was felled by a hammer!" Rune pleaded. "He came upon me as I lay here and wrested it away!"

"Fool!" bellowed Poleaxe, causing Rune to whimper and cringe against the ground. Trembling in fury, the Neidar warrior gazed around the plaza into the stunned, awestruck faces of his tribesmen. His fingers clutched the hilt of his broken sword—he came dangerously close to drawing the weapon and plunging the stub of sharp steel through Rune's craven heart.

At the last instant, he held his hand. "Clean this up!" he shrieked, gesturing to the whole square. "I will be back soon."

He paused only long enough to take another long drink from his jug of spirits, setting the container beside his chair before he stalked out of the square, through a wide gap that opened up in the ring of staring Neidar. The streets of the town were for the most part empty, and he took some small comfort from the fact there were none to witness his humiliation and despair. A bleak cloud seemed to hover over him, bearing him down as he stomped through the streets toward the shabby hut of the Mother Oracle on Hillhome's outskirts.

"Enter!" snapped the ancient oracle, even before he had raised his hand to knock on the door. Hesitantly, he pushed the frail barrier aside and entered the small, darkened room.

The old crone sat in the same place he had left her the day before. Her milky eyes were open, staring past him, and her gnarled hands were clenched into small fists, curled in her lap.

"So. You failed," she spit. "Tell me what happened."

He drew a breath and quickly decided against making excuses and dissembling.

"The mountain dwarves of Pax Tharkas attacked us while we were preparing to execute the Kayolin dwarf. We were taken totally by surprise. The Klar scooped up the two stones, and the prisoner escaped during the battle," he reported coldly.

"This is what I have seen," she said. "You let the gemstones slip from your hold."

"I did," Poleaxe admitted glumly.

"And you failed to prevent the dwarf maid from coming to me. I was forced to drive her away myself, last night. It took a great effort from an old, tired woman, but I succeeded."

"I am sorry, Mother," Harn said, ashamed. Once again his throat felt dry, his tongue thick in his mouth. He couldn't even muster enough saliva to present her with an excuse.

"This is unforgiveable," she said, but her tone was surprisingly gentle. She raised her wrinkled face, her nose twitching as the lids over her sightless eyes flickered up and down. "You have changed," she said bluntly. "You have grown but not naturally. How?"

He was startled by her statement, once more reminded that the Mother Oracle saw far and deep, despite her blindness. When he had awakened that morning, in the room where Gretchan Pax had eluded him, he had felt himself changed and grown. He had stared into a mirror and realized that he had changed physically. He felt in possession of a certain inner strength, a fateful power that he had not known as part of himself before. Anxiously he scratched at one of the bumps that had appeared on his face. It itched constantly, and despite his rubbing, he could not seem to ease the discomfort.

"I drank something," he said matter-of-factly. "It was something contained in a bottle of dwarf spirits, but it was not dwarf spirits. I tasted the difference."

She nodded, as if his explanation made perfect sense to her. "Good," she replied. "This I have also seen. This something, this potion, will help you to get the stones back. That is why I am not as angry as you might expect. You must retrieve them soon, of course. As for the Kayolin dwarf, you will have another opportunity to kill him, soon enough, when you recover the Bluestone and the Greenstone."

"But, Mother Oracle," Harn said, puzzled. "Surely the Klar are taking the stones to Pax Tharkas. And who knows where the escaped prisoner will flee?"

"Oh don't worry. He, like you, will follow the stones," she said confidently. "As to Pax Tharkas, you are destined to go there anyway. Destined to attack and capture it."

His mind reeled at the lofty goal the Mother Oracle had set for him. He knew that secure fortress well from the outside: its massive towers, the high wall, the vast battlements, the gate strong enough to withstand a dragon's might. He could only croak, "How?"

She shrugged, as if that were an issue of no great import. "The answer will come to me and it will come to you in good time. Do not fear. But for now you must act here, in Hillhome."

"What should I do?"

"The people are understandably shaken and angry. You must turn that anger to your cause with a demonstration of your vengeance, giving proof of your power and your command."

"Yes. I know just what to do. The other prisoners! There are two Theiwar in the brig. I will make an example of them. They will die in the Kayolin's stead. And then we will muster our resources and plan a counterattack that the Klar will not soon forget."

"Good," said the old dwarf woman, raising a withered claw. He knelt and kissed her hand. "Go. Plan. Conquer."

"Thank you, Mother Oracle," Harn declared.

And he did as she advised. As he returned to the town square, he no longer felt despair or humiliation; he felt calm, confident, in control. He took a deep draught from the jug that, not surprisingly, the townsfolk had left untouched beside his great chair. He was feeling better already as he looked across the square. The Neidar were there in teeming numbers, many hundreds, muttering and fretting. They grew silent as the big hill dwarf swaggered back and forth on the platform then flopped into his chair in one smooth gesture.

"Our vengeance begins this morning, and it will not be complete until total victory is ours!" he proclaimed. A few Neidar clapped or shouted in agreement, but he brushed their mild encouragement away.

He pointed. "There are still two mountain dwarves imprisoned in the brig," Poleaxe declared in a calm, measured tone. "Are there not?"

"Y-yes, Lord Poleaxe!" came the reply from none other

than Shriff Keenstrike, who was standing close by.

"Bring them here!" he ordered, deciding he liked, very much, being called "Lord Poleaxe."

Five minutes later the two captives, the Theiwar miners, were shoved into the middle of the plaza. Angry Neidar pressed in on all sides as Poleaxe spoke.

"Mountain dwarf filth!" he snapped as the two prisoners were shoved to their knees before him. He gestured to the bodies, to the destruction and detritus of battle around the plaza. "This is the work of your kinfolk! A treacherous attack, innocents slain—and then a cowardly retreat. Someone must pay! Someone *will* pay!"

One prisoner dared to raise his head and was smacked down again by a guard.

"Your tribesmen may have fled, but you are here, and you will receive the first taste of Neidar vengeance. Guards—bring me a block!" he cried, and several of his warriors quickly produced a broad, sturdy stump, setting it on the ground in front of the prisoners.

"Yarrow—is your blade sharp?" Poleaxe demanded of one of his bodyguards.

"Yes, lord. Sharp—and thirsty," replied the Neidar axeman with a glare at the two hapless prisoners.

"Good," Poleaxe replied. He gestured contemptuously to the pair. "Cut off their heads!" he ordered to an explosion of cheers and shouts from the crowd.

"Kill them!" cried many of the Neidar, pressing in, faces eager with bloodlust.

Only Slate Fireforge, far to the back of the crowd, watched the executions with any expression of sadness and dismay.

———DH———

Brandon kept following the high ground just below the summit of the ridge, moving steadily away from Hillhome, keeping the mountain dwarf column ahead of him in sight.

He was conscious of the captured sword at his belt, but that weapon wasn't going to be much use to him in his situation. He felt bitter regret at the memory of his cherished battle axe, no doubt treasured by some Neidar thief—possibly even Harn Poleaxe himself. Perhaps he would get it back one day. For the moment he had the sword.

And that, too, added to his sense that his luck was changing. After all, he was no longer a prisoner, he was armed, and his family's treasured stone was, at least, in the hands of mountain dwarves, not the vile Neidar. Things were indeed looking up.

The repulsed attackers maintained a pretty good pace as they marched swiftly toward the northwest. They had the advantage of the road, so Brandon was forced to jog along, climbing up and over obstacles, rocky outcrops and clumps of gnarled woods. He was puffing for breath, jogging near the crest, when he realized he wasn't the only person tracking the column.

A pair of dwarves accompanied by a large black dog was moving along the slope just below Brandon. Cautiously, he crouched behind a ledge of rock and observed the other pursuers. Then his eyes widened as he recognized the blonde-haired dwarf maid as Gretchan Pax, the historian who had spoken to him in the Hillhome brig.

What in Reorx's name was she doing out there?

Even as he wondered that, he found himself rather impressed by her field craft. Unlike him, she wore a bulky, apparently heavy, backpack, but she trotted along with ease and strength, hopping gracefully across the loose rocks of the high ridge crest. Her blue leggings and soft boots outlined the muscular curvature of her legs, and the sturdy traveling cloak she wore couldn't completely mask the alluring outline of her curvy shape.

Her companion, he was startled to realize, was a ragged-looking gully dwarf. The Aghar trailed behind her, apparently keeping up a steady stream of chatter, though they were too far away for Brandon to hear what was being said. Even as he wondered what odd circumstance could have thrown the unlikely pair together, he warily watched the dog that bounded close beside the two. The wind was in his face, so he didn't worry about his scent wafting down to the animal, but he made sure to walk stealthily, avoiding any untoward crunching of leaves or skittering of stones that might give him away.

What did Gretchan Pax want with the militant Klar? He couldn't guess the answer, but he didn't like the chance that she might discover him. Clearly she was friendly with the Hillhome dwarves, and he wasn't about to take any chances on her sympathy for him. Was she spying on the mountain dwarves for her own Neidar people? Somehow that explanation didn't ring true, but what exactly she was doing remained a mystery.

Brandon moved higher up the ridge, and when he came to a notch in the rocky crest, he moved across to the other side. He wouldn't be able to keep the mountain dwarves in sight, but he gambled that they would continue along the road, just as the winding ridge did.

Jogging along, he tried to come up with a plan. He knew he couldn't simply walk up to the mountain dwarves and ask them for the Bluestone back. He imagined the absurdity of the scene: "Um, that treasure you're carrying . . . it actually belongs to me . . ."

The only question was whether they'd kill him outright or simply laugh him out of their camp.

Of course, the strangers were mountain dwarves, and that, at least, gave him hope. Hylar and Klar clans, while not necessarily allied, were not traditional enemies in the manner of Hylar and Daewar, who were generally united in their hatred of the Theiwar and Daergar dark dwarves. He decided that he would follow along, wait for the Klar to make their camp, then go down and introduce himself. He hoped they would remember they had aided his rescue.

With any luck, he could at least join their ranks. As a kinsman from up north, they ought not to have any reason to distrust him on sight.

Of course, he remembered with a chill, Lord Heelspur and the assassins who had killed his brother were mountain dwarves too—albeit, Hylar of his own clan.

——DH——

Gretchan walked briskly along the ridge above the Hillhome road, wrapped in thought. Gus continued to prattle on about revenge, about the bold initiatives he was planning, the battles he would win. She merely ignored his boasts and blather, moderately grateful that he had something to talk about besides where the next meal was coming from. Her mind was working on deeper problems, and she was trying to come up with a plan.

Of course she had recognized the attacking dwarves as Klar clansmen. With Thorbardin sealed, it seemed likely they must have come from Pax Tharkas. She guessed the mountain dwarves would be returning to that fortress. Her guess was reinforced by the fact that the road they followed was the one leading to that great citadel.

"Oh, curse it all," she said as the afternoon wound into evening and the Klar's marching column remained a mile or so ahead of them on the road. They continued marching into the darkness, covering ground until almost midnight, until, at last, the company moved off the road and gathered into a cold, fireless camp in a small grove of pines.

"I need to go talk to them," she announced curtly.

Gus looked up at her and paled. "Talk to big fighter dwarves?" he gulped, his bravado fading in an instant.

"Yes. Now that they've stopped for the night. They won't hurt me, I'm sure. There's something I wish to know. But I want you to stay here, out of sight, and keep an eye on things for me. All right? And I can't take Kondike with me. I might have to move quietly, and he might spook the

265

folks I want to talk to. Make sure he stays put here, out of trouble. You did an excellent job of keeping an eye on Kondike before."

"Sure I did. I do that!" the Aghar promised. "I keep two eyes on him this time!"

"I knew I could count on you," Gretchan said, touched by her companion's obvious sincerity. There were evident risks in leaving the gully dwarf responsible for anything, but they were lesser risks than taking him along. She reminded herself that, back in Hillhome, he had managed to turn up in the right place at the right time.

"Just remember, don't make any noise. I'll be back in . . . call it two hours," she concluded, remembering the limitations of gully dwarf mathematical understanding.

Leaving Gus and Kondike hidden in a clump of rocks just off the road, she trudged toward the grove where she had seen the Klar make their camp. She was not looking forward to the encounter; the mountain dwarves of that clan were notoriously stubborn, unpredictable, and almost always rage filled. But she had to try to talk to them.

"Hey!" called a sentry, stepping out from behind a pine bole as she approached the camp. He brandished a heavy axe and peered suspiciously from beneath the canopy of the tree's branches. "Who goes?"

"It's me—Gretchan Pax," she announced, striding up to the dwarf.

"Who?" he demanded, squinting to get a good look. The white moon emerged from behind a cloud, washing the scene in illumination, and the Klar's eyes widened. "Why, hel—*loh* there," he said, grinning. "What can I do for such a pretty lady?"

"I need to have a word with your brave captain," she said with a sexy smile.

"Oh," he replied, somewhat crestfallen. "Well, Garn Bloodfist is by that big rock near the stream. I don't know . . . he didn't say anything . . . is he, uh, expecting you?"

"No, I'm a surprise," she said with a wink.

The sentry turned toward the camp. "Captain! There's someone here to see you. I, uh, think you'll want to talk to her."

The reply from the middle of the camp seemed, to Gretchan, like an inarticulate cry. She looked at the sentry, who simply shrugged and waved her in. "That's the captain for you," he muttered as she passed.

The mountain dwarves were extremely weary from their long day of battle, retreat, and hard marching. Most of them were wrapped up snugly in their bedrolls, snoring or nearly asleep. A few glanced up from their blankets as she moved among them, and she heard whispering and rustling as many of them sat up and blinked. The moonlight reflected in her hair, making it look like spun gold, and much of the snoring died out as the sleeping dwarves were nudged awake to have a look at the mysterious visitor.

Men, she thought as she followed the guard's direction toward the stream.

She found Garn Bloodfist wrapped in his cloak, glaring at the dark waters of the stream as it flowed past. At first she thought he was with someone—she heard him muttering angrily about "Revenge!"—but a glance around suggested no one else was present.

"Hello," she said unceremoniously, stepping to his side. "So you are the famous Garn Bloodfist. I need to talk to you."

"Who in Reorx's name are you?" he demanded, standing up and looking her over slowly and suspiciously. His eyes bulged from his bearded face and fixed upon her with a staring intensity she found strangely irritating.

Charm is wasted on this one, she realized. In a sense, that was a relief; it allowed her to cut right to the point.

"I saw your men at work today," she declared. "Quite a bit of butchery. I suppose you're very proud."

"And why shouldn't I be?" snapped Garn, his eyes darting this way and that. "We won the day!"

"That's as foolish a statement as I've heard in a long time. Win a day, and lose a year? Or a century? Is *that* what you're after?" she charged. Her voice grew stronger and more shrill. "You attacked a peaceful hill dwarf village! I suppose next you want to refight the Dwarfgate War? Maybe conjure up Fistandantilus to make another Skullcap!"

He gaped at her. "I repeat, who in Reorx's name are you?" he said, sounding a little less sure of himself.

"I am a highly respected historian," she said, shaking a finger in his face. "And I asked you a question. Why are you opening up old wounds and refighting the Dwarfgate War?"

Garn glared at the uppity female he had never seen before. "If you paid more attention to that history you claim to find so interesting, you'd notice that the Dwarfgate War has never ended. If we don't kill them, they'll end up killing us!"

She shook her head. "How can you be such an idiot? How can there be any hope for our people when fools like you will take any excuse to make war?"

"I am a warrior!" snarled the Klar, his hands twitching. He wasn't wearing a weapon, but he raised a fist, flexing it toward Gretchan's face.

She didn't back down; in fact, she shouted at him. "It was a tragic, foolish waste of lives—your own as well as the Neidar! You've inflamed the hill dwarves now. They'll be coming for vengeance soon enough."

"A waste?" Garn shot back, gloating. "If you're really such an important historian, then tell me if this looks like a waste." He pulled out a pouch and held it open so she could see, glinting in the pale light of the stars, two large wedges of colored stones. "Look!" he declared. "Unless I miss my guess, these are valuable dwarven artifacts that rightfully belong to the exiles of Thorbardin. It's a treasure like I've never seen!"

She stepped closer, eyes widening, inspecting the unusual colored stone. "Where do you think you're taking them? To Pax Tharkas?" she asked.

He glowered then thrust his bristling beard forward as if in challenge. "What if I am?" he demanded. "These stones are the spoils of our mission, and unless I miss my guess, they'll make Tarn Bellowgranite and even Otaxx Shortbeard sit up and take notice!"

She felt suddenly dizzy and sat down hard on a nearby rock. "What did you say?" she asked, her voice falling to a whisper.

"You heard me," Garn retorted. He scowled. "Say, what's the matter with you all of a sudden?" He looked around suspiciously. "Where did you come from, anyway?"

"I've been traveling . . . for a long time," she said in a small, disoriented voice. "I'm not sure I even remember where I come from anymore."

For the first time, Garn looked hard at the stranger. "Well, you can stay with us if you want to be safe. And we'll take you to the fortress with us," he offered a little too eagerly.

"No. I'm traveling with another party," she said curtly.

He blinked and his eyes narrowed. "What are you anyway?" he demanded. "Some kind of witch? Showing up here in the middle of the night, ten miles from Hillhome. Or is that your home?" he challenged menacingly. He took a step closer to her.

"Don't touch me!" she snapped. She stood, facing him down. When he reached toward her, she spoke a single word: "Stop!"

The word exploded through the night like a crack of thunder. "You are a witch!" Garn said angrily, struggling to push his hand forward against the unseen force that was blocking him. "Klar!" he shouted. "Take her!"

At least he tried to shout, and his mouth worked up

and down. But no sound came forth. Stunned, his eyes bulging, he stared at the mysterious dwarf maid, who glared at him with an expression that was not so much angry as distraught.

"I don't care where you're going," she said with a shrug, turning to watch the moonlight reflecting in the waters of the stream. The gemstones intrigued her. But narrow-minded dwarves such as Garn Bloodfist—Bloodthirst would be more appropriate—discouraged and depressed her.

Leaving him still struggling against the force of her command, she turned and walked into the night.

# TWENTY-ONE

## SAME NEW PROBLEM

Brandon neared the mountain dwarf camp just as dawn began to color the sky. The raiding party slumbered in a small field beside a winding stream, with a fringe of pine forest screening them. He had watched the camp through the night, and he moved carefully through the dim light, making sure not to crack dried branches under his feet or to rustle against the underbrush. He reasoned that, if he were able to walk straight up to the Klar captain and demonstrate he had entered the camp without meaning any harm, his chances of a moderately friendly reception would be significantly improved.

His plans were shattered by the appearance of four—no, six—armed Klar, who leaped out of the brush to surround him before he even reached the camp's perimeter.

"Hey," he objected, raising his hands in the middle of a ring of spears. One of the mountain dwarves plucked his sword from his belt while the others prodded him toward the center of the camp. "I just want to talk. I'm not an enemy!" he protested.

His protestations were to no avail. A half hour later, Brandon found himself a bound prisoner again, his wrists lashed together behind him, a sturdy chain shackled around his neck. The Klar were busy breaking camp and preparing to move out.

"What's the meaning of this?" he demanded of the captain. "I tell you, I just want to talk!"

"Ha!" said the dwarf who commanded the company. His eyes bulged as he thrust his face so close to Brandon that he could smell the Klar's rancid breath. He laughed, a gleeful, high-pitched sound that did not sound entirely rational.

"You're a hill dwarf spy, or I'm a gully dwarf," the captain hooted. "And you'd like nothing better than to follow us into Pax Tharkas!"

"You're wrong!" Brandon cried, appalled at the abrupt evaporation of his luck—again. "I'm a mountain dwarf!"

But the Klar captain, still chuckling, was already ordering his amused warriors onto the road.

And Brandon Bluestone, his neck chain tethered to two burly Klar axemen, was once again tugged toward a captor's lair.

——DH——

Harn Poleaxe sat in the darkness of his house, seething over the events of the day. Even the executions of the two prisoners, bloody and gratifying as that had been, could not erase the sting of defeat, frustration, humiliation. The Kayolin dwarf had escaped, vanishing into the wilds of Kharolis, and Poleaxe's hard-won treasure, the Bluestone that was going to vault him to greatness, had been stolen by the treacherous mountain dwarves.

Nursing another jug of dwarf spirits—his first one had not lasted until sunset—he scratched at the newest sore that had open up on his face. His fingernails came away red with blood. He put the neck of the bottle to his lips and leaned back, gurgling for a long time. The day had started with such fine portents and had degenerated into a disaster.

He deserved so much better!

His troubles started, he reflected, the previous night, when the seductive dwarf maid had eluded him and her companions had accosted him. That was followed by the trial that went awry, the botched battle with the Klar, and Brandon's scot-free escape.

Yet, he told himself, he was empowered, mighty and commanding and capable in ways that he could have only dreamt about before. And it was all the result of a potion.

He took another drink of dwarf spirits, and the powerful alcohol only seemed to enhance his abilities. Beyond that drink, he felt the potion's power coursing through his body, embellished by the spirits but not intoxicated. The enchanted liquid had changed and strengthened him, and once he had mastered his new powers, he would track down the mountain dwarves and the wench who had spurned him and all of them would pay. He would crush those opponents and any others who stood in his path. He would triumph, and in the end he would be Lord Poleaxe, master of all the hills!

He had been foolish to think of Brandon Bluestone as a naive blunderer; clearly the Hylar from Kayolin was dangerous in ways Harn hadn't understood.

Brandon had eluded him once. Next time he would die.

And Gretchan Pax would suffer.

His gorge rose as he recalled how she had spurned him, lied to him. How dared she! His lust surged as he recalled her beauty, her pride, her sparkling eyes and swelling breasts. Before he was done, she would *enjoy* submitting to him, by Reorx. In the end, it would be *she* who desired *him,* and only then would he spurn her. Oh, and she'd have to die as well.

The room was very dark, and he barely noticed the shape taking form in front of him. Only when the shape's two orbs, glowing like embers in the Abyss, opened did he feel the deep power, the mesmerizing presence of his visitor. He noted the great bat wings, smelled the fetid breath emerging from that fanged maw. The creature filled up all the space, darkening it like a great shadow, like a new and more intense form of night. The shape rose above him and stretched around him, a display of chilling power.

Harn Poleaxe dropped to his knees, gaping in a mixture of terror, awe, and reverence. "You! You will show me the way!" he gasped, certain beyond any doubt that the monster was his new ally, sent by the gods. The jug fell from his suddenly nerveless fingers, tumbling onto its side, but it was already so empty that none of the dregs spilled out.

The creature snorted, and again that foul breath washed over the hill dwarf. But it was like a perfume to him, anointing and blessing him, crowning his greatness. Harn Poleaxe shivered in delight and, pressing his face to the floor, waited for the monster to speak.

"Harn Poleaxe, you are a servant of the Black One," declared the creature. "It is his elixir that has empowered you and his will that you must obey."

"Speak!" Poleaxe begged. "Only tell me what to do, and I will do it. Tell me how I may strike at Pax Tharkas."

The creature hissed, a rasping sound that might have been taken for laughter. "You already know our master's will, I see. He will be pleased."

"I know his will, and I know mine! I am fated to wipe out the mountain dwarves in the fortress! I know what I must do. I must raise an army of Neidar, and we must attack the walls. But the gates, oh my lord! How can we take the gates?"

The thing made that noise again, and Harn was certain that it was a sound of amused pleasure. The red eyes glowed, and the maw gaped open again.

"Leave the gates to me," it said.

───DH───

Brandon stared upward at the massive towers and

wall blocking passage up the valley. He had seen Pax Tharkas portrayed in drawings and sketches, but the reality of the monument took his breath away. It was as if a part of the mountain range itself blocked their path—a massive slab with a flat, carved face, flanked by summits of utterly symmetrical, perfectly solid peaks. For a moment he forgot that he stood in chains, an abject prisoner of his fellow mountain dwarves. The legacy of that place, its all-encompassing majesty, seemed to banish all trivial emotions into the far corners of his brain.

For two weeks his Bluestone luck had held true. He had been treated miserably. His lowly status as a prisoner had been pounded home every day he had been marching with Garn Bloodfist's Klar.

For several days he had tried to convince the wild-eyed warrior that he was, in fact, a mountain dwarf of clan Hylar. Every time he made the claim, however, the Klar had grown more agitated, more paranoid. The Klar loudly accused Brandon of spying; he was convinced the Kayolin dwarf was a Neidar from Hillhome. He was fed stingily, poked and kicked, and threatened with execution if he didn't shut up.

At least Brandon caught a glimpse of the Bluestone and its companion Greenstone now and then when Garn took the colored stones out and studied them lovingly. Captain Bloodfist was proud of his prizes. His eyes seemed to shine in their glow, and he giggled and chortled as he carried them around the camp, endlessly enjoying their heft and beauty. It was clear, at least, that he treasured his treasures.

Other glimpses were less encouraging, however, as on the nights—about every forth evening—when Garn stalked, alone, into the darkness beyond the perimeter of his camp. He would shout and rail against the sky, the stars. Most of his words were garbled, and sometimes he would sob in abject grief or howl in a seeming frenzy of rage. On those nights, even his bravest warriors gave him a wide berth. When the captain returned to camp, exhausted from his ranting, he invariably slept through the following dawn, and the company was several hours late getting onto the trail.

But finally, they had reached their destination. The Klar had spent some time that morning, before they broke camp, in polishing their black armor and shields and cleaning some of the dust and grime from their hair, beards, and boots. They entered Pax Tharkas in a proud column of fours, each dwarf with his shield slung across his back, feet pounding the pavement in regular cadence, up the broad ramp leading to the massive wall.

The great gate in the center of the main wall was wide open. Brandon, in the middle of the column, was chained to a pair of burly warriors, the links fastened to the collar around his neck. Even so, he could swivel his head in awe, taking in the massive structure.

Even the atrium of Kayolin, which was essentially bottomless, was not as far across as the breadth of the massive hall. The whole place seemed to be hollowed out, at least on the ground level. There was a pile of rocks and boulders roughly jumbled in the center, but neither wall nor any other kind of partition divided the enormous space. Very high overhead he could discern a series of catwalks crossing back and forth and side to side through the upper reaches of the wall. The ceiling itself seemed to be lost in shadows, but he was certain that it was well over a hundred feet above his head.

"Bring the prisoner with me," ordered the captain. "We'll go see the thane."

A trio of Klar warriors fell in behind Brandon, whose wrists were bound behind him. At least one hundred other mountain dwarves were in view. Most were working, hauling, levering, and carrying large rocks to a series of lift cages at one side of the great hollow hall.

As they approached, one of those lifts was filled with rocks, and a dwarf rang a bell. Brandon watched as the container, which was little more than a sturdy wooden box attached to a block and tackle, creakingly rose into the darkness far overhead.

"Hold that work, there," Garn barked as several laborers approached an empty lift with the beginnings of the next load. The captain, the prisoner, and the three guards crammed into the box, and Garn signaled to the bellman. Once more the gong sounded, and that crate, like the other, began to rise into the heights overhead.

The lift climbed smoothly and swiftly with no yawing or pitching movements even as the floor fell away. Brandon estimated they were hoisted more than a hundred feet into the air before the cage slid snugly into a notched landing. There they found a dozen dwarves, some with shovels and picks, others cranking away on the block and tackle winch.

"Welcome back, Bloodfist," called one burly foreman. "At least you don't weigh as much as a box of rocks."

"Where's Tarn Bellowgranite?" asked the captain, ignoring the pleasantry.

A harsh voice answered him from out of the darkness. "Damn it, Bloodfist! Are you crippled? You know there's stairs you could climb—why did you waste the time of the load men?"

"I have a hill dwarf prisoner, my thane, and important treasure," Garn Bloodfist called as sternly as his leader had spoken. "I didn't want to waste any time in bringing you the news."

The captain turned and fixed Brandon with his piercing, intense eyes. "You will now meet the thane of Pax Tharkas. Mind your tongue, or I will have it cut out of your head."

Tarn Bellowgranite stepped into view, making his way along a dark, narrow wooden catwalk to the lift landing.

The dwarf looked old and tired, except for the undying spark of anger in his eyes. His head was bald on top, surrounded by a fringe of gray hair, and his shoulders slumped, his back bent, as he clumped along. To Brandon, he looked like a dwarf who had been carrying a great weight—greater than any box of stones—for a long, long time. The thane was accompanied by another elderly dwarf, a sturdy-framed fellow with white hair and a beard who, though his belly bulged perhaps more than he would have liked, still bore himself like a lifelong warrior.

"Greetings, my thane," said Captain Bloodfist, bowing low. His men did the same and, after a moment's hesitation and an elbow in his sides, so did Brandon. The Klar straightened and spoke again, addressing Tarn's companion. "Greetings too, General Shortbeard," he said. "I am glad that you, also, are here to receive my report."

"Well?" demanded the thane, looking Brandon up and down. "What manner of hill dwarf is this? Rather an unusually big fellow, to be sure."

"I keep telling this dummy, I'm not a hill dwarf!" the prisoner retorted, meeting Tarn's angry eyes with his own steady glare. "And I would expect better treatment from my own kinfolk in the mountain clans!"

"Shut up, you," declared one of the guards, delivering a ringing blow to the back of Brandon's head with the hilt of his sword.

While the Kayolin dwarf staggered, fighting the urge to slump to his knees, Garn spoke solemnly. "We caught this fellow following us back from Hillhome—he came from there, clearly. I believe he's a thief and a spy; he sought to pass himself off as a mountain dwarf, but you have heard his accent. Clearly he's not one of us. And my thane—"

Garn's breathing grew excited, and he was almost panting as he reached into his belt pouch to pull out the Bluestone and the Greenstone, which he set on a nearby workbench for all to admire.

"This is the booty the thief was after—the prizes we claimed from Hillhome. Look at them! I have a hunch they are valuable artifacts!"

The facets on the two wedges glittered and winked in the diffuse torchlight. Tarn Bellowgranite's eyes, like those of all the other dwarves, were drawn almost hypnotically to the pair of colored stones.

"Hmm, yes. Look at these, Otaxx," the thane said, addressing the one called General Shortbeard. "What do you think they are?"

"Where did they come from?" Otaxx asked Garn.

"The Bluestone is mine and it comes from Kayolin, just like me," Brandon interjected before anyone else could speak. "It was stolen from me by the leader of the hill dwarves, Harn Poleaxe. The other stone, the Greenstone, was already in the town of the hill homes when I was brought there—as their prisoner!" he concluded insistently.

"He keeps telling this preposterous story," Garn said, sounding more amused than upset. "All the way from Kayolin! Have any of you ever met a dwarf from Kayolin?"

As the thane regarded Brandon with frank suspicion, Captain Bloodfist continued enthusiastically. "These stones may be magical. Or think what even one would bring in the bazaar in Caergoth or Sanction. Wealth beyond imagining! The vital funds to outfit a proper army, to overwhelm the hill dwarf scum once and for all! Oh, that would be a glorious day for the mountain dwarves—and your Hylar legacy would be restored."

"I am a Hylar too!" Brandon shouted.

That was one interruption too many for Garn Bloodfist. Brandon felt Garn's blade pressing against his throat, colder by far than the metal collar encircling his neck. "I told you—cease your lies! Or do you want me to cut the tongue right out of your head?"

Brandon glowered but kept his mouth shut. His eyes appealed to the Hylar thane, who seemed preoccupied with his own troubles. But the Kayolin dwarf was surprised to see the old general, Otaxx Shortbeard, looking at him with an expression unlike all the others—pensive, even curious.

The old, weary thane gestured to the load men, who immediately started the empty crate descending toward the floor of the great hall again.

"This is the true Hylar legacy," Tarn Bellowgranite declared, waving his hand at the vast operation. "Restoring the great trap to operability. We are very close now; you see that the hall is nearly emptied, nearly done. These other matters are distractions."

"Yes, my thane, I know, I know," said Garn tersely. "You always preach patience."

But Brandon got the impression the Klar captain was humoring his ruler; Bloodfist's eyes narrowed in an expression very much like contempt as he scrutinized the older dwarf. "About the prisoner . . . I would like your authorization to lock him in the dungeon while his fate is determined."

Tarn was leaning over the catwalk's railing, looking at the dwarves who were busily filling the next lift. "You there! Watch that load; you're overbalancing to the left!" he barked. After a second he turned back to the Klar, blinking as if surprised to find him still standing there. He didn't spare a glance at Brandon. "Do what you must," he muttered.

Just my luck, Brandon reflected morosely. His fate would remain in the hands of the erratic, excitable Klar.

Without another word, Garn gestured to his guards, and Brandon was hustled into another lift crate, just emptied of its rock cargo. With a wave to the load men, the captain started their smooth descent back down into the cavernous hall.

"They go into Big House?" questioned Gus. He was staring in awe at the great fortress.

The column of mountain dwarves they had followed for so long was marching in through the vast central gate. That gate had been standing open during the whole of their approach, and the dwarves could see right through it and a second gate beyond to the valley on the other side of the massive wall.

"Yes, they're going into the Big House," Gretchan replied, her thoughts preoccupied. She, Kondike, and the gully dwarf were crouched behind a clump of boulders beside the road that approached the huge gate carved into the Tharkadan wall. There were many sentries on the wall in clear view, and no doubt others watching from concealed vantages. For the ninth or tenth time, she pushed Gus's head down. She didn't care to take any chances on being discovered.

Kondike was also watching warily. The dog's ears perked upward, nostrils flaring gently as they sampled the air and searched for any scent of danger. Gretchan kept a hand on the Aghar's shoulder as he squirmed and craned to get a better look. She was ready, at a moment's notice, to snatch the gully dwarf by the scruff of his neck and pull him back into concealment.

"We go into Big House too?" asked Gus hopefully.

"Well, yes and no," the maid replied.

"Yes and no you always say. What mean you yes and no?" asked the gully dwarf with a scowl.

"Well, we're both going to go inside," she said, eliciting a happy grin from the Aghar, "but we won't be using the front gate. I'm not sure the master of Pax Tharkas will be happy to see me. Anyway, I don't want to have to talk my way past those officious guards."

"Guards are fishes? We sneak?" Gus suggested brightly. "That fun. Aghar *great* sneakers!"

"I know," Gretchan said. "I'm counting on it. And I know just the place for some sneaking."

"Where that?" the Aghar asked eagerly.

"Well, it's a place I've never seen, but it's been well described in the histories. During the War of the Lance, some heroes used it to sneak in to Pax Tharkas so they could save many thousands of lives. It's an old place, disused nowadays, but I think it might just work."

"What old place this?"

"Come with me," Gretchan said. "And I'll show you the way called the Sla-Mori."

# TWENTY-TWO

## ANCIENT TOMBS AND MODERN PATHS

"This is the place." Gretchan pointed. She and Gus stood before the base of a tall cliff. For two hours she had been leading the gully dwarf and the dog along the rugged slope of the mountain valley, backtracking away from the great fortress, then moving off the road to follow a narrow, steeply climbing trail alongside a mountain stream.

Many times she had paused for rest, leaning on her staff, concentrating with her eyes closed. A few times, while she was thus engrossed, the Aghar had tried to offer helpful suggestions about what they might find to eat if they were to do some looking, or where they could go instead of that secret path that took forever to find, but he finally gave up, sulking, after she silenced him with increasingly short-tempered rebukes.

At last she had moved off the slope trail, pushing through tangling bushes and tree branches to climb up to that insignificant-looking spot of wilderness.

"What here?" demanded Gus. He squinted up the great cliff. "Golly. We not climb that!" he exclaimed.

"We don't have to," the dwarf maid explained patiently. "Just let me find what I am looking for . . ."

She spent several minutes probing the niches and cracks at the base of the cliff. Although she had spoken truly when she said she had never been in that place, she had studied many scholarly texts in which the Sla-Mori had been mentioned or played a prominent role, and her memory was very good for maps and history.

Soon she found what she was seeking. Reaching into a crack, straining upward as high as she could reach, she grasped a round knob of rock, an unusually long protuberance. Pulling it sharply downward, she stepped back and watched as a narrow panel of stone swung inward, revealing a wide, dark, musty corridor leading into the mountain.

The floor was covered with rubble, mostly dry rocks but in places there were pools of sticky mud, all coated with a layer of dust and grime. Gus started boldly ahead until, once again, her hand on his shoulder arrested his progress.

"We must tread carefully," she said. "Let's have Kondike lead the way."

Almost as if he understood what was expected of him, the dog paced ahead, stiff legged, into the secret passageway. He stepped easily over the broken rocks, sniffing alertly, his short tail erect. Gus and Gretchan followed close behind him.

In a few seconds, the door slid soundlessly shut, sealing them in utter darkness. Even as their dwarf eyes adjusted to the lack of light, Gretchan raised her staff and whispered a word. The anvil on the head of the pole began to glow with a soft illumination that penetrated into far corners and crevasses, lighting up the tunnel so they could see for quite a distance.

The corridor, they saw, meandered somewhat on its path—for at one time it had been a natural passageway, not a tunnel excavated from solid stone. True, there were signs of dwarven stone craft—regular arches to support the ceiling and buttresses in many places lining the walls.

Because of the rubble and the cracks and crumbles in the walls and ceilings, however, it still looked like a wild place, long neglected.

"This like tunnel to Thorbardin," Gus whispered. "We going to Thorbardin?" He wasn't all that enthused about the prospect of returning to his lifelong home.

"No. This is the Sla-Mori—the 'secret way' into Pax Tharkas. The elves used these halls for burial very, very long ago." But she was interested in the fact, if Gus could be believed, that similar tunnels existed in Thorbardin. She would have to remember to write that down.

"Bury bodies here?" asked the gully dwarf with an audible gulp.

"Yes," Gretchan said. Unlike her nervous companion, she was filled with reverence and awe to be in such a hallowed place. Her feet padded respectfully across the dusty stones, and in spite of the rubble and decay, she saw it as it once had been: a great hall, sacred to dwarves and elves alike, a symbol of alliance and peace as testified to by the name of the fortress itself.

"Pax Tharkas," she whispered to Gus, "translates roughly to mean 'Peace and Strength.' "

"Piece and strength," he mouthed, walking quietly beside her.

They came to a fork in the passage, and Kondike hesitated until Gretchan gestured with her staff toward the left. Again the dog led the way, picking up the pace slightly so the dwarves had to walk quickly in order to keep up. Despite his palpable fear, Gus hastened along, frankly more worried about being left behind than about any danger ahead.

Finally they came into a chamber so large, even the light from Gretchan's staff couldn't illuminate the far corners. It was a square vault with a series of columns lining the two side walls. In places, the ceiling had collapsed, dumping more rubble onto the floor, but in general the room was in better condition than the tunnel they had been following.

"Oh-oh. Dead guy! Who he?" asked Gus, suddenly freezing as he looked to the left.

"He was a great king," Gretchan said reverently as her eyes followed his. "He lived long ago, thousands of years before the Cataclysm. His name was Kith-Kanan."

"Kiss Caning," mouthed Gus.

The body of the legendary elf king, founder of Qualinesti, sat on a massive throne. Two tall statues of elf warriors loomed over him, sentries flanking the king's seat. The chair was set upon a raised dais, the monarch's body seated as if at rest, facing the vast chamber just as if he were hosting a vast crowd of lords, courtiers, and ladies.

Perhaps, Gretchan thought as a shiver of an imaginary breeze drifted over them, he did have a court full of ghosts to wait upon him. She had seen enough strange things in her life that she was not about to discount the possibility. The two looming statues to either side of the throne, each a stern-faced elf warrior, armed and armored and easily four times the height of a mortal elf, gave a strong suggestion of a watchful presence there.

Gus, meanwhile, couldn't fight his curiosity; he was creeping closer to the king's throne. He halted, gazing upward with trepidation, as Kondike padded over to stand protectively beside him. Gretchan, too, strolled over to look at the image of the ancient ruler. Kith-Kanan's flesh was not visible, for he had been entombed in a suit of full plate armor, including a helmet with a visor that covered his face. The armor had once been shiny silver, though it was blackened with age. Even so, the ornate scrolling on the greaves and breastplate was still visible; if anything, it was highlighted by the light film of dust.

"Kiss Caning elf king?" asked the gully dwarf, shaking his head in confusion. "In dwarf fort?"

"Yes," Gretchan said gently. "Kith-Kanan," she said,

emphasizing the pronunciation, "lived in a time when elves and dwarves worked together for the greater good of Krynn." She couldn't help the bitterness that seeped into her voice. "Now, it seems, even the different clans of dwarfkind are not content unless they are trying to kill each other every day."

"Not kill you!" Gus said fiercely, reaching up to take one of her hands in his grubby paws. "Gus not let them!"

"Thank you, my friend. I know you speak the truth from your heart, and that means a lot to me. I'm glad I could show you this place too. Now let's get going."

They left the corpse and statues and ghosts behind, proceeding through the darkened halls of the Sla-Mori. With her staff lighting the way, Gretchan found herself walking faster and faster, propelled by an eagerness even she didn't understand. Kondike loped along at her side. They came to a place where the cavern once had been blocked by a cave-in, but they were able to keep going since Tarn's laborers had obviously cleared the passage some years before. Other corridors and smaller passages branched off to the right and left, but Gretchan knew where she was headed. Her feet carried her rapidly along, around more twists and turns, and finally she reached an apparent dead end—a solid wall of stone.

Only then did she notice that Gus was missing. He must have fallen behind. She sighed in exasperation, trying to reconstruct when the intrepid Aghar had struck off on his own, until she realized she hadn't heard a sound from him for the better part of an hour.

"Hmm, that's not good. I hope you can stay out of trouble, little friend," she whispered to herself. More to the point, she hoped he wouldn't get into any trouble that would lead to her discovery. She was not ready to present herself to the lords of Pax Tharkas, not yet.

But she didn't intend to turn back and look for him. More eager than before, Gretchan pressed forward. She probed along the dusty wall and felt the outlines of an ancient carving, like a wheel with deep spokes engraved into the stone surface. Pushing her fingers into those grooves, she strained to move the mechanism. For a moment she feared that she wouldn't be strong enough, but suddenly it jerked and something broke free. The wheel in the wall rotated a quarter turn, and the great slab of stone blocking the passageway slipped to the side, opening the way into Pax Tharkas proper.

With a searching backward look, she determined that Gus hadn't caught up to her yet. She decided to leave the door open for the moment with the expectation that the gully dwarf was not far behind. Indeed, as the air deep within the fortress wafted past her nose, carrying the scent of garbage and miscellaneous refuse, she realized he probably wasn't the only Aghar in the place. Like most dwarven cities and fortresses of any size, Pax Tharkas no doubt hosted a thriving community of the little wretches, deep within the dungeons and tunnels where they were not—much of—a bother to the prevalent hardworking dwarves.

With her dog still shadowing her, Gretchan entered the dim corridors of the deep dungeons underneath what she knew was the East Tower of Pax Tharkas. Moving quietly, she slipped past dark, empty cells, climbed a narrow stairway to an upper floor, and continued to move farther into the fortress. She was approaching the next stairway leading up when she heard a key rattle in the lock overhead, and a door opened to reveal flickering torchlight.

Silently the dwarf maid and the shaggy, black dog shrank back into the darkness, a whispered word extinguishing the light glowing on the end of her staff. They drew deeper into a narrow side corridor off of the main dungeon hall. They would be almost impossible to see back there, even with strong dwarf eyes.

Sure enough, a small party of dwarves clumped by, ten paces away from her, but none of them even glanced her way. Two of the guards were escorting a prisoner, and she wasn't too surprised to recognize Brandon Bluestone, once again a prisoner.

Gretchan had spent much of the past two weeks watching the Kayolin dwarf's suffering. She had seen him captured by Garn Bloodfist's Klar the morning after she visited the mountain dwarf camp, and had observed him locked in chains, and dragged roughly along by his uncaring captors. She had followed closely, observing the company's progress all the way to Pax Tharkas. She knew he couldn't expect any better treatment from the hard-headed Hylar and Klar who lived there.

And Daewar, she reminded herself curtly. After her conversation with Garn Bloodfist, she knew without a shadow of a doubt that there was at least one Daewar there.

She waited in the silent darkness as she heard a metal door open, followed by the coarse laughter of the two guards as they tossed their prisoner into his cell.

"Don't worry," one of them taunted. "We'll be along with some food by next week at the latest."

"Until then," chortled the other, "you can always snack on the rats."

Gretchan frowned but held her tongue as the guards again clomped past her hiding place and climbed the stairs toward the next-higher level. Only when she heard the door slam behind them did she emerge, Kondike quietly trailing, to move into the main corridor.

There was only one cell with a closed door, so that must be where Brandon was being held. There was a small grid of bars in the door, providing a window into the cell, and she pressed her face to that opening before speaking in a whisper.

"Brandon? Brandon Bluestone of Kayolin?" she asked.

Seated on the bench that doubled as a bunk, he looked up with an expression that mingled consternation and pleasure. Their eyes met and even in the lightless conditions—she did not want to risk illuminating her staff again—they could recognize each other. She braced herself, preparing for another angry outburst, but instead the prisoner threw back his head and laughed heartily.

"Do you make a habit of visiting *every* prisoner in *every* dungeon?" he said, still chuckling. "Or is it just me?"

"Actually, it's just you," she admitted. "I saw you get taken by Garn's men, and then I saw them leading you into the dungeon and I followed you here. I wanted to, uh, see how you are doing. I hope they haven't beaten you—too badly. Have you had anything to eat?"

He shrugged from his seat on the bench. "So far, my survey of Neidar versus Klar hospitality has failed to arrive at any conclusion. But my research—as you can see—continues." Brandon's voice took on an edge of sarcasm. "I'll share the final result with you, for your book, if you want."

She bit her tongue on a sharp reply, as always sensitive to the progress—or lack thereof—of her book. "I'm sorry this happened to you again. I . . . I wish there was something I could do. About your bad luck, I mean. And I wasn't too nice to you last time we spoke; I wanted to apologize for that too."

Say something, she screamed silently. For a long heartbeat, he only sat there, studying her.

Finally, he rose and came over to the door, leaning his face close to the bars. He was really quite handsome, she told herself, even if he was still dressed in the same filthy garb he had been wearing for two weeks of marching through the mountains. His hair was uncombed but rich and thick and a pleasant shade of brown. It was draped low on his forehead, almost covering one eye with a rakish, very intriguing effect. His beard, once neatly trimmed, was unkempt, but it parted to reveal a neat set of white teeth.

"Uh, actually, I'd been wishing for the chance to say the same thing to you. I could have been more pleasant when you visited me in the brig," he admitted.

She was taken aback by his frank statement. It seemed almost un-dwarf-like! She realized that, when she first had met him, she had wanted to get him talking about his homeland, to learn about Kayolin from a dwarf who had lived there; then, it was only her research, her book, that mattered. At that moment, though, she found herself just wanting to get to know him, to understand him.

"You really are from Kayolin, aren't you?" she said. "I should have believed you."

"All my life," he replied. "Until the last few months."

"How did you come to be in the south hills?"

"It's a very long story," he said with a bitter chuckle.

"I have plenty of time," she replied.

And so he told her the long story. He told her all about the vein of gold he had discovered and about his brother's murder and Ham's murderous betrayal. He discussed his father's grief and his hopes, the treasure he had sent south with his son, and about Poleaxe's treachery in stealing it from him.

"That's where you found me, in the Hillhome brig. Waiting for execution, it turns out," he concluded.

"Wait. You mean, you think Harn Poleaxe intended to have you killed?" she asked.

"Intended, tried, almost did," Brandon said bitterly. He described his sham trial and his perilous predicament when he'd been shackled to the timber frame with tinder and firewood piled around his feet as the Klar attack began. "If the Klar hadn't attacked when they did, I'd have been cooked to a cinder in the next hour."

"That Poleaxe! He's even worse than I thought," Gretchan said. She told him all about Poleaxe's attack on her and fleeing Hillhome.

"The bastard!" Brandon spit, his knuckles whitening as he gripped the bars of his cell door.

All of a sudden Gretchan felt terribly weary and discouraged. She slumped against the door. "It's not just Poleaxe. There's Garn Bloodfist and Tarn Bellowgranite—and the high king in Thorbardin. All they can think about, it seems, is how they can make war against their fellow dwarves."

"Wait. You've been to Thorbardin?" Brandon said. "Is that your home?"

"No. I come from . . . far away from here," she said. "But all my life I've studied Thorbardin, talked to dwarves who lived there—even some who want to go back."

"But it remains sealed against the world, doesn't it?"

"Yes. And when I finally accepted that I'd never be able to visit the place, I decided to come to Pax Tharkas, to meet the dwarves here, who left Thorbardin only a decade ago. That's the closest I can get to chronicling Thorbardin, for now."

"I see. And where will all this research and chronicling lead?"

She sighed. "My great ambition is to go to the Great Library, in Palanthas. I want to ask them to take me in as an aesthetic or a student. I just want to read, to study, to learn about the dwarves of the past."

"All this talk of the past!" he challenged her, shaking his head. "What about the present or the future?"

Gretchan looked at him through the narrow bars and shook her head. "You've seen the present," she admitted sadly. "War and false trials and treachery and theft. What kind of future do you think the dwarf race has?"

"Oh, it can't be as bad as all that, can it?" he objected.

She couldn't help but place her own hands over his, and when his fingers clutched at hers, she felt a giddiness she had never felt before. It was as if he would never let her go.

And she would never want him to release her.

Gus was busy wandering through the tunnels of the Sla-Mori. He strolled into one room full of crypts, and when one of the coffin doors started to squeak open, he fled, dashing at top speed through the darkness. He scrambled over piles of loose stones, investigated shadowy niches, and discovered a chamber where a massive chain emerged from the ceiling to be fastened to a heavy iron bracket sunk right into the stone of the floor.

Once or twice he tried looking around for Gretchan, but he felt certain she was just a few steps ahead of him, and there was simply so much to see, he couldn't be bothered to worry about her. Little insect critters scurried out of his path, too fast for him to catch even one, but they reminded him he was getting hungry. Luckily he found a piece of old, rotten timber with a sumptuous yellow mold growing along one crumbled edge. He feasted on that rarity, spitting out the larger pieces of wood, until he felt sated. He got up to start walking again until, finally, he realized that he was very, very much alone.

He hastened down the darkened hallways, tripping and falling over many a loose rock, anxiously seeking the dwarf maid who had become his companion, his rescuer, his best friend—his goddess! He wanted to call out to her but didn't dare risk attracting attention to himself. So he trekked on, moving as fast as his stubby little legs would carry him.

He came to a door that was standing open. The other side of the door smelled refreshingly like Agharhome, the gully dwarf slum where he had lived nearly all of his life. He slowed to an easy stroll, wandering down a winding corridor with wet, slimy walls that reminded him of home. Then he caught an especially familiar, favorite scent, the stink of wet fur and a fleshy body.

Rat! He saw the creature scampering to the side, scuttling underneath a low shelf. Instantly Gus dropped to his hands and knees, clawing after the creature, reaching his stubby fingers under the shelf. He felt its naked tail, squeezed hard, and pulled only to feel it yanked away from his grip by an even more forceful tug.

"Hey! Rat mine!"

The protest came from a female gully dwarf who popped into view on the other side of the shelf. She held the wriggling rat in her hands and deftly twisted its body, snapping its neck.

"No, rat mine!" Gus retorted, planting his fists on his hips and glaring at the female. He had been startled by her abrupt appearance but managed to overcome his instinct of flight to stand in place and face her down.

She glared back at him, stubbornly clutching the rat. Her nose, Gus saw, was impressively large, swelling out from between two round cheeks. Her hair was reddish brown, tangled, and long, straggling over her round shoulders except where her large ears caused the matted tresses to extend almost straight out to the sides.

In that moment he remembered Slooshy and how they, too, had fought over a rat on their first meeting. He had claimed the rat and taken it away from Slooshy then lost it when it slipped out of his hand. Then Slooshy died. The memory made him feel terribly sad.

"Me Gus," he said, pointing a pudgy thumb at his chest. "You keep rat," he added graciously.

The female Aghar scowled suspiciously, looking him carefully up and down. "Berta," she said finally. Reconsidering her first impression, she gave the rat another twist, wrenching the little body into two parts.

"Here," she said, extending the hindquarters toward Gus.

Wide eyed, he took the morsel, and for two minutes the pair of them sat companionably on the ground, tearing off bits of the still-warm meat, chewing, and spitting as they discarded the larger bones, the feet, and the tail.

"This your big house?" Gus asked after a satisfied belch. He gestured to the yawning caverns, the dungeon passages and the shadowy stairwell around them.

"No," Berta said. "Me live Agharhome, over there two steps." She pointed into the distance. "Come into Paxhouse for food sometimes, though."

"You have Agharhome here?" asked Gus, amazed and delighted. "With highbulp? And clans?"

Berta seemed to think about that before she shrugged. "Got clans," she said. "But no highbulp right now. Him killed by big bluphsplunging doofar dwarf."

"Oh," Gus said, slumping sadly. Life for the gully dwarves seemed to be pretty much the same from one Agharhome to the next.

Berta flashed a grin, pivoting around to kneel on the floor and look him over carefully. She reached out and touched his arm, nodding in satisfaction. "Hey, you be new highbulp?" she asked. "Highbulp Gus!"

Gus gaped at her in astonishment. He couldn't be a highbulp! Highbulps were smart! Highbulps were powerful! Highbulps were masters of the Aghar, and he wasn't the master of anything.

"Gus make good highbulp," Berta pressed. "You brave, but no bully—not take rat from me like old highbulp would."

The little Aghar's mind was reeling. His new friend had presented him with an astounding idea, and even though it was unthinkable, she made him feel very strong and brave. Maybe he would make a good highbulp.

Only then did he think of his other friend, Gretchan. Immediately he bounced to his feet, suddenly panicked by the thought she had been gone for a long time. "I gotta go!" he cried. "Now!"

He sprinted away, leaving Berta staring open-mouthed after him. Where was the highbulp going? she must have wondered.

The highbulp was miserable about Gretchan. How could he have been so careless as to lose her? He lost his goddess, best friend, the most beautiful person ever to speak to him or show him an ounce of kindness.

Distraught, he wandered through darkened dungeon halls. He was weary and despairing, but he wouldn't give up. And finally his efforts were rewarded, as after many miles of walking—at least two, he figured—he came upon Kondike, lying on the floor of the dungeon, his head sleepily resting on his forepaws. At Gus's approach, the big dog raised his head, and his tail thumped against the floor in greeting.

Gus knew Gretchan wouldn't be far away from her beloved dog, and indeed, he promptly spotted the historian. She was leaning against the door of a dungeon cell, talking to another dwarf in hushed tones. Then, before the Aghar's disbelieving—and horrified—eyes she leaned in and kissed the other dwarf full upon the lips.

# TWENTY-THREE

## STORM CLOUDS GATHER

After another meeting with the Mother Oracle, only two days after the Klar raiders had been repulsed, Harn Poleaxe had taken the next step in his increasingly detailed and ambitious scheme. Following the ancient one's instructions, he had kindled her fire, brewed her tea, and stood back, drinking from his jug of spirits and scratching at the multiple sores across his face and arms, as she cast the liquid onto the floor to watch it puddle and melt in the midst of the sticky debris. She studied its signs and meditated. When she finally spoke, it was with great authority and conviction.

"You must summon the Neidar warriors from all across the hills," the Mother Oracle counseled in her blunt fashion. "Bring them to you here, and unite with them for strength. Form an army to destroy the mountain dwarves in Pax Tharkas!"

Harn was thrown by the grandiose idea. How many hill dwarves from towns a hundred miles away would care to follow him, he wondered. How many would even know his name?

"It will take some work, but they all share your goal,

and many more than you know will have heard of you!" the Mother Oracle cackled, reading his mind. "The Klar from Pax Tharkas have been raiding these lands for ten years. There is not a Neidar anywhere in the Kharolis range that doesn't hate and fear that troublemaking clan."

"Will they come?" Poleaxe asked, feeling intrigued as he began to imagine the possibilities. He took another drink and pondered the glory: a great army, at his command!

"You alone can make them come and unite!" the oracle hissed, her whisper hoarse and dry and like a knife that penetrated to the core of his being. "You have seen the way the dwarves of Hillhome responded to your leadership! Put your orders in writing, and send them with fleet messengers. The Neidar will surely answer your call!"

"I will, Mother Oracle!" he crowed, clenching his bloody fingers into a fist.

She nodded as if pleased. For a long time, she held her white, sightless eyes upon him, and he squirmed, even twitched around to see if someone were behind him. He turned back with the uncanny sensation that the blind, old woman was studying him.

"You must look the part of a commander," she said. "Find a great war helm—one with a plume of feathers, so that all will see you on the field."

"A splendid idea!" he agreed.

She reached out a bony finger, touched a bleeding spot on his cheek, and nodded. "And make sure it has a visor," she added. "A plate of metal that you can lower to protect . . . and shield your face."

And so he had done just as advised. Harn spent the next day drafting an eloquent call to action, a rather lengthy missive detailing, with minor exaggeration, the cruelties of the mountain dwarf attack against Hillhome, and the irreplaceable treasures that had been stolen from the hill dwarf coffers. He reminded the Neidar all through the Kharolis range of the long years of injustice, brutality, and violence wreaked upon their peaceful villages by the mountain dwarves of Pax Tharkas. That fortress, his missive read, was chock-full with treasures that the Hylar had stolen from many hill dwarf towns, villages, and homesteads.

He hinted, without claiming so directly, of an ally who would smash the gates of the mighty fortress and allow the Neidar army to charge inside and extract their vengeance. With each word that he wrote, he felt the growing power of his leadership, the compelling force of his will, transferred to the page. Somehow, the strength of his irresistible will would be communicated across the whole of the hill country.

At the same time as he was writing the letter, his lieutenants were gathering volunteers and fleet horses. When the missive was finished, some two dozen riders had assembled. Secretaries made multiple copies of the letter, and each rider took one of those epistles and departed at a gallop. Harn Poleaxe stood proudly in the plaza of Hillhome and watched them go, well satisfied at the momentous events he had put in motion.

Even as the horses thundered away, the town's best weaponsmith, Kale Sharpsteel, brought him a new helmet. It was tailored to cover his whole head, resting on his breastplate and shoulder pads, and was topped with a great plume of black and white stork feathers. The smith averted his eyes as he handed the metal cap to Lord Poleaxe, and Harn immediately placed it over his head. He lowered the visor with a flick of his finger and found that he could see clearly through the wide eye slits Sharpsteel had perfectly placed. The lone drawback was the fact that he had to raise the visor in order to take another drink of spirits.

Only then did the hulking dwarf swagger back to the private sanctuary of his own house. The hearth there had grown dark and cold, but that didn't matter to him; increasingly, he had become contemptuous of concerns such as food and warmth and even light. Drink, however, retained its eternal appeal, so he went immediately into the cellar, drawing himself a mug from a recently tapped keg. Removing his new helmet, he scratched at his face and sat down in his most comfortable chair.

He was waiting for someone. No, *something,* he corrected himself. He didn't have long to wait.

The monster arose from the floor, its webbed black wings emerging first from the very ground, followed by its crimson eyes and that terrible fanged maw. Poleaxe trembled in a mixture of terror and delight as the creature, the being he had chosen to believe was proof of his own elite status, once again made its presence known to him.

"Have you sent out your summons?" hissed the thing.

Harn Poleaxe didn't even stop to wonder how the creature knew about his plan.

"Yes!" Poleaxe boasted. "I have dispatched two dozen messengers to more than fifty villages and towns. I expect to raise an army of at least two thousand valiant dwarves."

"All hill dwarves, yes?"

"Hill dwarves, every man sworn to the destruction of the mountain dwarf outpost in Pax Tharkas," the warrior pledged stoutly. "Their longtime enmity and treachery will be punished, and my people will once again rule the hills of Kharolis."

"That is good. My master will be pleased," replied the creature silkily. "And when will you make this war? Time is short."

"We march on Pax Tharkas in ten days or less," vowed the new warlord of Hillhome.

"Again, that is good," hissed the creature.

"And you will be there too?" Harn said. "You will do as you say, break down the gates of the fortress?"

Again the creature hissed, a long, sibilant sound as its jaws gaped and its red eyes flared. "The gates," it murmured, "will not be a problem."

# THE SECRET OF PAX THARKAS

—DH—

Otaxx Shortbeard found Tarn where he almost always could be found: up on the catwalk along the Tharkadan Wall, supervising the progress of his great task.

"Almost done now," said the old Daewar general, watching in approval as another load of rocks was dumped from the lift, individual dwarves bearing the stones onto the unthinkably heavy pile of the reloaded trap.

"Aye," Tarn said, allowing himself a tight smile. "I predicted completion by the end of the year, but now I'd guess we're no more than a month away."

"I remember that hall, when we first claimed this place," Otaxx said, looking down into the huge, almost empty chamber below. "Rocks filling it halfway up the walls and worse. No way to open either gate, not even so much as to let a goat crawl through."

"Now with the gates open, wagons can roll down the road. We can open up trade with Haven or Tarsis, bring new traffic here. Finally restore some life to this old backwater."

"True, true," Otaxx said, gazing below. Indeed, the piles of rocks that still remained down there were already neatly shunted off to the left and right. The central part of the hollow wall, where the two gates allowed passage, had been cleared the previous year.

"You look troubled, old friend," Tarn said, clapping his old battle commander on the shoulder. "What are you thinking about? You should be proud at this happy time."

"Ah, we've known each other too long for secrets," said the old dwarf. He stared across the vast hall, but his gaze was focused on somewhere much farther away. "I've been remembering Berrilyn, more and more these days. When our work here is done, I'd like to travel into the east, to see if I can . . . well, not find her, not anymore. I don't fool myself about that. But learn what happened to her, to all of them. I'd like to look for Thoradin."

Tarn nodded. He, too, had known love at an early age. Belicia Slateshoulders, his true love, was dead, that he knew for certain, but if he didn't know, he would be tempted to go and look for her himself, just as his old friend was tempted to do.

"Do you think you'd have any mere chance of finding them? Of finding her?" the thane asked.

Otaxx could only shrug. "I'll always hate myself if I don't try."

———DH———

"Here, I brought you some warm soup."

Gretchan's voice brought Brandon out of his solitude and misery, and he quickly pushed himself to his feet and crossed the cell to the securely locked door. He touched her hand where her fingers were wrapped around the bar, his stomach growling as he smelled the rich broth.

But it was not the food that lightened his heart as much as the dwarf maid who brought it.

"Thanks," he said with a slight chuckle. "But how are you going to get that bowl through the bars?"

She laughed with him. "I knew you'd point that out right away. Here's the way we'll do it. I'll hold it up, and you put your lips against the bars. I'll pour it right down your throat."

"Sounds all right. Be careful, though." He gestured to his tattered and stained tunic, unwashed and unchanged in the weeks of captivity and travel. "I'm wearing my best shirt."

She lifted the bowl, and he sipped, feeling the soup warm his throat and his belly. Almost magically, strength and energy began to spread through his body, suffusing his limbs, brightening his eyes, lifting his spirits.

"Did you bring this right from the royal kitchen?" he asked, wiping his lips after he'd finished.

"Hardly. Nobody knows I'm down here yet," she said.

"I'd like to keep it that way for as long as possible." Gretchan held her pipe in her hand, exhaling smoke through her nose, and Brandon relished the sweet smell of burning leaf. He had come to associate that scent with their pleasant visits and was delighted by the way the odor lingered for hours even after she departed.

"I hope you're being careful," he cautioned. He didn't know how she managed to hide in the fortress, but she'd visited him virtually every day he'd been in the cell. The memory of her last visit, and the expectation of her next, kept him from descending into utter despair.

"Maybe you shouldn't come here anymore," he said, hoping she'd ignore him. "It's too dangerous."

She waved away his objections. "Your stories are finally starting to get interesting," she teased. "For your ancestor to be climbing Garnet Peak on the very day the Cataclysm occurred, for example. It almost makes me believe in all your tales of bad luck!"

"That's when it started," Brandon admitted morosely. "Nothing left of him but his axe, and I left that in Hillhome!"

"Who knows? Maybe you'll have a chance to go back and get it someday," she suggested. "Now, tell me again, when did the governor of Kayolin decide that he should start calling himself a king?"

"You know all my sore points," he said with a grin, touching her hand again. "No, let's talk about you for a change. I don't really know very much about you, do I? I know you don't come from Thorbardin or Pax Tharkas or Kayolin. So when are you going to tell me more about yourself?"

She sighed and looked at him affectionately. "In due time, I will," she said. "But I'm begging you to be patient with me. Can you?"

"Sure, of course I can," he said. His eyes twinkled. "Especially if you bring me some more soup tomorrow."

Garn Bloodfist studied the two wedges of green and blue stone. He propped them on the desk in his office near an oil lamp, its wick set to burn bright. He was dazzled by the shiny pure colors, seduced by the flickering facets that danced across the desk and the floor and sparkled along the walls. Eyes shining, he studied the reflections, giggling in sheer pleasure.

"Where did you come from?" he inquired of the objects.

It was not the first time he had spoken to them. For two weeks he had been studying them with every waking moment, wondering about their origins, their value. He had even gone out onto the upper parapet of the East Tower and asked answers from his father when Dashard Bloodfist appeared to him in the night sky. Though he preferred his nocturnal communions in the wilderness, such was his fascination with the two stone wedges that he was willing to risk the uneasy looks, the whispered gossip, that inevitably resulted from his seemingly unbalanced behavior.

Only Garn knew that his father was real, that his memory, the proof of his horrible betrayal, was the flame that kept the Klar warrior's fiery spirit burning so bright. And Garn Bloodfist was not afraid of the uncanny, the unexplained. Indeed, he was becoming increasingly convinced there was something supernatural about the stones. It wasn't so much the result of any special observation, though he did spend hours handling and scrutinizing the stones. It was more like a deep, growing conviction.

It was his conviction, more than anything else, that caused him to reevaluate the prisoner he had dragged back there all the way from Hillhome. Who was Brandon Bluestone? Why had he possessed the Bluestone, as he claimed? And why had he risked his life to confront the Klar? Was it to retrieve the fascinating colored stone?

In truth, Garn didn't believe his prisoner was simply another treacherous hill dwarf. There was something exotic, foreign, about him that aroused other suspicions, though, and the Klar commander had waited long enough to act upon his suspicions. Scooping the two stones back into their bag, Garn locked the precious stones in a vault and started down to the dungeon, determined to get some answers.

He was startled, but not shocked, to encounter a gully dwarf at the bottom of the stairway leading into the dungeon. The wretches were common enough pests around there, but he didn't like the thought they were often straying beyond the boundaries of their filthy town.

"Get out of here, you!" he snapped. "Or I'll knock your head right off your shoulders!"

Much to his surprise, the little fellow didn't budge, but instead stood there, glaring up at him, almost as if he had something he wanted to say.

"What is it, runt?" demanded Garn. "Don't you understand plain speech?"

"Prisoner complaint!" spit the Aghar with surprising vehemence. He gestured down the corridor toward the cell where Brandon Bluestone was imprisoned. "Him not locked up good enough!"

"He escaped?" Garn asked, startled until the gully dwarf firmly shook his head.

"Not escape. But not locked up enough!"

"What do you mean?" asked the Klar captain with exaggerated patience.

"Uh, him visited by nice, pretty maid. Nice, pretty maid all right, real important historian. Prisoner fools her. Gretchan visits him—and him not locked up good enough!" With that, the angry Aghar spun on his heel and sprinted away into the darkness, toward Agharhome.

Garn stared after him, amazed and alarmed. First of all, that was a pretty long speech for a gully dwarf. Then, too, he remembered the historian named Gretchan Pax very vividly; her sudden appearance in the midst of his company's camp had unsettled him more than he dared to admit. Her foul powers had paralyzed him in the mountain camp that night. She was either a witch or something much worse. Who was she really? Why was she there? And what was her purpose in talking to the prisoner?

Every answer he could imagine caused him worry.

——DH——

Gus strutted proudly through the dungeon of Pax Tharkas. He was getting to know the place fairly well, and indeed, not far away he had found himself a second home in the scummy tunnels of Agharhome, on a comfortable sleeping pallet. The pallet had been graciously offered up by Berta, who volunteered to sleep on the cold stone instead, and Gus allowed himself to feel a measure of gratitude toward the dirty little gully wench.

She even continued to call him "highbulp," which he found a delightful and inspiring title. Thus far, the rank was not acknowledged by any other of the tower's Aghar population, but Berta kept telling everyone that Gus was the new highbulp, and she kept telling Gus himself that, in two days, the rest of the bluphsplunging doofars in Agharhome would recognize his exalted status as well. In point of fact, he didn't really care if the others called him highbulp. It was enough that Berta did so and that she would share the occasional rat or other morsel she acquired. Her pallet was nice too.

But right at the moment, he was thinking of a different female. He was very proud of his boldness in speaking to the great Hylar prince, and he wanted to boast about his deed. Up till then he had been in a jealous snit for days and had avoided Gretchan Pax. Speaking to the Klar prince had made him feel better. Gretchan didn't seem even to care if he was alive, but he had been doing some very good spying, and he knew right where to find her.

Gretchan had made her quarters, all unknown to the Tharkan garrison, in a small, dry, secret room just next to the dungeon halls. The chamber was clean and warm, and she always seemed to find good food to eat; she was constantly taking food to the prisoner. Gus felt another stab of jealousy but set his chin, marching onward.

Coming to the secret panel, which was concealed behind a weapons cabinet in one of the rooms that would have been used to garrison dungeon guards, should there ever be enough prisoners down there to require a garrison, Gus pulled the cabinet door open and knocked on the wooden back wall. Immediately he heard a low growl from beyond the panel.

"Kondike! It's me! Gus!" he whispered loudly.

Moments later the panel was pulled aside and Gretchan Pax was beaming down at him. "Gus!" she said very sweetly, the gully dwarf had to admit. "I was afraid I'd lost you! Come in."

"No lose Gus!" he replied sarcastically, stepping into the room as she held the door open for him. "Gus no lose Gretchan either."

"Well, now you have found me and I'm glad," she said. "This is a good hiding place, but I didn't think anyone else knew where I was."

"I follow!" Gus bragged happily. Then his features twisted into a dark scowl, and his tone became accusing. "Follow when you visit big kisser dwarf in jail!"

"Why Gus!" Gretchan chided, her eyes widening and her cheeks colored by a tinge of embarrassed redness. "Have you been spying on me?" she asked sharply.

"No! I mean yes!" the Aghar replied, gazing steadfastly at the floor to avoid Gretchan's beautiful eyes. His big toe jutted out the front of his worn boot, and he used it to mark irregular circles on the floor. "Not Gretchan, but Gus spy on big kisser dwarf!"

"All right now, Gus. I'm serious. What are you talking

about? What's the big deal about this big kisser—oh, his name is Brandon, damn it. What about him?"

"I not like big kisser dwarf. Him bad for you. Big dwarf general gonna lock him up more better! Him not locked up enough!" Gus stated bluntly.

"Oh, isn't that sweet. Are you jealous?" Gretchan asked amusedly. She started to laugh then caught herself, her expression growing stern. "Wait, what's that about a big dwarf general? Did you talk to someone?"

"Yep. Gus brave, talk to Klar chief. Him gonna lock up prisoner more better. You and I then go away like before. Forget big kisser dwarf!"

"Oh, Gus, you didn't!" the dwarf maid gasped, kneeling down to grasp the gully dwarf firmly by the shoulders. Her eyes were large, serious, and concerned. "Did you . . . did you tell the Klar general that I am here, that you saw me visiting the prisoner?"

"Yes!" he declared hotly.

"Oh, that's terrible!" she said, shaking her head as her eyes moistened with tears. "Garn Bloodfist will be angry, and he's already so twisted up with hate. There's no telling what he might do! How could you do this to me?"

"To you? Big kisser dwarf bad; him do to you! Klar gonna make him stop!"

"You don't understand!" accused Gretchan. "Brandon doesn't mean any harm to you or anyone else. He keeps ending up in jail, but he's innocent; he did nothing wrong! Now you might have cost him his life!"

"Life?" gulped Gus. "N-no! Not life. Just lock him up better!"

The dwarf maid stamped her foot angrily. She was furious, so angry she was shaking. Gus took a step backward, feeling suddenly very miserable. "You little fool!" she snapped. "You've just ruined everything! Oh, just get out of here! Go away, I tell you!"

Stunned by her outburst, his heart breaking under the

onslaught of her harsh words, Gus could only retreat out through the secret door still cracked open behind him. He wandered, feeling forlorn, back into the dungeon, haunted by the sound of Gretchan's sobs coming through even after the door had slammed shut.

# Twenty-Four

## Roads and Gates

Garn Bloodfist went straight to the thane, finding him—as always—on the catwalk high inside the Tharkadan Wall. Tarn Bellowgranite was supervising the placement of the rocks, nearly all of which had been lifted up from the floor where they had lain for more than eighty years. Bloodfist clenched his fists, shaking his head in a physical effort to remind himself to be calm when all he wanted was to grab Tarn by the shoulders and shake him into some sense of alarm.

The thane cut the Klar captain off before he could speak. "This last step is crucial," Tarn explained, gesturing at the complicated mechanism of gears and chains and pulleys, clearly entranced by the sight and taking no notice of the fact that his listener was trying to get a word in edgewise. "The counterbalance is important; it's why the simple pull of a lever is enough to dump half a million tons of rock down into the gateway."

"Yes, I see," Bloodfist said, stopping himself from rolling his eyes. How long had he feigned interest in a task that, to his mind, was endless and meaningless?

"I'm glad you do see, my captain," replied the old dwarf. Garn was startled at the earnestness with which his ruler addressed him. "For this great task is almost completed. At one time I felt that it would not happen during my lifetime; now I think the chances are good that I will see the final rocks raised into the trap before the end of this month.

"But when I'm gone, my valiant Klar, this great mechanism, this fortress, these hallowed towers will all be the responsibility of you and the other clan captains. I want you to welcome this trust, and I trust you will prove worthy of the task you shall inherit."

"My liege," Garn said, driven by exasperation to disrespectful bluntness. The image of his father's gashed and bleeding body, the mute plea for vengeance he saw every time he looked skyward into those dying eyes, would not allow patience. "I believe you have done a great service to the Hylar and Klar exiles by your work here in Pax Tharkas. But I want you to know: my goals remain higher. Pax Tharkas is a splendid base for us, a fortress we can use to launch the next campaign. But you must know that I am still determined, before my years are through, to regain our status in Thorbardin itself!"

Tarn Bellowgranite sighed. "I understand your ambitions, my bold warrior. But I hope you will come to see that you are advocating a hopeless and destructive course. Thorbardin is sealed from within, and any intrusion by ourselves, or anyone else, would surely be met with crushing force. No, Garn, Jungor Stonespringer might as well have caved in the mountain on that entire dwarven realm, for it is lost to us and the surface world forevermore."

"I know there is bitterness in your heart, my thane; surely it was a rank betrayal that brought us to exile! You know it cost my father his very life! But I think you are letting it cloud your judgment!"

"Don't be a fool!" snapped Tarn. "The Hylar and the Theiwar would unite against you in a finger snap. The Daergar would not be your friends either! You would invade Thorbardin with a few hundred warriors and meet an army of ten thousand!"

Garn took a deep breath, conscious of the eyes—and ears—of the nearby laborers who had paused in their work. He trembled at the rebuke, and his own eyes bulged while his hands clenched into fists. With every fiber of will, he reminded himself that Tarn Bellowgranite was a revered figure among the Hylar exiles. It would be foolish to display overt contempt for the thane. So he hung his head with a humility he did not feel. "I accept your reasoning, my liege. Please accept my apologies. I spoke not from the head, but from the heart."

"I understand, Garn. It is not easy to live as we do, with the memories of past greatness all around us. But we must be strong and our path must be reasoned."

Had the old, senile thane abandoned all hope of future greatness? Garn wanted to scream the question aloud, but instead he bowed and walked meekly away.

Yet his passive demeanor marked a growing anger and a fierce determination. He had come to speak to Tarn Bellowgranite about a different matter, and as it turned out, he had not been allowed a chance to even broach the issue. He was still shaking, and only with a conscious effort was he able to unclench his fists. Reorx curse him—it was Tarn Bellowgranite who was the fool!

Never mind. He didn't need his thane's permission to make important decisions! By Reorx, the fool was so busy lifting his rocks, he didn't care what else went on in the world anymore.

Garn maintained his apartments in the East Tower, claiming one floor of the tower for his own use and garrisoning the three hundred dwarves of his mobile company on the floors just below. He strode onto the uppermost of those garrison floors, where a number of his warriors were playing gambling games while others were busy sharpening their weapons or catching up on their sleep.

He nodded to two of his oldest followers, burly mountain dwarves with a great capacity for violence and an almost non-existent penchant for analyzing the moral aspects of whatever tasks Garn Bloodfist assigned them. "Crank, Bilious," he barked. "Come with me, and bring your swords."

The two armed dwarves willingly accompanied him down the long series of stairways leading to the ground level and into the dungeon below that. The two thuggish Klar warriors asked no questions as Garn led them into the deepest levels of the east dungeon. They were always eager for action and oblivious to causes or motives.

"We're going to put an end to some irritating mischief," the captain explained as they reached the lowest level. "This prisoner is proving to be more trouble than he can possibly be worth."

They advanced into the portcullis room, the square chamber connecting to the deepest dungeon passage, and here Garn came up short as he spotted a ragged little figure sleeping in the corner.

"You again?" he barked, rousing the gully dwarf with a sharp kick. "Didn't I warn you to get lost?"

"Oh, great prince!" cried the miserable creature, throwing himself on the ground at Garn's feet and salaaming the Klar. "Thank you for come here!"

"Get out of my way," the Klar captain growled. "I have work to do!"

"Oh, not with dwarf prisoner, no!" insisted the gully dwarf with startling conviction. He stood defiantly in the path of the mountain dwarves. "My mistake. Go away!"

"What's this?" muttered Garn, almost amused.

"Move, you," declared Crank, whipping out his sword and waving the blade at the bold Aghar.

"You move!" declared the runt, dashing forward and biting the armed mountain dwarf on the knee.

"Hey! Ouch!" howled Crank. "You miserable little half-pint!"

He swung his blade, but somehow the gully dwarf, who was almost under his feet, scampered away. Bilious also moved to cut him off, blocking him from fleeing through the door deeper into the dungeon. "Where do you think you're going?" the menacing warrior demanded.

The two armed dwarves closed in on the Aghar, but the little fellow dived to his belly and scooted right between Crank's legs.

Garn had been chuckling, but he had had enough. "Cut him down and be done with him!" snapped the Klar captain. "We've got more important things to do!"

The mountain dwarves spun and pursued, and the gully dwarf dashed out the door. But Bilious had anticipated the move and leaped to block the Aghar's escape. The dirty gully dwarf found himself trapped, his back to the corridor wall, one armed mountain dwarf inside the square room, the other blocking his passage down the corridor. Bilious stabbed, aiming low, and the Aghar sprang upward, flailing with his hands, clawing at the mold-slick stone on the dungeon wall. There was nothing to grab there on the surface of the wall itself, but his hand came into contact with a metal lever jutting up from a narrow slot.

The gully dwarf seized the lever with both hands, intending to pull himself up and away from his attacker's blade. Instead, his weight caused the lever to drop sharply, plunging him onto his rump on the floor. A catch was released and unseen chains made a rattling noise as Bilious charged, stabbing wildly. The frantic gully dwarf tumbled out of the path of the attack, and the three enraged mountain dwarves stumbled over the Aghar, sprawling across the floor of the dungeon.

The chains rattled louder and faster, metal clanging against stone, as the two portcullis gates dropped into their deep sockets on the floor. Two metal grates closed off the chamber, blocking the way into the halls of prisoner cells and also closing the way back up into the East Tower. The small square room was, for all intents and purposes, a cell in its own right.

And Garn Bloodfist, Bilious, and Crank were all trapped inside.

——DH——

The army of hill dwarves snaked its way through the rugged terrain, skirting the Plains of Dergoth, advancing on Pax Tharkas from the south. At its head marched Harn Poleaxe, hailed as "Lord Poleaxe" by one and all. He sat astride a horse, a mighty sword resting in his lap, while all the rest of his army advanced on foot. The plumed helm rested on his head, and he kept the visor closed—except when he took a drink—because he had seen that his dwarves were shaken by the sight of his increasingly bloody, lumpy face. Still, he barely noticed them, strung out in a column more than a mile long behind him. His eyes, for now and forever, were fixed ahead, on the future.

And the future would be found in Pax Tharkas.

Harn had been pleased and rather surprised when more than three thousand hill dwarves had answered his summons to war. They had come from the farms and villages and towns of the Neidar scattered throughout the valleys and plains below the lofty summits of the High Kharolis. Marching eagerly, singing ancient songs of war, gathering from pairs to platoons to companies as they converged on Hillhome, they had responded to his call with a cheerful eagerness to make war and a seemingly unquenchable thirst for revenge.

Some of the Neidar were grizzled veterans, bearing scars earned during the War of Souls or the Chaos War or, for some of the eldest, even the War of the Lance. They limped and cursed and argued, but they marched and were ready to fight. Far more of them were strapping adults or callow youths, unblooded and unscarred but eager to face the ultimate truth of battle. Some were drunk, others were crazed, but most were hale and hearty.

All of them shared an abiding hatred of the mountain dwarves. That hatred had seethed and simmered for years and, finally, had its fuse lit by Poleaxe's message. All had seen the damage, felt the injustice, of the Klar raids that had terrorized their lands for the past decade. An assault against Pax Tharkas had been considered a hopeless, quixotic notion. But they had been swayed by the eloquence of Harn's appeal.

"Aye-uh," said Axel Carbondale, a legendary captain of axemen through the course of three wars, upon his arrival in Hillhome. "I couldn't have said it any better myself."

"I've been *trying* to say it for years!" declared Carpus Castlesmasher, mayor of Bloodford, a hero who had been decorated five times for his company's doughty defense against draconians and ogres over the past decades. "But you said it in a way that all the Neidar understand," he admitted, his eyes shining with admiration as he offered Harn Poleaxe his sword and his life.

There were more than four hundred pikemen from the villages around the Plains of Dergoth. Nearly twice that many hill dwarves armed with crossbows and daggers came from small woodland villages. The foothill mines produced five companies of heavy infantry, each dwarf protected to the eyelids by heavy plate armor and bearing axes that could split the shield, or the skull, of any foe with a single blow. Swords were sharpened, spare spears fashioned, and provisions collected from every field, silo, and barnyard.

They had gathered on the slopes around Hillhome, camping in the great square and in the fields just beyond the town, carousing in the inns every night and generally driving the good citizens of the town to cower in their homes, bar their doors and windows, and wait for the scourge to be gone. Fortunately for them, Poleaxe was eager to start the expedition.

He summoned all the captains, and as many of the men who could squeeze there, into the plaza of the town. They crowded in there to hear him with battle lust in their hearts. He wore his helm, seeing that all would come to recognize the lofty plume of black and white feathers. The visor was lifted, and he took frequent sips from the jug he carried.

"I want you to hearken back to the days of the Dwarfgate War, my hill dwarf kinsmen!" he had declared when the last recruits arrived and the volunteer army stretched as far as the eye could see. He stalked back and forth on the raised platform in Hillhome's square, his voice booming out, ringing across the plaza, carrying even to the ranks of dwarves packed into every side street. His listeners were rapt, absorbing every word. When he turned his blood-spotted face, more than half covered with bloody warts, toward those in the front rows, they stared back at him in a mixture of horror and awe. But they absorbed his words and thumped their chests in response to his commands.

"These mountain dwarves in Pax Tharkas are the hated Klar, the arrogant Hylar! They are the ones who sealed Thorbardin against our kind long ago, when the gods sent the Cataclysm raining down upon our world! And they are the ones who visited such terrible devastation upon us when the wizard Fistandantilus, wanting only fairness for our ancestors, sought passage through the undermountain lands."

He drew a breath, letting the powerful images of the past, each evoking a tragic racial memory, wash over the gathered fighters. Taking a long drink, he allowed the tension to build before he spoke again.

"This Hylar captain who struck Hillhome out of the calm of a peaceful morning, whose warriors slaughtered our women and children and left their bodies to bleed in the street, he should be the first to die . . . and then all the arrogant ones like him. I ask you, my clansmen, are we to put up with Hylar arrogance forever?"

A resounding "No!" roared from a thousand and more throats—at least from the throat of every hill dwarf who was close enough to hear what Poleaxe was saying. The rest filling the streets, the throng extending to the far outskirts of town, also cheered and shouted as the message that was passed to them increased in shrillness and hate.

Then a murmur, followed by a hush, spread through the gathering, moving in reverse of Harn's message, like a wave flowing from the town's outskirts toward the central square. Poleaxe was surprised to see that the wave originated from the narrow lane where the Mother Oracle lived, and as he watched, he saw the crowd of hill dwarves parting to allow one, still unseen from the square, to pass. He allowed himself to hope.

She came! The old dwarf crone hobbled forward, leaning on a crooked staff, her shawl wrapped tightly around her skinny frame, exposing only her wrinkled face, her pale, blind eyes, and the clawlike fingers of her hands. The hill dwarves gawked at her rare appearance—she hadn't been outside of her hut in years—and gave her a wide berth, pressing onto the sidewalks and alleys as she tottered along the center of the street.

As she entered the square, the whole town fell silent, and a wide path appeared in the throng as it became clear that she was making for the raised platform where Harn Poleaxe stood. He hopped down to the ground and took her hand as she reached the edge. Still holding the jug in his other hand, he guided her up the steps and onto the dais.

"Behold, my Neidar!" Harn bellowed. "The Mother Oracle has come to bless our endeavor!"

The cheer that washed over them was sudden, loud, and sustained. Harn, who loomed over the old woman, was conscious of her stature, as if she were the large one. He stood back and, as the warriors settled in to listen, the crone raised her hand and waved it in the air. The Neidar, as a group, sighed in pleasure as if a physical blessing had been bestowed.

"My beloved hill dwarves," she began, in a high-pitched voice that, somehow, seemed to carry to all the many thousands of ears in attendance. "Today you embark upon a mission that is blessed by Reorx himself. For ever is our god a foe of injustice, and never has a people suffered greater injustice than his Neidar.

"The mountain dwarves have wronged you, tortured you, made war upon you for many centuries. For all those years, you have been patient and virtuous, disdaining the vengeance that is so rightfully yours. Yet each crime against you, each murder and theft and injustice, has been catalogued by the Master of the Forge. And soon, my Neidar, that record of wrongs shall be made right!

"For know: you march on a quest that is greater than your own desires, mightier than the wrongs that have been done just to you warriors alone. You march to right the wrongs that have been done to all your people, for all the years of the world. You march in righteousness! You march to vengeance! And most of all, you march to victory!"

At her last word, she clenched her talonlike fingers into a fist. A cloud of smoke erupted from the place where she stood, provoking gasps of awe. Even Harn Poleaxe took a step back, gaping in astonishment as the smoke dissipated and he discerned that the old dwarf woman was gone. He raised his jug and took a long drink, aware of the murmurs growing into a dull roar from the gathered throng.

Poleaxe stood tall, raising his long arms over his head and clasping his hands together into a single triumphant fist. The power of the potion pulsed through him, and he felt as though he could smash down the walls of Pax Tharkas with the blows of his own flesh.

But he had an army to carry those walls.

"My Neidar!" he cried, and his voice was like the roar of a bull ogre. "March with me! Make war on the mountain dwarves! Carry their fortress, and end their miserable lives!"

And, he told himself with a private smirk, he had an even more potent ally in reserve—a creature whose desire for killing and vengeance rivaled his own. As the roars of approval rose from the throats of his troops, he sensed the power of his great band, and he knew they were invincible.

"Now, hill dwarves! Now we march! We march to avenge our ancestors! We march to punish our foes! And we march to bring the Neidar to the greatness that has ever been denied!"

The final roar swelled like thunder, carrying through the town, into the air, up and over the ridges of the surrounding hills. The noise had echoed, like terrible thunder or the crashing of powerful waves, as the hill dwarves zestfully hoisted their weapons and marched to war. Even then, a week's march north of the town, drawing ever closer to their ancient objective, the songs of war and victory rose from the Neidar throats, resounding from the mountain ridges, carried on wings of battle toward the ears of Reorx himself.

——DH——

"Open this gate, you miserable runt—you filthy gully dwarf!" roared the dwarf captain, pounding his fists against the bars of the portcullis. "Or I'll tear your arms off and stuff them into your useless mouth!"

Gus huddled on the floor, just on the other side of the closed portcullis—wisely staying far enough away that the trapped mountain dwarves couldn't reach him with their swords, which they had poked through the grid as soon as they realized they were trapped. He was too terrified to do anything, much less run away.

The Aghar stared, open mouthed, at the enraged dwarves. He wasn't sure how they had managed to get trapped, though in the back of his mind he suspected it had something to do with the lever he had grabbed. The eyes of the great captain bulged so far from his face that it seemed as though they might pop right out of his head.

"I only want to climb wall," he protested. "I not try to drop gate!"

His pleadings only seemed to inflame the dwarves. The big captain practically foamed at the mouth, while his two big henchmen each took hold of the nearest gate. Working together, straining until sweat streaked their skin and veins bulged on their foreheads, they were able to lift the massive barrier only scant inches before it crashed back down and they collapsed, gasping for breath.

"I tell you—if you don't open this gate immediately, your fate will be a suffering that your worst nightmares could never imagine." The captain's eyes were wild, bulging, and staring, and he snarled like a wild animal, straining to reach through the closely set bars.

Gus, having endured some very terrible nightmares in his pathetic life, found the threat to be ominous indeed. But he simply didn't know how to raise the gate, and all the blustering warnings in the world weren't going to change that. He was terribly afraid of the big, furious dwarves, but it gradually dawned on him that he might sneak away from there and, so long as the gate remained closed, his antagonists wouldn't be able to chase him.

Thus, he wheeled and sprinted off into the darkness, hearing the sounds of the infuriated Klar cursing echoing through the dark passage behind him.

He came to the wardroom leading to Gretchan's secret room, but she had been so upset before, he didn't dare approach her. A big mess, he thought miserably, it's all a big mess.

Still running, he realized he was headed toward the passage where the Kayolin dwarf was imprisoned, which terminated in a dead end not far beyond Brandon's cell. As long as he was in the neighborhood, he might as well see if the bad kisser dwarf was still alive. He peeked in.

There came a sound from inside the cell, and a fist appeared, clutching the bars on the door. "Hello?"

The question was tentative, suspicious. Gus looked upward and saw Brandon's face appear in the small, barred window. The Hylar, upon seeing a mere gully dwarf staring back, shrugged his shoulders and moved back into the cell.

Gus thought for a moment, feeling helpless and afraid. The bad kisser dwarf didn't seem so bad up close, and he hadn't even tried to kiss Gus.

He ought to do something, he told himself, thinking of the trapped angry dwarves and all the mistakes he had made. There was only one thing he could think of: he went back to the secret door outside of Gretchan's room. Mustering all of his courage, he knocked on the wooden panel, suddenly worried that she might not be there.

And when she opened the door, she did not look as mad as she had been when he had so anxiously retreated from her presence a day or two earlier.

"Hello, Gus," she said, frowning down at him. "What do you want this time?"

He wanted to throw himself into her arms and beg forgiveness, but instead he mustered all of his noble character and spoke to her.

"Mean dwarf prince comes to hurt prisoner. I sorry for before and try help. They locked up now, but they still want to come here and hurt him, us. We gotta get prisoner out of there, or else . . . or else . . ." He sniffled loudly and wiped away a tear.

To his immense relief, Gretchan did lean down and pat him on the shoulder. "Thank you for coming," she said, all very matter-of-fact, as though she had known he was coming and what he would say. "That was very brave. Now what do you mean, 'locked up'?"

"Here, let me show," he said, tugging her hand, pulling her out of the garrison room and into the corridor. "Wait here," he whispered as they came closer to the place. "You listen."

He strolled forward around the last corner and was immediately spotted by the big dwarf captain, who was down on his knees, grunting as he tried to budge the cage.

"You! Gully dwarf! Come here, damn your eyes! Turn that lever and pull this gate up, or so help me Reorx—"

Gus didn't wait to hear more. He raced back around the corner and was surprised to see that Gretchan was laughing. At first he was insulted, but then his chest swelled with pride as she clapped him on the back and whispered, "Well done!"

Then she frowned. "But you're right. We have to get Brandon out of here before they're freed, or they'll ... I don't know what they'll do, but I don't want to find out. We'd better hurry. Others will be coming down to see what happened to them."

With Gus and Kondike racing along behind her, she hurried to the cell where the dwarf was imprisoned. Pressing her face to the grate, she called to him. Immediately he appeared.

"Trouble," she said. "No time to explain, but we've got to get you out of here now."

"I'm all in favor of that," Brandon replied. "But how? Did you bring a key?"

She shook her head. Pulling her little silver hammer from her belt, she warned the dwarf: "Stand back."

"Why?" Brandon asked incredulously, giving a slight chuckle. "In case the hammer breaks and a piece goes flying?"

"Suit yourself," Gretchan replied. She hoisted the little tool, which had a head shaped much like the anvil on her staff, and swung it lightly against the latch on the cell door.

The explosion was so deafening, Gus covered his ears.

Wood splintered and iron screeched as the portal was blown off its hinges, the bulk of the heavy door sent flying back into the cell, where it knocked Brandon onto the floor. The heavy wooden beams forming the door were shattered, and the lock itself had shattered into a hundred metal shards.

"How did you do that?" gasped Brandon, sitting up in astonishment and pushing the wreckage of the door off himself. Aside from some nicks and bruises, he looked only a little worse for wear. "It looked like you only tapped it!"

"Looks can be deceiving," she replied slyly. "Now do you want to have a long conversation, or do you want to get out of there."

"Get out!" Brandon replied, shucking away the broken beams and pushing himself up. He glared at her. "But you could have warned me."

"I tried," said Gretchan, grinning.

The big mountain dwarf stepped to the door of the cell then stopped. "Wait. I know you carry that hammer with you everywhere; you had it in Hillhome. So you could have done this anytime? Gotten me out of here?"

"I told you—there's no time to talk!" she snapped in agitation.

"Damn it, I want some answers!" Brandon growled. "You've been feeding me, bringing me soup—by Reorx, you kissed me through the bars of the cell! When all this time you could have let me out with one swing of your hammer! It's like I've been some kind of caged pet!"

She snorted but then looked away, abashed. In another moment, her face hardened. "Look. We can talk about it later. For now, I'm getting away. Are you coming along?"

"Oh, I'm coming, all right—if only to get those answers you promised!" Brandon muttered, emerging into the dark corridor. "Who's that?" he said immediately, pointing to Gus and wrinkling his nose.

Gus sulked and pointed back at Brandon, wrinkling his nose in similar fashion.

"Oh, that's just Gus," said Gretchan. "He helped save your life. After he almost got you killed. It's another long story for later. Now come on!"

"Where are we going?" asked Brandon as she led all three at a trot back out of the dead-end corridor.

"Just trust me," she said. "This place is full of surprises, and I've been learning a lot of them."

# TWENTY-FIVE

## A SECRET REVEALED

Help! Help us someone! Open these gates!" Garn Bloodfist shouted for the hundredth time, stalking around the small, square room where he and his two men were caged by the falling portcullis trap.

"I don't think anyone can hear us, Captain," Bilious suggested unhelpfully.

"Of course they can't!" the Klar officer screamed. "Help me make some louder noise, you worthless scum!"

For a time all three of the trapped Klar shouted and hollered until they all were too hoarse to make any sound above a croaking rasp. "What are they doing up there?" demanded the captain in a whisper. "Are they all asleep? Drunk?"

"I think we're too far away for them to hear us," Crank speculated none too brilliantly.

"Your weapons!" Garn said, suddenly struck by inspiration. "Bang them against the bars!"

Crank and Bilious obeyed his order with enthusiasm, drawing their swords and smashing the flats of the blades against the metal bars of the portcullis, raising a din that crashed against their ears with deafening force. The sounds rang and echoed and swelled through the subterranean passage, making an unworldly clamor. Even when the tip of Crank's blade broke off, the two swordsmen kept up their banging until—finally—a curious Hylar sentry came wandering down into the dungeon to see what all the noise was about.

"Open the gates! Lift the portcullis!" croaked Garn, his voice grown hoarse from more than an hour of shouting. After gaping in momentary astonishment, the rescuer obligingly pulled down on the lever, with each tug of the mechanism working the winch, lifting the two gates an inch at a time. Watching impatiently, the Klar captain wanted to strangle the fellow for taking such a long time, but that would have to wait until he had caught up with the blasted Aghar and the imprisoned Kayolin dwarf.

When the grate was some two feet off the floor, Bloodfist threw himself down flat and squirmed under the barrier, to be quickly followed by Crank and Bilious.

"Finish raising it!" he called back to their rescuer before plunging deeper into the dungeon. His feet pounded on the cold stone floor as he sprinted around corners so fast that he bounced off the walls, putting his head down and urgently charging forward again.

Even before he reached the corridor where Brandon Bluestone was imprisoned, he had the sickening feeling they were going to be too late. Running down the last stretch, he grimaced in almost physical pain as he saw the open doorway to the cell. Skidding to a stop beside the empty chamber, he glared at the wreckage of the splintered door and roared out curses, kicking through the debris as if he expected to find the prisoner hiding there.

"What happened?" asked Crank, gaping stupidly. "Did that gully dwarf knock the door down?"

"Don't be an idiot," snapped Garn. "*She* did this! She's here, somewhere, working against me. She's a witch, I tell you; I knew it the first time I saw her! And that gully dwarf told me: she's lurking right *here*, in Pax Tharkas!" He stared up and down the corridor as if he could command Gretchan to appear simply by the dint of his willpower.

But of course, that would never happen.

Instead, he ordered Crank to run back to the garrison hall and alert the company of Klar warriors.

"Make sure they are all armed. Send half the men down here to start searching in the dungeon. Have the rest disperse through the East Tower. We must catch them before they escape."

His father's bloody face seemed to shimmer in the air before him, and the Klar captain let out a wail of grief and fury that ensured Crank would sprint back to the tower at full speed. Drawing his own sword, Garn Bloodfist held his weapon tightly, striding through the dungeon of Pax Tharkas on a mission of punishment and revenge.

----DH----

Two Neidar scouts came down from the ridge, dragging a body between them. They tossed it onto the road before Harn Poleaxe. The army commander, peering through the eye slits on his helmet visor, saw a dead dwarf with pair of crossbow bolts jutting from his back.

"He was a lookout—Klar," said one of the scouts, spitting on the corpse. "But he won't be doing much looking out—or anything else—anymore."

"Good work," Poleaxe said. He raised his visor so he could take a drink, and while he drained his jug, he looked up, scanning the steep ridges that flanked the road along which his army marched. His advance parties were swarming all over those heights, but even so, he knew it was unrealistic to think they would be able to approach the fortress unnoticed. After all, it was the only route an army could use to get into the pass from the south, and the mountain dwarves were sure to have many more sentries posted.

But the Neidar still hoped for a surprise attack. "Get

back up there, and find us another one," he ordered, and the two hill dwarves—both of whom were dressed for agility and silence in leather armor and soft walking boots—turned back to the heights at a jog.

Harn tossed his empty jug to Rune, who followed immediately behind the army commander, leading a mule that was bearing two kegs of dwarf spirits strapped to its panniers. As a reward for his assistant's loyalty, Harn had given Rune the axe he had taken from Brandon Bluestone. The Neidar, who had been badly beaten during the prisoner's escape, wore that weapon proudly, strapped to his back where all could admire the splendid craftsmanship, the keen steel edge.

The kegs were the exclusive refreshment of Harn Poleaxe, and they had been full when the army departed Hillhome. Rune, who took care to refill the jug alternately from the left and right keg so as to keep the mule's load even, promptly turned the spigot. Poleaxe fidgeted in his saddle, scratching at the blisters that marred both cheeks and his entire forehead, until his subordinate, with a deep bow, brought him the freshly filled vessel. Harn took a deep drink and once again waved the column forward.

As the army neared the enemy stronghold, the ranks of the Neidar had tightened and the marching songs ceased. Morale was high; that was apparent from the joyful determination Poleaxe saw in every face, in the way the dwarves carefully sharpened their weapons at each night's camp, in the way the scouts ranged eagerly and swiftly onto the surrounding heights.

On the tenth day of the march, several of his scouts had reported a glimpse of the fortress's towers around the next bend of the winding but only gently climbing pass. To the best of Harn's knowledge, no mountain dwarf lookout had survived to carry word of their approach to the Pax Tharkas garrison, but of course, if such a sentry had indeed slipped away from his scouts, it was likely that the hill dwarves would not know about it.

So they established a camp a half day's march from their objective, protecting it with a full set of defensive preparations. Instead of sleeping in a meadow on the valley floor as they had done each previous night of the march, where fresh water would be readily available, the Neidar unrolled their bedrolls across a series of plateaulike surfaces crowning the ridge to the west of the road. They carried a plentiful supply of water up to their compounds, and the captains posted double the number of usual guards to make sure they stayed watchful in shifts throughout the night.

In the center of the large camp, Poleaxe met with his two most important lieutenants. Axel Carbondale and Carpus Castlesmasher, who had been among the first to join the campaign and swear loyalty to Poleaxe, came to the commander at his small campfire, and together the three of them plotted their maneuvers for the morrow. In the darkness of the camp, Harn removed his helmet to give him free access to scratch his itching sores. He ignored the discomfited looks of his lieutenants as he addressed them while inspecting his bloody fingers.

"We're going to carry the day, I promise," Poleaxe said. "We have an ally who can't be defeated." He ignored the surprised looks exchanged by his two lieutenants. "I will command a third of the troops directly, leading the men from Hillhome and the eastern towns. We'll make the initial assault, but I want both of you to bring up your own wings closely behind me." Seeing the two lieutenants accepted those orders without objection, he continued.

"Carbondale, you'll lead all the Neidar down from the western slopes; that's about a third of the army. When we come through the front gates, you'll be on the left, and I want you to make for the West Tower."

"Aye, my lord," said Axel, frowning.

"Carpus, you'll be in charge of the right wing—the

dwarves from south of Cloudseeker. Your task is the opposite of Carbondale's; you'll be on the right flank as we attack, and once we're inside the Tharkadan Wall your objective will be the East Tower."

"Very well, my lord. But—"

Harn Poleaxe raised his hand, his eyes narrowing as he smiled slyly. "You want to know how will we breach the main gates?" he guessed.

"Aye-uh," Castlesmasher allowed. "How, indeed?"

"I have a plan for that, but I can't reveal it, not yet. Just have your men prepared to move out with the dawn," Poleaxe explained breezily, watching as the two lieutenants again exchanged surprised, and slightly worried, glances. He held out the jug that, only rarely, did he let out of his hand. "Here, my brave dwarves. Share a toast with me to our ultimate victory."

In fact, Harn was reluctant to reveal the identity of the creature just yet. For one thing, he himself didn't know its precise nature, and he didn't want his men to be apprehensive. He well knew the traditional dwarf bias against the magical and supernatural. He feared the possibly damaging effect on morale if the troops knew he was relying on such a creature to spearhead the attack. Once the battle was joined, however, he was confident that bloodlust would compel the Neidar to follow him gloriously into battle.

As he had thought, the unexpected offer of dwarf spirits was enough to distract his men from their questions. Each took a healthy swig before Carpus held the jug out and Harn snatched it back.

Lord Poleaxe took a deep drink himself then stretched and yawned, making it clear the meeting was over. As each of the two Neidar would be returning to a different camp, on elevations separated by deep ravines, Harn wasn't worried about them getting together to speculate through the night.

And, indeed, he needed to be alone to complete the last portion of his own battle plan. After Carbondale and Castlesmasher had made their farewells and disappeared from sight, Harn Poleaxe arose and walked through the perimeter of his camp. He made his way out onto a slender promontory with sheer cliffs falling away to either side. At the far end of the promontory, he came upon a large boulder and settled himself on a ledge where he had a view over the tumbling ridges of the tangled mountain range. Drinking steadily, he felt his senses growing keener, more perceptive. A thrill ran through him, manifested as a physical shiver. He scratched contentedly, pulling away a large scab from his forehead and ignoring the blood that ran into his eyebrows.

Far in the distance, where its blocky shape was outlined by a few flickering torches, Poleaxe got a glimpse of one of Pax Tharkas's two massive towers. The red and white moons were both high and nearly full, but scudding clouds moved quickly past them, mostly leaving the mountaintop vantage masked by shadow.

Harn didn't have to wait for long. He sensed the monster almost instantly because of the chill that brushed against his skin even before he saw the minion. In the darkness, his first visual clue was the pair of red eyes, glowing like embers, that flashed open just a few feet before his face. The Neidar gradually discerned that the monster was hovering in air, just beyond the top of the precipice, and that it regarded the hill dwarf commander with a curious expression. Those black, batlike wings flapped slowly, a leisurely cadence that was surely not enough, by itself, to float the massive creature in the air.

"You have made your plans," the creature stated in its eerily dry voice, so suggestive of wind rustling through the limbs of winter-barren trees.

"I have. My army is eager and ready to strike on the morrow. I personally will lead the first charge and you will see that the gates fall before me. Is that not correct?" he said.

The creature responded with an elaborate and somewhat disconcerting shrug. "That may not be necessary after all," it replied.

"Those gates are supposed to be ten feet thick!" objected Harn Poleaxe, who was not used to being challenged. "We have no siege engines, no war machines. If, I tell you, the gates are closed, we won't be able to get in! They must be taken down! You must do as I say!"

"I must do nothing!" replied the monster. Its voice did not increase in volume, but its fiery eyes flared furiously.

"I—I apologize for my discourtesy," Poleaxe said immediately, feeling his bowels turn to water in the face of that horrific rebuke. "But how can we carry the fortress against those gates?" he asked somewhat plaintively.

"I flew over that place just moments ago," replied the creature. "The gates are open now, as they have been every night for the past month. You may be able to carry the entrance by storm even before the mountain dwarves know you are upon them."

"If you say so, I will try," pledged Harn. "But what if that doesn't work?"

"You must attack as soon as you can. Do not rely entirely upon me."

Poleaxe knew they still had a long way to go; they would have to negotiate several twists and turns and something of an uphill grade before reaching their objective. "We will be in position to attack some time in the middle of the afternoon," he calculated.

"Very well. Do so. And if you are outside of the fortress when night falls, I will emerge with the darkness to smite them. But remember, you must attack as soon as possible."

"I shall, my . . . my lord," Harn replied. He might have been daunted by the task before him, but as the monster flexed its wings, Poleaxe felt a new invigoration. He watched the beast, but it did not leave. Instead, he came to him and wrapped him in an embrace of shadows. The hill dwarf tingled to a strange sensation, a piercing joy as the intangible essence of the thing seeped directly through his skin.

Moments later, it was gone, but it was with him as well. Tingling with energy, possessed, finally, by the full power of his dark master, Harn leaped to his feet. He drained the last swallows from his jug and knew that he and his men were ready.

There could be no turning aside, not anymore. Harn Poleaxe, and the black creature within him, would lead the charge.

———DH———

"Where are we?" asked Brandon as he followed Gretchan up a narrow, winding staircase that spiraled up through a shaft so confining that his shoulders brushed the walls and he had to duck every time they reached another of the ubiquitous, and solidly built, arches.

"We're climbing the East Tower," she replied, pausing to breathe heavily. "This is a secret stairway, not the main route. That's why the ceiling is so low," she noted somewhat apologetically. "But I thought you'd prefer it to Main Street."

"I do," Brandon agreed, gasping for breath. He, too, was exhausted by the climb and welcomed the respite, however brief. Looking over his shoulder, he saw that Gus and Kondike were also weary and panting. The gully dwarf had plopped down on a step, while the dog, tongue hanging out and flanks heaving, watched his mistress attentively.

"Seems like a long way up," the Hylar remarked sourly. He was still coming to grips with the ease with which she had smashed his cell door after his long days languishing in the filthy cell.

"Take heart—we're almost halfway there," she replied.

"Halfway! That's encouraging. Aren't we allowing ourselves to be trapped, caught like a bear in a tree, so to speak, if we keep climbing higher?" He even found himself wondering if he could really trust her but quickly acknowledged that he didn't have any other choice, at least not right at the moment.

She shrugged, which didn't do a lot for his confidence. "Maybe, but I don't think so," she said. "I'm betting we're going to find a way into the Tharkadan Wall. There's a whole network of catwalks and tunnels up in the top of that space where I think we can hide."

"You're holding all the cards," Brandon admitted. "Lead on."

They resumed the climb, hoisting themselves up two steps at a time, trying to avoid noise and conversation as they continued to the top of the tower. The stairway wound back and forth, a series of flights in a column without windows. Occasionally they passed wooden doorways, but Gretchan ignored each of those in her steady progress up.

Finally the dwarf maid paused at a landing, she and Brandon catching their breath as they waited for Gus, red faced and puffing, to join them. When he did, she opened a nearby door. They entered a huge, square room lit by sunlight streaming through narrow windows on two of the walls.

"Daylight," Brandon said, feeling something akin to deep pleasure. "I'd forgotten what it looks like."

"Daylight not so great," Gus scoffed. He stomped off to one of the windows, crossing his arms over his chest while he looked out.

"What's eating him?" Brandon wondered aloud.

Gretchan smiled. "I think he's jealous of a certain big kisser dwarf."

"Big kisser—oh," the Kayolin dwarf replied, blushing slightly as he stared at the Aghar's back.

"Gus did a certain amount of uh, spying down there in the dungeon," she explained.

"Why *did* you leave me in there?" he challenged.

"Did you ever think that it was maybe to keep you safe?" she shot back heatedly. "After all, every time you were out on your own, you ended up in some kind of trouble!"

He blinked, surprised at her vehemence and her answer. "That's the curse of the Bluestone luck," he retorted, wishing he had a stronger comeback.

"Maybe it's not just luck!" she snapped. "Maybe it's the choices you make! Did you ever think of that?"

"I—damn it, no!" he admitted angrily.

"Anyway," she said, seeming to force herself to calm down. "Do you want to go back or come with me?"

"Like I said," Brandon replied through clenched teeth, "lead on."

He wondered where they were going. When he looked around, he saw a massive chain rising up from a hole in the floor in the center of the room. Each link was roughly as long as he was tall, with the metal bands themselves as thick around as his muscle-bound thigh. The chain rose up at an angle then nestled into a groove around the outer rim of a giant wheel. The wheel appeared to serve as a gear, and the chain extended straight from the top of the wheel to a hole leading into the Tharkadan Wall itself.

"That's part of the ancient trap," Gretchan said, taking note of Brandon's astonishment. "It's anchored to the bedrock outside the fortress itself. So even if the towers and the wall are destroyed, the rocks can fall and the pass can be sealed."

"And from what you tell me, Tarn Bellowgranite has spent all the years of his exile loading that trap so that it can be used again if the pass is threatened," Brandon said, shaking his head in disbelief.

"Yes," Gretchan replied. She sighed. "But not just that. I think he wants to open the pass to trade caravans and commerce as well. That would be a more useful renewal of its legacy, if you ask me. Though there are no guarantees it will come to pass."

Another door to the room burst open, and Tarn Bellowgranite and Garn Bloodfist, accompanied by a half dozen armed dwarves, rushed inside. They were followed by the white-bearded elder, Otaxx Shortbeard, who was ruddy faced and panting after the long climb.

"There they are!" cried the Klar captain, pointing to Brandon and Gretchan as he waved his soldiers forward. "Take them!"

"Stop!" shouted Gretchan, stamping the butt of her staff against the floor. The shaft made a surprisingly loud bang when it struck the stones, and to Brandon's surprise, the men-at-arms froze. From the gaping looks on their faces, they were as surprised as he was. Each tried to move his feet, swaying and struggling, but it appeared as though the Klar warrior had been nailed to the floor.

"See, my thane!" shouted Garn, who could talk though he couldn't move his legs. "Behold that sorcery! She *is* a witch! I sensed it that night she came to me, beside the river!"

"Oh, be quiet!" snapped the dwarf maid.

Brandon desperately wished for a weapon, but he was as unarmed as he had been in his cell. And Gretchan had only that little hammer. He didn't like their chances if it came to a fight, and he didn't think her magic and bravado—impressive as it was—could hold the mountain dwarves at bay for long.

Struggling to move, the Klar captain cuffed one of his dwarves, knocking him to the floor. "Fool," he cried. He loomed over the fallen soldier and glared at Gretchan, clenching his fists, but he seemed unable to make any further advance.

Beyond Bloodfist, Tarn Bellowgranite sighed, suddenly looking very old. He took out a cloth and mopped his bald pate, which was slick with sweat. He looked at Gretchan, and his expression grew cold.

"I don't know who you are or why you have come here to vex us. You've managed to spook my bravest captain, and he tells me you've taken the liberty of breaking a prisoner out of my dungeon. How do you explain yourself? Are you indeed a witch?"

Gretchan was looking past the thane at the old general. "You there. Are you the Daewar Otaxx Shortbeard?" she asked.

"I am," he replied stiffly. "And I, too, demand that you answer my thane's questions."

"You are in no position to make demands," she said. Then, softening her tone, she added, "I am not a witch." She raised her staff, and the miniature anvil atop the pole suddenly glowed with a golden light even brighter than the sunlight spilling in through the windows. "I am a priestess of Reorx," she said. "And I have been traveling the lands of the dwarves for a long time, studying our people, trying to understand why we do what we do."

"The Reorx of the mountain dwarves or of the hill dwarves?" challenged Garn Bloodfist belligerently.

"He is the same god, you fool!" she snapped. "And his heart is breaking to see the strife that exists between his two tribes."

"So you sympathize with the Neidar, then." The Klar sneered. He pointed at Brandon. "Witness, my thane, that she has freed the hill dwarf spy from his cell in the dungeon."

"I tell you again for the last time: I'm as much a Hylar as Tarn Bellowgranite!" Brandon declared, fists clenching as he took a step toward the Klar.

"More, actually," Gretchan said calmly. "For you are only a half-blood Hylar, are you not, Thane?"

Tarn nodded, staring intently at the priestess. "Yes, my mother was a Daergar," he said. "This is not a secret. But who are you, and why do you come here and cause all this commotion? You seem to know very much about us, yet you have revealed very little about yourself—save that you are a cleric of our shared god."

"Yes, you are a cipher," Otaxx Shortbeard said to Gretchan, sounding more curious than angry. "You rightly called me a Daewar. But what clan are you from? And where is your home?"

"I am a Daewar too," Gretchan said. "My home . . . my home is in the east."

"Do you mean . . . Thoradin?" asked the old general in a tone of wonder.

She nodded. "Yes. I left there more than a decade ago, intending to return to Thorbardin, to see my people's ancestral home, to meet my kinfolk and the fellow clans. But the undermountain kingdom was sealed before I arrived in the Kharolis."

"Then . . . you mean to say . . . ?" Otaxx was still wrestling with the incredible revelation. "Did Severus Stonehand actually reach Zhakar? Did the Mad Prophet lead the Daewar to a new home in the old mountains? For years we have believed that his entire expedition ended in disaster, that everyone perished. Please—I must know!"

"Severus Stonehand and most of the Daewar did reach the Khalkist Mountains," Gretchan said. "The way was difficult and spotted with tragedy. But he survives and most of his people survive in the caverns that were once the home of the Zhakar dwarves. They still endure many struggles, and Thoradin itself—at least, as it once was—remains an elusive dream. But clan Daewar survives."

"By the grace of Reorx," Otaxx said, his eyes tearing. "It is as if my deepest wish has been granted. My thane, this is wonderful news!"

"This is all damned irrelevant!" snapped Garn Bloodfist, eyes all but bursting out of his skull. Forgetting that his movements were frozen, he cuffed his man-at-arms and pointed at Brandon.

"Seize him—take him back to his cell!"

Before the poor man-at-arms could react, however, another door burst open and a gasping, red-faced watchman, one of the sentries posted atop the Tharkadan Wall, staggered into the room.

"There's a column of hill dwarves in sight!" he announced, panting for breath following his long run down from the parapet. "Thousands of them! They're two miles away, and they're fast nearing the gates!"

# TWENTY-SIX

# KIN'S BLOOD
# AND BLOOD FEUD

"Is this attack your doing?" Tarn Bellowgranite demanded coldly. His eyes never left Gretchan's. "Perhaps you are the true Neidar spy—come here to divert us! You hold us here, captive to your magic. And all the while your allies in the hill dwarf army are creeping up on the fortress, readying a surprise attack!"

"I tell you, she cannot be trusted!" Bloodfist declared, shaking his fist, straining to move his feet from where the priestess's magic had stuck him to the floor. "Her whole story is a lie—a distraction, as you have well guessed, my thane."

"No!" Gretchan protested, her voice breaking. "I know nothing of this attack; I'm against all wars and attacks!"

"I can't afford to believe you," Tarn Bellowgranite declared. "Not when my fortress, my whole community, is at risk. Release us at once! I command you, treacherous witch!"

"I'm telling the truth!" she insisted, wincing as if the thane had struck her.

Brandon listened, trembling with barely controlled anger. If he'd carried a weapon, he would have turned it against the Hylar thane and his bloodthirsty captain.

"What are your orders, my thane?" asked the messenger from the top of the wall, whose eyes darted around, confused, as he listened to all their strange talk. He was the only one of the Pax Tharkas dwarves who was not immobilized by Gretchan's spell.

"Get word to the garrison troops at once!" Otaxx Shortbeard ordered when it seemed that Tarn could not tear his eyes away from Gretchan. "Order the gates closed."

"Free us at once!" Garn shrieked, eyes bulging. "Your treachery is further proved with each passing second!"

The priestess stepped to Brandon's side and took his hand. "Be ready to move quickly," she whispered and shifted toward the far wall of the room, the place where the chain disappeared into the Tharkadan Wall. To Gus she instructed: "Gus, I want you to listen closely now. It's time for you to go. Go safely, go down below, to Agharhome. I know about your . . . friend down there. She's a good friend and she misses you. I know that she's been looking for you."

The Aghar stared up at her, enchanted and dumbfounded. His eyes welled up with tears. She knew everything, it seemed.

Her gaze flickered over to Garn Bloodfist as she gave the gully dwarf a good-bye hug. "And don't let a mountain dwarf bully scare you. You're one of the bravest dwarves I've ever known."

"You have seen the proof yourself!" Garn insisted, reaching out, grasping Tarn's arm in one of his hands. "She's a witch! An enemy! A traitor!"

Gretchan stamped her staff onto the floor, and the silver anvil on the head of the staff pulsed with light. "I am a priestess of Reorx! I serve the Lord of the Forge and seek only the betterment of dwarfkind. Sometimes it seems that dwarves themselves are the biggest obstacles to their own happiness!"

She lifted the staff from the floor, holding it in both

of her hands as she gazed raptly at the men-at-arms who had been frozen by her command. "I free you," she said. Then she looked at Garn, shook her head, and turned her gaze on Tarn.

"Thane Bellowgranite, I am no enemy, no traitor, nor am I a witch. I seek a better world for *all* dwarves! That means mountain dwarves and hill dwarves." She smiled wanly and winked at Gus. "Even gully dwarves. We're all the favored children of Reorx."

"The Neidar are even now launching an attack against us—and surely you know the story of what the dwarves of Thorbardin did to me—to clan Daewar as well—to all of those who remained behind!" Tarn protested. "The fanatics of Thorbardin rose up in revolution, were blinded by ideology and rank greed. They threw me out of my own kingdom! How can you suggest that I find common ground with them?"

"Because it's the only way! You must find a way to forgive them, to lead your people into the future."

"Impossible!" roared Tarn, stepping forward hesitantly, as if uncertain that his feet really had been freed. He shook his head ruefully. "You may not be a witch, but you are a sorry idealist." He turned to his veteran commander, finally, when he was convinced that the spell had been broken. "General Shortbeard, see to the garrison. Get the troops on the walls, the auxiliaries taking care of ammunition. The gate crew should start turning the capstan; we don't have much time."

"Aye, my thane," declared the elder officer, limping toward the door . . . but not before he cast a speculative glance at Gretchan over his shoulder. He finally charged from the room, his voice booming with command; he still sounded like a dwarf general, even if he wasn't as spry as he used to be.

Meanwhile, Tarn's eyes flashed with anger as he pointed firmly at the priestess. "You will leave this place and never return! And this one"—he pointed at Brandon but spoke to the dwarves closest to Brandon—"Garn is right for once; take him back to his cell!"

"Go—now!" Gretchan said, seizing Brandon's hand and sprinting to the wall of the large room. He saw her idea at once: the gap where the heavy chain passed through the wall into the interior of the Tharkadan trap. It would be a narrow squeeze between hard stone and even harder iron, but the Kayolin dwarf followed Gretchan as both leaped into the narrow notch and scrambled like monkeys along the links that disappeared beyond the hole.

Garn's dwarves came charging after. One Klar lunged after Brandon, reaching for his foot, but Brandon kicked him in the face, knocking him backward with a satisfying crunch of bone. The dwarf fell and his companions tripped over him. By then, Brandon was chasing Gretchan into the darkness. It was only later that he wondered about the gully dwarf and the dog Kondike.

----DH----

"The gates are open, Lord Poleaxe!" shouted one of the hill dwarf spearmen, hoisting his weapon over his head and shaking it joyfully.

"I can see that, you fool. Now keep running!" Harn commanded. He took a deep, satisfying gulp from his spirits and felt the potent liquor augmenting the potion, pulsing through his bloodstream with eerie, arcane force. He wanted nothing so much as to drive his sword through an enemy's flesh, to warm his hand in the flow of fresh blood.

"Move! We must get there before the damned mountain dwarves have a chance to close it in our faces!"

In fact, every Neidar in the army was running as fast and hard as he could. The prospect of a surprise attack against the vaunted fortress drove them to an impressive burst of speed. They were running so hard that they didn't have any breath left to give voice to their battle cries.

Harn, in the very front rank of the surging column, could scarcely believe his eyes. He saw the two towers, the massive, square citadels that flanked the walls, rising like mountains before him. Even at more than a mile's distance, he had to crane his neck just to see the tops of the spires. And that vast wall, stretching like a cliff across the whole breadth of the steep-walled valley, looked like an utterly impassable obstacle, a perfect defensive bastion.

Except that the broad, tall gate was standing open, almost as if the mountain dwarves were extending a welcome to their cousins from the hills.

The mountain dwarves looked to be taken completely by surprise. The advancing column passed farms and pastures and mines, all lying in the very shadow of Pax Tharkas, and when he looked to the sides, Harn saw terrified mountain dwarves running for shelter, climbing the ridges, or darting into their mines. Apparently, Harn's army had eliminated or eluded all the sentries. Otherwise, there would have been a warning signal, and those outlying dwarves—together with their livestock—would already have sought shelter in the fortress.

As the road leveled out the voices of the hill dwarves rose in a great war chant. No one felt fatigue; there was no flagging in the onrush. The roaring of the battle cries mingled with the pounding of feet against the stone-paved road as the hill dwarves came on like a surging wave.

They drew close enough to see all the activity on top of the massive wall: dwarves peering through the battlement and more and more of the garrison troops rushing into sight. They would harass the charge, Harn knew, but they were too late to stop it. The only thing that would hold them back was that massive gate. His heart pounded from the exertion and excitement, and he raised his sword in one hand, his jug in the other, as he scrutinized that huge barrier, desperately afraid it would start to close. How long would it take them to move such a massive, heavy object?

He didn't know the answer, but with each step he took, his hopes grew higher; for still the gate stood open and showed no sign that it was starting to swing shut.

─────DH─────

"Chase them! Catch them!" ordered Garn as the priestess of Reorx and the dwarf from Kayolin disappeared into the chute surrounding the heavy chain.

When the Klar tried to scramble into the narrow slot to pursue Gretchan and Brandon, the first two got stuck—encumbered as they were by heavy breastplates and their swords. While they took forever trying to squirm free and unstrap their metal armor, the rest of the party sprinted out the side door, shouting and making their way toward the catwalks above the great, hollow chamber of the Tharkadan Wall.

With Gretchan gone, Garn suddenly felt his legs freed. He didn't know what he should do, though; he was eager to join the pursuit but knew he'd better get his company in position to defend the fortress against attack. Damn the witch! Damn the hill dwarves; surely it was part of their conspiracy! And damn Tarn Bellowgranite, standing there with a dull look on his face, for being too old and foolish and for having left them vulnerable to attack!

Even as the last of the pursuers disappeared, another scout ran into the room with a report from the wall. He addressed Tarn breathlessly, his eyes darting looks at a clearly glowering Garn. Neidar were advancing at a run, the scout said, and had approached to within a mile of the gates. The man had just finished his report when Mason Axeblade, the garrison commander, raced in, also looking for Tarn Bellowgranite.

"What are your orders, my thane?" Axeblade asked.

"Which way are they coming from?" Bloodfist interjected before Tarn could reply.

"The south!" reported the scout excitedly. "They've come up the pass from the Plains of Dergoth."

"It's the dwarves of Hillhome," the Klar captain calmly explained to the thane. His heart was pounding in fierce excitement, but he resisted the urge to thump his chest, to shout a battle cry. Instead, he stared into Tarn's eyes. "They've come to seek revenge," Bloodfist noted pointedly. He couldn't suppress his grin as he saw Tarn looked dazed, as if he couldn't find his tongue.

"There are thousands of them, Captain," said the messenger, darting looks at the two dwarf leaders. "This is far more than the company of one or even five towns. It's as if all the hill dwarves mustered under a single commander."

"We've got to get the gates closed before they get here," muttered Tarn Bellowgranite. Then he seemed to wake up, come alive. "Put every available dwarf on the capstans!"

"At once, my liege!" pledged the Daewar, Captain Axeblade.

"No, my thane! Captain Axeblade, stay a moment," Garn Bloodfist declared in sheer delight. "It is too late. We have made one mistake; let's not make another, fatal one. Don't close the gates at all. The circumstances couldn't be more advantageous!" he exulted. "We can let them into the fortress and kill them all!"

"But—how?" the thane objected. "Once they're inside the Tharkadan Wall, they can carry the battle to the towers, fight us wherever we try to stand."

"Not if we move fast, my liege. This is a Reorx-sent opportunity. I pray, we must take advantage of it!" Garn strode to the window, staring out over the narrow valley. The file of hill dwarves, rushing forward in a dense column, was just coming into view around a bend in the valley wall. They moved with surprising speed, and even from a mile away, the hoarse, basso rumble of their war chants could be heard. "Let them come in!"

"What do you mean?" asked Tarn, moving to the window to join his captain. "How could that be to our advantage?"

"Yes—what's your plan, Captain?" demanded Axeblade impatiently. "Spit it out, man—there's no time to waste!"

Garn obliged. "We allow them into the wall, through the open gate. Our force is divided in two, and each company backs up to the base of one of the towers. We hold there for as long as we can until the whole Neidar army has packed the hall. Packed, I say, like figs in a crate—just where we want them: caught and doomed."

"You mean—we drop the trap on top of them?" asked Tarn in disbelief.

"Yes! We can lure them inside the wall then allow our own troops to make a fighting withdrawal, finally taking shelter in the bases of the towers. When only the Neidar are left in the wall, we release the trap we have long prepared. A hundred thousands of tons of rocks will fall on them, and every single one will be crushed."

"But . . ." Tarn shook his head, avoiding meeting his captain's gaze. "But so many deaths . . . and all the work . . . the trap just restored. The work would be wasted—"

"Not wasted, my thane!" insisted Garn. "This is the perfect use. We can finally wipe out our enemies with one blow! Think about it: the task just finished, the trap ready to drop. And here come the hill dwarves, right where they can destroyed.

"It can only be the will of Reorx himself!"

———DH———

Gus and Kondike stood rooted to the spot, watching as Gretchan and Brandon made their escape. Gretchan had whispered good-bye to the little Aghar and told him to take care of the big, shaggy dog . . . and to get away as best they could, during all the ruckus.

He was momentarily distracted by the sight of dwarves running in and out of the door, cursing, shouting orders, all of them ignoring him and Kondike, fortunately.

He remembered what Gretchan had told him to do—go to Agharhome. Indeed, the memory of Berta was a powerful allure, suggesting safety and a hiding place and good, Aghar food. The deep cellars under the tower would certainly provide a refuge from all the chaos and talk of killing and war.

But he could see that the dwarf maid and the big kisser dwarf were in terrible danger, and he wouldn't abandon his beloved goddess or—he realized with a gulp—her big kisser friend.

So with Kondike racing at his side, he turned and darted through the door where many of the dwarves had departed, chasing after Gretchan and Brandon. He stopped at the first side door, and after vigorously working the latch, he yanked it open. He didn't know where it led but heard feet running all around him. So why not?

He found himself up on a high catwalk, teetering above the floor of the vast, hollow Tharkadan Wall. The walkway led to his right and was suspended from the ceiling by wooden supports. It swayed slightly under his weight, and it looked like a very long way down. But again, he heard feet running all around him. Gus bit his lip and took a hesitant step forward.

"Come on, Kondike!" he urged, finding his balance and setting off at a clip.

"Gus!" It was Berta, crawling out of a nearby hole above the catwalk. She dropped down onto the platform, causing it to sway again, and Gus grabbed onto the railing.

"Berta! What you do in this bluphsplunging place? Go home! Be safe," he barked authoritatively. In truth he was as frightened for her as he was for himself, he realized.

"I no go!" she snapped, planting her fists on her hips. "I come look you. Two days I look you! Where go Highbulp

Gus, I say? Now I find you here!" She rolled her eyes. "I no go!"

"Well, come with me, then," he said in exasperation. "But don't look down. I gotta find my friend Gretchan and her friend the big kisser. They need help!"

"Who Gretchan?" demanded the female Aghar, narrowing her eyes suspiciously, even as she obligingly jogged along beside her fellow gully dwarf. "What big kisser?"

The walkway was made of wooden boards with a railing to either side. Looking to his left, Gus spotted the big chain extending horizontally above another catwalk. Below the chain was a stone shelf, a notch in the far edge of the wall before the long drop to the floor of the hollow wall. Gus couldn't see Gretchan and Brandon, but he sure heard a lot of footsteps and stomping around; Gus decided they must be somewhere near that chain.

"She go there probably, I think," he said, pointing at the heavy links. He spotted a place where the chain passed through another hole in the wall, vanishing into shadowy darkness. "I go there too!" he declared. "You come? I don't promise but maybe fun!"

"Wait! How?" Berta demanded. "You crazy doofar? You gonna fly?"

"I make big jump!" Gus boasted, sounding more confident than he really felt.

He eyed the gap, not sure if he could make the leap. He'd have to jump over to the chain then lower himself down to the catwalk so he could follow the chain into the next dark tunnel. If he didn't catch the chain, he might take a bad fall; the catwalk or stone ledge wouldn't be so bad, but the floor itself was a long way down. At least two feet, Gus guessed.

"I go now!" he said, perched on the edge of the walkway. "Coming or not?"

"No!" Berta screamed. "You get splattered!"

"I gotta try help Gretchan!" he insisted.

Gathering his courage, he vaulted from the catwalk, just managing to cover the distance and grab onto the chain before lowering himself to the walkway below him. "Whew!" he said, glancing over his shoulder at Berta, who had her hands over her eyes but was peeking through her fingers. "Boy, I really brave!" Removing her hands, she smiled proudly.

The entry through the hole in the wall was only about two long steps away from him, and he started toward it at a run.

Except that he had forgotten about the dog. Kondike stood anxiously on the upper catwalk, barking, bouncing back and forth from foot to foot. Before Gus could think of any way to stop him, the big dog came after the gully dwarf, launching himself into space, stretching toward the curving links of the chain.

But, unlike the dwarves, the dog didn't have hands to grasp the chain. He clawed at a link, tumbled on his back onto the catwalk, and rolled over the edge.

# TWENTY-SEVEN

# DWARF BLOOD

**O**taxx Shortbeard strode along the battlement atop the Tharkadan Wall. The platform was more than a hundred feet above the ground, and he had a clear view of the approaching Neidar column—and of the mountain dwarves who had rallied to the defense.

Hundreds of his people, Hylar and Klar and the occasional Daewar who, like himself, had refused to follow the Mad Prophet, manned the top of the wall. The warriors wore their armor, including breastplates and helmets, and in many cases they carried shields as well. Two fighters stood at every notch in the crenellated rampart, peering down at the attackers, occasionally raising a shield or ducking behind the stone wall to deflect the aim of the sporadic arrows being launched by the Neidar.

Behind the front rank of warriors was a long single rank of mountain dwarf archers armed with short bows. They were the younger males and the females, who were not as brawny as their armored comrades but could send a veritable shower of arrows raining down from the wall—and would do so as soon as Otaxx gave the command.

Beyond the archers were the auxiliaries, mainly children and elders, whose job was to bring up fresh supplies of arrows and to establish caches of other ammunition. Some of those dwarves had kindled fires, while others readied kettles in which they would heat oil or water to dump on the enemy once they reached the base of the wall so far below. Still others hauled small boulders, establishing those weapons in neat piles just behind the battlements. The rocks couldn't be hurled as far as the arrows, but when the enemy was just below, they could be rained down with devastating impact.

"The gates?" demanded Otaxx when he saw Tarn Bellowgranite approaching. "I don't hear them closing yet."

"They're not," replied the thane, shaking his head reluctantly. "Garn has a plan: he wants to let the Neidar into the Tharkadan Wall."

"And crush them all with the trap?" guessed the old Daewar at once. He whistled. "Dangerous, but it might work."

"Aye. And if it does, we'll be free of the Neidar menace for good," Tarn acknowledged, sounding as though he were trying to convince himself as much as his general.

By that time, the first rank of the hill dwarves had reached within a hundred paces of the wall. The road column had spread out into a front more than a hundred dwarves wide. At a signal from the leader, who was distinguished by a massive helmet topped by black and white feathers, they rushed forward at a sprint, howling the glory of Reorx and their hatred of the mountain clans at the top of their lungs.

Long ago Otaxx had ordered markers to be installed beside the road, at every twenty paces, for just such a showdown. Because of those white posts, the bowmen knew the exact range to their target.

"Archers, fire!" the general barked. "Range is one hundred paces."

The first volley flew like a swarm of locusts, dark shafts

filling the sky, showering down upon the leading ranks of the hill dwarf attackers. Dozens fell—it looked to the general as if every Neidar in the first rank, save the hulking captain brandishing his great sword in the center of the line, was slain by the initial volley. But the next ranks continued to surge forward.

The archers reloaded quickly and fired again and again, each bowman—or woman—shooting as fast as individual skill allowed. The missiles continued to pepper the assaulting formation, sending dwarf after dwarf to the ground, writhing or dying, but still the furious charge continued. The surviving Neidar roared their fury, a wave of sound that rose up and over the wall. They came on, the column pressing together in the very shadow of the high wall, for it was too wide for all of them to pass through the gate at once.

The burly mountain dwarves picked up rocks and hurled them into the mass of targets packed so tightly that it was hard for any missile to miss. Skulls were crushed, shoulders and breastbones shattered, spines snapped, and limbs broken under the onslaught, which in a few seconds left nearly a hundred hill dwarves battered and bleeding on the road.

But the momentum of the attack was barely dented, and the first of the attackers were racing through the lofty, wide-open gate.

"Keep up the barrage," Otaxx ordered his men. "Take down as many as you can before they get to the gates!"

He turned and addressed the thane of Pax Tharkas. "It's time to take the fight inside," he said and ran to the door in the tower, ready to command the battle erupting inside the Tharkadan Wall.

——DH——

"Death to the Hylar!" cried Harn Poleaxe, sprinting at the head of the long hill dwarf column.

He could scarcely believe his eyes: the great gate of Pax Tharkas still stood open! His warriors scrambled over the rough ground, streaming past the mines and the fields, charging toward that lofty, inviting opening.

The barrage from the parapet was devastating, but Harn felt as though he were somehow invulnerable. Every dwarf in the first rank with him perished in the initial volley of arrows, but somehow—even though he was the largest target in the line—he escaped injury. Was it the potion of the dark one that protected him? Or was it that he was blessed with the favor of Reorx? No matter—he never felt more alive and more confident of success.

"Onward, Neidar!" he shouted, waving his sword. "Remember Hillhome!"

They rushed toward the yawning entrance to the great wall. Harn was thrilled that the minion's prediction had proved true—he never even paused to wonder why that gate hadn't closed up yet, even though the defenders must certainly have had a good half hour's warning of attack from the time the first hill dwarves came into view.

A scattering of mountain dwarves stood in that gateway. No more than a dozen defenders were in position to face the rush of a thousand hill dwarves, so Poleaxe wasn't surprised to see them break and run as the attackers drew closer. The Neidar were within the very shadow of the looming entrance.

Some of the mountain dwarves fled to the left, while others ran to the right.

"Split up!" ordered Poleaxe, flush with the anticipation of victory. He led a huge number of his warriors to the left, while another large contingent, under the command of Carpus Castlesmasher, veered right.

The whole of the great vault of the Tharkadan Wall loomed above them. Mountain dwarves formed defensive lines at the opposite ends of the massive hall, but Poleaxe could see that his troops would easily overwhelm their surprisingly slipshod defense.

"Take them all!" he howled. "For the glory of Reorx and the graves under the mountains!"

He raised his visor, turning his bloody face upward as he took a long drink. His dwarves poured through the open gate, spilling through the vast hall beyond. The jug was empty, but even that didn't matter; Harn simply cast it aside, raised his mighty sword, and joined in the attack.

——DH——

Meanwhile, high above the battle, Gretchan led Brandon along the chain for a hundred feet, crawling as fast as she could. The great links extended through a horizontal passageway, and there was barely enough room for a big dwarf such as Brandon to scrape his way between the heavy iron links and the stone tube through which they passed.

At least they had left Garn and his warriors behind.

Then the dwarf maid abruptly swung her feet down toward a shaft plunging through the stone framework. Brandon followed her, and they both dropped onto a lofty catwalk, more than a hundred feet above the fortress floor.

"Hey!" barked a Klar sentry, startled by the two dwarves who had dropped to the platform very close to him. He started to draw his sword, but Brandon sprang at him and felled him with a single sharp punch to the jaw. The sentry collapsed, out cold, but as the Kayolin dwarf grabbed at the Klar's sword, the weapon bounced off the catwalk and plummeted all the way down to the floor of the wall's interior. Shrugging at yet another incidence of rotten luck, he turned to follow Gretchan as she started along the catwalk.

To their left Brandon saw the massive wooden platform, piled high with many tons of boulders. Chains and gears connected to the front of that platform, while massive hinges fastened its back to the fortress wall. Huge steel pins held the platform in place, and he could see a smaller cable linking those pins to a block and tackle mechanism and a large lever, mounted on a heavy, notched gear. When the lever was cranked, Brandon could see, the cable would gradually pull the pins free—and when they were removed, the whole platform would swing downward, sending the rocks tumbling to the floor of the great hall.

The din of noise rose below them, and they looked down to see the army of hill dwarves rushing into the fortress through the open gates.

"Why didn't they close the gate? It looks like they aren't even trying to keep them out!" Brandon asked.

Gretchan grew pale and looked at him in horror. "It's Garn's plan, I'll bet!" she declared. "He's letting them into the hall so he can crush them with the rocks! They'll all be killed!"

"Serves the bastards right," the Kayolin dwarf said, which was his honest gut reaction.

Gretchan glared at him then shook her head in exasperation. "Look, I can understand why you hate them; they didn't treat you with any decency or fairness. But can't you see that if Garn causes a massacre, the feud with the Neidar will never die? Their hatred of mountain dwarves will be worse than ever. This moment will scar our race every bit as bad as what happened after the Cataclysm; we will *never* outgrow it!"

Brandon grimaced. Already the clash of battle filled the vast interior of the wall. He could see more of the hill dwarves rushing in through the open gate, while the mountain dwarf garrison formed two lines, defending the approaches to each of the two towers and slowly bottling the attackers in the center. Gretchan was right: Soon Garn Bloodfist's lines would be able to pull back, out of the danger zone, and the Tharkadan trap would plunge a mountain's weight of rocks right on top of the clustered attackers.

"What can we do about it anyway?" he asked.

"I don't know!" the priestess declared, despairing. "But we have to do something!" She looked around, desperately trying to think. "I'll try to find the thane and change his mind. Can you warn the hill dwarves? Tell them what Garn has planned? Maybe they'll withdraw from here before it's too late."

Brandon gazed at the surging, violent battle and heard the furious cries, fueled by centuries of hatred. A number of Neidar were in the middle of the tower, unable to reach the front lines because of the congestion. Maybe, possibly, they could be made to listen to reason.

More likely, of course, they would tear him to shreds. That would be in keeping with the Bluestone luck. All his logic, all his life's experience told him that it was sheer insanity to even consider going down there, into the midst of the enemy army. If they didn't kill him, the imminent release of a thousand tons of rock would probably do it anyway.

He shrugged, feeling helpless and more unlucky than ever, but he could only look at Gretchan and reply, "I'll try."

—DH—

"Form to the right and left!" shouted Garn Bloodfist, directing his mountain dwarves to take up defensive positions within the hall, trying to contain the attackers within the vast space of the Tharkadan Wall. His voice was shrill, and he fairly shivered in anticipation of the massive slaughter he was about to trigger. The plan was working to perfection! Even then, his Klar were withdrawing from the center of the hall, gathering at the base of the West Tower.

Meanwhile, Mason Axeblade had taken command of the Hylar defenders in front of the East Tower. He stood with his line, shouting similar orders. The Neidar crowded into the space between the two lines, more and more of the hill dwarves charging in through the open gate. The two mountain dwarf lines were thin, no more than a single rank with shields and swords, but that was fine with Garn. They were forced back steadily by the charging hill dwarves until the center of the hall was full of Neidar eager for battle but mostly unable to reach the ranks of the defenders.

Garn's men, the troops of his loyal Klar company, fought with the discipline that had been instilled in them by constant drill and practice. They maintained their close ranks, shields up to protect the entire line as they stabbed and hacked, parried and thrust. The hill dwarves were hampered by the close quarters, and many of them bled and died; they were unable to break the tight line of mountain dwarves. But slowly the defenders fell back until they were packed in a semicircle against the base of the West Tower.

Within that tower other warriors opened the doors leading from the vast chamber of the wall into the interior of the sturdy tower. One by one the Klar started slipping through that door, the rank of the line tightening up to fill in the gap left by each withdrawing warrior. The captain grinned fiercely. His scheme was working to perfection.

It was finally time to move to the next phase of the plan. One of the lift baskets that had been used to haul rocks up to the trap was sitting on the floor, within the protective semicircle of the embattled Klar. Garn leaped into that lift and gave the signal to his men waiting above. Immediately they started to haul him upward until he rang the bell for them to halt, allowing him to survey the field from twenty feet up in the air.

From the lift basket, the Klar captain saw that his troops at both ends of the great hall were furtively retreating as commanded. The central space of the Tharkadan Wall was full of Neidar attackers, many of them simply milling about because they couldn't get at the shrinking number of defenders. Only then did Garn ring the bell. Immediately, willing hands hoisted the crate and its lone occupant up higher, toward the shadowy attic where the Tharkadan trap was primed and ready.

———DH———

"Kondike!" Gus cried as the dog slipped and fell from the catwalk.

Frantically the gully dwarf scrambled down into the niche, where the great chain passed around another gear. Sobbing with relief, he saw Kondike had landed on the ledge below him. The dog was panting and holding his right forepaw up. He was perched on a stone shelf that was built in to the surface of the wall itself, and somehow had stopped himself from falling down to the floor below.

How could he get down there to help the goddess's dog? Frantically the gully dwarf looked around.

Gus spotted a wire, twisted around the center of the gear for some mysterious purpose. Maybe he could use it! He reached up and grabbed at the end, but it was too stiff; he couldn't budge it.

"What you do?" demanded Berta, who was watching him from the upper catwalk.

"Try to get wire for catch dog. Help me!" he called. He spotted a piece of wood near her foot. "Give stick me!"

"Who Gretchan?" Berta demanded to know instead.

"What?" asked Gus, startled by the question. He slumped back onto the chain and stared at her.

"Who Gretchan?" She pouted. "You say she friend? She friend, or Berta friend?"

"Gus got two friends!" he retorted. "Help me get wire!"

"No!" she replied petulantly. She crossed her arms over her skinny chest and extravagantly turned her back.

"Berta my friend!" he shouted. "You my bluphsplunging bestest doofar friend! Now help me!"

She finally handed him the stick. He poked the end of it into the coil of wire and pulled. Somewhat amazingly, the end of the spool came free and he was able to grab it with his hands.

His stubby fingers pried at the stiff metal, slowly unspooling it from the hub.

Finally, he pulled it free.

# TWENTY-EIGHT

# A MOUNTAIN STANDING

"All right, all right, I'll try to warn them about the trap," Brandon repeated. He gestured to a nearby lift cage, one of the platforms that had been used to raise the rocks off the floor of the great hall. It was not a mere man-basket, but a wide freight lift, a square surface more than twenty feet long on a side. "Can you maybe lower me in that?"

"Yes," Gretchan said. Her face was pale, but she embraced him, kissing him quickly. "Thank you. I can't think of another dwarf in the world who'd be willing to do what you're doing."

"Yeah, well . . . if they throw me in the dungeon again, promise you'll come to visit me, all right? And bring your hammer."

Eyes misting, she kissed him again. "Good luck," she said through her tears.

"That's not very likely," he replied.

Still, her words gave him some hope as he stepped onto the lift platform, which was nestled into the docking port beside the catwalk. He winked at Gretchan, trying to look nonchalant as she started turning the crank, even though he felt a knot in his stomach. The lift swayed slightly as it came free and started to descend. He wished he had a weapon.

She dropped him quickly, the lift plunging with almost dizzying speed toward the middle of the long hall. Brandon had to grab the supporting line and hold on for his life. The Neidar, he could see, were thronging to both sides of the cavernous entrance, striving to push through the ranks of their comrades to strike at the thin, slowly retreating lines of mountain dwarf defenders.

"It's a trap!" Brandon shouted when the lift was still twenty feet above the floor. He waved toward the open gate. "Get out of here! They're going to crush you with rocks from overhead!"

A few of the Neidar, milling nearby, stared up at him in surprise. Some pointed their weapons at him but were restrained by others who were listening to his shouts. They collected around the lower lift dock, regarding him with more curiosity than hostility.

"The mountain dwarves let you through the gates on purpose," he shouted, dropping still lower, pointing at the open entrance. "They want you all in the hall, under the trap. See how they're pulling back, letting you fill up this space? As soon as they back into the towers, they'll drop a mountain's worth of rocks on your heads!"

Several of the hill dwarves warily began to edge toward the open gates, pushing through the stream of attackers still spilling in to the great fortress. Others glanced at their comrades uneasily, wondering about the mountain dwarf tactics—the plan that was unfolding just as Brandon said it would. The sun was low in the sky, rays of dying light spilling in through the tall gates, illuminating the battle raging at the foot of the East Tower.

Already the two ranks of the defenders had withdrawn almost completely out of the center of the hall. Doors opened behind them at each far end as, one by one, the Klar and Hylar warriors slipped away into the towers themselves, leaving smaller and smaller pockets of their companions to pretend a defense of the interior.

The lift slammed to rest on the floor, knocking Brandon over. But he stood up and held up his empty hands before anyone could approach him—a gesture he hoped the Neidar would take as proof of his nonhostile intentions. The dual battles raged some distance away, but more than a hundred hill dwarves had gathered around the platform. It rested on a docking shelf a couple of feet above the ground, so it almost felt like a small stage. Turning through a circle, Brandon exhorted the dwarves to all sides.

"Get out of here while you can!" he shouted. "Spread the word. There's a whole shelf of rocks up there"—he gestured toward the ceiling—"thousands and thousands of tons of them! The mad Klar is waiting for the chance to dump it on the lot of you!"

"What about you?" one of the Neidar shouted hostilely.

"Yes, me too!" Brandon shouted back. "I'm risking my life to warn you!"

As more of his listeners looked upward, more turned and made for the gate, many of them shouting and gesturing to the Neidar still pouring in to turn around and go back. The purpose of the Tharkadan trap was well known to all dwarves—hill dwarves as well as mountain dwarves had been saved the last time it was used, long ago during the War of the Lance. Any enemy breach in the old days would be defended by filling the interior with rubble. Most of the hill dwarves thought that mechanism had been destroyed beyond repair. They didn't realize that Tarn Bellowgranite had dedicated himself to restoring it.

"You!" the voice shot through the din of the battle, and Brandon turned to see Rune charging him. "Bastard! Spy!" shouted the hill dwarf, raising a battle axe over his head as he sprinted closer. The sight of the enemy who had so tormented him inflamed Brandon with a fiery determination to fight—and kill—his old enemy.

And even more significant to Brandon's eye was that battle axe itself: the Neidar Rune carried Brandon's own weapon, the family heirloom that had been Balric Bluestone's, stolen from Brandon upon his first capture. The Kayolin dwarf growled an almost animal sound and flexed his knees, stepping toward the edge of the platform. Even though he was unarmed, he eagerly awaited the hill dwarf's charge, and he looked almost foolishly vulnerable to his frenzied attacker.

With a howl of rage, Rune sprang upward, hesitating only slightly in the face of Brandon's reckless advance. That was all the opening the Kayolin dwarf needed. He stepped back nimbly, and Rune stumbled as he tried to land on the lift platform, which was a few feet higher than the floor. Brandon lowered his shoulder and charged, driving into his opponent's solar plexus, plunging too close for the long-hafted weapon to come in to play.

The two dwarves tumbled to the platform, rolling to the side, and Brandon—his muscles fueled by long weeks of frustration and indignity—drove a fist into the underside of Rune's jaw. The hill dwarf's head snapped back with a crack of bone as his spine fractured. He fell dead, and Brandon snatched the axe from his lifeless fingers before his body even stopped twitching.

Still tense from the sudden combat, he raised the axe over his head and shouted at his dumbfounded observers. "I'm telling the truth! Get out while you can!"

The flow of the attackers coming in the gate had slowed dramatically as they heard the warnings from Brandon and from other fleeing Neidar, and in another few moments, the advance had stopped altogether, the front rank of hill dwarves remaining outside the gate, peering nervously upward and edging back. More and more of Brandon's listeners were streaming toward the gate as well.

Getting the attention of the dwarves actively engaged

in combat was a tougher challenge, the Kayolin dwarf knew. "Warn your comrades!" he exhorted his listeners. "Get them out of here—as many as will listen. There's no time to waste!"

Some of the Neidar did head toward one or the other pocket of battle, though more thought ill of the risk. Brandon stayed on the lift platform, waving and shouting, drawing the attention of more and more Neidar. Then he heard an enraged shout, a voice that compelled his attention.

"My prisoner!" roared Harn Poleaxe, rushing toward him from the skirmish at the base of the East Tower. The enemy commander stood head and shoulders above his men, his own hulking size augmented by the helm with its lofty plumes.

"He's condemned to die! Don't listen to him, you fools!" cried the Neidar commander, swatting at several dwarves. He shouted at the warriors waiting outside the gates. "Attack! Hit them now while the hour of victory is at hand!"

Looking shamefaced and sheepish, the hill dwarves tried to swallow their fears and move, albeit reluctantly, back into the hall. Harn had his sword drawn as he charged toward the mountain dwarf, through the ring of Brandon's listeners, his face contorted with rage. Brandon was shocked to see that face, scarred as it was by blisters and scabs, lumpy and misshapen, swollen like an overripe melon too long in the sun.

"He's the spy we had in chains!" cried Poleaxe to warriors left and right as he raced toward Brandon. "What kind of idiots are you—letting him talk you out of our great victory? Leave him to me; my sword will put an end to his lies."

Brandon, with relish, raised his axe, the haft so familiar that it felt like an extension of his own hands. He met Harn at the edge of the lift platform, parrying the Neidar's first blow with a crossing block, but he was sent stumbling back, overcome by the big hill dwarf's strength. Harn sprang upward onto the lift platform, raising his sword to brush aside Brandon's return slash, a powerful overhead swing. His face was crazed, more monstrous than dwarf, and he closed in with a rush. The two blades met with a ringing clash, and again Brandon stepped back, astonished at Harn's strength.

Harn had always been a big, sturdy dwarf, but it was obvious to Brandon that he had grown in size and power since their journey from Kayolin. It all had started, Brandon remembered, on the day Poleaxe had presided over his trumped-up trial in Hillhome's square. The dwarf had seemed magically enhanced that day and from that day on. Brandon understood that he was in the fight of his life and that he was at a clear disadvantage with his opponent.

For several seconds the two dwarves circled each other on the lift platform. Brandon was grateful, at least, that the rest of the hill dwarves didn't rush to their leader's assistance. Not that Harn needed help in any event, but as the hill dwarves pressed closer to the lift to watch the fight, they seemed more curious than angry.

Harn charged in a bull rush, and the Kayolin dwarf parried and blocked, skipping nimbly to the side and falling back. He avoided the corners of the square platform, knowing he'd be trapped if he let Poleaxe force him into one of them. The big Neidar came at him again, swinging his sword over his head and bashing it down with the full weight of his brawny muscles and his white-hot rage. It took all of Brandon's strength to hold his axe up, canting the blade at an angle to deflect the enemy's blows. He couldn't hope to stop Harn's blow, but at least he could knock it aside.

Dusk had fallen outside, but the pitch of battles inside the tower only mounted in fury. The Neidar had nearly attained their victory as the last of the small pockets of mountain dwarf defenders fought to little effect outside the doors leading into the towers. One by one the garrison's warriors were escaping through those doors.

Harn shrieked and foamed in growing frustration as Brandon continued to dodge and weave away from him. The Neidar watching the duel were muttering their disappointment in their champion as the Kayolin dwarf used his venerable axe to bash aside another series of crushing blows. Out of the corner of his eye, Brandon noticed many hill dwarves making their way toward the great gate and the growing darkness outside, casting nervous glances upward as they hurried to depart.

Apparently Harn Poleaxe, too, noticed the beginnings of a withdrawal, for he abruptly turned to face the warriors retreating. "Get back here, you cowards!" he roared.

And Brandon saw his chance. Harn's attention was distracted for only a split second, but that was enough time for the Kayolin dwarf to strike. He lunged and drove the blade of his axe down through the shoulder plate of Poleaxe's metal armor. The weapon cut through skin, sliced the bone of the hill dwarf's ribs and shoulder, and penetrated the flesh and lung below.

With a wheezing gasp, Harn Poleaxe stumbled away, dropping to his knees while Brandon wrenched his deadly axe free of the ghastly wound. The hill dwarf coughed, and blood spumed out of his mouth. Eyes staring, he looked at Brandon in disbelief. He tried to speak, and more blood spilled. Swaying on his knees, he dropped to his face and lay motionless in a growing pool of sticky crimson.

Exhausted, panting, holding his bloody axe with the blade pointed down, the mountain dwarf felt no sense of victory—only a weary relief. He slumped to his own knee, trying to catch his breath, hearing the distressed muttering of the surrounding hill dwarves. He wondered if they were going to attack him; he didn't really care if they did. But his ears pricked up; they weren't talking about him and Poleaxe. They were muttering in fear.

Only then did he raise his eyes to see the cause of their fright. Harn's lifeless body was twitching unnaturally, bulging and squirming at the back, the legs, the head. It was as if the Neidar's flesh were a sack containing some writhing creature—a creature that wanted very much to get out.

Abruptly the body burst open, spattering blood and bone and flesh in an explosive spray. Immediately a great shape, winged and black as night, rose from the ravaged corpse like an apparition, looming above the dead Neidar. It fixed a monstrous gaze on Brandon and opened eyes that glowed like the very fires of the Abyss.

————DH————

Gretchan had worriedly watched Brandon's descent. She couldn't hear his words over the clash of swords and the shouts and cries of the battling dwarves, but she could see he wasn't being attacked immediately and seemed to be attracting more and more listeners. She was awed by his courage but even more so by his goodness toward a former enemy. She'd never known that kind of dwarf before, and she shook her head in amazement.

She had started back along the catwalk when the door to the tower opened, admitting Tarn Bellowgranite, Otaxx Shortbeard, and Garn Bloodfist to the open-sided platform where the control lever for the Tharkadan trap was cocked and ready.

Garn immediately started for that lever.

She rushed to stop him. "You can't do this!" she cried.

"Don't try your sorcery, witch, or I'll have you killed!" The Klar sneered.

"I can't stop you with magic," she admitted truthfully, addressing the thane and the general even as the Klar captain moved to block her path. "You have to stop this madness for your own reasons, with your own hearts! Thane Bellowgranite, is this the legacy you want to leave to history? A catastrophic massacre of your own race? A taint on your reputation and on dwarf hearts that will be worse than the wounds left by the Cataclysm?"

"That is *not* my legacy!" Tarn replied testily. "It is not my choice. We are hard pressed, under attack by foes; you can see that yourself. We must defend ourselves!"

"This is not the way to win!" Gretchan cried. She gestured over the edge of the catwalk to the two small pockets of battle swirling down below. "Look, your garrison has almost completely withdrawn. They'll be safe in the towers—they could hold those doors for weeks, I'm certain, if they had to. You have, in fact, safely defended Pax Tharkas. You don't have to go the rest of the way. You don't need to kill all those hill dwarves."

"The priestess is right, my liege," interjected Otaxx, causing Tarn to raise an eyebrow and Garn to curse under his breath. "Each tower is a fortress unto itself. And we command the top of the wall, as well. We can threaten the Neidar with the trap and force them to withdraw, but we don't need to crush them to every last man."

Tarn Bellowgranite scratched his beard, considering that reasonable suggestion.

"Don't tell me you're going to listen to this witch?" Garn Bloodfist spit at Tarn Bellowgranite's feet in disbelief. His eyes darted wildly from the thane to Gretchan to the lever that would release the trap.

"My thane, this is a historic opportunity," he cried. "Never again will our enemies be so completely in your power. We must act—now!"

"The Neidar will be your enemies forever if you do!" Gretchan insisted. "If you kill all those in this army, you'll be faced by ten times as many, all of them out for blood, next time. You can never wipe them all out, and future generations will dream of blood revenge. This is not the way to peace and unity among the dwarves!"

At that moment, the clamor from down below suddenly

dwindled. The reason was the last of the mountain dwarves had withdrawn from the hall, leaving the vast space filled with milling, confused hill dwarves who, for the moment, were unable to reach their enemies. Those enemies sheltered behind stoutly barricaded doors. There was no one left to fight.

"If you won't act, I will!" cried Garn, lunging to the lever that would release the trap. He seized the shaft and pulled, activating the big flywheel that would tug the cable and pull the pins holding up the trap door. The mechanism of the Tharkadan trap began to groan.

At the same time, a shrill cry keened through the hall below them. Gretchan looked down to see a black shadow, large as a giant and a hundred times more menacing, rise above the floor.

Brandon Bluestone, a bloody axe in his hand, stood alone before it.

—DH—

Gus had unspooled a long section of cable, winding it off of the big stone wheel. He scaled down the wire while Berta, still grumbling about Gretchan, grudgingly held the line above. Gus swayed back and forth dizzyingly, but he'd almost reached the ledge where Kondike was trapped. The dog barked and wagged his tail eagerly, watching the Aghar descend toward him. If Gus could just reach Kondike's side, he thought he could wrap the cable around the dog and, with Berta's help—or maybe even some big dwarves—lift the stranded animal to safety.

Abruptly the hub above him, the great stone from which he had removed the wire, began to spin. He couldn't know that Garn had pulled the lever, had started the mechanism in motion. He could only see that the massive stone wheel was spinning with increasing speed.

But even though that hub had been connected to the gear itself, bearing the huge weight of the chain, the gear didn't move. In his effort to save the dog, Gus had unspooled the cable that connected it to the flywheel. The Aghar slid down the vibrating cable, remembering to hold onto the end of it as Kondike gave him a sloppy lick on his face.

But for the first time, he wondered what it was he held in his hand. He looked at the spinning wheel, the disengaged gear, and he knew exactly what had happened.

"Oh, no!" he wailed, slumping next to the big dog. "I broke it!"

———DH———

The dark creature rose like a black tower above Harn Poleaxe's ravaged corpse. The monster was taller than a giant, and it exuded menace with its great, arching, black wings and hideously glowing eyes. The huge maw gaped like a cave mouth, studded with jagged fangs like stalagmites and stalactites. Brandon needed all of his strength just to keep his grip on his axe. His knees shook and his guts churned at the sight of the horrific thing.

What remained of Harn Poleaxe was shriveled and ghastly, like a discarded suit of skin. The monster reared above the bloody mess and looked toward Brandon, who felt helpless in the gaze of those horrid red eyes. The creature swelled even larger, looming to an impossible height, flaring those black wings, and casting its gaze over the whole of the great hall. The fanged jaws gaped, and a roar bellowed forth, the sound reverberating from the walls, shaking the very bedrock of the floor.

The hill dwarves around the lift platform recoiled in horror, many of them running out the fortress gate, others whispering prayers to Reorx and staring in wide-eyed fear. The monster roared again, and Brandon found some control of his limbs, stumbling away in abject fear. Still clinging to his axe, he sprang down from the platform and staggered across the floor, feeling those crimson eyes burning into his back.

He felt a shocking chill and looked back to see the black beast pounce after him, springing like a massive winged cat. Brandon ducked to the side, falling and rolling across the floor as the monster came down on the spot where he had been. All around, the hill dwarves were fleeing, shouting in panic and dismay, thronging into a packed bottleneck in their frantic efforts to get out of the massive gate.

The monster spun and roared again, the blast of sound actually brushing Brandon's hair and beard like a gust of wind. He could never outrun it, he knew, so he raised his axe and his voice, roaring a war cry of his own.

"For Bluestone and Kayolin!" he cried, rushing forward with his axe upraised. The monster reared, wings flapping, as if it couldn't believe the dwarf's effrontery. Brandon swung his axe, the ancient blade of his ancestors, the keen steel slashing through the talons of the monster's foot with a hiss like red-hot metal touching water. The beast howled in fury. With one backhanded blow, it knocked the dwarf to the side, sending him tumbling like a gaming pin. It took all of Brandon's concentration to hold on to his axe as he rolled across the floor.

"Behold the true power of Harn Poleaxe!"

Gretchan's shouted voice rang out amid the suddenly eerie silence of the great hall. She was riding down in a second lift platform, her staff grasped in her hand, her golden hair shimmering in the light from the glowing anvil of Reorx. She pointed to the monster but addressed the gawking, awestruck hill dwarves who still remained in the hall and were trying to decide what to do.

"This is the corruption that ate away his soul! This is the power that drove him to this mad war—that almost resulted in death on a scale you can't even imagine."

The lift continued to drop, bringing her down to the docking station next to Brandon.

The creature's red eyes glared in fury and hatred at the priestess and her shining light. As she neared, it raised up taloned foreclaws as if to shield its face from the burning glare. Growling and shivering, it stood its ground, and when she raised the staff in challenge, it flapped and, instead of recoiling, stepped closer to her.

Gretchan's face was locked in a grimace of determination. She put both hands on the staff, bracing her feet as if she were trying to withstand a gale of wind—and, indeed, when the monster bellowed again, her hair blew back from her head like a golden plume. The light on the head of the staff wavered, and the monster roared another exultant challenge, taking a second step closer to the dwarf priestess.

She shook her head to ward off the onslaught, hair cascading in a halo, and raised her voice in the face of the beast's challenge.

"Good hill dwarves!" she cried. "Is *this* the kind of master you serve? A creature of darkness, of foul magic and even more foul gods? Haven't you been deceived enough by Harn Poleaxe, who was a slave to that master?"

The lift came to a rest on the floor. Brandon stood on shaky legs, breathing hard, his fingers clenched around the haft of his axe. The Kayolin dwarf stumbled toward her as she pointed to him.

"This dwarf, whom you would have killed under Harn's orders, risked his own life to try and save you. He warned you of the trap, which the Klar captain was ready to spring, and if those stones had fallen, he, too, would have perished under their weight, as well as most of you. But he was willing to take the chance to save Neidar lives . . . and work toward peace."

The beast roared, wings flailing, and it reared high, snarling and snapping toward the priestess. With a sudden lunge, it sprang toward her.

"Begone!" cried Gretchan. She pounded the base of her staff against the platform with a thump that echoed through the vast hall. Her talisman pulsed with light, so bright that even the hill dwarves couldn't look at it.

But the creature waved a massive paw and seemed to wipe that light away. Roaring again, it pressed closer, looming five times Gretchan's height, throwing back its head with the fanged maw gaping. It pounded taloned fists against its chest, the sound thrumming like a massive drumbeat through the cavernous hall.

The priestess struggled to stand, to hold her staff, but the force of the monster was too great. She stumbled back, almost falling. The light of Reorx's forge flickered again and faded.

In the sight of her peril, Brandon found his nerves and his strength. He raised his axe and charged, bringing the weapon in a great downward sweep as he approached the creature from the flank. He couldn't reach its head or even its torso, but his axe blade sliced through the beast's thigh, cutting the black flesh, tearing through enchanted sinew and bone. The thing wailed in savage pain and staggered, sinking down as the limb collapsed underneath it.

"Go!" Gretchan shouted again, her voice pitched to a piercing scream. Her staff blazed anew, the white light searing into the creature's face, burning, charring, killing. Shrieking and writhing, the dark monster slumped, weakened, and vanished, leaving the hill and mountain dwarves staring in horror.

Brandon staggered up to Gretchan and took her in his arms. She collapsed with a sob, and for long heartbeats they held each other. Only gradually did they become aware of the eyes of the Neidar, many hundred of whom still remained in the hall, watching them in awe and apprehension.

"Let the killing cease, in the name of Reorx." Gretchan spoke almost in a whisper, but her voice carried through the whole vast chamber.

"Peace," said the hill dwarf called Slate Fireforge as the restive Neidar looked warily around the vast chamber, as if expecting another attack. "Let's talk about this for a moment."

"Good idea," replied Gretchan Pax.

————DH————

Mason Axeblade took charge of Garn Bloodfist, who was on his knees, sobbing and wailing at the failure of the trap. The Daewar captain secured the rebellious Klar's wrists with manacles and ordered two of his Hylar warriors to lock him up in the dungeon.

Tarn Bellowgranite and Otaxx Shortbeard descended to the floor of the main hall, where some of the Neidar remained. The hill dwarves' morale had been badly shaken by the death of Poleaxe and the manifestation of the monster, and the vast majority had been only too willing to march back out of the fortress. Some had headed straight home, no matter how many miles away. Many others camped on the flats outside the wall, huddled around hundreds of fires that dotted the field for an expanse of nearly a mile.

Within the Tharkadan Wall, torches burned all around the big room. The bodies of the slain were being collected and prepared for burial, hill and mountain dwarf corpses arrayed side by side. Two hill dwarf captains, Slate Fireforge and Axel Carbondale, met with Tarn and Otaxx to parley.

Gretchan and Brandon were there too, while Gus and Berta sat with Kondike off to the side, watching the bigger dwarves with mingled awe and skepticism. The two gully dwarves had managed to capture the attention of a couple of Hylar men-at-arms, and those sturdy dwarves had been able to hoist both Gus and the dog back up to the catwalk.

"When Gus escaped from the black wizard, he inadvertently brought a bottle of the wizard's brew with him," Gretchan was explaining to everyone between puffs on her pipe. A bluish haze of sweet smoke surrounded her.

"I don't know what it was, but it obviously had some kind of corrupting effects. It was in a bottle of dwarf spirits, and Harn Poleaxe stole it from my room in Hillhome. I have no doubts that he drank it and became the tool of that darkness we saw looming just a short time ago."

"And you killed it?" Otaxx Shortbeard asked in awe.

"I don't think so," Gretchan said honestly. "But it was banished by the power of Reorx, through my staff—and Brandon's axe."

"How did Reorx wield my axe?" the Kayolin dwarf asked dubiously. After all, he rather thought that he, himself, had struck the killing blow.

Gretchan merely smiled. "Remember the story you told me: how that axe was carried by your ancestor, who was on a mountaintop the day the Cataclysm struck."

"Balric Bluestone, yes," Brandon remembered.

"They never found him, but they found his axe. Do you think that was just luck?"

"Not *my* family's luck," he acknowledged. "Not on that day."

"You're right. It wasn't luck. It was the will, the gift, of Reorx. That steel blade has been blessed by our god; there is no other way it could have wounded that creature."

Brandon looked at his weapon, which he had lovingly cleaned and polished, with a new appreciation.

At the same time, the thane of Pax Tharkas cleared his throat. "You say the gully—er, Gus—escaped from a black wizard?" Tarn asked, scratching his head dubiously. "Where is this wizard, then?"

Gretchan shrugged, drawing another puff from her pipe. "Gus came out of Thorbardin. He's an honest fellow, I think we've all seen. So I believe him. It must certainly have been a Theiwar black-robed magic user."

"You seem to know an awful lot about our people," Otaxx Shortbeard observed.

Gretchan expelled the smoke from her nose and looked at him seriously. "I was taught about our people ever since I was a little girl. My mother wanted me to know the place she had left behind as well as the new world she and the rest of the Daewar were trying to create in old Thoradin."

"Hmm. I remember you said your mother traveled with the Mad Prophet. The name 'Pax'—it's not a family name I recognize, and I spent most of my life among those Daewar," the old general admitted.

"Well, it's not my given name. I chose it for myself." Her eyes were wet as she looked at Otaxx. "My mother's name was Berrilyn Shortbeard . . . and I don't think she ever forgave herself for leaving you behind."

"Berrilyn . . . ?" The old dwarf rocked backward. "But . . . then . . ." His voice choked, and his eyes swam with tears.

"I am your daughter, born in Sanction," Gretchan said gently. "For these past forty years, I've been growing up and determined to do my researches for a history of the dwarves on Krynn. But in my heart, I was also looking for a way to return to my clan home. I thought it was in Thorbardin until, just days ago, I learned you were here, in Pax Tharkas."

The others watched silently as father and daughter embraced. Brandon wiped away a tear, and even Gus sniffed loudly—an outburst of sound that allowed them all to laugh.

"And this Bluestone that Garn brought from Hillhome— that is really your family's treasure, stolen by this hill dwarf villain?" Tarn asked Brandon.

"Yes," he replied. "Harn said he was willing to pay a fortune for it—a thousand times a hundred steel pieces. But I think he was waiting for the chance to steal it instead."

"Why do you suppose he wanted it so badly?" Slate Fireforge asked.

"He had two of them, you know," Brandon pointed out. "There's a green one as well. Garn took them from him."

"And I believe there's a third, somewhere," Gretchan said. "A Redstone. There are some intriguing legends about the Tricolor Hammerhead. It's a weapon that can only be made by merging all three of those precious stones together, to form a hammer of unprecedented power. I believe that's why Harn sought the Bluestone. I think there's an old dwarf woman in Hillhome, he called her the Mother Oracle, who planted the idea in his head. Some stories suggest the Hammerhead is a device so powerful, it's capable of smashing open Thorbardin's Gate."

"Oh, now I remember! Thorbardin wizard's war," Gus piped up. He had been trying to keep up with the conversation as Berta patted a dirty rag against his bleeding forehead. "I wonder if war start yet?"

"The same wizard or a different one?" asked Tarn Bellowgranite sharply.

"Black wizard's war," the Aghar replied. "He's gonna kill all the thanes. If they not kill him first."

"Oh, is that it?" the weary thane said sadly. He exchanged a look with his old friend Otaxx. They seemed to understand more than what they told. "So civil war comes again to Thorbardin. A black Theiwar's army versus Jungor Stonespringer's fanatics. It would serve them both right—if not for all the innocents who will perish."

"I wonder . . ." Mason Axeblade said, his voice trailing off hesitantly. The Daewar captain had been a silent observer up to that point.

"You wonder what?" Brandon asked.

"I wonder about this hammer and this war you speak of. It seems to me at least possible that, if we can find the Redstone and put it together with these other fabled stones, then we might have a tool that would smash open the gates of Thorbardin. And if there are two factions inside, trying to tear each other apart . . ."

"We might find in that conflict a chance to go home again," Tarn Bellowgranite concluded.

# EPILOGUE

Willim the Black had worked hard to restore his operation. He had recruited forty new apprentices, twenty-seven of which remained alive even after four weeks of training. More would be lost in the weeks to come, but he was encouraged by the rate of success displayed by the group so far. They were hard workers, and the survivors showed real Theiwar spirit—they had not blanched even as they witnessed the failures, their former colleagues, meeting their fate in Gorathian's pit.

All the apprentices, of course, were Theiwar, as that was the only clan of dwarfkind with any magical aptitude. And the Theiwar of Norbardin, when it came to war, would be Willim the Black's sole hope of success. He visited them as often as he dared, magically transporting himself into the homes of those he knew he could trust or intimidate. From some of those homes, he had claimed his apprentices, and even knowing the risks, they had all come willingly, for there was great power waiting for those few who succeeded.

In those same houses, and in others, he had planted the seeds of his rebellion, recruiting agents to do his bidding, spies to keep him apprised of developments. After all, Willim the Black was well known among his clan, and if he was not even mildly loved, he was tremendously feared, and that, to a Theiwar, was the greatest asset.

The black-robed wizard had also gone invisibly throughout Thorbardin, passing through the cities and the warrens, observing the state of the people. Stonespringer's rulership grew ever more restrictive, more controlled by the fanatical king. His edicts were enforced by an ever-growing army of brutal thugs, Hylar and Daergar mainly, who walked the streets of Norbardin, accosting females who dared to show themselves in public, demanding tribute from the honest merchants and craftsmen who tried to survive there. Aghar had all but vanished from public view, though to Willim that was the lone positive result of his enemy's reign.

Stonespringer had long made a habit of placing his most loyal subordinates in key roles, so they controlled nearly all of the key positions in Thorbardin's society. The Theiwar were treated as lower-class citizens, denied roles of influence or power. But that fact, Willim knew, would work to his own advantage, eventually. His people had little patience for those who would master them and little tolerance for arrogance and abuse. One day, those resentments would bubble to the surface, and civil war would begin anew. Until that time, Willim would train his new apprentices, assemble components for his spells and potions, and prepare.

It was against that backdrop that the black minion returned to the wizard in his laboratory. The creature had failed, Willim saw at once, in that the potion of mastery had been lost, though it had been employed in a worthy cause. For that reason, the wizard did not condemn the beast to an eternity of suffering, but merely locked it away in a cage of magical bars, so when the time was right, the monster could once again be unleashed with a charge to make right its abject wrong.

And Willim had one more ally, out on the surface world. An ally that dwelled among the outer dwarves and worked his will as her own . . . an ally that had no eyes but, like Willim, could see very well indeed.

# APPENDIX

# COLD STONE SOULS

An essay by Gretchan Pax

*The penchant for internecine warfare is not unique to humans or ogres or goblins or any of a host of other races known for savage brutality and devastating conflict. It seems that wild young peoples cannot refrain from destroying themselves or their kin in the convulsive violence of great wars. Ogres, goblins, and others of that ilk live lives of constant violence, raiding and thieving and making war for sport. Theirs is an existence wherein the strong always lords power over the weak. So it is too with the tangled affairs of humankind, for man never seems to weary of endlessly battling over land, treasure, trade, and religion.*

*Perhaps it is more surprising that even among the elder peoples of Krynn, most notably the elves and the dwarves, such squabbling has been a source of historical feuds dating back to the Age of Starbirth. Neither is it surprising that such conflict continues even in the modern, civilized Age of Mortals, wherein we now all live. While visionary leaders have arisen through the centuries, they have been unable to stem the never-ending forces of destruction and chaos. As in the case with all conflict, it seems that wars between* related peoples have the capacity for greater violence, deeper cruelty, and longer-lasting schisms than strife waged between less closely aligned populations. For the elves, this truth is most evidenced by the long and seemingly irreparable rift between the ancient realm of Silvanesti, and the newer (though still venerable) nation of Qualinesti. In fact, it may be observed that the conflict between these two nations actually outlasted the nations themselves.

In the case of the dwarves, the schisms between these "Peoples of the Rock" are most vividly etched by the experience of the Cataclysm, when the gods rained their destruction down upon the world. As all the peoples of Krynn reeled from the chaos, expecting annihilation and violent death, the mountain dwarves in their great under-mountain fortress of Thorbardin sealed the gates of their kingdom, locking their blood-kin, the hill dwarves, out of the shelter, leaving them exposed to the rain of disaster tumbling downward from the skies.

It was an act of monstrous selfishness—to be sure, an act born of fear—and it left clan-splitting scars that continued to fester, to become infected, to burst into poisonous disease, whenever these two mighty branches of the dwarf tree meet. It infuses the memory, the very beings, of mountain and hill dwarves alike, shaping hatreds and prejudices and always serving as a ready source of fear. It is that legacy, as well as the pounding impact of the Cataclysm itself, that has shaped the conflicts that, to this day, result in battles and violence and brutal campaigns motivated by greed and envy.

During the dawning ages of Krynn, dwarves established mighty nations in three distinct parts of Ansalon. Thoradin was the First Home, birthplace of the dwarf race and a long-standing nation of industrious, productive peoples. In the very center of the continent of Ansalon, the Khalkist Mountains formed the roof over Thoradin, a fortress that neither man nor giant nor dragon could assail. But Thoradin could not stand against the gods, and the Cataclysm destroyed much of those hallowed halls, leaving only the remnant—soon to become diseased and corrupt—of miserable Zhakar.

Mightiest of all the dwarven nations was great Thorbardin, started by dwarves who came from Thoradin, though before long the Second Home of the dwarves outshone the first in size, population, and splendor. The undermountain realm beneath the peaks of the high Kharolis housed great cities, a teeming transportation network, and great manufacturing centers. Here the Hylar, the Theiwar and Daergar, the Daewar and the Klar, and even the wretched Aghar, dwelled side by side in their subterranean cities, centered around the vast Urkhan Sea.

Hundreds of miles to the north rise the Garnet Mountains, and they, too, are home to an underground nation of mountain dwarves. Kayolin is not so large as Thorbardin, and it hasn't attracted as much attention from potential antagonists. Kayolin has survived through the ages with fewer convulsive changes than either of the other great nations, and today it approaches a status of national identity that is all its own.

And beyond the mountain dwarves, the true historian cannot ignore the Neidar, the hill dwarves. Indistinguishable from each other by appearance, the hill dwarves are descendants of dwarves who long ago chose to live on the surface of the world rather than underneath it. Because of this, the Neidar are more dispersed than the mountain dwarves. They lack any concentrated nation along the lines of Kayolin or Thorbardin, and the hill dwarves live in many parts of the world, usually in towns or villages that are nominally independent, but sometimes these communities become part of whatever surrounding surface nation, usually human-controlled, in which they find themselves.

The three major dwarven realms of the world, which in the past were linked through trade, culture, and easy land routes of travel, were divided by the Cataclysm. The dwarves of the Khalkist, in the rugged mountains south of Sanction, were essentially cut off from all contact with the two other great dwarven kingdoms. It was the expedition of the Mad Prophet, Severus Stonehand, who brought dwarf culture back to the First Home. Though the Daewar exiles face many challenges, including fiery mountains and hostile neighbors, they strive to forge a new nation upon the ruins of the old.

My initial studies concerning Kayolin have been limited by a lack of access. However, it is known that the dwarven nation under the Garnet range has been spared much of the tumult that has rocked Thorbardin. Ruled by a governor who is technically subordinate to the high king in Thorbardin, Kayolin has been a de facto independent state since the time of the Cataclysm. Prior to that devastating event, much overland trade linked the two nations. But with the creation of the Newsea, the land connection between Kayolin and Thorbardin was severed, and with it most communication and virtually all trade between these two hallowed lands ceased.

Still, Kayolin is known to be involved in affairs of Northern Ansalon, including having forged at least a loose alliance with the empire of Solamnia. That dwarven realm is the source of the highest-quality steel in the world, and its mines, delving ever deeper, continue to tap into the closely held mineral wealth of Krynn. Its great city, Garnet Thax, is a wonder of subterranean architecture, with its many levels arrayed around the virtually bottomless shaft know as the Governor's Atrium.

Lacking contact with the other dwarven realms, some Kayolin dwarves have advocated complete independence. I have a report from a reliable source that the governor has taken to calling himself "king" and that Kayolin no longer *views itself as a member of the greater dwarf society. I have been unable to confirm this information with my own observations, but events have conspired to make it possible for me to visit Kayolin sometime in the near future.*

*In Thorbardin itself, the kingdom has been usurped. The former thane of the Hylar, the last legitimately appointed high king in all dwarvendom, was Tarn Bellowgranite. He was driven from his realm by a revolution led by another Hylar, Jungor Stonespringer. With several hundred followers, Bellowgranite withdrew to the fortress of Pax Tharkas, where he is expected to live out his days.*

*The fanatical dwarves who ejected him seem determined to turn their backs upon the world. They have sealed both of the great gates that connected Thorbardin to the outside world. Foreign dwarves and the rare representatives of other races were simply rounded up and, in many cases, executed. This is the harsh truth of Thorbardin today: it is a nation, and a people, which has completely and utterly turned its back upon the rest of the world.*

*One day, however, that world may come and find them.*